*Folktales*
OF THE WORLD

GENERAL EDITOR : RICHARD M. DORSON

FOLKTALES OF
Hungary

EDITED BY
Linda Dégh

TRANSLATED BY
JUDIT HALÁSZ

FOREWORD BY
RICHARD M. DORSON

THE UNIVERSITY OF CHICAGO PRESS

The University of Chicago Press, Chicago
Routledge & Kegan Paul, Ltd., London
© *1965 by The University of Chicago. All rights reserved*
Published 1965. Printed in the United States of America
82 81 80 79 78   7 6 5 4 3
Paper   ISBN: 0-226-14024-5
Library of Congress Catalog Card Number 64-19846

Foreword

In Hungary today one finds some of the most interesting folktale research being carried on anywhere in the world. So a Finnish folklore scholar has recently written, giving the palm long held by the folklorists of his own country to those of an up-and-coming rival.[1]

Yet this new zeal has developed only since 1953, when the journal *Acta Ethnographica* announced that its "reborn science" recognized the connection between scientific theory and the practical tasks of building socialism. Breaking with the tradition of its predecessor, *Ethnographia*, which had printed articles entirely in Hungarian, the new journal began publishing research papers of high merit in English, Russian, German, and French. Now the activities and achievements of Hungarian folklorists, present and past, became visible to Western eyes. For the century and a half since the Grimm brothers issued the first scholarly collection of folktales (in 1812 in Germany), stimulating collectors throughout the countries of Europe to follow their example, little had been heard from Hungary, a racial and linguistic island between the Balkan and the Baltic states. Only one edition of value made its way into English in the nineteenth century, *The Folk-Tales of the Magyars*, translated and edited by W. Henry Jones and Lewis L. Kropf and published in 1889 by the Folk-Lore Society

---

[1] Lauri Honko, in a review in the *American Anthropologist*, LXV (Feb., 1963), 142, of *Folklore Research Around the World*, ed. R. M. Dorson. The organization of contemporary folklore research in Hungary is reported on by Tekla Dömötör, "Ethnographische Forschung in Ungarn 1950-62," *Hessische Blätter für Volkskunde*, LIV (1963), 665-74.

of England. The fifty-three tales in this volume were selected largely from the pioneer works of the poets and authors János Erdélyi (1814–1868) and János Kriza (1812–1875).

The earliest count of Hungarian tales, made in 1867 in a paper to the Kisfaludy Society in London, set the known repertoire at two hundred and forty narratives.[2] By 1901, when Lajos Katona, the first comparative folklorist in Hungary, analyzed some twenty collections of tales, the number had grown to six hundred. In 1955, when Ágnes Kovács reported on the Hungarian tale-type index under preparation, she estimated the national stock at six thousand folktales.[3]

The vigorous collecting and interpretation of Hungarian folklore since the second World War are responsible for these gains. Gyula Ortutay, the leading Hungarian folklorist of the present day, has described this renaissance. His eighty-page essay, "The Science of Folklore in Hungary between the two World Wars and during the Period subsequent to the Liberation," published in *Acta Ethnographica* in 1955, indeed forms one of the most revealing documents in the history of folklore scholarship. It casts the whole story of folkloristic researches in his land—a story told with candid and elaborate detail—into a Marxist-Leninist drama. All the preliminary spadework, with its false starts and mistaken assumptions, is a prelude to the final struggle and triumph of the Soviet-inspired school over the bourgeois positivists. Nor is this an idle academic dispute, for, as Soviet political leaders have asserted, folklore is the people's literature, and accordingly a major instrument of propaganda, which folklore scholars must utilize to advance the socialist cause. Nevertheless, the smoke-

[2] Reported in *The Folk-Tales of the Magyars*, collected by Kriza, Erdélyi, Pap, and others; translated and edited, with comparative notes, by the Rev. W. Henry Jones and Lewis L. Kropf (London, published for the Folk-Lore Society by Elliot Stock, 1889: Publications of the Folk-Lore Society, XIII), p. xxii. The paper was read by László Arany, himself a noted collector.

[3] Ágnes Kovács, "The Hungarian Folktale-Catalogue in Preparation," *Acta Ethnographica*, IV (1955), 444. Kovács writes ". . . Katona's scheme of types is, nevertheless, still in force, and his work still serves as a model for arranging the types of Hungarian folktales."

screen of ideology should not obscure the high merits of Ortutay and his school.

The three cardinal heresies of folklore theory are declared by Ortutay to be intolerant nationalism and chauvinism, romantic idealization of the peasant folk, and acceptance of erroneous Western ideas.[4] These errors, with glimpses of countervailing virtues, can be perceived in the work of nineteenth-century collectors. They are perpetuated in the more advanced studies made in the period between the two World Wars. The heresies are at length routed by the new school of dialectical folklorists, led by Ortutay himself, emerging after the liberation of Hungary in 1945 from Hitler and the fascist regime of Horthy. With such yardsticks against which to measure his countrymen, Ortutay is able neatly to pigeonhole the folklorists of the past hundred and fifty years.

Thus praise is meted out to János Erdélyi, who compiled three volumes of *Folksongs and Legends* from 1846 to 1848, because he displayed insights into social theory and recognized that the rudest peasants possessed the finest specimens of folkprose and folk-poetry. His celebrated contemporary János Kriza, although a more accurate collector, sympathetic to the serfs, and a skilled fieldworker who first understood the need to explore fully a homogeneous geographical or ethnical society, unhappily displayed a bigoted chauvinism. In 1863 his volume of folktales and folksongs titled *Wild Roses (Vadrózsák)* generated a violent polemical and legal dispute with the Rumanian scholar I. Grozescu, who cast doubts on the alleged Hungarian origin of two ballads. This so-called Action of the Wild Roses inflamed the passions of east European ethnologists and folklorists for decades, and produced the error that Ortutay labels a hostile nationalism. Thus the early Hungarian folklorists contemptuously criticized Rumanian and Slovak publications, and treated all oral products of the folk as going from, and never to, Hungary. Instead of stressing ties with their east European neighbors, investigators of customs and traditions influenced by the Western

[4] Gyula Ortutay, "The Science of Folklore in Hungary between the two World Wars and during the Period subsequent to the Liberation," *Acta Ethnographica*, IV (1955), 5–88.

comparative method, like Lajos Katona before and Sándor Solymossy after the first World War, emphasized Hungarian affinities with the remoter countries of western Europe. In the period
of the Hapsburg Monarchy, following the Compromise of 1867,
this opprobious Hungarian nationalism reached its peak.

In condemning nationalism, Ortutay treads slippery ground,
and he hastens to make clear the distinction between the chau-
vinistic and socialistic brands of nationalism. Insofar as they pro-
tested against Hapsburg political and economic exploitation of
the people and asserted a true spirit of independence, the early
nationalists were proper patriots, and the discovery of the nation's
folk-literature abetted true patriotism. But the cause of the
Hungarian people must be associated with the similar cause of
other east European peoples, as the famed patriot Kossuth asserted
in his exile. In the modern period, the music-folklorists Béla
Bartók and Zoltán Kodály are glorious, right-thinking nationalists.

A second heresy, idealizing the peasantry of a pastoral paradise, further accounts for the sterility of much Hungarian
folklore research prior to the enlightenment. Ortutay labels this
error "romantic, idyllic, Narodnik (populist)." He sees its most
grievous by-products as the separation of the country peasants
from the city workers, and the divorce of folk-literature from its
economic and social context. An unhistorical and unrealistic
mentality thus developed among the collectors of folklore, who
regarded all peasants in a blissful light. These sentimental collectors failed to appreciate that the peasantry too is divided into
social classes, and that only among the poorest serfs, exploited by
"vampiric and despotic" peasants, do the folk arts truly flourish.[5]
Standard series such as the *Collection of Hungarian Folk Poesy*
(*Magyar Népköltési Gyüjtemény*, Vols. I–XIV, 1872–1924), and
Ethnography of the Hungarian People (*A Magyarság Néprajza*,
Vols. I–IV, 1933–37), betray the faults arising from the romantic
notions of the folk. The older volumes are filled with un-

---

[5] Some support for Ortutay's thesis can be found in the case of the
Norwegian peasantry; not the superior *bönder*, but the lowest servants
and cotters, proved to be the best carriers of tradition (Oscar J. Falnes,
National Romanticism in Norway, New York, 1933, pp. 53–54).

systematically arranged and accidentally procured materials; the more recent ones, influenced by the Finnish school of historical-geographical folklorists, present arid comparisons of motifs and types, and arbitrarily divide the spiritual and material realms of folk culture.

Here the third heresy manifests itself. Hungarian folklorists have unwisely accepted the positivism and comparativism practiced by scholars in western Europe. For example, the Finnish method reduced folk-narrative to skeletal abstracts and classifications, and then sought far-flung international parallelisms to swell the count. Meanwhile, this method ignored the social, historical, creative, psychological, and aesthetic factors that would explain the cultural products of the Hungarian peasantry. Another error fostered by Western bourgeois mentality is seen in Freudian psychoanalysis, which had seduced Géza Róheim (1892–1953). Beginning and ending his notable career with studies of ancient Hungarian mythology, Róheim strayed in between, spending his mature years in western Europe, in Australia, in the United States, and writing on a variety of non-Hungarian subjects with his fanciful psychoanalytical interpretations.

More tragic, in the eyes of Ortutay, is the case of János Honti (1910–1944), who died a martyr's death in one of Hitler's concentration camps, and might well have found the right methodology had he lived out his full life into the years of the Liberation. In the short but brilliant span allowed him, Honti began as an orthodox Finnish-method comparativist, constructing a Hungarian tale-type index before he had even taken his final examinations to teach grammar school.[6] While a third-year student in the faculty of philosophy at the University of Budapest, in 1931, Honti published a treatise on his theory of the relation of folktales and heroic legend, *Volksmärchen und Heldensage*.[7] Years of study in Paris during the 1930's strengthened his international outlook. From 1935 on his views underwent a change, and he spoke for a freer, more flexible science of folktale study, which

[6] *Verzeichnis der Publizierten Ungarischen Volksmärchen*, FF Communications, No. 81 (Helsinki, 1928), pp. 3–43.

[7] *Volksmärchen und Heldensage*, FF Communications, No. 95 (Helsinki, 1931), pp. 3–60.

would turn from purely philological problems and classification of texts, types, and motifs—in short, the Finnish method—to philosophical inquiries into the narrative world-view and concept of reality of a people as revealed in its folktales.

An article of 1936 in the Irish folklore journal *Béaloideas*, "Celtic Studies and European Folk-Tale Research," presented his system.[8] By now Honti had formed friendships with the younger generation of Hungarian folklorists, especially Ortutay, whose personal feelings for Honti shine through his dialectical critique.

> The tragedy of his abruptly finished life is therefore a veritable symbol of how the Hungarian folklore scholars tried to find guidance between the two World Wars in the West, and how their aspirations ended in disappointment and bewilderment . . . all these scholars had finally come to see the insolubility of their problems and face the bankruptcy of their life-work. This was the reason why our scientists suffered bitter disappointment, fell victims to a wayless pessimism, longed to quit their country, and had lost their roots in the home soil; and all this was determined by the fundamental contradictions of the Hungarian society between the two World Wars.[9]

Ortutay admits to having shared in Honti's pre-Liberation errors, such as the failure to relate folk-literature to social and economic realities. He dedicated his English edition of *Folk Tales of Hungary* to Honti, and edited a volume of *Selected Studies of János Honti* in Hungarian (both published in Budapest, 1962).[10]

Even before the spread of the gospel according to Marx and Lenin, right-thinking scholars could have anticipated the socialist doctrines of folklore theory; now the new Hungarian school dis-

---

[8] Honti's article (*Béaloideas*, VI [1936], 33–39), has been sharply criticized by Kenneth H. Jackson, *The International Popular Tale and Early Welsh Tradition* (Cardiff, 1961), p. 133, n. 63, for asserting the Irish origin of certain international tales.

[9] "The Science of Folklore in Hungary," p. 55.

[10] Information on Honti is given in the review-essay by Vilmos Voigt of *Selected Studies of János Honti*, in *Acta Ethnographica*, XII (1963), 195–201. "He was the first prominent Hungarian folklorist to investigate the theory of the whole epic popular tradition. . . ."

covered a glorious predecessor, made to order and cut to the cloth
in the figure of the persecuted priest Lajos Kálmány (1852–1919).

The resurrection of Kálmány commenced in 1940, in an inaugural lecture given by Ortutay at Szeged University and
printed the next year, in which the speaker extolled the priest's
progressive outlook. In a later paper Ortutay declared that Kálmány's collecting work had an "epochal importance in the annals
of Hungarian science." But when Kálmány died in a lonely flat
in Szeged, his body lay untouched for several days, while rats
gnawed at his books and manuscripts. Friends recovered ten
bundles of manuscript which, according to the author's will, were
placed in the Hungarian National Museum. Eight of these were
later transferred to the Ethnological Archives of the Ethnographical Museum, where in 1949 a small study group directed by
Linda Dégh began to examine them. The group eventually proposed publication of the materials to the Ethnographic Society,
and the first of five projected volumes, a mammoth tome of 824
pages, appeared on the centenary of Kálmány's birth, in 1952,
under the general editorship of Ortutay. Dégh prepared the first
volume for the press, and supplied an extensive analysis of Kálmány's theoretical ideas. The detailed, laudatory review in *Acta
Ethnographica* was written by a Homeric scholar, Károly Marót,
whom Ortutay has applauded as an oustanding contemporary
Hungarian student of folk poetry.[11]

The collective tribute of the New School to Kálmány cited
both his accurate methods and his perceptive social theories. He
collected widely from the village goose-herds and peasants, and
trained his students to do likewise. From one peasant alone,
Mihály Borbély, he obtained sufficient tales to fill a whole book,
Traditions, thus anticipating the Soviet technique of studying
the personality within a community. Refusing to tamper with
and restyle popular songs and tales, the priest incurred the wrath
of the authorities, who barred publication of many of his
materials. Kálmány understood the need to collect intensively in

[11] For Kálmány see Marót's review of *Kálmány Lajos Népköltési Hagyatéka*, Vol. I (*Lajos Kálmány's Posthumous Collection of Folk-Poetry:
Part I, Historical Lays and Soldiers' Songs*), in *Acta Ethnographica*, III
(1953), 469–72; and Ortutay, "The Science of Folklore in Hungary," p. 14.

a homogeneous area, and to relate the texts of folk-literature to a cohesive society. His accuracy extended even, at this early date, to recording folksong tunes. He appreciated the fact that among the poorest peasantry throve the noblest specimens of folk-poesy. His sympathies for the peasants living under feudalistic and ecclesiastical tyrannies led him into bold protests. In dedicating a book to Count Lajos Tisza, he blamed Hungarian landlords for the ruin of villagers fleeing from Szeged. The priest promptly recognized the crucial significance of the October Revolution in Russia, and in February, 1918, warned his bishop that the Hungarian people were eagerly awaiting the confiscation of church lands.

In the first posthumous volume of Kálmány's collections, the editors arranged 243 popular songs and lays according to historical periods and social movements: Old National Historical Lays, Songs of the National Movement, Soldiers' Songs from the First Half of the 19th Century, Serfs' Songs, Songs of the War of Independence and the Age of Resistance, Hungarian Soldiers in Service of Foreign Interest, The Soldier's Life in the Age of Francis Joseph, Songs of the World War.

Will a disinterested folklorist accept this high evaluation of Kálmány's work? He can credit the testimonials to Kálmány's collecting skill and industry, but he will question the socialist theories imputed to him, particularly since Marót admits that Dégh has been obliged to reconstruct them on the basis of scanty notes and the tendentious character of his collections.

Ortutay has put on record his gradual abandonment of Western theories and the adoption of Soviet ideology into his folklore research. During the mid-1930's he read Finnish historical-geographical folklorists such as Antti Aarne and Kaarle Krohn, German psychological ethnologists like Frobenius, English functional anthropologists such as the Polish-born Malinowski and Evans-Pritchard, and French sociologists like Durkheim, seeking guidance to laws of behavior in primitive society. But his own field experience failed to confirm their hypotheses. From the "village-exploring" movement among ethnologists ("community studies" in the language of American sociologists) he

acquired his respect for and insistence upon fieldwork data as
the court of first and last resort in which to test all theories. Then
his encounter with a Russian study of an individual folk-nar-
rator, Mark Asadowskij's *Eine sibirische Märchenerzählerin*
(1926), opened his eyes to the Russian-Soviet methods of folklore
investigation. Turning now from the West to the East, he found
sharper concepts of the peasant community and traditional culture; Soviet fieldworkers compared features in the performance
styles of individual narrators and epic-singers to reconstruct folklore forms existing in given historical epochs.

Even while the second World War was under way, in 1940,
Ortutay launched his movement, with the publication of the
series *New Collection of Hungarian Folk Literature*. In these
volumes Ortutay and Dégh investigated the personalities of outstanding folk-narrators. István Banó analyzed the diverse styles
of storytellers within a single ethnic unit, in Baranya County, to
uncover the social and psychic factors producing stylistic diver-
gences. Ágnes Kovács explored the complete tale-repertoire of a
single village and reported on the social habits influencing and
controlling narrative art. Together Ortutay and his co-workers
inquired into the components of communal tradition, and the
individual creative forces operating within the anonymous, orally
transmitted village culture.

A sharp debate ensued. Scholars of the old school reared in the
Finnish method—Bertalan Korompay, the type-index compiler
János Berze Nagy, even János Honti—criticized the prominence
given the storyteller's personality, and feared havoc to their technique of motif-analysis. But by 1953, when *Acta Ethnographica*
commenced, the new school had completely triumphed, and the
series has continued to the present day along the same lines.

The eleventh and most recent volume in the series is *Legends
of Karcsa* (*Karcsai Mondák*), collected, introduced, and annotated by Iván Balassa, former director of the Ethnographic
Museum and presently vice-director of the national department
of museums.[12] Between 1958 and 1961 the collector obtained some
400 legendary traditions from a single village, of which 280 were

[12] Published by Akadémiai Kiadó, Budapest, 1963, 626 pp.

told by one informant, forty-four-year-old László Lénart. An endpaper map indicates the sites of the events described in the legends. Balassa begins with an ethnographic description of the village community, discussing the social opportunities and functions of legend telling, and then sets down the legend texts. These are divided into I, Historical legends; II, Legends of persons, animals, plants, and objects with supernatural knowledge; III, Legends of supernatural beings. The scholarly apparatus includes annotations to the legends, a comparative bibliography of Hungarian and European collections, a dialect glossary, an index of the supernatural beings and an index of place names, biographies of the three main informants, and eight photographs of storytelling scenes, including one of the collector tape-recording a legend narrator. This is a model legend collection, from which Linda Dégh, who served as publisher's reader, has reprinted eleven texts in the present volume.

The new school of Hungarian folklorists has initiated bold and imaginative enterprises. A case in point is the investigation into the industrial folklore of the Hungarian working class reported on by Tekla Dömötör in an issue of *Acta Ethnographica* devoted to similar projects for east European countries. The principles governing the inquiry are clearly enough rooted in Soviet dogma: the affinity of peasantry and city laborers; their common poetry of lamentation and distress; and the ignoring of this creative folk art by reactionary regimes. But the quest itself, hunting folklore in the industrial metropolis, is of the greatest interest to folklorists everywhere, and has never been systematically undertaken. Dömötör introduces her essay in this vein:

> The systematic disclosure and study of Hungary's industrial folklore was started a few years ago by members of a co-operative Group for the Research of Workmen's Folklore, a body formed under the aegis of the Hungarian Academy of Sciences. Research work of this kind was not without precedent in Hungary, for workers' songs, further ballads inspired by the tragic lot of the industrial workers, were recorded also in the past by some of our folklorists, among them by the most outstanding representatives of

the profession such as Béla Bartók, Zoltán Kodály and Lajos Kálmány. These songs and ballads, closely related to the folk songs of the peasantry, are not infrequently but industrial variants of peasant songs, telling of the doomed life of young men and young girls pining away in factories, or miners slaving in collieries; particularly moving is the lyrical poetry of the agricultural proletarians who emigrated to America at about the turn of the century and converted into industrial workers.[13]

The reason for the neglect of industrial folklore in the 1920's and 30's is given as the prejudices against the working class of the Fascist government in Hungary, following its overthrow of the republic in 1919. Actually the simple fact is that folklorists from the initiation of their field early in the nineteenth century have associated folk traditions with the countryside.

The study group, directed by Linda Dégh, attacked its problems resourcefully. Instead of collecting at random, the members decided first to analyze the ethnography—the social, economic, and historical conditions—of the working class, and then to set up specific, clearly focused field projects. The relative youth of industrial society in Hungary, dating back only to the 1830's and '40's, insured an excellent opportunity to observe the historical process transforming country folk into city folk. Three main streams flowed into the new working class: craftsmen in the old guilds, skilled workers from all parts of the Austro-Hungarian monarchy, and rural peasants. After 1919 the Horthy government blocked immigration and the working class became solidified. In order to probe into the diverse population elements of these workers, the Co-operative Group devised special inquiries:

1. Mode of life and folklore of a large-scale industrial works in the capital city of Budapest.

2. Mode of life, culture, and folklore of skilled iron workers, of unskilled workers in the building trades fresh from the country, and of apprentices in the new industrial center of Dunaújváros.

[13] Tekla Dömötör, "Principal Problems of the Investigation on the Ethnography of the Industrial Working Class in Hungary," *Acta Ethnographica*, V (1956), 331. The complete article is on pp. 331–49.

3. Mode of life, folklore, and professional and revolutionary traditions of the coal miners around Salgótarján.

4. Collection and analysis of revolutionary industrial songs of the period from 1860 to 1945.

5. Collection and analysis of the traditional customs and folklore of the agrarian proletariat, the navvies, and certain categories of small craftsmen, chosen as an intermediate group between farmers and laborers. The navvies, a seasonal migrant labor force working on heavy irrigation and road construction projects, commanded special interest because their lives compelled them to share both agrarian and industrial traditions.

These research tasks were still further refined. Thus in the study on coal miners, the fieldworkers entered two contrasting villages, Kishartyán and Karancskeszi. In the first, although the male population consisted almost entirely of miners or factory workers, the old folk traditions were found to be well preserved; in the second, where 38 per cent of the men were agricultural laborers, the village nevertheless had lost its heritage of folk art and folk poetry—due, according to the report, to the hostility of the local authorities and village teachers. In Budapest, the ethnographer-collectors reported on such matters as May Day celebrations, housewarming ceremonies, workers' weddings and red-carnation burials, dancing parties of tradesmen, and changes in attire of laborers and miners. In addition they collected vigorous forms of prose narrative, mainly legends, anecdotes, and jokes attached to the different occupations and trades, as well as autobiographical and local stories from real life containing suggestions of traditional motifs. Márton Istvánovits recorded and analyzed a whole volume of peasant tales from a factory hand living for many years in Budapest.

In the domain of folk-narrative alone, recent Hungarian research has registered notable achievements. Linda Dégh began in 1947 a series of field expeditions, lasting over a period of thirteen years, to the village of Kakasd in Tolna County, where a colony of Szeklers had been repatriated after the second World War. The Szeklers, a distinct linguistic and ethnic group, originally living on the inner slope of the eastern Carpathians, participated in uprisings against the Vienna government in the eighteenth century, including the insurrection of Ferenc Rákóczi. After armed reprisals in 1764, the survivors fled, first to Moldavia, then north to Bukovina. In the year 1946 some 40,000 Szeklers were resettled in the counties of Tolna and Baranya, in place of expatriated Germans. The village Dégh chose to investigate had been colonized from one of the most archaic of the Szekler communities in Bukovina, and she reaped rich harvests. These are made manifest in a bulky dissertation submitted to the Hungarian Academy of Sciences in 1956, "Folk Tale and Society: Practice of Story-Telling in a Szekler Settlement," and published in revised form by the German Academy of Sciences in Berlin in 1962, titled *Märchen, Erzähler und Erzählgemeinschaft*;[14] and two volumes of collected texts, one entirely filled with the repertoire of a single tale-teller, Mrs. József Palkó.[15] This kind of fieldwork suggests the folkloristic studies of immigrant groups in the United States which have long been contemplated but not as yet realized.

The care and exhaustiveness of the Hungarian folktale catalogue being prepared by Ágnes Kovács further compels admiration. Building on the earlier indexes of Katona, Honti, and Berze Nagy, Kovács and her helpers have planned a highly informative catalogue. Since about 95 per cent of the 6,000 Hungarian narratives are unavailable in the world languages, and a complete translation would be prohibitive, the catalogue offers a structural analysis of the more than 500 tale-types identified by Berze Nagy (256 fairy tales, 209 jokes and anecdotes, 55 animal tales), supplemented with synopses of the variants, a distribution map, and a full translation of a representative tale for each type. The cataloguers not only examined the better known tale-collections, but also hard-to-find narrative material buried in reviews

[14] Akademie-Verlag, Berlin, 1962. The subtitle is "Dargestellt an der ungarischen Volksüberlieferung." Pp. 435. This work received a Guiseppe Pitré folklore prize in 1963.

[15] Volumes VIII and IX in the *New Collection of Hungarian Folk Literature*. The titles in English translation are *Folk-Tales from Kakasd*: I, *Tales of Mrs. Palkó*, II, *Tales of Mrs. Palkó, Gy, Adrásfalvi, Mrs. Sebestyén and M. László*. Akadémiai Kiadó, Budapest, 1955, 1960. Pp. 509, 399.

and newspapers. In addition, they prepared lists of manuscript collections and of popular publications, such as school readers and chapbooks, reproducing folktales.[16]

As well as energetically collecting traditional tales, Hungarian folklorists have also closely scrutinized their content. In the tape-recorded repertoire of 243 tales and 13 legends of storyteller Lajos Ámi, collector Sándor Erdész observed numerous references to geographical and cosmogonical concepts.[17] He interviewed Ámi —who in 1959 received the title "Master of Folk Arts" from the cabinet of the Hungarian People's Republic—on his ideas on the structure of the world, and found them to be identical with the world-view of the folktales, and with the general belief-system of the Hungarian peasant. An example of a taped question and answer follow:

> "What holds the firmament?"
> "In my opinion the firmament is set down on the rim of the earth as a tent when it is placed. It is in that shape like a tent when it is fastened down because it is supported by the Earth. The firmament is so low at this point that the swallow has to drink water kneeling on the black cotton-wood."

In one of the tales told by Ámi he thus comments about a wandering hero, "When he got to the end of the world where the swallow drinks water kneeling on the black cottonwood because he wasn't able to straighten up, he found an old-looking house there." The tale and the belief mesh. In common with his fellow peasants in northeastern Hungary, Ámi conceived of the origin of man in these propositions:

1. Once the Earth and the Sky almost touched.

2. The original home of the first couple was not on the Earth but in the world above from which they descended.

3. The first couple were covered with hair which they lost through the use of a plant with magic properties.

[16] Kovács, "The Hungarian Folktale-Catalogue in Preparation," *Acta Ethnographica*, IV (1955), 443–77.

[17] "The World Conception of Lajos Ámi, Storyteller," *Acta Ethnographica*, X (1961), 327–44.

Erdész reconstructs the universe as seen physically and historically by Ámi. He traces Ámi's concepts to early Christian sources
synthesized with oral mythical traditions and rationalized by
the Hungarian peasant's practical turn of mind.[18] This method of
folktale analysis is highly suggestive for the social and intellectual
historian.

If Hungarian folklorists are strongly influenced by Soviet
ideology, they are nonetheless receptive to Western ideas and
conversant with Western scholarship. This synthesis is indeed
their major accomplishment; fluent in English, Russian, and
German, they are bringing to a confluence ideas about the creative
role of the narrator and the social function of his audience shared
by American, English, Scandinavian, and German as well as
Soviet scholars. In two richly documented treatises, "Some Questions of the Social Function of Storytelling" (1958) by Dégh,[19]
and "Principles of Oral Transmission in Folk Culture" (1959)
by Ortutay,[20] this common viewpoint is persuasively advanced.
Ortutay indeed calls attention to the views of Cecil Sharp, the
great English folksong collector, in stressing the possibility of
enrichment as well as deterioration in folksong variants. And he
gives full credit to the Finnish historical-geographical school for
crystallizing the concepts of type and motif and formula, without which the fluid processes of oral transmission could not be
measured. Dégh, in assembling a small anthology of comments
on the storytelling habits of itinerant tradesmen, soldiers, fishermen, agricultural workers and the like in Hungary and many
other countries, considers the function of oral narration among
contemporary social groups in much the same way as do American anthropologists in nonliterate societies.

It is fortunate for the English reader that some of the work
of talented Hungarian folklorists like Ortutay and Dégh has

[18] Sándor Erdész, "The Cosmogonical Conceptions of Lajos Ámi, Storyteller," *Acta Ethnographica*, XII (1963), 57–64.

[19] *Acta Ethnographica*, VI (1958), 91–146.

[20] *Acta Ethnographica*, VIII (1959), 175–221. An inaugural lecture delivered at the Hungarian Academy of Sciences, April 6, 1959.

been made available in English translation.[21] The present volume forms a notable addition to these resources.

Richard M. Dorson

[21] The English edition of *Hungarian Folk Tales*, selected and edited by Gyula Ortutay (Budapest: Corvina, 1962), 544 pp., makes accessible a lengthy historical essay by Ortutay on "The Hungarian Folk Tale" (pp. 7–71). A German edition, *Ungarische Volksmärchen*, was issued by the same publishers in 1957. Ortutay's selection of 69 tales draws in part from some of the older and less reliable Hungarian collections.

Introduction

The aim of this book is to give the reader a taste of the various forms of oral narrative as they are found today in Hungarian villages. For this reason the principal goal in selecting the material was not to assemble the most beautiful specimens from the entire body of Hungarian folktales, but to attempt a trustworthy presentation of the folktale as a living art, displayed through recent collections covering material of the past twenty years. With this endeavor in mind I wish to serve a double purpose: with the help of modern recording techniques, to make available a body of authentic Hungarian material for international folklore research; and to acquaint the interested reader with the oral art of the Hungarian peasant.

Oral folk narrative is still a popular form of entertainment in the Hungarian village of today. The past twenty years have seen the development of scientific methods in folktale research which aim at studying the tales in their social context, taking into account the community from which they have sprung and investigating the correlations between the storyteller and his audience. Of course, the scholar still considers the comparative study of the texts. Thus in the course of the past twenty years fieldworkers have discovered a considerable number of eminent storytellers, and have written monographs on the art of outstanding individuals and of the communities from which tales, jests, legends, and other oral traditions have flowed in great abundance. The collectors have exhausted the entire tale treasure of their informants, recording their narratives by means of shorthand or tape-recorder; they have studied the occasions of storytelling and investigated the active and passive co-operation of the listening audiences (Ortutay, 1955, 1957). For some time now researchers in folktale study have sought to answer the fundamental question as to the exact nature of a community's tale-corpus, and for this reason the same narrative is being recorded at intervals as recited by the same narrator. Scholars are examining the transmission of folk tradition from older to younger generations and between storytellers of the same generation. By means of this research they hope to obtain insight into the laws of variation, deterioration, disintegration and revival in oral tradition; further, they are attempting to grasp the process in which the ethnical crystallization of the various types takes place (Dégh, 1959, a, b; 1962).

The extraordinary richness of Hungarian oral literature may be rightly regarded as a characteristic of the historical life story of the Hungarian peasantry. In the course of our history, the Hungarian peasant had been made to bear a double brunt, suffering not only from national oppression, but at the same time bearing the burdens which lay heavily on the serfs. When serfdom was abolished in 1848, the general condition of the peasantry in no way improved; indeed, if possible, it took a turn for the worse, as from serfdom the peasants plunged into the state of agrarian proletarians. Large estates joined forces with bank capital and helped to bring about the feudalistic form of Hungarian capitalism which saw the number of have-nots grow into "three million beggars." These agrarian proletarians embraced every layer of the poor peasantry, from permanent farmhands, cottars, day laborers, and seasonal hired labor to the floating masses of construction laborers. And as has been clearly demonstrated by our folklorists, rural sociologists, and students of village life, the poor peasantry alone must be regarded as the depository of the Hungarian folktale. They are the preserver of our oral folk literature. For the poor peasant, storytelling provided an escape from sordid reality; it was his silent revolt and his wishful correction of social injuries.

The changed conditions brought about by the reallotment of land in 1945, however, did not bring about immediate changes in every respect. The Hungarian peasants, confined within the limits of their particular illiterate art, due to centuries of oppression, were not able to break completely with their traditional culture which was firmly rooted in a magico-religious ideology. Yet the past fifteen years have brought about many changes in village life. Thanks to modern housing and up-to-date farming systems, a great many of the everyday utensils of the peasants have found their way into museums and present-day collectors would have to search hard to find farm implements used in olden days. Communication facilities, electricity, radio, t.v., and other cultural benefits, e.g., public libraries, the cinema, and frequent performances of traveling theaters, have helped greatly toward levelling the differences betwen rural and town life. The desire to acquire knowledge has grown beyond all imagination; not only do the young continue with their studies after having completed the eight grades of compulsory primary and inter-mediate school, but adults all over the country desire to make up what they missed in education in their younger days, or wish to obtain higher qualifications by attending special courses. With the changed circumstances, however, are disappearing the communal opportunities for storytelling favorable to the preser-vation of oral tradition. Although some of the old storytellers, particularly in more secluded regions, or those of exceptional talents, will still captivate an interested audience with their narra-tives, their role in the life of the village community is rapidly waning. In the past two years, since 93 per cent of the Hungarian peasants have begun co-operative farming, a striking change has become apparent also in their tastes; they are abandoning folk tradition in preference for written literature.

Several of the old storytellers are still alive and occasional opportunities still arise for them to tell their stories. These occur especially at family gatherings during wintertime, or to audiences of women assembled to perform some collective task, or to work-ing brigades during the breaks in their daily work, or at some unexpected intervals due to machine repairs. Well-known story-tellers may get invitations to the village cultural center, where they recite the most popular pieces of their repertory at the request of their audiences. Localities which are still favorable for telling and listening to stories are the workmen-hostels for con-struction workers, lumberjacks, miners, and other workingmen.

Further, the centuries-old custom of storytelling has been kept on to this day in the barracks where each soldier is called upon to tell a tale after lights are out. If there happens to be one who cannot tell a story, he is ordered by way of punishment to shout into the stove, exactly as his predecessors were made to do a hundred years ago: "Oh, mother! Haven't you brought me up to be a big brute of an ass, who hasn't even been taught to tell a tale!"

It should be noted that today interest in tales of magic, at such gatherings as we have just mentioned, shows a definite decline, with a marked shift toward jokes, anecdotes, and mythic legends. This is further evidence of the vitality of these genres, which have kept their currency to this day all over Europe, even in the oral tradition of the most highly cultured nations on the continent.

The sources for Hungarian folk narratives preceding the eighteenth century are evidently of much the same nature as those of other peoples. Apart from the anonymous twelfth-century chronicler who, in the *Gesta Hungarorum*, makes mention of *"de falsis fabulis rusticorum,"* there are only sporadic hints in the sermons of preachers that the common people found greater pleasure in listening to "idle stories by which they are lulled to sleep, or to the old wives' tales narrated in the spinning-rooms" than to the pious teachings of their preachers. So much so that, according to some records dating from the fifteenth century, the preachers deemed it best to interlard their sermons with popular tales and pointed anecdotes in order to draw greater flocks into the churches and to make them listen more intently to their teachings. Indeed, it is quite understandable that these tales or elements of tales appeared only occasionally in this or that historical reference, or in sermons, since they were not held in great esteem. They were looked upon as the appurtenances of everyday life, and as such, little regard was paid to them.

The tale served as a sort of currency used by the itinerant student, the wandering minstrel, and the discharged soldier in the course of their wanderings; they paid with their stories for whatever hospitality they received during their journey. They told their tales in the market places to the crowds, at the tables of the great nobles, or to the members of the squire's household, and to the landlord and his guests at a roadside inn. Tales were recited by the household servants too, to lull their master or their mistress to sleep. Storytelling was certainly not considered an art of any kind; it was a simple form of entertainment, to help people to pass from reality into the realm of fancy. Tales were handed on by word of mouth since it was not considered worth the trouble to record them, at least not until, all over Europe, general interest began to turn to the common people.

From the sixteenth century onward, our sources become more numerous. Elements of Hungarian folk narrative appear in the Hungarian adaptations of world literature (e.g., *Gesta Romanorum, Legenda Aurea, Historia Septem Sapientum*), in the exempla, in legend and fable collections, and in chapbooks. Jests and anecdotes become a part of the content of almanacs, and the stories telling of incidents attached to the Hungarian Hercules, Miklós Toldi, or to King Mátyás the Just, become the forerunners of our folk legends. At the same time we hear of the witch who can work an evil charm on milk by causing it to spoil, and of other persons endowed with supernatural powers, capable of all sorts of magic practices, described to the minutest detail by the clergymen.

At the end of the eighteenth century, evidently as a result of the European Enlightment and the Romantic movement, interest in folk literature developed also in Hungary. To encourage inquiries into the oral tradition of the Hungarian serfs, appeals appear one after the other, urging students to follow in the footsteps of Herder and Bishop Percy. Henceforth collecting of folk narrative appears as a common cause with another vigorous movement, the struggle for the recognition of the Hungarian language as a national language, a desire inseparable from the fight for independence of the Hungarian people suffering under the oppression of their Hapsburg rulers.

Among the first collectors of folk tradition a number of eminent Hungarian authors can be found. These writers wished to propagate the cause of the common people by inserting elements of folk tradition into their work. For instance, in one of his plays written in 1793, Mihály Csokonai Vitéz includes the tale of the grateful dead (Type 506, *The Rescued Princess*), putting it in the mouth of a serf. Stimulated by the example of the Grimm brothers, György Gaal became our first tale-collector. He found his first informants among the soldiers of a Hungarian hussar regiment which was stationed in Vienna. Gaal was on friendly terms with their commander, who in an order of the day called upon his soldiers to write down the tales they knew. Thus a number of manuscripts were obtained (e.g., Private János Kovács humbly reports to the colonel that "There was once behind the beyond . . ."). A small volume of Gaal's collections, translated into German, appeared in 1822. A few years later the Hungarian Academy of Sciences took the initiative in the promotion of folk literature and succeeded in developing it into a nation-wide movement. As a result a work of three volumes was issued in 1846–48, edited by János Erdélyi, under the title *Folksongs and Legends*, which, among many other items, contained thirty-five tales. A few years later a collection of tales was issued by Erdélyi. At the same time vigorous work was done by János Kriza, a young Transylvanian theologian who had become acquainted with Herder's ideas during his college years in Berlin. After returning to his country he organized his friends, mostly teachers and clergymen, into a network of collectors. In his *Wild Roses*, a collection of folk literature, issued in 1863, there are included twelve tales, but his recently published posthumous work contains a much larger body of material. It was about this time that Arnold Ipolyi, explorer of the primitive religion of the ancient Magyars and author of *Hungarian Mythology* (1858) organized an association for the collection of folk traditions; a part of his phenomenal collection appeared in 1913. From the 1860's onward, collections appeared in a steady flow; mention should be made, among other works, of László Merényi's three books and László Arany's collection of tales, recorded as he remembered them from childhood.

With such publications the first phase, marked by a strong trend to render the texts in a simple and popular style, came to an end. Parallel with these collections, a number of works treating theoretical issues begin to appear. Imre Henszlmann, stimulated by the mythological theory of the Grimms, attempted in 1847 a systematic classification of the Hungarian folktales, at the same time comparing the Hungarian material with its European counterpart. In 1867 László Arany chose the Hungarian folktale as a topic for his inaugural address at the Academy of Sciences.

Meanwhile, the general aim of collecting underwent a change, and mere aesthetic considerations gave way to the scientific analysis of the texts. *A Collection of Hungarian Folk Traditions*[1] (1872–1924) groups, in fourteen volumes, a great mass of material according to regions and individual villages (e.g., Berze Nagy's collection from Besenyőtelek). A few gifted storytellers had now been discovered. Collectors with a linguistic interest, like Antal Horger and Béla Vikár, used shorthand to insure literal accuracy in recording the texts. Lajos Kálmány's *Traditions,* a collection of tales and legends from the southern counties of Hungary, issued in 1914–15, was an outstanding work. The second volume, following Bünker's and Radloff's example, contains the narratives of a single narrator, a young farmhand named Mihály Borbély.

At about this time Lajos Katona emerged as the first Hungarian folklorist to attain international prestige. He was not a collector himself, but an important theoretician who helped to shape the further course of Hungarian folklore studies. To his assiduous work we owe the first Hungarian type classification. This was issued in 1903–04. As the editor of the periodical *Ethnographia,* and as one of the founders of the Hungarian Ethnographical Society, he set the guiding principles for folklore research. As early as 1908, he had established connections with the Folklore Fellows in Helsinki, a Hungarian section of which was formed, shortly after his untimely death, by a group of enthusiastic folklorists. Prominent among these were János Berze Nagy, Sándor Solymossy, Gyula Sebestyén, and Béla Vikár. Particularly important had been the scholarly activities of Berze Nagy. His *Hungarian Tale Dictionary,* completed in 1912, has unfortunately perished. His huge *Hungarian Folktale-Types,* which elaborated on the principles of Katona, had been perfected by 1930, although for financial reasons its publication had to be

[1] This and following titles are given in English translation.

postponed until 1957. As regional superintendent of schools in the county of Baranya, he organized a group of able teachers into a collecting team whose efforts resulted in the three volumes of the *Hungarian Folk Traditions in Baranya County* (1940). The Hungarian section of Folklore Fellows, through a series of informational lectures, attracted many public and grammar school teachers working in the country. These teachers prepared several collections with the assistance of enthusiastic high school and university students. The publication of further volumes of *A Collection of Hungarian Folk Traditions*, however, had come to a stop for lack of funds following the first World War. But the huge collection, part of it raw material and part containing a multitude of manuscripts ready for press, has been preserved in the Ethnological Archives of the Ethnographical Museum. It is now current practice for all fieldworkers to send a copy of each collected specimen to this archive so that researchers may have access to it.

Material belonging to the second period of collecting is of only relative authenticity, for, following the pattern set by international tale-research of those days, much greater stress was laid on topical accuracy than on the verbatim recording of the texts. The main aim of the collectors was directed to record well-rounded and complete "types," instead of observing folk narrative as a living art and as a function of a given community. Therefore they had no interest in storytellers who would dish up mixed types and "spoil" the texts by turning them into a medley of indiscriminately linked elements. The ideal story was seen in the stereotype. As for the methods of recording, the collectors followed various procedures: some would write down the narrative immediately after hearing it; others preferred to make a composite recording of the same story heard repeatedly during their collecting. This kind of "accuracy" characterizes also the dialect transcriptions; the collectors used the local vernacular to denote deviations from the standard language usage. It is understandable, therefore, that claims to indubitable authenticity could not have been made until due regard was paid to the ethnological-sociological aspects of the narrative—that is, when the researcher ceased to regard the folk narrative as a phenomenon in itself, separate from the time and locality and community to which it belonged, and learned to treat folk traditions as an integral part of popular culture (Bronislaw Malinowski, *Myth in Primitive Psychology*, 1926).

Such new trends appear for the first time in our collections with Gyula Ortutay's *Peasant Stories of the Nyír* and *Rétköz* (1935) and with his tireless efforts toward faithful recording of the texts. It was Ortutay who, influenced by Asadowskij's famous report on a Siberian storyteller (FFC No. 68), first elaborated and adopted a sociological method for folktale research in his analytical monograph on Mihály Fedics, the Hungarian storyteller (Ortutay, 1940, 1955).

Further volumes from various authors have appeared successively from 1940 in the serial publication of the *New Collection of Hungarian Folk Literature*. So far eleven publications have been issued; all of them attempt to reveal the individual and collective creative process in their interrelations, through the analytical study of a given community's tale treasure. This kind of research requires the greatest accuracy in text recording. It has been already revealed by our recent recordings that our old collections are unsuitable for clarifying such important issues as, for instance, variations due to the individual storyteller and to the community, stylistic differences, ethnical features, and so forth. With our recently collected material, the entire character of the Hungarian folk-narrative corpus has been cast in a new light and these new aspects called not only for the revision (Kovács, 1955) of our old tale-type index, but necessitate the reclassification of material belonging to other genres of our oral literature. Not only are techniques required which insure greater accuracy for recording, but the recording has to register to the minutest detail every factor which might have a bearing on the formation or the background of a given text, or which would explain the changes due to alterations in the social environment. In point of fact, to explain the exact nature of the folk narrative, research must be directed to the community as a whole. By furnishing a social basis for the approach to folk narrative, we will undoubtedly create a more solid foundation for interethnical research and also for investigations concerning the life story of any literary genre in folk literature (Marót, 1948, 1949; Dégh, 1959 a, b; 1962; Ortutay 1960, 1961).

The selections in our present volume, barring the *märchen*, reflect the popularity of their respective genres. Owing to limitations of space, I had to disclaim any pretension even to relative completeness within each genre. For this reason I endeavored to pick out the most typical Hungarian specimens and, from the internationally known tale-types, those variants which have taken on specific features on Hungarian soil. Thus I could not include variants of those types which, although a characteristic part of the Hungarian tale-body, are known with very little deviation elsewhere in Europe. The scanty number of *märchen* may seem disproportionate, particularly as more than half of the Hungarian tale-body belongs to this type. Apart from the local legends, there is no other genre which can contest with the *märchen* in popularity. However, owing to their great length—they frequently run from forty to eighty pages—it was not possible to include more than eight of these tales. These eight tales are all, with one exception, hero-tales (although tales containing as their principal character an ill-fated heroine, e.g., Types 403, 425, 450, 706, 707, are popular enough in this country). I have picked out these particular hero-tales because they are representative specimens of the Hungarian folktale, while those of the abused heroine follow the well-known pattern of the European versions.

One of the main features of Hungarian folk narrative, a feature which becomes most strikingly apparent in the *märchen* and is more or less characteristic also of the other genres, appears in the circumstantial manner of narration. There are two particular ways in which this trait may become manifest.

The first we shall consider is the multiplicity of episodes. The tale is always augmented by a considerable number of related episodes, elements, or types, integrated into the narrative, or by the linking together of two or more independent tales. Other characteristic features are the indiscriminate blending of elements, the contamination of different types and the phenomenal variation of the co-ordinate and subordinate episodes, cleverly linked up to form a coherent chain of events. Indeed, the better

acquainted the collector becomes with the plot-constructing techniques of the Hungarian storyteller, the more he will be convinced that clear-cut types are concepts needed only for the
scientific classification of tales, and are not very common in
reality; they are a framework which hold a string of episodes
and motifs chosen *ad libitum* by the individual storyteller. The
truth of this statement is easily substantiated by the fact that of
the literary tales—such as the tales of Andersen, Grimm, or the
inspiring adaptations of the Hungarian Elek Benedek—only
those have become really popular which have had their counterpart in our folk tradition. In such cases the book variant has
helped toward their preservation but with little or no rationalizing
effect on the plot construction. Although I have striven toward
consistency of texts in selecting the narratives for this volume, it
has been impossible to find any two *märchen* which would not
overlap at least at one or two points. For instance, in Nos. 2 and
5 we find the identical incident of the dragon's fight on the
bridge; in Nos. 3 and 6 the hero of the tale appears three times
consecutively in the church and afterward claims that he had been
at home all the time. As for complexity of plot, No. 8 deserves
our attention in respect to elements borrowed from other tales.
The plot of these tales is usually so intricate that it reminds us
of the popular adventure story. Investigations are being carried on
to clarify the extent to which the structure of these tales is due
to *ad hoc*, individual impulses and to what extent it remains un-
changed. We are also attempting to determine whether there
exist structures which are originally rigidly stable or loosely
flexible and thus do or do not permit of individual inventiveness.

The second factor which contributes to the lengthiness of the
tales is the narrator's circumstantial, epical style of narration.
The threefold recurrence of the same episode is typical of these
tales; sometimes these episodes accrue in length when they are
related a second or a third time in the story. The first appearance
of an episode may be prior to the first test of the hero, when it
is usually put into the mouth of some magic helper in the form
of an advice; second, it is retold when the test actually takes
place (see No. 5); and it may be repeated a third time, in the
words of the hero, as he gives an account of it to another person.

There are tale-types in which the denouement involves the self-revelation of the disguised hero (as in Type 706, *The Maiden Without Hands*), and the narrator then recites the whole story all over again, with no change whatsoever in the second retelling except for heightening the tension by a dramatically expressive style. Another typical feature of the narrative manner of the Hungarian storyteller shows in his fondness for relating with great accuracy every detail as to time, locality, and tasks in connection with some incident; usually he displays considerable skill at colorful descriptions of royal splendor, of beauty, ugliness, or poverty and in the faithful presentation of his hero's frame of mind by describing his moods and thoughts and agonies in course of his wanderings and adventures preparatory to his heroic activities (see No. 3). Further, the narrator frequently lingers over some often unimportant episode, or goes to excessive lengths in the satirical presentation of certain elements, as for instance in the description of the dragon-killer's animals in No. 8. Sometimes considerable space is devoted to personal experiences or to local issues which are integrated into the story.

A strong individual stamp may and usually does emerge in the story, but strict adherence to the general framework of the tale and the use of stereotyped formulas is a positive must for the storyteller. These well-known patterns have become an indispensable part of the tale, whether the story is told by a gifted raconteur or only by some occasional storyteller with less experience and of more modest talents. I shall give here some of the most frequently used phrases which might have lost their original idiomatic flavor in the translation. To indicate the long wanderings of the hero, we usually find this stereotyped expression: "(he) was going and was going on and on against seven times seven countries . . .". It is left to the imagination of the narrator to continue with some absurd notion to further express the remoteness of his hero's destination. The *táltos* horse, carrying the hero through the air, puts the question, "How shall we go? Like wind or like thought?" And his master answers, "Just so, my dear horse, that neither you nor I may come to any harm." The old woman living in a forest is addressed in this manner: "May God give you a good day, my dear granny." She answers, "It's lucky for you to have called me your 'granny,' else I would have devoured you right away." The hero coming to some strange part of the world is accosted thus: "How come that you are here where not even a bird would come?" And the princess "is so beautiful that you could look at the sun, but not at her." It has become an unwritten law for the storyteller to give a word-for-word account of the recurring incidents and to repeat verbatim every dialogue that belongs to them, thereby expressing the special rhythms of the *märchen*.

These typical features of the *märchen* arise from the particular conditions under which they were told and heard. Although the tales reflect the concepts and values which had been long preserved in the feudal-patriarchal ideology of the Hungarian peasant, and although the elements and topics of the tales have been born in the village community, yet, instrumental in forming them into an artistic whole has been the fact that these tales offered the only, and an indispensable, form of spiritual entertainment. This is true also for certain non-village communities. Storytelling, especially the telling of magic tales, is a certain pleasure for men working far from their village homes. (The role of the female storyteller in a village community is of only secondary importance.) At workingmen's hostels and in the provisionary barracks accommodating farmhands, herdsmen, fishermen, lumbermen, construction laborers, or itinerant artisans, plenty of opportunity arises for a skilful storyteller, who in the course of his variegated activities has moved about to many places and seen many things, to find an interested audience for his stories. Men exhausted by a day's hard work find listening to tales a welcome recreation before going to sleep.

At these places the Hungarian storytellers, the most eminent of whom are represented in this volume, found real inspiration. We know of several storytellers who could carry on with a tale from six o'clock in the evening until daybreak the next morning; others could spin out one and the same story to make it last from one evening to the next over several weeks. And after continuing for a while with his tale the storyteller would occasionally cry out "Bones!" just to check on the attention of his audience, and if only a few answered "Meat," evidence that most of the listeners had gone to sleep, he would stop his tale. He would continue the next evening, after they had all agreed on the proper starting place. We know also of narrators who declared that they could make their story as long as they wished, or who told of rival storytellers who had a different tale for each day of the year. Although this may sound like an exaggeration, our recordings do indeed bear evidence to the fact that some narrators had as many as one hundred or two hundred tales in their repertory (Dégh, 1957). For instance, the recently recorded tale treasure of the seventy-two-year-old illiterate night-watchman, Lajos Ámi, contains 254 narratives (Erdész, 1962). Unfortunately, their great length prevented the inclusion of any of his tales in this volume.

The art of folk narrative plays an important role in many traditional manifestations of village life. There are a number of collectively performed tasks, such as spinning, the husking bee, stripping feathers, or bottling fruit. There the assembly, to enliven their tedious work, amuse themselves with singing songs or telling tales. In wintertime, family gatherings or friendly meetings offer similar opportunity for recreation of this kind. If there is in the village a storyteller of some repute, he is sure to get an invitation to tell his tales. But then he had better keep a check on his rambling fantasy at such occasions, as the village young are too impatient to listen to a long drawn-out narrative, and he himself would get easily confused by their ceaseless comings and goings and whisperings and by the fidgeting children. Therefore in the village community only a short or an amusing or a thrilling story can hold the interest of the audience. There are storytellers who have specialized in telling anecdotes and local legends and owe their popularity to accomplishments in these genres. There are also the droll storytellers who display considerable histrionic talents in reciting their amusing adventures and experiences. Although they do not know any narratives of the traditional kind, still their audiences never tire of listening to their stories.

The tale is kept alive in the community through the narrative art of outstanding storytellers, but the traditional tales must not be regarded as the possession of the individual storyteller but as the common property of the whole community. It has been found that in a community where storytelling is a living art there is usually not a single individual who is unacquainted with most of the traditional tales. Many of the people can even give an outline recital of these tales if requested, but most villagers are no more than passive bearers of the traditional folk literature (Dégh, 1959). Children become acquainted with oral traditions in the course of their adaptation into the life of the village community. The young children hear the tales from the older children who learn them, one way or another, from the grown-ups. For instance, to teach a child hoeing, the father will keep his son at work by telling a tale. When the child stops working, the father discontinues his tale. Thus a child becomes acquainted with the raw material of oral tradition; time will show whether or not he possesses the talents which make a skilful narrator.

A clear-cut distinction between the various kinds of folk narrative would be difficult to draw, as usually one genre follows the other and they are recited alternately to suit the whims of the listeners or the moods of the storytellers. Wonder tales are commonly not expected to be taken as the truth, whereas mythological legends are accepted as true. However, there is a close relation between the wonder tale and the local legend, as both have sprung from the same magic conception of the world which has lived on in our popular beliefs to the present day. Yet there are indications that in spite of the revolutionary changes which the Hungarian village has undergone during the past fifteen years, it will be the *märchen* or wonder tales and not the deep rooted local legends which will first yield to the rationalizing impacts of a higher civilization. I have attempted to select the most characteristic specimens of Hungarian local legend material, and have furnished the necessary explanations concerning the texts in the notes at the end of the book.

It should be mentioned here that elements which have their origins in popular beliefs occasionally lend to the fanciful world of the fairy tale a semblance of realism. For example, the queen takes advice from a village witch; "water is cast" to cure the prince from the effects of an evil spell. There are also tales which are based on myths and therefore have more easily adapted themselves to local beliefs, so much so that some variants have lost all their typical tale features (e.g., Types 365, 407, 449, 506, 756). Again, there are a number of local legends which in their structure have assumed every characteristic feature of the tale, or which appear as a transitional type between legend and tale (see Nos. 70–72). In these narratives we frequently find elements and incidents which otherwise belong to the *märchen* (e.g., the water of life; the healing grass; the threefold test; the horse of the coachman endowed with magic power talks exactly like the táltos horse of the tale hero, "How shall we go? Like wind or like thought?").

The variegated group of anecdotes and jests makes up, according to A. Kovács, 12 per cent of our tale corpus. Collecting work in this genre, as compared with the *märchen*, has been less vigorously pursued. Especially has the obscene tale been neglected by most collectors, and only one or two variants have been noted down even of the most popular specimens. However, the most recent collections have already revealed a considerable number of tales of this genre.

In the area of anecdotes and jests the Hungarian storyteller's characteristic amplifying technique appears in the concatenation of jests which contain a single episode. The form lacks epic structure, and instead there prevail brisk dialogues with no connecting text.

In these jests there becomes apparent a highly censorious sense of social criticism, often associated with rabid anticlerical feelings. This criticism had its roots in the antagonism of the common people against their masters and superiors (see Nos. 9, 10, and 14). The heroes of these stories are mostly cunning servants. Justified by their moral superiority and undeserved sufferings, they are made to mete out justice which often seems harsh and cruel in its outcome, but is never unfair. These jests and anecdotes are, indeed, excellent satires, directed against the village boss, the overbearing official, or the bullying squire held up to ridicule by a released soldier, or their own coachman, or a gypsy lad play-acting the simpleton. Because of the long drawn-out period of Hungarian feudalism, several new types thus sprang into being, differing from the well-known international types, and of the already extant ones many have gained in plasticity.

A distinct group of anecdotes (Nos. 14–17) attached to the figure of King Mátyás should be mentioned here, with the note, however, that they do not belong to the historical legends. Aside from the well-known versions, there are some twenty types which have not been reported outside the Hungarian material.

There is no clear-cut demarcation line between religious tales and anecdotes in Hungarian folk literature. Tales and anecdotes which have grown up around the figures of Christ and St. Peter have become widely popular.

The animal tales are meant exclusively for audiences of children. The tales of lying serve as an interlude, a sort of emotional relief-valve, told between two tales meant to be taken seriously.

The Hungarian body of historical legends consists of relatively meagre material. From the point of view of the community their role is minor, and excepting the fairly rich material contained in the *betyár* legend cycle, they were usually related with an instructional purpose, to acquaint the young members of the peasant family with some local events of the past, or they were recited for the entertainment of the more politically or historically minded, well-to-do peasant farmers. As for the poor peasants, they took very little interest in the history of their "lords." They cared to hear only of events which had some bearing on their own hard lot and of heroes such as King Mátyás or Prince Rákóczi or Lajos Kossuth who had done something for the welfare of their people. In matters of form the historical legends are found to be the most roughly structured; usually they tell of a single episode with no effort at epic elaboration. Even our most outstanding narrators have shown themselves reluctant to narrate historical material, on the plea that, not having experienced these events themselves, it would not be right to tell lies about them. As for the tales, that is a different matter; in them lying is not considered improper.

The so-called "true stories," a form of narrative which has only recently shown a vigorous development, are not represented in this volume, for several reasons. They are far too long, they are topically unsuitable on account of their marked local character, and they are recited in an untranslatable idiom. In fact, only quite recently, since the traditional genres have apparently lost some of their attraction to the folk, has the collectors' attention turned to this new group of narratives. They deal with a variety of topics; the stale hunting stories together with the Münchhausen adventures and war reminiscences, stories telling of unforgettable or thrilling or dangerous or amusing experiences, are lavishly enriched with the most colorful bits of biographical references. The newly established industrial centers draw their labor power predominantly from the village young men, and the first phase in their new life as industrial workers begins when they are thrown together in workingmen's hostels. Here little interest is shown in the traditional tales, for the newcomers, who have come from widely different parts of the country, are wont to exchange the everyday experiences of peasant life, giving their accounts with the accurate detail of an ethnographic description. After several retellings these accounts may develop into fixed stereotypes, but their distinct placement in folk literature presents a problem (Dobos, 1958).

One finds an uneven distribution of folk narrative throughout the area where the Hungarian language is spoken. Thus the Great Hungarian Plain, covering the vast area between the river Danube and the Tisza, and the stretch west from the Danube to the Austrian border, is poor in folktales. The reason is that during the days of serfdom these parts of the country were inhabited by free peasants endowed with special privileges, holding fertile lands. After the Revolution of 1848 they soon developed into a class of peasant bourgeoisie. This layer of peasantry never indulged in tale-telling. In their frantic, self-imposed toil, driven by their hunger for more land, they did not find leisure time for telling tales. Nor had they been forced by poverty to seek imaginary satisfaction by identifying themselves with the poor hero of the fantasy world of the folktale. At best they amused themselves with telling jokes or anecdotes, but for tale-telling, the typical entertainment of the poor peasant, they had only contempt. On the other hand, these peasants possessed a keen and conscious interest in history, which explains their bent for the historical legend.

As pointed out, the telling of tales is primarily a corollary of labor performed outside or far from the village. It was, therefore, not the soil-bound landowning peasant residing in the village who depended on the tale for his principal amusement, but the hired agricultural laborer, moving about in groups or with his family from one farm to another. Until 1945 the estates of the aristocracy and the clergy, with their ten to hundred thousands of cad.holds (1 cad.hold = 1.42 acres) extended over vast areas of the country. It was the miserable and primitive conditions of life of the residents of the manorial villages and farmsteads which have helped to develop the tale as folk art at its highest. Between the two World Wars, however, a decline in the telling of tales became apparent. By 1945, as a result of various causes, local and otherwise, such as industrialization, growing class consciousness of the workers, and large-scale migration to the cities, only a few major areas were to be found where tale-telling had been kept alive. Of course, there are still villages where tales have survived in the memory of the villagers who are willing enough to recite them on request. And there are places where the once famous raconteurs, now silenced for lack of listeners, are still living.

As for the local legends, they have kept their popularity to this day in all parts of the country, principally in the northeast region, in the counties of Zemplén, Szabolcs, and Szatmár. It is in this large area, inhabited in days of yore mainly by serfs, where the tales and legends have persisted most vigorously. But today, in place of the great farmsteads, we find villages, and the only reminiscences of the former vast estates are the manor houses which have been converted into social welfare homes for aged and ailing peasants. In this area the entire material of the communities rich in oral traditions and the tale and legend treasure of the outstanding tale-tellers is now being sought out and recorded by our collectors.

Another area of the Hungarian language territory which offers rich material in folk narrative is the independent and autonomous Hungarian community of the Székelys in Transylvania (Rumania). The Székelys have contributed some of the most colorful and archaic specimens to our tale corpus. This ethnic group has never known serfdom, but from the Middle Ages on has enjoyed the privileged status of a military force guarding the eastern borders of Hungary. Due to its geographical isolation and its peculiar historic destiny, it has succeeded in preserving the treasures of its oral literature. Today there are two ethnic groups living within the borders of our country with similarly flourishing oral traditions. Both of them, the Bukovinians and the Moldavians, were resettled in Hungary from Rumania in 1946. The larger group, the Bukovinians, settled in thirty-eight trans-Danubian villages, the minor group of Moldavians settled in six villages in the same area.

The fact that the richest tale material is to be found in the eastern and northeastern regions of the Hungarian language territory raises the question of interethnical relationships. There certainly must be some connection between the rich folk traditions of Szabolcs-Szatmár County and the treasure of folk literature of the neighboring Carpathian Ukrainians. For many centuries there has been constant contact between the peasant inhabitants of the two areas; there are also many immigrant families of Ruthenian origin who have already become Magyarized in their adopted country. Many examples could be given to show the beneficial interaction of these relationships in enriching the folktale-body on both sides.

But of even greater influence has been the interplay of Rumanian and Hungarian folktales. It is certainly not mere chance that the narrative tradition of the Rumanians of Transylvania rises high above the tale material found elsewhere in Rumania, just as the tale corpus of the Transylvanian Magyars (Székelys) surpasses that of the other Hungarian ethnic groups. Evidently the fantastic imagery of the Rumanian folktale and its peculiar mysticism must have exercised considerable influence on the style of the Székely folktales, a feature that contrasts with the typically realistic manner of presentation of the Hungarian folk narrative. And there are several other analogies of types and variants, which suggest close relations between the tale corpus of the two peoples; in fact, it would be no easy task to analyze the extent to which borrowing and lending between them has taken place.

Hungarian folk narrative plays an intermediary role between the folk literatures of western and eastern Europe. The characteristic tale-types of both West and East European folk tradition have come to form a part of the Hungarian repertoire. Undoubtedly, the strongest impact is always that which comes from the neighbors. Thus, aside from the Rumanian and Ukrainian, the influence of the south Slavs should be mentioned here. Quite frequently these influences manifest themselves in identical local redactions of international types in the folklore of both peoples.

From the end of the 1920's onward, our folklorists have turned their attention to the "eastern elements," i.e., the elements bearing on the primeval religion of the ancient Magyars (Solymossy, 1922, 1930; Diószegi, 1957). Explanatory comments, where they seemed necessary in connection with magic and local elements in our tales, have been duly enlarged upon in the notes, but our present knowledge is still far from complete in regard to these matters. Evidently, there are many elements in our folk traditions which indicate Finno-Ugrian linguistic affinities and are reminiscent of our relations with the Altaic Turks. Indubitable reminiscences of shamanism, totemism, and animism are traceable here and there, deformed or transformed, but all the same recognizable in our folk narrative body. At the same time, there are many elements from primeval sources which have entered our folklore through Indo-European intermediaries, especially through contacts with German and Slavic peoples. When research workers have furnished all the data required for the thorough analysis of the historical aspects of our tale corpus, it will become possible to trace the origins of these elements.

What is even more important from our point of view is to answer the question of how the internationally known types, motifs, and episodes have converged into such distinctively Hungarian forms. Hungarian features appear not only in the topics of these narratives, but reveal themselves in the manner and style of narration as well as in a number of inconspicuous and seemingly insignificant details. This applies just as well to the folktales of all other peoples. As Anatole France has so concisely expressed it, "They assume the hue of the sky, the smell of the earth and in them the very soul of the people unfolds itself."

The principal motive of this book is therefore to suggest the contribution of Hungarian oral literature to the universal stock of folk narrative.

LINDA DÉGH

A NOTE ON THE PRONUNCIATION OF HUNGARIAN

The Hungarian orthography is very regular so that once a few simple rules are learned, any word can be easily pronounced to the satisfaction of the average speaker of Hungarian.

All words are accented on the first syllable. What appears to be an accent mark over some vowels indicates, not accentuation, but lengthening of the vowel. In the case of *á* and *é*, the pronunciation is changed as shown below.

The approximate English equivalents of the Hungarian vowels are: *a* as in banana; *á* as in arm; *e* as in get; *é* as the *a* in fade; *i* as in ski; *o* as in ornament; and *u* as in Ruth. The umlauted *ö* is pronounced tensely, somewhat like the *e* in earn. There are no diphthongs; every vowel is given its full value without gliding. A *y* following a vowel is pronounced as *i* in ski.

The consonants, except for *c*, *s*, and *j*, are much as in English. The *c* is pronounced as *ts* as in hats. The *s* is pronounced as *sh* in shine. The word Cecus-becus, found in the title of tale No. 25, is thus pronounced tse-tsu-sh be-tsu-sh. Combinations of *c* and *s* together and with *z* (which alone is pronounced as it is in English) are as follows: *cs* as *ch* in church; *cz* as *ts* in hats; *sz* as *s* in same; *zs* as *g* in genre or the *z* of azure. The letter *j* is pronounced as *y* in yet.

A consonant followed by *y* in Hungarian is palatalized and softened so that *gy* in Nagy becomes Nadzh. *Ty* as in gatya becomes gatcha and *ny* as in Kálmány becomes Kálmánh.

Contents

I MÄRCHEN

1 The Son of the Cow with a Broken Horn   *page*   3
2 Csucskári   15
3 Handsome András   28
4 Pretty Maid Ibronka   46
5 The Tale of a King, a Prince, and a Horse   57
6 The Tree That Reached Up to the Sky   77
7 Péterke   99
8 The Story of the Gallant Szérus   109

II JOKES AND ANECDOTES

9 Whiteshirt   129
10 The Parson and the Poor Man   136
11 The Squire and his Coachman   141
12 Lazybones   142
13 A Stroke of Luck   147
14 A Hussar Stroke   149
15 King Mátyás and the Hussars   161
16 A Deal that went to the Dogs   168
17 King Mátyás and his Scholars   171

III RELIGIOUS TALES

18 Why Some Women are Grouchy and Some are
    Slovenly   175
19 How People Got a Taste of Tobacco and How
    They Took to Dancing   177
20 When Jesus Became Thirsty   181

21   When Jesus Grew Tired   *page* 182
22   St. Peter and the Horseshoe   183
23   The Little Innocent   186

IV   ANIMAL TALES

24   When a Magyar Gets Really Angry   191
25   Cecus-Becus Berneusz   192
26   Mányó is Dead   193
27   The Dogs and the Wolves Converse   194
28   Three Kids, the Billy Goat, and the Wolf   196
29   The Goat That Lost Half His Skin   197
30   The Yellow Bird   199

V   TALES OF LYING

31   When I Was a Miller   203
32   When I Was a Kid of Ten   207

VI   HISTORIC LEGENDS

33   The Fairies of Karcsa   213
34   When the Tartars Came   215
35   The Valiant Fish Trapper   215
36   The Kidnapped Child   217
37   Rákóczi Legends:
 a   A Hunting Adventure   218
 b   Rákóczi and His *Táltos* Daughter   219
38   How We Saw the Last of Forced Labor   220
39   Captain Lenkey's Company   221
40   Lajos Kossuth and Sándor Rózsa   223
41   Kossuth Wanders Through the Countryside   224
42   A Piece of Roguery   225
43   Outlaw Jóska Gesztén Goes His Own Way   226
44   Jóska Gesztén Makes His Getaway   228

VII   LOCAL LEGENDS

A   THE HERDSMEN LEGEND CYCLE

45   The Two Herdsmen Who Used Black Magic   231
46   The Herdsmen and the Wolves   232

47	The Herdsman's Magic Cape	*page* 234
48	The Cowherder's Bull	236
49	Uncle Gyuri's Bulls	237
50	The Herdsman's Dog	238

B   THE COACHMAN LEGEND CYCLE

51	The Magic Whip	240
52	The Magic Calk	243
53	The Count's Horses	247
54	The Carter and His Wheel	249
55	Knowledge Obtained at the Crossroads	253

C   WITCHES

56	The Witch that Came with the Whirlwind	256
57	The Man Who Understood the Language of Animals	257
58	The Witch's Doughnuts	259

D   OTHER PERSONS ENDOWED WITH EXTRA-ORDINARY KNOWLEDGE

59	Three Funny Stories About Magic	264
60	The Miller and the Rats	269
61	Why Men Grow Old	270

E   THE *GARABONCIÁS* LEGEND CYCLE

62	The Black Bull and the *Garabonciás*	273
63	The Dragon Rider	276
64	The Man Who Lodged With Serpents	280
65	The Grateful *Garabonciás*	283

F   SUPERNATURAL BEINGS

66	The Lover Who Came as a Star	285
67	The Witches' Piper	287
68	The Man Who Lost His Shinbones	288
69	The Unquiet Surveyor	289

G · LEGENDS THAT HAVE ASSUMED THE FORM OF TALES

70   A Dead Husband Returns to Reveal Hidden Treasure   *page* 291
71   The Midwife and the Frog   296
72   The Devil's Best Man   300

Notes to the Tales   305
Glossary   353
Bibliography   355
Index of Motifs   361
Index of Tale Types   363
General Index   365

Part I
Märchen

· *1* · *The Son of the Cow with a Broken Horn*

Once upon a time there was a poor man. The man was so poor that he possessed nothing apart from a curly-tailed pig. And so fond was he of that pig that he often went without food and gave what he had to the pig to keep it alive.

One day it so happened that his wife died, and their little child was left motherless. As the funeral costs exhausted whatever means he still had, he fell on such evil days that the child had to be given into service at the age of six.

So his father gave him into service, and the boy became a cowherd. Day after day he was tending six cows and three calves at the pasture. And for himself he had nothing more than a few ash cakes for the whole day.

One of the six cows under his care had a broken horn. Since the farmer was keeping him on such scanty food, the boy took to sucking the udders of the cow with the broken horn. And the cow did not mind it at all. She let him do it just as if he had been her own child.

One day when the boy was taking a suck from the cow with the broken horn he heard her say, "Listen, my boy. Do not feed yourself at my udder, but when you feel hungry, screw off my uninjured horn and you'll find in it food enough to last as long as I live, and to last for your lifetime. And when you have had your fill, screw my horn back where it belongs."

The child did as he was told. Whenever he felt hungry, he went to the cow with the broken horn and screwed off its horn and did himself well with steaks and stew and whatever else he found in it. And he did not care any longer whether he got any food or not from the farmer because he always had a bellyful before he went home.

Well, the farmer who had taken him into his service had three daughters: a girl with one eye, a second with two eyes, and

a third with three eyes. And it caused their mother to think long
how it came about that the boy was growing healthier and
stronger in spite of the poor food she gave him.

So she said to her daughter with one eye, "Go and see what
that child gets himself to eat while he is with the cows. To be
sure, I let him go without a scrap of food today. I want to know
how he manages for himself."

The girl with one eye went at once, but when she came to the
pasture where the boy was grazing the cows, he had already had
his fill, thanks to the cow with the broken horn.

The girl went home, "On my honor, I haven't seen anything,
mother. But cheerful enough he seemed, whistling and dancing
and singing to himself."

"Just wait," the farmer's wife thought to herself. "I'll send
my second daughter, the one with two eyes, tomorrow, and she'll
go straight with him when he takes the cows to the pasture."

And so she did. Next morning when they rose, she packed
only a chunk of stale bread for the child, but for her daughter
she gave a generous and toothsome snack. And then the two
went driving the cows to the pasture.

When they came to the pasture, they found a good place to
sit down. While the cows were grazing, the boy and the girl set
to their lunch. The boy was munching the chunk of stale bread.
And the girl had plenty of good food, but she ate it all up and
did not offer a morsel to the child.

The boy was thinking to himself, "I wish you'd drop off to
sleep. I'd go straight off to my cow to have my fill."

And so it happened. As soon as they finished having their
snacks, the girl with two eyes stretched herself on the grass and
dropped off to sleep. And the little boy went over to the cow,
screwed off her horn, and took his fill of what he found in it.
All along the way homeward the little boy was whistling and
singing merrily.

At home the farmer's wife questioned her daughter, "Now tell
me, didn't you let the child eat your dinner?"

"No, I didn't. Not a morsel."

"Hm-m-m. Doesn't he look cheerful? And I wonder why he
does."

And she went on questioning her daughter, "Do tell me now. Didn't you drop off to sleep while you were with him?"

"Oh, mother, I didn't go to sleep. Maybe I dozed off just for a little while because the heat made me feel drowsy out there in the pasture."

So that was that. The next morning the woman again gave the child a chunk of stale bread. She called her daughter with three eyes, two in front and one at the back of her head, and sent her off together with the child.

When they came to the pasture they set to their snacks. The little boy was munching stale bread. The girl with three eyes had all the good things to eat and was generously provided with them. But not a morsel did she offer the child.

The boy was thinking to himself, "Before long you'll drop off to sleep."

And she did. The boy was keeping a close watch on her and saw that she closed her eyes. But he did not know that she had kept open the one eye at the back of her head. When he saw her with both eyes closed, he went to the cow with the broken horn and screwed off her horn and had his fill out of it.

The girl with three eyes saw what he was doing because she was spying on him with her third eye. But the child did not know it. All the way home he was whistling and singing so merrily that it was good to hear it.

The woman questioned her daughter with three eyes, "Now, let me hear. Is there anything you can tell me?"

"I dare say, mother, there is. I saw the boy feed from the horn of the cow with the broken horn."

And the cow heard the words and said to the child, "Listen, my boy. The sooner we get away from here, the better. If we do not, you will starve to death, and I'll soon be slaughtered. So when the sun goes down, sit on my back and I will take you to the mountains. We'll live there, and I will take care of you as long as I live."

And that is what happened. When the day was closing in and darkness fell, the child got on the back of the cow. The cow set off with him, but she did not pass through the entrance gate;

instead she went to the back yard and through the wicket gate so that nobody should see them leave.

And when the morning sun rose they were well on their way, riding beyond the beyond, up to the great mountains. Then the cow with the broken horn stopped before a cave. "Here we are going to dwell until you grow up," she said.

And so it was. Time wore on. One year after the other. The boy grew into his eighteenth year. The cow with the broken horn said to him, "Have a try at that big tree here. I want to see whether you are strong enough to pull it up by its roots."

The son of the cow then set to pulling the tree up, but he did not have the strength to do it at the first go. He did pull up the tree, but not by all its roots.

"Now, listen," said the cow to him. "I'll go on looking after you until you grow strong enough to pull up that other big tree."

Time wore on. A couple of years went by, when the cow with the broken horn said to her son, "Now. Get hold of that tree. Let me see whether you can pull it up."

The boy set to it. At one go he had the tree out by its roots.

The cow then said to her son: "I see now that you are strong enough to be on your own. Go see the world and try your luck. I am old and I feel that the end of my days is drawing near. God help you, my dear son. We'd better part now. I am going this way, and you should go the other. But here, take this dagger from me. When you see that the blade is rusty, you will know that I am no more. When you see its blade lean and bright, you just say what you wish and it will help you in whatever trouble you may find yourself."

The two then parted. The cow with the broken horn went one way. Her son went the other way. He went all alone, making his way through the wilderness. As he was wandering on and on, he came to the edge of a forest. And there he saw a man pulling up a tree just as a woman would pull up hemp.

He walked up to the man and said, "I say, fellow. It seems to me you have plenty of brawn. What if you measured your strength against mine?"

The Treepuller answered, "The stronger will throw down the weaker, and the weaker will have to serve the stronger."

So they started wrestling together. The Treepuller threw the son of the cow with the broken horn with all his might so that the boy sank into the ground up to his knees. And at this he got into a rage and threw the Treepuller with such might that he sank waist deep into the ground. Then the Treepuller cried for mercy and said, "Let me serve you, and I will be your loyal servant as long as I live."

And they shook hands and became companions. Then they set off together to try their luck in the world. They set off and wandered on and on. One day they saw a man who was breaking down a hill, shoveling away the stone as if he were shoveling earth.

The son of the cow with the broken horn then called to him, "I say, fellow! You seem to have plenty of brawn. What if you measured your strength against mine?"

The Hillbreaker answered, "Why not? Let's go to it."

The son of the cow with the broken horn walked up to him and said, "Here I am, fellow. Put your shovel down and let us try each other's strength."

Then they went for each other. Strong as Hercules were both wrestlers, and neither could throw the other. Then the Hillbreaker tried a trick and threw the son of the cow with the broken horn with such might that the boy sank knee deep into the ground.

Angered at this, the boy leapt forth; he grabbed hold of the Hillbreaker and threw him with such might that he sank into the ground waist deep. And then the Hillbreaker begged for mercy, "Oh, do not hold it against me if I have offended you. Spare my life and as long as I live I'll follow you through thick and thin."

The son of the cow with the broken horn held out his hand, "Man proposes, God disposes. So let us be friends as long as we live." And they shook hands. From then on each did what the other asked him to do. But the son of the cow with the broken horn, being the strongest of the three, became their leader. And so he said to his two companions, "Now let us be getting on and see what is in store for us."

And they walked until they came to a mountain. There a man was kneading iron just as women knead their dough. The son of the cow with the broken horn walked up to him and said, "I say, fellow! You seem to have plenty of brawn kneading all that iron just the same as a woman kneads her dough. What if your measured your strength against mine?"

The Ironkneader then answered, "Why not? Let's go to it." And he seized the son of the cow with the broken horn and was squeezing him in a mighty grip as though he were working up a mass of dough.

But the boy was holding his own. He grabbed hold of the Ironkneader and threw him with such force that he sank waist deep into the ground.

And then the Ironkneader cried for mercy. "For the better part of my life I have been kneading iron, but never before have I met your equal. Let us be friends. Why should we go on fighting. Let there be no hostility among ourselves and let us see to it that none of us comes to harm. Let's be companions as long as we live."

They shook hands and the four became friends. They went and wandered on and on. When the day was closing in they came to a house. They spent the night in that house and no harm came to them.

In the morning, the son of the cow with the broken horn said, "Listen, friends! Why shouldn't we stay in this house? There is no occupant in it, and there is room enough for all four of us. We could make ourselves comfortable here and have a good rest." Then he said to the Treepuller, "You'll stay at home and do the cooking. You'll have a meal ready for us when we are back from stalking."

And that is what happened. The three of them went on hunting, and the Treepuller stayed at home to cook their dinner. And while he was preparing millet mush, all of a sudden a little man, a manikin, bobbed up in front of him and said, "Will you let me eat of this meal?"

"Not if I can help it, unless you take it."

"And how I will eat!" said the manikin. "What's more, I'll throw it on your belly and then eat it."

Meantime the mush was done to a turn. The little man then threw down the Treepuller and, standing on his belly, ate up the mush. And when he finished eating he went away.

And the Treepuller got on his legs and helter-skelter set to preparing something else for his companions. But the meal was not half cooked when the three arrived. "What have you been doing, friend?" the son of the cow with the broken horn asked him with no malice. "Did you drop off to sleep? Were you just idling away your time that you could not get dinner ready for us?"

The Treepuller made no excuses but said, "Well, I'm just a bit behind time, but we won't remember it when we have had our fill."

Next morning when the sun rose, the son of the cow with the broken horn said, "We'll go out stalking and you, Hillbreaker, do the cooking for us today."

So it was. The Hillbreaker stayed at home, and the three of them went hunting. The Hillbreaker set to preparing their dinner. He had the meal almost ready when the little man was there again, standing right in front of him. He said to the Hillbreaker, "Will you let me eat of the hare stew you're cooking?"

"Not if I can help it," said the Hillbreaker. "Not if I saw your two eyes start out of your head. There are four of us to eat of this stew and hungry as hunters are we. We want to have our fill."

Said the manikin to him, "Just wait! I'm going to throw it on your belly and then eat it up."

Meantime the stew was cooked. The little man then threw the Hillbreaker down and ate the stew which he had thrown over the man's belly. When he left the house, the Hillbreaker got on his legs and in great haste set to stirring up the fire and to preparing a new meal. He chopped the meat, but it was not half cooked when the three companions arrived.

"Haven't you got our dinner ready yet?" the son of the cow with the broken horn asked him. "Didn't you drop off to sleep? Were you idling your time away? Well, make it snappy! You seem to be handier at cooking than the other fellow was; I see you've got the meal half cooked. Maybe you can have it ready by the time we've unpacked."

And they went into the house and unpacked the things they had brought back with them. When they came out, the Hill-breaker called to them, "Come on. Your dinner is ready." They went to have their dinner. It was a substantial meal, and they had their fill. When they finished eating, they stretched out and slept till midnight.

The son of the cow with the broken horn was first to wake. He cried out, "Hey, friends. There's something going on outside."

And they went out and looked round, but there was nobody in the wood near the house. They turned in and went to sleep again.

In the morning when they rose, the son of the cow with the broken horn said, "Well, Ironkneader, it's your turn today to stay at home and do the cook's services for a day. Let's hope you'll prove a more capable cook than your mates and won't drop off to sleep. Off we go stalking. See to it, Ironkneader, that you have the meal ready by the time we come home."

"It will be all right!" he promised.

And the three went stalking game. Two of them knew well what was awaiting the Ironkneader, but neither of them dropped a single word about the little man nor of what had happened to them. They went stalking and returned with a good bag. As they were coming home, and were drawing near the house, they saw that smoke was still coming strong from the chimney. They came to the house and the son of the cow with the broken horn said, "It seems, friend, that you too, are behindhand with our dinner. Well, let's hope you'll have it ready while we do the unpacking."

The three then took the bag into the house and unpacked what game they had brought in a neat row, putting one carcass on top of the other. Then they turned toward the kitchen.

"Come on! Your dinner's ready," the Ironkneader called to them.

They set to it at once. When they had their fill, they lay down and slept.

In the morning when they rose, the son of the cow with the broken horn said, "I am going to stay at home today. I'll do the cooking. Maybe I can get dinner ready at the proper time."

The three went stalking. On their way they were telling one another how they had fared when they stayed at home. "Just wait and see," they said, "how our friend, the son of the cow with the broken horn, will come off."

The son of the cow with the broken horn set to work at once and was busy preparing dinner for them. He had their meal half cooked when the manikin, who had thrown his comrades down, bobbed up in front of him and said, "Will you let me eat of this meal?"

"Not if I can help it," said the son of the cow with the broken horn. "Not if you wait for it till you are blue in the face."

Said the little man, "Just wait. I will gobble it up. I'll throw it on your belly and then eat it." He made for the son of the cow with the broken horn to throw him off his feet.

The two were soon grappling, but the son of the cow with the broken horn seized the little man and held him in such a tight grip that the manikin could not budge. He snatched up the big ax which they used for chopping wood and flung it at a bulky stump which had been left near the kitchen as it was too heavy to be moved. The ax made a cleft in the stump where it struck it. Into that crack the son of the cow with the broken horn pressed the beard of the little man so that he was caught by it and could not move. Then the son of the cow with the broken horn went and finished the meal which he was cooking. He took the stew pot to the porch where they always ate their meals. The stew was now piping hot, and they could have set to it at once. By the time his three companions arrived it was getting quite cold.

"We'd better sit down to our meal at once before it gets ice cold," the son of the cow with the broken horn said. And they set to it and did themselves well.

When they had their fill, the son of the cow said to them, "Now I know what happened to you and why the three of you were late with the dinner. Why didn't you tell me about it? I dare say, you were ashamed to reveal what cowards you had been and to own up that a little man like that manikin had proved more than your match. I showed him what's what and captured him. Come and see!"

He led them to the back of the house where the little man was held captive. When they came to the stump, there was no manikin there. They followed up the tracks left by the tree stump the dwarf had dragged along when he escaped. After going along for a while, all traces of him were lost. The night was closing in and it grew too dark to see anything at all.

The son of the cow said to his companions, "Let's go back to the house. There will be another day to go in search of him."

They went back and lay down and went to sleep. When they arose in the morning, the sun was high in the sky. When they went out into the courtyard they saw that there must have been a heavy rain during the night. They had their breakfast, and then set out to continue their search. Three of them set off: the son of the cow with the broken horn, the Ironkneader, and the Hillbreaker. The Treepuller stayed at home to cook the dinner.

When they reached the spot where they had left off their search the night before, they saw that all trace of the little man had been lost. Then the son of the cow with the broken horn said, "As there's nothing else we can do, let's go stalking in some other part of the woods." They went and were looking right and left.

Suddenly the Hillbreaker cried out, "Look, look! What's that bustle going on yonder there?"

"Let's go and see what it is."

As they drew nearer, they caught sight of lots and lots of tiny tents with hundreds of manikins swarming round them. The many tiny tents stood around a bigger tent. The son of the cow with the broken horn said to his companions, "I'll go and find out what those small hustlings are yonder there," as he could not make out exactly what they were.

The Ironkneader said, "Let me go, comrade."

But it was well past noontime and the three felt hungry already. Said the Hillbreaker, "And why shouldn't we come here tomorrow in the early hours so that we should have more time to look around? As it is, it's going to be late enough when we get home."

Before long the evening was closing in on them. They gave a lot of thought to the Treepuller, who could not imagine what was keeping his comrades so long. When they were back at home, the son of the cow with the broken horn said to him, "We've kept you on tenterhooks, haven't we? Here we are. Let's have our supper."

They set to it, and they did themselves well because they were very hungry. When they finished eating, they went into the house for their night's rest. The Treepuller and the Ironkneader were already in bed when they were startled by a voice calling from outside, "Come out if you are such hardy fellows!"

At once the Treepuller and the Ironkneader got out of bed and were ready to go outside, but the son of the cow with the broken horn called out, "We have no mind to go out now. In the morning when the sun rises, we shall go out. It's too late now, and we couldn't see for the darkness. Tomorrow we'll see what there is to be seen."

And that is what happened. They stayed inside the house. All night the three took turns keeping watch. All night they heard the voice calling, "Come out if you are such hardy fellows!"

But the challengers could not make their way into the house. The four inside kept watch till morning. When the sun rose and the four companions looked out of the window, they saw a big crowd of manikins filling every bit of space around the house. There were as many of them as there was grass in the meadow.

Seeing them the son of the cow with the broken horn turned to the Treepuller and said, "How long could you stand up to it, comrade?"

"Until I am in blood up to my mouth."

And then he asked the Hillbreaker, "And how long would you stand up to it, comrade?"

"Until blood reached over my head."

And then he turned to the Ironkneader, "And you, comrade, how long would you stand up to it?"

"Until my raised arm only would stick out of the blood."

Then the son of the cow with the broken horn said to his three companions, "Here goes! Let's buckle on our swords."

The four comrades buckled on their swords and rushed out of the house. At them! The four went for the enemy. They were hitting out on all sides, cutting off heads as if they were just so many turnips. The enemy fell in great rows like grass under slashes of a scythe. In less than a couple of hours, the Treepuller stood in blood reaching up to his shoulder. About a quarter of an hour later, the Hillbreaker stood in blood reaching up to his eyes. It was not quite half an hour later, and only the hilt of the Ironkneader's sword was to be seen sticking out of a flood of blood. It was then that the son of the cow with the broken horn remembered his mother, the cow, and wondered if she were still alive. Looking at the blade of his dagger, he saw that it was gleaming bright. He cried out, "My dear fostermother, I wish I could see you."

And no sooner had he said this than the cow appeared. She said, "Where are you, my son?"

But all he could answer was, "It's all up with us."

The cow's heart sank. She burst into a flood of tears. Her flood of tears turned into a river and carried away that torrent of blood. The cow said in great sorrow, "I cannot find my son nor his three companions."

Her son and his three companions turned into fish in the river. The cow with the broken horn said, "Take heed of my words, all fishermen! None of you who will make a catch of these fish shall be able to sell or eat it unless you can guess what sort of fish it is. If you do, the fish will turn into human shape again. Then, my son, you and your comrades will show your gratitude to the fishermen and take vengeance on the manikins who brought about your misfortune."

It so happened, and before long the son of the cow with the broken horn was caught in a net, together with his companion, the Hillbreaker. The fishermen were put to great trouble getting them out of the net. Struggling hard, one of the fishermen cried out, "I dare say, they are as strong as men." And his words worked the miracle. They saw one fish turn into the son of the cow with the broken horn and the other fish turn into the Hill-breaker. The other two have not been caught to this day.

Then the son of the cow with the broken horn said to the Hillbreaker, "Now let us go and get even with the little men for what they have done to us." And they went to seek their revenge.

The Hillbreaker hurled a big hill over them. The hill buried the manikins, and not one little man was left to be seen. But since there was such a countless lot of them, their hustling and bustling kept the earth on the hill forever moving. The son of the cow with the broken horn then called a curse down upon them and said, "May all of you turn into ants!"

And since that day there are ants in this world.

And perhaps my tale would have been longer if they had not been turned into ants. So that is the end of my story.

·2· *Csucskári*

Beyond the beyond. Beyond the seven seas, and beyond their farthest shores, there lived a poor Gypsy who had three sons. Time passing, the sons grew in strength and understanding so that they began to grasp how difficult it must have been for their parents to care for them till they grew up to be young boys. They said to their father, "Father! We know how great your cares are and how little your earnings and what many troubles you have. We have decided to leave our home right now. It's enough for you to look after mother. Now please, damn us in the sight of God and man and take us into the Németi thicket so that we may live there in the thicket hereafter."

Grieved as he felt at these words, their father promised to do as they wished because he knew that he was an old man and that he could no longer provide for them. So he took his three sons to the thicket and left them there to themselves. What did the three young boys do there? They sat down beside the road and amused themselves with making small heaps of dust.

In far off time, beyond the memory of living men, there was no sun, moon, or stars in the sky. There was only darkness. In those days there reigned a king beyond the seven seas. The king had three hundred and sixty-six councilors. The three hundred and sixty-six councilors were ordered to go in search of the far off countries which lay beyond the seven seas or even farther beyond their shores. They were ordered to go on and on until they found the man who could fix the sun and the moon in the sky. If they found that man, the king would give him half of his kingdom and his daughter in marriage. So the three hundred and sixty-six councilors went off to search. They did not go very far. No further than the edge of the forest where the three Gypsy lads made their abode.

The eldest councilor then said, "Listen, my good companions. We have been ordered by his majesty, the king, to make it known to rich and poor, to young and old, and every living soul that whoever could fix the sun and moon in the sky, would get half of the kingdom. So the three young Gypsy boys living yonder there in the thicket might be told as well."

He went then to the three Gypsies and told them about the state of things. The youngest boy said, "We have well understood the difficult task in your words. Pray do not go any farther. Return to my king and lord and tell him that I am willing to fix the sun and moon in the sky on the condition that I get half of his kingdom. First, he must send the god of this earth to us."

The three hundred and sixty-six councilors then returned to their country. "Here we are, sire. Your majesty, please keep us in your most royal grace."

'Well, how did it come off? What can you tell me?"

Says the councilor, "We have found three Gypsy boys. They are willing to do what you wish on the condition that the god of the earth is sent to them."

"Well, well. There are three hundred and sixty-six of you; so you had better take counsel with one another. I give you a whole day to figure out who that might be."

A day went by and the three hundred and sixty-six councilors were none the wiser. "To tell the truth, sire, your majesty, we are at our wits' end."

"I dare say, if three hundred and sixty-six of you could not hit upon the right answer after racking your brains for a whole day, how could I help you, having only one head to think with? You had better go back to the Gypsy boys and ask them who the god of earth might be."

So they went back to the three Gypsy boys to ask them in the name of the king who the god of the earth might be.

"Well, when you go back to the king, tell his majesty that he should send the papist priest to us because we're of the papist faith."

The councilors went back and reported to the king that the three boys had asked for the papist priest. Without delay the priest was carried off in a fine coach to fetch the three Gypsy boys from the thickest thicket in the forest. So the three Gypsies and the priest came back in the coach. At once they went to the king's palace.

"Here we are, sire. Your majesty, we have come here to make out a contract with you."

They went to the king's residence and there the king and the three Gypsy boys sat down to draw up a contract. On their part, the three Gypsies bound themselves to fix the sun and moon in the sky; on his part, the king bound himself to give his daughter in marriage and half of his kingdom. When all this was settled, it was put down in the contract by the youngest Gypsy boy. He put it down in letters of gold without the use of a pen. He wrote it with his little finger. The youngest Gypsy, called Csucskári, turned out to be a *táltos*.

This done, Csucskári made his two brothers take an oath on the hilt of seven swords that they would obey him in all things and would not take heed of what they might see or hear. Then they set off on their journey. They wandered on and on till they came to the fringe of a wild, wild forest. Here Csucskári sees a big oak tree. On its top he sees a leaf. On the leaf is written in letters of gold that he who dares to pass the forest would hear a great crackle. He would come across a boar who would go at him and tear him to pieces. Then in a creek he would find a sow. Inside the sow there would be twelve wasps, shut up in a small box. The man who would take hold of the box and release the wasps would have the power to fix the sun and the moon in the sky.

No sooner had he finished reading what was written on the leaf than Csucskári set himself to make a small arrow in the way young boys do. When he got it ready, he took aim at the boar which was just breaking forth from behind the trees.

Says the boar, "Hey, Csucskári. When you were smaller than a hundredth part of a grain in your mother's womb, I knew that I would have to fight you, but don't think of doing away with the sow. She has nine piglets. I dare say, the piglets have to be raised by their mother. I know very well what you have in mind, and that you've resolved to fix the sun and the moon in the sky so that there be light again. Have a heart, Csucskári! After you've ripped open the belly of the sow to take out the box with the wasps, sew up the wound so that she may raise her nine piglets."

In great anger, Csucskári set forth to the forest to search for the sow. When he found her, he took his jackknife and cut her belly open. There he found the twelve wasps shut up in a small box. He slipped the box into his pocket and began to sew up the wound. This done, he set forth on his journey. He came to a house. He went in and called out, "Good day to you, my good woman." (He saw a woman in the room.)

"Good day to you, Csucskári. When you were smaller than a hundredth part of a grain in your mother's womb, I knew that my husband, the dragon with twelve heads, would kill you."

"Don't you worry about it. Do tell me, pray, what sign there is of his coming."

"When he gets within twelve miles of his home, he grips his mace, which weighs twelve hundred pounds, and hurls it at this castle with such force that it makes the cornerstones crack."

Csucskári turned his head and saw at a glance that the mace had already found its way home and made the cornerstones crack. In great anger, he picked up the mace. Brandishing it over his head, he hurled it away with such force that it traveled more than twelve miles back the way it had come. Then he walked to a nearby ditch which was spanned by a short bridge. He climbed under the bridge and there he made himself a sort of sword which he thrust through the boards of the bridge when he heard the dragon coming. No sooner was the dragon riding on the bridge than his horse tripped over the sword.

"Heigh-whoa! May your blood be lapped up by dogs. What's that? Haven't you done twelve good miles this day without as much as a false step. I guess it's Csucskári who is playing a nasty trick on us. If I knew for sure, I'd make him pay with his head."

At these words Csucskári leapt forth from under the bridge.

"Ho, ho! my twelve-headed friend. So that's what you are after. To take my head? Nothing doing. You can wait for it till doomsday. A poor reward, I'd call it, for all the trouble I'm taking to fix the sun and the moon in the sky so that we may live in light instead of darkness."

Says the dragon with twelve heads, "Never mind about that now. You'd better tell me how you want to fight me. Is it to be the sword, or shall we measure each other's strength in a fist fight?"

"It is neither by the sword nor in a fist fight that we are going to settle this. My father was neither a cattle driver nor a cowherd, so why should I bother about your challenge." With this he stepped forth and with two swift strokes cut off the twelve heads of the dragon.

He set off again. He came to a house. He went in and called out, "Good day to you, my good woman."

"Good day to you, Csucskári. When you were smaller than the hundredth part of a grain in your mother's womb, I knew that the dragon with ten heads would fight you because you killed his brother."

Said Csucskári, "Don't you worry about it. Do tell me, pray, what is the sign of his coming?"

"When he gets within ten miles of his house, he grips his mace, which weighs a thousand pounds, and hurls it at this castle with such force that the weathercock on the top of the roof will make an about-face."

No sooner did he hear this than it all happened as she had foretold.

Again Csucskári hid in a nearby ditch spanned by a short

bridge. Again he thrust his sword through its boards. When the dragon with ten heads came riding up the bridge, his horse suddenly tripped over the sword.

"Heigh-whoa! May your blood be lapped up by dogs. What's that? Haven't you done ten good miles this day without as much as a false step? I know this is all Csucskári's doing. To be sure I'll make him pay for it. He killed my brother, the dragon with twelve heads, and I'll take his life for it."

Enraged by this furious talk, Csucskári leapt forth from under the bridge. "Come on, comrade, let's see whether you can take my life." And with no more bandying of words the two rushed at one another. All the clock round they were dealing each other blows with the flat of their swords. And another day went by in trying their strength against each other by the point of their swords. Each fighter was an equal for the other. It was Csucskári who brought their fight to a close by dealing a blow with his sword, cutting off all ten heads of the dragon at one mighty sweep.

This done, Csucskári set forth again. He wandered on and on, till he came to a house. He went in and inside the house the wife of the dragon with eight heads gave him an uppity welcome. "Hey, Csucskári! What business have you here? You've killed the two brothers of my husband. Now he's going to finish with you, and you're going to die either by fire or by water or by the point of his sword."

"Don't you worry about it. But do tell me, pray, what sign there is of his coming?"

"There is no sign. There he comes."

"Heigh-ho, wife, I smell a stranger there in my house."

"There is no smell and there is no stranger you could smell. It must be your comings and goings that take you far from your home which fill your nostrils with strange smells." (You see, she concealed from him that Csucskári was there.)

"Look here, woman, tell me the truth at once, or I'll kill you outright. What is the strange smell I smell in my house?"

"Since I cannot keep it from you, I'd better tell you. Csucskári is in there."

"I could have guessed that it was Csucskári. And what of your false words to me? Have you grown so fond of him? Step forth at once, Csucskári. Tell me by what death you choose to die."

"You'd better ask what death you'd choose for yourself."

"Not so fast, fellow. Do you think that because you've killed my two brothers you can do away with me as well? Come on. Let us measure each other's strength by the point of our swords." (You know. He took it for granted that he would finish with Csucskári.)

All the clock round they were measuring each other's strength by their swords, but each found in the other his equal. In strength they were one and the same.

When finally Csucskári felt that he was near the end of his tether, the dragon called to him, "Listen, Csucskári. It seems to me that a valiant fighter like you is now at the very point of death. I know that you are a great champion, so let us agree upon taking a day's rest and after it we may start all over again in some other way."

The day gone, the two went at each other with their swords. Said the dragon, "Listen, comrade, there's nothing doing. In strength you're my equal and I am yours. So from now on we'll turn into flames; you'll be the green flame and I shall be the red flame."

When the red flame became so fierce that it almost destroyed Csucskári, the distressed champion lifted his eyes to heaven and right above his head there was an eagle croaking away mournfully.

"Right you are, bemoaning the ruin of the hero who is striving to fix the sun and the moon in the sky so that there may be light for all. Go now, pray, and bring water in your mouth and on your wings, and let it run over the red flame. And in return I will give you his eight heads, and the flesh and hide of a whole cattle herd, and above it there will be light." But look! The red flame is still going stronger than the green flame.

So the eagle brought water in his mouth and on his wings and let it run over the red flame so that it began to die down at once. Then Csucskári gripped his sword and at one mighty sweep cut off the eight heads of the dragon.

Then the spouses of the three dragons set out: the wife of the dragon with twelve heads, the wife of the dragon with ten heads, and the wife of the dragon with eight heads, and together they marched off to see their old father-in-law.

The old dragon asked his eldest daughter-in-law, "Well, my dear daughter, what curse would you put upon Csucskári who killed your husband, the dragon with twelve heads?"

"Well, dear father, only this: I would bring hunger upon him and then make him find a loaf of bread of which a single bite would make him burst into twelve pieces."

"Right you are, my eldest daughter-in-law. Well, what about you, my second daughter-in-law? What curse would you put upon Csucskári who killed your husband, the dragon with ten heads?"

"Only this: Within a mile from the place where hunger comes upon him, I would make him thirst so much that he would almost perish with thirst. Then I would make him pass a well so that when he drinks of it, its water would make him burst into ten pieces."

"Right you are, my second daughter-in-law. So what about you, my dear youngest daughter-in-law? What pains would you put upon Csucskári who killed your husband, the dragon with eight heads?"

"I would make him pass a pear tree laden with the biggest and finest pears so that when he'd take a bite into a pear it would make him burst into eight pieces."

While this went on, Csucskári shook the insides out of a tom-cat. Then he slipped into its skin and jumped onto the lap of the youngest daughter-in-law. She said, "Well, dear mother, what curse would you put upon Csucskári who killed your three sons?"

"As for me, I am going to sit on the shovel blade and ride after him and burn his buttocks."

Hearing this, Csucskári defecated on the lap of the youngest daughter-in-law and took off.

"We may as well go to hell now. All of us. Csucskári has overheard us talking. There is nothing now we could do against him."

Then Csucskári set off and wandered on till he came upon his two brothers.

"Well, how are you, brothers?" he said when they met.

"Since you are asking us, brother, we have great hunger."

"You say that you are hungry!" And Csucskári threw up his arm. All at once a table was spread before them. The two brothers set to it hungrily, but Csucskári being a *táltos* didn't touch anything, neither food nor drink.

When the two finished eating Csucskári made them take an oath on the hilt of seven swords that they would let him be the first in everything they would do hereafter, or else they would perish by a horrible death. "Do not fear, my good brothers. I have the sun and the moon in a small box, right here in my pocket. Hereafter I shall win myself a royal palace, and until then our lives are still at stake."

They set off again and wandered on and on. They had gone a long distance when, goodness knows by what trick, the hag with the iron nose began to burn their backs.

Says the eldest brother to Csucskári, "Oh, what terrible hunger has come upon us, my dear youngest brother. Believe me, I can hardly make out your features in my pangs of hunger."

"Do not worry, brother. I see a loaf of bread yonder there. It won't take us long to get there and then we can have our fill of it. (It was the loaf put there by the magic power of the wife of the dragon with twelve heads.) "Just keep your courage up till we come to that bread. But remember, you must let me go first."

They go on and reach the loaf. Csucskári takes the loaf in one hand and makes the sign of the cross over it. And lo! red blood flows forth from the bread. (Thus he did away with the wife of the dragon with twelve heads.)

They go further. Says the eldest brother, "Alas, Csucskári. My thirst is so great that my mouth has dried completely."

"Do not worry, brother. I see a well over there. We are going to have a drink from it, but I must go first."

When they reached the well, Csucskári drew forth his penknife and made the sign of the cross over the water. And lo! red

blood flows forth from it. (Thus he did away with the wife of
the dragon with ten heads.)

They go further. Says the eldest of the brothers, "Look,
Csucskári. I see a pear tree yonder there. How I wish I could
pick a pear or two for myself."

"Do not worry, dear brother. In less than a minute you can
pick a pear or two for yourself, but I must go there first."

Then Csucskári made for the tree and took one of its pears.
He cut the pear in two, and lo! red blood flows forth from it.
(Thus he did away with the wife of the third dragon.)

At this the old hag with the iron nose came up, riding fast on
a shovel hot enough to burn her buttocks. The three wanderers
were near despair. How could they flee before her? Where should
they run for dear life? Suddenly they saw a shack not very far
off. Says Csucskári, "Let us find our way to that round shack
yonder. We might be safe there."

They went to that shack. In the shack they find a man who
was a blacksmith.

Csucskári says to him, "Listen, brother smith. As long as we
live, we are going to serve you, all three of us, only save our
lives from the old hag with the iron nose. She is the mother of
the dragon with twelve heads and she is after us to take our
lives."

"Look here. I'll save your lives on the condition that you will
serve me as long as you live. If you fail to obey me, just see what
I might do to you. Look at that manikin here. He is about two
inches in size, but I can tie him into three hundred and sixty-six
knots when I get angry."

Young Csucskári wanted to see at once how this was done.
So the smith showed him how he tied the manikin into three
hundred and sixty-six knots.

Then the hag with the iron nose came to the door and called
in, "Heigh, my friend! Didn't Csucskári with his two brothers
come here?"

"So he did, mother."

"Then you must give them to me at once," she said. "He has
killed my three sons. Three champions they were, and you
would not find their equal, not in seven counties."

Says the smith, "Oh, mother, you'd better forget about it. It's not so simple at all with a fellow like that Csucskári. If I were to give him to you through the window, he might run away; if I were to give him to you through the door, he might knock you off your feet and get away. But listen, mother. Come what may, I am going to cut a hole in the wall and through this hole I will push him out. You must stand there. Open your mouth and catch him. Then you can bite him into pieces."

And that's what happened. Csucskári made a hole in the wall. The smith took a big pot, big enough to hold sixty quarts, and filled it with lead. He began to melt the lead in the pot.

When they finished what they were doing, Csucskári took hold of the pot and the smith called out through the hole, "Hey, mother! You'd better put your mouth close up to the hole so that not an inch of Csucskári may slip past it, or he might get away."

Saying this he poured all sixty quarts of the melted lead into her mouth. Then he went out to see what happened. The hag with the iron nose lay dead as a doornail.

Great joy came upon Csucskári because the hag they feared so much was destroyed. Still he had his worries. How were they to get away from the smith? If in his anger he could tie a manikin into three hundred and sixty-six knots, to be sure there would be a good many hundred knots more for Csucskári.

The smith had a wife. Csucskári fell in love with her and as she loved him too, he soon asked her to reveal to him what secret strength her husband possessed. What was it that made him able to move easily through heaps of steel, reaching up right to his knee, and by what trick could he tie up a man into three hundred and sixty-six knots?

At noon the smith came home to have his meal.

"Oh, my dear and wonderful husband," his wife said to him, "I have been living with you for some thirty years now, but I have never asked you wherein lies that magnificent strength of yours."

At that the smith fetched her such a blow in the face that she passed out for twenty-four hours. A little time after, she asked her husband again, "My dear husband, do tell me, pray, wherein lies your magnificent strength?"

"Listen, wife. As you are so keen to find out, though heaven only knows whether I shall not be sorry for it, I am willing to tell you. Look at that chain mail I always wear for a shirt. Without it, I possess no more strength than any other human being."

"Oh, dear husband, if I had known it before, I would have had it gilded for you."

When the day turned to night and the smith went to sleep in his bed, his wife took off his shirt and gave it to Csucskári. At once Csucskári slipped into the shirt. Then he goes to his sleeping brother and ties him into three hundred and sixty-six knots to test the magic power of the shirt. Then his unties his brother.

Midnight came. The smith wakes from his sleep. At once Csucskári goes up to him. "Listen, brother smith. I am not going to serve you any longer."

Says the smith, "And why not, may I ask? Didn't you make a pledge that all three of you were to serve me as long as you live?"

"Indeed, we did, but that was some time ago."

"Just listen, brother. I know that all this is my wife's doing. I dare say, you have enough guts to oppose me, what with tying up your brother, though you could not have done it without having taken my strength from me. But here you shall remain."

At this Csucskári seized the smith and tied him into three hundred and sixty-six knots.

"Oh comrade, didn't I spare your life and your brothers' lives? Surely, I may trust your kind heart and you will untie me before you leave this place."

Csucskári untied the smith and with his brothers took leave of him. They set off and wandered on and on until they came to a spot not far from the royal palace where they had made the contract with the king.

"My dear brothers, after all the trouble I went through, let me now take a little rest so that I may sleep for a while."

It was not really that he wanted to have a sleep. It was only to put his brothers to the test. You know, he did not really need any sleep because he was a *táltos*.

Said his two brothers, "Indeed, you deserve some sleep brother, after all your troubles."

Said his second brother, "My dear brother, Csucskári, you can make yourself comfortable when we reach the king's palace. There you can take off your clothes and take a bath. That's where you should take a rest."

But Csucskári did not take heed of his words. There and then he lay down and soon was snoring away in sleep. His eldest brother than drew forth his razor and began to sharpen it. His younger brother asked him, "What are you doing, brother? Didn't you have a shave yesterday? Surely, you don't need one today."

"I am going to cut Csucskari's throat so that I may marry the king's daughter and get half of his kingdom."

"And could you cut your brother's throat in cold blood knowing that it was Csucskári who did all the fighting and endured the many hardships? What else did we but follow him about, and surely that did not amount to much." And he called to the sleeper, "Wake up, my dear brother Csucskári! Our eldest brother is going to cut your throat."

"I knew it, my dear brother. I was not sleeping. It was only to test the true feelings of your hearts for me. But now you must disown our eldest brother and pledge yourself to have nothing to do with him, whatever state you may rise to in this world. He may not even hope to be taken on as a herdboy for your turkeys." (That is what Csucskári said to his second brother.)

After that they took leave of him, and Csucskári and his second brother set out for the king's palace. When they came to the palace, they went in. "Good day to you, sire. Your majesty, I have brought the sun and the moon for you but on the condition that you give your daughter in marriage and half of your kingdom to my brother and not to me because I am a *táltos*."

"That's all right by me," said the king.

Then they did justice to their agreement. The twelve wasps were released, and the sun and the moon were fixed in the sky. And so there was light.

Throughout seven countries the drums went rolling and all the dukes and counts and great lords came together to celebrate

the wedding. For seven years and seven winks the wedding feast
went on.

And if they are not dead, they are still alive to this day.

• 3 • *Handsome András*

Once upon a time, in a certain part of the wide world, there
lived a poor man. So poor was he, that not even a flea would
have done well on him. The poor man had a wife and a son,
and until the child reached his seventh year, the man together
with his wife went to work on farms. They worked hard as
hired hands to make both ends meet. They lived as miserably
and as poor as church mice, and often they had to go without
a meal. But when the child reached his seventh year, he had
grown into such a handsome young boy that it would have been
hard to find his peer in seven countries. And soon the rumor of
his good looks went around and reached other lands, and it
became known what a handsome youth he was. The only trouble
was that he had no name because he had not been christened
as yet. But before long, a fitting name had been found for him
and he was to be called Handsome András. As soon as he had
a name for himself, he said to his parents, "Well, my dear
parents, make me ready for a journey as I am going to leave you.
I shall go and seek service somewhere and try my luck in the
great wide world. I am not going to endure any more starvation
at home, nor do I want to remain a burden to you. I have had
more than enough of living in poverty."

And what astonishment it gave them to hear that, young as
he was, he was willing to earn his bread in the service of
strangers. They tried to argue with him, but to no avail, so firmly
was he resolved to set out on his journey. Since he would not
change his mind, there was nothing else they could do but let
him have his way. They got provisions together for his journey
and packed his bag with an ash cake, and some baked potatoes,
and a big cabbage and a couple of onions, and a small pouch of

salt, so that he should not be wanting in food while on his journey, and until he had found a suitable place for himself.

András took leave, bidding farewell to his father and mother, and the folks he knew. Some of the people returned his farewell with taunts and called to him to watch his step while he was on the road, and to keep out of the mudholes and mire, because if he did not take care to keep his clothes and shoes clean, he would soon be infested with lice and covered with filth and would go to the dogs. But he paid no heed to their raillery and went on his way. The girls burst into bitter tears when they saw him leaving. Not a single girl had dry eyes in the village, such was the grief caused by his departure. It would have pleased them no end to make him change his mind and keep him at home, but he had no interest in them and proceeded on his way. And he went on and on, over hill and dale, over hedge and ditch, straight ahead, until he came to a big forest. And in the forest he came to an opening. On its farther side he found a big cave and a stream of pure water running past it. And there András settled down.

He took some food from his bag and made a fire to cook himself a meal. No sooner had he finished unpacking his provisions than a golden feathered pelican alighted from above and dropped a letter, written in glittering gold ink, right before him on the ground. It made him wonder what sort of a bird it was that had brought a letter there. And when he picked it up to have a look at it, didn't he find his very own name written on the letter? That was a surprise, indeed! Who on earth could have sent him a letter in that part of the world, where there was not a soul who knew him? He began reading, and would you have ever guessed that on the outside it said: "This is to Handsome András—to be delivered into his hand only." And when he turned it over to look inside, there was written in silver ink: "I say, Handsome András! I've seen a painted picture of you. But I'd like to see your living self, just to make sure that you are really as good-looking as I think. I want you to come here, to our beautiful Fairyland. And when you set off just follow the track of my pelican bird. This letter is from Fairy Rózsa, the daughter of the far-famed fairy king. It is from Fairy Rózsa, the most beautiful princess in Fairyland, who keeps you in her thoughts. Let me see you soon.—Fairy Rózsa."

András picked up his bag and, slinging it over his shoulder, he set off at once, without taking a night's rest. He kept close behind the pelican and followed the bird over hill and dale, over sea and land, over hedge and ditch, over rocks and wood, until he ran out of provisions and had not a scrap of food left in his bag. He had spent all his strength in the long journey and felt unable to go any further. But that was not all. The worst of his troubles came when his beard and his moustache had grown to such length that he could wrap that vast amount of hair round his waist twelve times and still it was trailing along behind him so that he could not help but trip over it. And once as he fell, he went down straight into a deep pit, and as hard as he tried, he could not get out of it. There was nothing he could do but remain in the pit.

"I guess," he thought to himself, "there is no Fairyland at all. Someone has just fooled me with that letter. But come to think of it, how could the pelican have known that I am the best looking young fellow in the world? Maybe there is a Fairyland after all, as the birds there seem to have more sense than most of the folks I know around our parts. Anyway, the trouble is that I shan't be able to ever get there, as I haven't got a scrap of food to live on. And I have grown old, with all my strength spent, and I've lost my good looks. What else can I do but wait for death? Oh, if only just once I could have set eyes on the beautiful fairy maid, there would be still a glimmer of hope for me! But now I'm done for."

As he was speculating about this and that, at the bottom of the pit, suddenly he beheld a bearded little man, about two inches high, standing right in front of him.

"I dare say, it was lucky for you to think of Fairy Rózsa, or else I would have devoured you, or torn you to pieces. But now get quickly on my back and I will take you to the border of Fairyland. And then I will show you which way to go."

As it seemed best to follow his advice, András got on the little man's back. In less than a wink the dwarf carried him out of the pit. András was holding fast onto his hair and, "fog before and fog behind him," the manikin shot forward. He made a long leap and two jumps, and there they were, right above Fairyland. But when the dwarf came down to the ground with András, he stopped and said, "Well, now you must get off my back and proceed on your journey alone, going always eastward. It is not a long distance from here to reach the Fairy Castle, which revolves on the paw of a cat with seven skins. And soon you will hear a voice coming from the castle, and it will sing, 'Come this way, Handsome András! Here is the Fairy Castle.' Well, so long."

No sooner had he said that than the manikin vanished out of sight as if the earth had swallowed him up. And in his place there stood the golden feathered pelican.

Again András set forth, following the bird. Before long he came to a lake. The water in the lake was quite white. "I guess," he thought, "I could bathe in that nice lake. Anyway, it's a long time since I had my last bath." And the next thing he did was to get out of his clothes. It did not take him long, since they had been worn to tatters, leaving half his body bare. After he had stripped he went into the water. When he had stayed in the water just a minute or two he felt so hot that he thought it best to come out at once. And Lord! what did he perceive upon coming out of the water: he had lost his hair, his beard, his moustache, even his eyebrows while he was in the lake. And the water made him young again, young as a new born babe, but strong in his body as if he had muscles of steel.

He walked to the spot where he had left his clothes, but hell's bells!—all his clothes were gone. What's happened to them? Who's taken them? "Well," he thought, "it's a pretty scrape I've got myself in. How can I go to Fairyland? To be sure, Fairy Rózsa would turn me out at once, if she saw me appear before her without a stitch of clothing." And all the while his eyes went searching around in the hope that he might catch sight of the thief who had stolen his clothes. And suddenly, he caught a glimpse of a glittering thing. It was lying not far from him, under a cactus tree, at the edge of a bed of reeds. "What's that? I must have a look at it." He walks up to the cactus, and my! there are garments as beautiful as you could wish. Never before had he seen anything like them. And there they are: a pair of spurred copper boots, with their uppers creased like an accordion. And to match them, there were a pair of brass tights, braided neatly with tulip patterns. But that was not all. When he beheld a silver vest and a coat, and a cocky gold hat trimmed with a cockade and a peacock feather, and lying beside them, a diamond studded sword, its steel glittering in all the colors of the rainbow, his amazement was so great that he just stood there gaping, with his eyes popping out of his head. "Well," he thought, "what a fine looking lot they are. But what good are they to me, if they belong to someone else?"

All at once, there was the pelican again. And it was carrying a second letter in its mouth and it dropped the letter on the garments and then flew off again. "Why shouldn't I have a look at that letter and see what it says," he thought. Lord bless my soul! Here's what's in the letter: "These garments are for Handsome András to make up for the lost ones, so that he should be able to make his appearance before me, in Fairy Castle. And he should make haste and lose no time so that I may see him soon. In the inside pocket of his vest he will find some food. Goodby till then—from Fairy Rózsa."

To be sure, he didn't need to be told twice to get into the garments and to buckle on the diamond studded sword with a belt glittering in all the colours of the rainbow, and to cock over his eye the little gold hat trimmed with a peacock feather. Then he reached into the inside pocket of his vest to take out some food, but alas! there was no food at all, only a beautiful rose with petals in seven colors.

"I dare say," he thought, "an untruthful maid that Fairy Rózsa must be. Didn't she write to me about food, when there's nothing but a rose. Though I feel hungry enough to devour a piece of rock. But as there's nothing else, I am going to find out how it smells."

But as soon as he brought the rose to his nose, there! he was holding a plate in his hand. And there was such a lot of food and drink and money on the plate, that he found it difficult to hold. He almost dropped it with surprise. Hadn't he taken a rose from the inside pocket of his vest? And lo! there he was now holding in his hand a large plate of gold, painted all over with beautiful flowers in the brightest of colours. And the food and drink and money he found on the plate would have served well a hundred such youths. Well, he sat down under the cactus tree and set to his meal. But when he took out the first spoonful, he could hardly believe his eyes, because there was no food at all, only tiny little birds, covered with feathers of diamond, of gold and silver. And when he brought the spoon to the plate again, all the tiny ones opened their mouths in expectation.

"What a girl is Fairy Rózsa! The most cunning and artful of all girls in Fairyland. Wasn't it a clever trick to play on me! But just wait till I stand face to face with you, Fairy Rózsa. You'll get a kiss from me that will make the earth tremble under your feet." Then he put the plate on the ground and set out. When he took a few steps he turned and looked back, but the plate was gone. "No worry," he thought. "It was God who gave it to me, and it was God who took it from me; it will be God who'll give it back to me as sure as God is three in one." And he set off and was walking for seven days and seven nights, and he did not stop anywhere. Suddenly the tune of a sweet song caught his ears, but it sounded so far off that it was scarcely audible. He stepped out in the direction of the sound; and as he came closer and closer to it, he was able to make out the words:

"Come, oh come, and do not tarry,
Let my yearning heart be happy.
How I wish, to see you here
Handsome András, dearest dear."

"Oh," he thought, "how I wish I could see you, my pretty and beloved Rózsa." And to think of her made his spirits rise, and he felt as hopeful as ever, so that he stepped out more briskly. But during his long journey he had worn such great holes in his copper boots that his toes were showing. And his legs felt so tired that he had to proceed on his knees. And as he was crawling along on his knees, he came to the top of a big mountain. There he stopped to look about, but confound it all! the Fairy Castle still loomed so far off, that he could hardly see anything of it at all. But even that was the lesser worry because he could have managed somehow to make his way to Fairyland on his knees, if only the other side of the mountain had not been covered with smooth and slippery glass. And so smooth and slippery was the slope, that even the flies descending it would go slipping down and break their necks. So what was he to do? How could he get safely down the slippery glass? He was sure that as soon as he stepped on it, he would go rolling down the slope and arrive at the foot of the mountain in such shape that a knitting needle would not be sharp enough to pick up what there remained of his bones. "Well," he thought, "I've come as far as this, but it seems I cannot go any farther. So I'd better look for a cave or a hollow in a tree where I can spend the rest of my life, as I see there's no other way down the mountain toward Fairy Castle. To be sure, if some winged creature does not take pity on me and does not help me to get away from here, I shall die of hunger."

But it was time to move on, as it had begun raining and the day was drawing to a close, and he was in need of shelter. As he went along he came to a fir tree with thick and bushy boughs. He figured that if he climbed the tree he could spend the night in safety from the beasts roaming around in the forest. He started climbing, but the tree was so high that after seven months' climbing he still had not come near the top. Growing tired of climbing, he chose a thick branch and on it he lay down and rested for three days and three nights. And all the time he was feeding on the prickly leaves and berries of the juniper. And he drank the resin which was under its bark. And after three days and three nights he set off again. And he went climbing forth along the branch and he went until he beheld a beautiful wreath which was fastened at one end to the branch he was climbing. And the opposite end of the wreath was tied to the top of the highest spire in the Fairy Castle, which was revolving on the paw of a cat with seven skins. The wreath was thus suspended by its two ends and was dangling in the air, seven miles above the ground. "Well, so far, so good. But how can I get through this dangling wreath? If I am caught by the wind it will be the end of me and there will be no one to pull me back. However, let the future look after itself. Come what may, I'm going to take my chance and if I have to pay with my life, at any rate I shall die in Fairyland for Fairy Rózsa."

And he went climbing across the wreath, and made his way safely to the top of the highest spire in the castle. But the spire was revolving so fast that he found it impossible to gain a foothold. What else could he do, but look for some other way to get down? And as time wore on, it happened again that his beard began growing very fast, and it grew until it was seven hundred feet long. Then András took his jackknife and cut a long lock off his hair and divided it into twenty-one strands. And he made a rope of them, tying each to the other's end. And when he had the rope ready, he fastened one end to the wreath and the other to his sword, and he lowered it to the ground. But it was not long enough to reach down to the ground. Then he cut off his long beard and tied it to the rope to make it longer. It was still not long enough. Then he cut his yellow moustache, which he wore twisted in a corkscrew curl. But when he tied it to the rope, it was still too short to reach down to the ground. Then he cut his eyebrows, which had grown to such length that they made a knot of nine coils on his head. And still the rope was not long enough to reach down. But as there was nothing else that could be used to make the rope longer, he began letting himself down, holding onto it.

When he reached the end of the rope, he beheld an open window opposite him, not far from where he was. And in the window there were roses and tulips, delighting the eyes with their beautiful colors. And behind them there stood a young woman, of such great beauty that never before had human eye beheld the like of her. Then Handsome András swung forward and landed in the open window. But the beautiful maid had gone. She was only one of the comeliest parlor maids of Fairy Rózsa. But when she saw that a handsome youth was letting himself down on a hair-rope, in the direction of the window, she hastened to her mistress, to report to her the arrival of the long expected visitor, Handsome András.

Oh, dear! Oh, dear! How angry she grew at the maid's report. How could she tell her such a whacking lie? And in her anger she landed her a blow in the face that sent the maid sprawling

on the floor. At that very moment a second maid came in, to
report the arrival of Handsome András. She, too, got a box on
the ear for having told a lie to her mistress. But an instant later
a third maid came in to inform her that the long expected visitor
had arrived. Well, that was the last straw. Fairy Rózsa struck the
maid on the mouth so mightily that all her teeth were knocked
loose. And just a few seconds later, there was a knock on the
door. "Come in," said Rózsa, and Handsome András stepped
into the room. There was no end of amazement that the far-
famed Handsome András had truly arrived at the castle.

András saluted Fairy Rózsa as befitted her, and told her who
he was. And then he said to her, "Well, beautiful fairy maid, in
your letter you invited me to come to Fairyland. So I have come,
that I may take a close look at you and that you may judge my
looks for yourself. Now tell me what you wish me to do."

Said Fairy Rózsa, "All right, András. I see that you are really
handsome and you can keep your wits about you. But it is my
wish and my condition that you cannot marry me until you
have curried the three filthy horses in the stable and cleared away
the dung, because I want these three horses to draw the coach
which will take us to our wedding. If you can complete this task,
I will become your wife, but if you fail, I will have you impaled."

How his heart sank at her words. So that's why she had made
him come here, to clean the stable and to curry horses. Well,
if so, let it be. He goes to the stable, and there are three fine
horses tied in their stalls. Three roans they were; one the color
of gold, the other a silver-grey, and the third a copper-red.
András did not waste time, but stripped himself to the waist,
got hold of a shovel, and set to mucking out the stable. And he
toiled and toiled until the sweat came trickling down all over
his body in seventy-seven streams. But the faster he did the
shoveling, the more muck there was in the stable. It made him
wonder, and he sat down on the threshold and buried his face
in his two hands and began to weep. And so completely did he
give himself up to despair that the tears came rolling down his
cheeks in huge drops. He was at a loss, indeed. What should he
do to the three darned horses to stop their endless defecating?
Surely, he'd never get through clearing away all that mess, not

if he worked till doomsday. But what could he do with such filthy beasts that went on defecating as if a machine were at work in their insides? And as he sat there, brooding over his troubles, one of the horses (all three of them being *táltos* horses) began to speak to him. "What makes you so worried, Handsome András?"

"There's enough to make me worry. Haven't I been ordered by Fairy Rózsa to clean the stable and to curry the three of you? Can't you see that I am unable to do either, not if I went on toiling till I was blue in the face?"

"If that's all," said the *táltos*, "don't worry your head about it. Go and lie down in the left corner of the stable and put the shovel across the broom at your feet. And have a good sleep till tomorrow morning. And when you hear me give a loud snort, get up and prop the shovel and the broom against the hinge, but put both of them upside-down, with the business end upward. And when you turn round, you'll find our coats gleaming and spotless, and the stable well cleaned out. Then come to me and put your hand into my left ear. In it you'll find a copper nut. Crack the nut open, and you'll find in it a fine silver sword and garments woven of gold. Get into the garments and buckle on the sword. Then go into the courtyard and get on the top of the muckheap. There you must seek until you find a dogrose bush. Just give it a slight touch three times with the tip of your sword. Then get hold of the bush and pull it out. Underneath you'll find a soiled saddle and a bridle covered with mould. Put the saddle and the bridle on me, and I will do the rest. Then go and look for a place where you can lie in hiding, concealed from human eye. And do not come out of hiding until you hear me neighing three times."

Handsome András did as he was told. When the morning came and he heard the *táltos* horse give a loud snort, he quickly leapt to his feet, took hold of the shovel and the broom, and propped them against the door. Then he drew forth the copper nut from the left ear of the *táltos* horse. He cracked it open and took out the silver sword and the golden garments. He got into the garments and buckled on the sword. Then he went out and on the top of the muckheap he found the dogrose bush. He touched it three times with his sword. Then he took hold of the bush and pulled it out by the roots. Underneath, he found a saddle and a bridle half eaten away by rust and mould and at least seven hundred years old. He took them to the stable and put them on the copper-red roan. Then he went and hid himself under the tail of an old buffalo that was a hundred years old. And there he lay in hiding until he heard the *táltos* horse give three neighs.

And this is what Fairy Rózsa was doing that morning. She went to the stable to see how Handsome András was getting on. When she saw that all was in perfect order, she looked around for András to praise him for the good work he had done. But she could not find him anywhere. She asked the *táltos* horses whether they had not seen a handsome youth in the stable. But they shook their heads in denial and said that they had not seen anyone except the old stableman. She was getting anxious about András. Where could he have gone without a horse, without food, without money, and without knowing anyone thereabouts? "I hope he didn't ask my swans to take him away without my leave?" And she summoned her swans, but not one of them was missing. But there was no trace of András. "No fear," she thought to herself, "he will show up when he gets hungry. He must be around somewhere, as I know he did not leave by the castle gate." So she gave orders that as soon as he appeared the *táltos* horses should blow at him such air as would make him fall asleep. And then they must call her back by neighing because she was leaving now to go to White Pearl Chapel, and she would not be back before noon.

And so saying she stepped into her glass coach drawn by her swans. She touched them lightly with a white violet, and the swans rose with her into the air and, "fog before them and fog behind them" they were gone as if the earth had swallowed them. Then the *táltos* horse gave three loud snorts, and at once András left his hiding place and came forth. The *táltos* horse then said, "Well, Handsome András, lead me out and get on my back. I will take you to Honey Lake. That's where you'll find White Pearl Chapel and Fairy Rózsa is there attending Mass. And as soon as I descend from the air, get off my back and stroke my head three times. And I shall vanish out of sight. Then you must cross yourself with your left hand and the moment you do so, you'll become the most handsome youth that ever walked this earth. And lots and lots of people will want to shake hands with you. But you must neither look at nor speak to anyone. Fairy Rózsa herself will walk up to you to shake your hand. But do not look at her. She will smile at you and tell you how she loves you, but do not listen to her. Go into the chapel and when the priest says 'Amen' at the end of Mass, come out at once, and make quickly back to the spot where you got off my back. Then give three snorts, and I shall appear. Then jump quickly on my back, so that we can get home before Fairy Rózsa arrives. And you must keep in mind what you have now heard or you will come to grief."

Well, András did as he was told. When Fairy Rózsa went to church, András got on the back of the *táltos*, and the horse rose off the ground, up into the sky, so high that it went head on into the moon, sending it seven miles upward. Then the horse went forward, stepping from one star to the other, just as if it were going up a flight of stairs.

Suddenly the *táltos* horse went gliding down toward the earth. It came down under a beautiful palm tree which stood on the shore of Honey Lake. There András got off his back and crossed himself with his left hand—and the very moment he did so, his beauty become such that it outshone the splendor of the sun. Then he raised his left hand and stroked the head of the horse three times. At that instant the *táltos* horse vanished from sight. Then he made for the chapel, but the fairy maids came swarming round him, and it was not easy to get out of their way as all of them were eager to shake hands with him and none of them would have resisted long in becoming his betrothed. When Fairy Rózsa came over to shake hands with him, he neither looked at nor spoke to her. He went into White Pearl Chapel and took a seat in the men's pew. He closed his eyes and ears to everything, except the sermon. And when the priest said 'Amen,' he rose and left the chapel and made his way back to the shore of Honey Lake. When he got back under the palm tree, he gave three whistles, and the copper-red *táltos* roan appeared. Quickly he jumped on its back, and off they went, and the *táltos* horse was going at such speed that in the trail of dust that rose in his wake there was no telling which way they had gone. But Fairy Rózsa did not spare her seven swans and drove furiously in pursuit of András. But all in vain. Back at home, she went at once to the stable to see whether she would find András there. And there is András hard at work shoveling out the muck, and he is streaming with sweat, and he is clad in his tattered filthy rags, the same he was wearing when he appeared in the castle.

"Let me hear, András," she said, "where you have been all the time when I was looking for you."

"Where else, but in my skin."

"Steady, steady! But where did you go?"

"Nowhere. All the time I was inside the stable."

"Do not lie to my face. You weren't here."

"To be sure, I was here. I was sleeping under the tail of that old buffalo. And if you do not believe me, just go and look for yourself and you'll find my night cap still there."

Verily! She found his night clothes where he said they were.

"Since I got up this morning, I've been tending these filthy nags. There wasn't time for me to go anywhere."

"Just think, András! Didn't I see you this morning in White Pearl Chapel?"

"Not me, princess."

"Well, never mind then."

And that was all that passed between them so Fairy Rózsa did not get any nearer the truth. The next day came. Rózsa went to church again. This time she went to the Crystal Chapel on the shore of Milky Lake. Before she left she went to the stable to see how András was getting on with his work. And there she finds him, working up to his knees in muck, his face covered with a layer of dung so thick that radishes would grow in it. Without speaking to him, Fairy Rózsa left the stable and stepped into her glass coach, drawn by fourteen swans. And off they carried her, swift as the whirlwind.

And this time András did not need telling twice. At once he went to the copper-red mare and with his right hand reached into the mare's right ear. There he found a silver hazelnut.

He cracked it open and took out the finest garments woven of pure gold and a sword to match. He got into the garments and buckled on the sword. The mouldy saddle he snatched up with a pitchfork and slung it on the back of the silver-grey filly. Then he swung into the saddle. He was filled with ardent longing to be at the place where he could see Fairy Rózsa. No sooner had this thought flashed through his mind, than the silver filly leapt into the air, and did it with such fervor that it carried the stable some fourteen miles upward into the sky, and only then and there did it shoot through the stable roof, so that there was no living soul to see which way it went. And the silver filly stepped on the rainbow paved Milky Way [orig., the Warrior's Path] and went on until it reached the Milky Lake. There it descended on the shore of the lake and stopped at the foot of a turnip tree. And András followed the same course as he had on the Sunday before. He neither spoke to, nor looked at anybody, although the whole congregation were keeping their eyes on him while he was in the chapel. And when the priest said "Amen," he just turned out of the door and vanished as if the earth had swallowed him up.

Well, soon after, Fairy Rózsa is leaving too, her fine long veil trailing along behind her as she goes. She steps into her glass coach, and the swans drive off with her, and they go like the wind, so that even the clouds are put to flight. But they could not catch up with Handsome András. Back at home, she went at once to the stable. There is András toiling hard, up to his armpits in muck, a revolting sight to the eye indeed. But she does not mind asking him, "Well, András, where have you been today? Didn't I see you this morning in Crystal Chapel, near the Milky Lake?"

"Not me, princess. What do you think? There's no getting through with these darned horses. It seems to me, I just go on forever and ever trying to rub them clean and yet they are all of a muck. And then, neither have I got a Sunday-best to go out in. Sure, I wouldn't think of leaving the stable in my filthy and tattered clothes."

"That's funny. I saw someone that looked exactly like you."

Well, that was what passed between them, and she left the matter at that.

And the third Sunday came. And Fairy Rózsa went to the stable to see how András was getting on with his work. There he is, scraping the horses with such violence that it made the stable shake. Rózsa left without saying a word. She got into her glass coach, and the twenty-one swans drove off at great speed, going eastward.

Then the copper-red *táltos* horse spoke again: "Well, dear master, put your hand under my tail and there you will find a bean with a hole in it. Crack it open and inside you will find garments sparkling like diamonds and a sword to match. Get into the garments and buckle on the sword. Then get on the back of the golden-haired filly, but keep a good hold, and when you're brought to the place where you'll find Fairy Rózsa, behave just as you have done before. Neither speak to nor look at anyone. Go into the Diamond Dew Chapel, and when Mass is over, leave as quickly as you can, so that Fairy Rózsa might not catch up with us, or we'll be done for."

Well, András did as he was told, and on that Sunday too they arrived home without mishap. Fairy Rózsa went to the stable and found András frantically going about his work so that she did not dare to question him. And as soon as she was back in her room, she fell into a fit for sheer anger that she had lost track of the handsome youth, and in her desperation she went off in a swoon so deep that her maids had to throw nine tubs of cold water over her to bring her round. When she came to, she sent at once for András to ask him whether he had not been in this or that chapel in the morning. But András said, "What do you think, princess! Can't you see that my clothes are soiled all over? Who would be wanting to go to church in such sorry rags?"

"Well, you can leave now."

And when he left her, Rózsa fell so seriously ill that she went off in a deadly faint. The priest and the doctor were sent for, and all the wise men and women were summoned to her bed. But not one of them knew the cure for her illness. There was sorrow and despair all over Fairyland at the news that the most beautiful of all fairies was lying on her death bed.

Then the *táltos* horse spoke up again, "Come on, András! Your hour has struck. Take the silver nut out of my left ear, and the sword and the garments out of the nut. Get into the garments and buckle on the sword and put the saddle on my back. And then let us make for the garden of Fairy Rózsa. But hold on to the saddle because I shall be prancing and dancing in front of her window, and my dance will cure all her ailments."

Well, András got into the garments and saddled the *táltos* horse. As soon as he got on its back, the horse took a long leap and they came down in the garden of Fairy Rózsa. And there the *táltos* started prancing and dancing so beautifully that nothing of the like had been seen there since the days of Adam and Eve.

And Fairy Rózsa beholds the dancing horse through the window. Her eyes are starting out of her head for sheer amazement. And she calls out to him, "Oh, come in, you handsome youth! What a long time I have been looking for you."

But without so much as a glance at her, András was off and back to the stable. Quickly he slipped out of his garments, tucked them away, and began currying the horses.

Then Fairy Rózsa sent one of her maids to find out what András was doing. And at once the maid came back to report that he was in the stable in his soiled garments currying the horses.

Hearing this, Fairy Rózsa threw herself down in such great fury that her maids feared she would break through the earth and go down to its deepest bottom. This time fourteen tubs of cold water had to be thrown over her to bring her round. But her bitter disappointment, that once again she had missed shaking hands with the handsome youth had such ill effects that her state turned from bad to worse.

The *táltos* mare then spoke again, "Well, dear master, you'll find a golden hazel nut in my right ear. Take the golden garments and sword out of it. Put them on and put the saddle on the back of the silver-grey filly. Today it's the silver filly's turn to take you to the garden of Fairy Rózsa. And go at once because she is close to breathing her last. But you must neither look at her nor pay heed to her words, no matter what she says."

András did as he was told. The silver filly took a long leap and there they were in the garden of Fairy Rózsa. And the silver filly went prancing and dancing so that she shook the palace to its foundation.

Fairy Rózsa felt it too and went to the window to see what it was. My gracious! There was the filly spinning round and round, swift as wind, and not since Noah's days had there been a dance like this. And on the filly's back there sat the handsome youth robed in golden garments. In tears she implored him to come in to her, but he turned a deaf ear to her gracious invitation. And when the grooms appeared to help him down from the horse and to lead him to the princess, the filly gave a jump and two leaps and vanished out of their sight.

The grooms went running to the stable to see whether they would find András and the horse there. And what do they behold! There is András, in his soiled garments, standing in muck up to his knees, and beside him there is the filly, and András is busy currying the horse. Back the grooms rush to the palace to report to the princess that they had found András scraping the horse, and himself all in muck, so that it was a proper eyesore to look at him.

Again Fairy Rózsa threw herself down in a temper, and if they had not got hold of her she would have cracked her skull. So only her big toe came out of joint. But in her great rage she went quite blue in her face, so that this time twenty-one tubs of cold water had to be thrown over her before she looked like herself and came to her senses. And then she went on lamenting and weeping bitterly, until it had brought all the people of the city to the palace and they were crying over her grief that she had fared ill again with the handsome youth.

Then the *táltos* mare spoke again, "Well, András, lose no time in going to Fairy Rózsa, because her soul is just about to leave her body through her mouth, and if she opens her mouth it would be flying out at once in the shape of an owl, and then you would lose Rózsa forever. Get quickly now into your golden garments and mount the golden-haired filly, and leap to her window, so that you may find her alive."

Well, András did not have to be told twice to get into his garments. He saddled the filly, and they dashed out of the stable through the vent hole. And in a wink there was András, prancing the golden filly under the window of Fairy Rózsa. And as she caught sight of them, she gasped and her soul slipped back into her belly, and in her great joy her eyes came popping out of her head so that her maids had to use an iron stick to push them back into their right place.

Then she called the youth by his name, "Oh, my beloved Handsome András, cease teasing me. Come here and let me kiss you."

Well, as he was quite fed up with living in the stable, there was nothing else to do but to go to Fairy Rózsa and to take her in his arms. And he gave her a kiss that left a burning red mark on her chin. But Rózsa did not need to be told twice either. And she was smothering him with her kisses, kissing him on the nape of his neck and on his spine, and on every possible part of his body, until there was not a spot left where she had not kissed him. And then she called him into her own room and she dressed herself in garments of gossamer gauze spangled with pearls, and she combed her hair that glittered with all the colors of the rainbow. And when she was ready, they went to the priest and were married. And they had a wedding feast, the like of which had not been seen since the beginning of things. It lasted for seven years. There was meat and drink in plenty, but you had to look sharp to get a bite of it. I was there myself, but I had to do with a hoe-cake with curd cheese, and a plateful of stuffed cabbage, and potatoes and sour milk. It was a fine meal, God bless them for it.

That is all to the story. If you don't believe me, find out for yourself. And the young pair lived happily. And András' parents were sent for, and with them came a host of their in-laws, and the lot of them lived happily, and if they are not dead they are still alive to this day. God bless them all in Fairyland, and God bless us here.

·4· *Pretty Maid Ibronka*

There was a pretty girl in the village. That is why she was called by the name of Pretty Maid Ibronka. But what of it, if all the other girls—and what a bevy of them used to gather to do their spinning together—had a lover to themselves, and she alone had none? For quite a while she waited patiently, pondering over her chances, but then the thought took hold of her mind: "I wish God would give me a sweetheart, even if one of the devils he were."

That evening, when the young were together in the spinning room, in walks a young lad in a sheepskin cape and a hat graced with the feather of a crane. Greeting the others, he takes a seat by the side of Pretty Maid Ibronka.

Well, as is the custom of the young, they start up a conversation, talking about this and that, exchanging news. Then it happened that the spindle slipped from Ibronka's hand. At once she reached down for it and her sweetheart was also bending for it, but as her groping hand touched his foot, she felt it was a cloven hoof. Well, great was her amazement as she picked up her spindle.

Ibronka went to see them out, as on that evening the spinning had been done at her place. Before separating they had a few words together, and then they bid each other good-by. As is the custom of the young they parted with an embrace. It was then that she felt her hand go into his side, straight through his flesh. That made her recoil with even greater amazement.

There was an old woman in the village. To that women she went and said, "Oh mother, put me wise about this. As you may know, for long they have been wagging their tongues in the village, saying that of all the village girls, only Pretty Maid Ibronka is without a sweetheart. And I was waiting and waiting for one, when the wish took hold of my mind that God would give me a sweetheart, even if one of the devils he were. And on that very same evening a young man appeared, in a sheepskin cape and a hat graced with a crane feather. Straight up to me he walked and took a seat by my side. Well, we started up a conversation, as is the custom of the young, talking about this and that. I must have become heedless of my work and let the spindle slip from my hand. At once I reached down to pick it up, and so did he, but as my groping hand chanced to touch his foot, I felt it was a cloven hoof. This was so queer it made me shudder. Now put me wise, mother, what should I be doing now?"

"Well," she said, "go and do the spinning at some other place, changing from here to there, so you can see if he will find you."

She did so and tried every spinning room there was in the village, but wherever she went, he came after her. Again she went to see the old woman. "Oh mother, didn't he come to every single place I went? I see I shall never get rid of him this way, and I dare not think of what is going to come of all this. I do not know who he is, nor from where he came. And I find it awkward to ask him."

"Well, here's a piece of advice to you. There are little girls in the village who are just learning to spin, and they find it good practice to wind the thread into balls. Get yourself such a ball, and when they gather again at your place for the spinning, see them out when they leave, and while you are talking to each other before parting, fuss about until you can get the end of the thread tied in a knot round a tuft in his sheepskin cape. When he takes leave and goes his way, let the thread unwind from the ball. When you feel that there is no more to come, make it into a ball again, following the track of the unwound thread."

Well, they came to her place to do the spinning. The ball of thread she kept in readiness. Her sweetheart was keeping her waiting. The others began teasing her: "Your sweetheart is going to let you down, Ibronka!"

"To be sure, he won't. He will come; only some business is now keeping him away."

They hear the door open. They stop in silence and expectation: who is going to open the door? It is Ibronka's sweetheart. He greets them all and takes a seat at her side. And as is the custom of the young, they make conversation, each having something to tell the other. Amid such talk the time passes.

"Let's be going home, it must be close to midnight."

And they did not tarry long, but quickly rose to their feet and gathered their belongings.

"Good night to you all!"

And they file off and leave the room, one after the other. Outside the house a final good-by was said, and each went his way and was soon bound homeward.

And the pair drew closer to each other and were talking about this and that. And she was manipulating the thread until she got the end knotted round a tuft of wool in his sheepskin cape. Well, they did not make long with their conversation as they began to feel the chill of the night. "You better go in now, my dear," he said to Ibronka, "or you'll catch cold. When the weather turns mild we may converse at greater leisure."

And they embraced. "Good night," he said.

"Good night," she said to him.

And he went his way. And she began to unwind the ball as he was walking away. Fast did the thread unwind from the ball. And she began to speculate how much more there would be still to come, but no sooner than this thought came into her head, than it stopped. For a while she kept waiting. But no more thread came off the ball. Then she started to rewind it. And bravely she followed the track of the thread as she went winding it into a ball again. Rapidly the ball was growing in her hand. And she was thinking to herself that she would not have to go very much farther. But where would the thread be leading her? It led her straight to the church.

"Well," she thought, "he must have passed this way."

But the thread led her further on, straight to the churchyard. And she walked over to the door. And through the keyhole the light shone from the inside. And she bent down and peeped through the keyhole. And whom does she behold there? Her own sweetheart. She keeps her eye on him to find out what he was doing. Well, he was busy sawing the head of a dead man in two. She saw him separate the two parts, just the same way we cut a melon in two. And then she saw him feasting on the brains from the halved head. Seeing that, she grew even more horrified. She broke the thread, and in great haste made her way back to the house.

But her sweetheart must have caught sight of her and briskly set out after her. No sooner had she reached home in great weariness and bolted the door safely on the inside, than her sweetheart was calling to her through the window: "Pretty Maid Ibronka, what did you see looking through the keyhole?"

She answered: "Nothing did I see."

"You must tell me what you saw, or your sister shall die."

"Nothing did I see. If she dies, we'll bury her."

Then her sweetheart went away.

First thing in the morning she went to the old woman. In great agitation did she appeal to her, as her sister had died. "Oh mother, I need your advice."

"What about?"

"Well, I did what you advised me to do."

"What happened then?"

"Oh, just imagine where I was led in following the thread. Straight to the churchyard."

"Well, what was his business there?"

"Oh, just imagine, he was sawing a dead man's head in two, just the same way we'd go about cutting up a melon. And there I stayed and kept my eye on him, to see what he'd be doing next. And he set to feasting on the brains from the severed head. I was so horrified that I broke the thread and in great haste made my way back home. But he must have caught sight of me, because as soon as I had the door safely bolted on the inside, he was calling to me through the window, 'Pretty Maid Ibronka, what did you see looking through the keyhole?' 'Nothing did I see.' 'You must tell me what you saw, or your sister shall die.' I said then, 'If she dies, we will bury her, but nothing did I see through the keyhole.' "

"Now, listen," the old woman said, "take my advice and put your dead sister in the outhouse."

Next evening she did not dare to go spinning with her friends, but her sweetheart was calling again through her window,

"Pretty Maid Ibronka, what did you see looking through the keyhole?"

"Nothing did I see."

"You must tell me what you saw," he said, "or your mother shall die."

"If she dies, we will bury her, but nothing did I see looking through the keyhole."

He turned away from the window and was off. Ibronka was preparing for a night's rest. When she rose in the morning, she found her mother dead. She went to the old woman, "Oh, mother, what will all this lead to? My mother too—she's dead."

"Do not worry about it, but put her corpse in the outhouse."

In the evening her sweetheart came again. He was calling her through the window, "Pretty Maid Ibronka, tell me, what did you see looking through the keyhole?"

"Nothing did I see."

"You must tell me what you saw," he said, "or your father shall die."

"If he dies, we will bury him, but nothing did I see looking through the keyhole."

Her sweetheart turned away from the window and was off, and she retired for the night. But she could not help musing over her lot; what would come of all this? And she went on speculating until she felt sleepy and more at ease. But she could not rest for long. Soon she lay wide awake and was pondering over her fate. "I wonder what the future keeps in store for me?" And when the day broke she found her father dead. "Now I am left alone."

She took the corpse of her father into the outhouse, and then she went as fast as she could to the old woman again: "Oh, mother, mother! I need your comfort in my distress. What is going to happen to me?"

"You know what's going to happen to you? I may tell you. You are going to die. Now go and ask your friends to be there when you die. And when you die, because die you will for certain, they must not take out the coffin either through the door or the window when they carry it to the churchyard."

"How then?"

"They must cut a hole through the wall and must push the coffin through that hole. But they should not carry it along the road but cut across through the gardens and the bypaths. And they should not bury it in the burial ground but in the ditch of the churchyard."

Well, she went home. Then she sent word to her friends, the girls in the village, and they appeared at her call.

In the evening her sweetheart came to the window. "Pretty Maid Ibronka, what did you see looking through the keyhole?"

"Nothing did I see."

"You must tell me at once," he said, "or you shall die."

"If I die, they will bury me, but nothing did I see through the keyhole."

He turned away from the window and took off.

Well, for a while she and her friends kept up their conversation. They were only half inclined to believe that she would die. When they grew tired they went to sleep. But when they awoke, they found Ibronka dead. They were not long in bringing a coffin and cutting a hole through the wall. They dug a grave for her in the ditch of the churchyard. They pushed the coffin through the hole in the wall and went off with it. They did not follow the road, but went cross-country, cutting through the gardens and the bypaths. When they came to the churchyard they buried her. Then they returned to the house and filled in the hole they had cut through the wall. It so happened that before she died, Ibronka enjoined them to take care of the house until further events took place.

Before long, a beautiful rose grew out of Ibronka's grave. The grave was not far from the road, and a prince, driving past in his coach, saw it. So much was he taken by its beauty that he stopped the coachman at once. "Hey! Rein in the horses and get me that rose from the grave. Be quick about it!"

At once the coachman comes to a halt. He jumps from the coach and goes to fetch the rose. But when he wants to break it off, the rose would not yield. He is pulling harder now, but still it does not yield. He is pulling the rose with all his might, but all in vain.

"Oh, what a dummy you are! Haven't you got the brains to

pick a rose? Come on here, get back on the coach and let me go and get the flower."

The coachman got back onto his seat, and the prince gave him the reins which he had been holding while the other went for the rose. The prince then jumped down from the coach and went to the grave. No sooner had he grasped the rose, than it came off at once and he was holding it in his hand.

"Look here, you idiot, with all your tearing and pulling you could not get me this rose, and hardly did I touch it and off it came into my hand."

Well, they took off, driving back home at great speed. The prince pinned the rose on his breast. At home, he found a place for it in front of the dining room mirror so that he should be able to look at it even while he was having his meals.

There the rose stayed. One evening some leftovers remained on the table after supper. The prince left them there. "I may eat them some other time."

This happened every now and again. Once the servant asked the prince, "Did your majesty eat the leftovers?"

"Not I," said the prince. "I guessed it was you who finished off what was left."

"No, I did not," he says.

"Well, there's something fishy about it."

Says the servant, "I am going to find out who's in this—the cat, or whoever."

Neither the prince nor the servant would have guessed that the rose was eating the remains.

"Well," said the prince, "we must leave some more food on the table. And you will lie in wait and see who's going to eat it up."

They left plenty of food on the table. And the servant was lying in wait, but never for a moment did he suspect the rose. And the rose alighted from her place by the mirror, and shook itself, and at once it turned into such a beautiful maiden that you could not find a second to her, not in all Hungary, not in all the wide world. Well, she sat down on a chair at the table and supped well off the dishes. She even found a glass of water to finish off her supper. Then she shook herself a little and back again she was in her place in front of the mirror, in the shape of a rose.

Well, the servant was impatiently waiting for day to break. Then he went to the prince and reported, "I've found it out, your royal majesty, it was the rose."

"This evening you must lay the table properly and leave plenty of food on it. I am going to see for myself whether you are telling me the truth."

And as they were lying in wait, the prince and the servant, they saw the rose alight from her place. She made a slight movement, then shook herself and at once turned into a fine and beautiful maiden. She takes a chair, sits down at the table, and sups well on the dishes. The prince was watching her as he sat under the mirror. And when she finished her supper and poured herself a glass of water and was about to shake herself into a rose again, the prince clasped his arms round her and took her into his lap.

"My beautiful and beloved sweetheart. You are mine, and I am yours forever, and nothing but death can us part."

"Oh, it cannot be so," said Ibronka.

"To be sure, it can be," he says. "And why not?"

"There is more to it than you think."

Well, I just remember a slip I have made in the story. Here goes then. On the day she was buried, her sweetheart appeared at her window as usual. He called in to her. But no answer came. He goes to the door and kicks it open: "Tell me, you door, was it through you they took out Ibronka's coffin?"

"No, it was not."

He goes then to the window, "Tell me, you window, was it through you they took the coffin out?"

"No, it was not."

He takes himself off to the road, "Tell me, you road, was it this way they took the coffin?"

"No, it was not."

He goes to the churchyard, "Tell me, you churchyard, was it in your ground they buried Pretty Maid Ibronka?"

"No, it was not."

Well, that is the missing part.

Fervently the prince is now wooing her and tries to win her consent to their marriage. But she resorts to evasion. And finally she made her condition, "I will marry you only if you never compel me to go to church."

Said the prince, "Well then, we could get along without you going to church. Even if I sometimes go myself, I shall never compel you to come with me."

Here is another part of the story I missed telling in its proper order. As he did not get any the wiser from the answer of the road, and the churchyard either, he said to himself, "Well, I see I must get myself a pair of iron moccasins and an iron staff and then I shall not stop until I find you, Pretty Maid Ibronka, even if I have to wear them away to nought."

The time comes when Ibronka is expecting a child. The couple are living happily, only she never goes along with him to church. Day follows day, the years slip by. Again she is with child. They have already two children, and they are no longer babes, but a boy of five and six years of age. And it is their father who takes them to church. True enough, he himself had found it strange enough that only his children went with him while all other folks appeared together with their wives. And he knew that they rebuked him for it and said, "Why does not your majesty bring along the queen?"

He says, "Well, that is the custom with us."

But all the same he felt embarrassed after this rebuke, and next Sunday, when he was getting ready with the boys to go to church, he said to his wife, "Look here, missus, why won't you come with us too?"

She answered: "Look here, husband, don't you remember your promise?"

"How then? Must we stick to it forever and aye? I've been hearing their scorn long enough. And how could I give up going to church when the kids want me to go with them? Whatever we were saying then, let us forget about it."

"All right, let it be as you wish, but it will give rise to trouble between us two. However, as I see you've set your mind on it. I am willing to go with you. Now let me go and dress for church."

So they went, and it made the people rejoice to see them together. "That is the right thing, your majesty," they said, "coming to church with your wife."

The mass is drawing to a close, and when it ends, a man is walking up to the couple wearing a pair of iron moccasins worn to holes, and with an iron staff in his hand. He calls out loudly, "I pledged myself, Ibronka, that I would put on a pair of iron moccasins and take an iron staff, and go out looking for you, even if I should wear them to nought. But before I had worn them quite away, I found you. Tonight I shall come to you."

And he disappeared. On their way home the king asked his wife, "What did that man mean by threatening you?"

"Just wait and see, and you will learn what will come of it."

So both were anxiously waiting for the evening to come. The day was drawing to a close. Suddenly there was someone calling through the window, "Pretty Maid Ibronka, what did you see through the keyhole?"

Pretty Maid Ibronka then began her speech: "I was the prettiest girl in the village, but to a dead and not to a living soul am I speaking—and all the other girls had a sweetheart—but to a dead and not to a living soul am I speaking. Once I let it out, I wish God would give me one, even if one of the devils he were. There must have been something in the way I said it, because that evening, when we gathered to do our spinning, there appeared a young lad in a sheepskin cape, and a hat graced with a feather of a crane. He greets us and takes a seat at my side and we are conversing, as is the custom of the young. And then it so happened—but to a dead and not to a living soul am I speaking—that my spindle slipped from my hand. I bent to pick it up and so did my sweetheart, but as my groping hand touched his foot, I felt at once—but to a dead and not to a living soul am I speaking—that it was a cloven hoof. And I recoiled in horror that God had given me a devil for a sweetheart—but to a dead and not to a living soul am I speaking."

And he is shouting at the top of his voice through the window. "Pretty Maid Ibronka, what did you see looking through the keyhole?"

"But when at the parting, as is the custom with the young, we embraced, my hand went straight through his flesh. At that I grew even more horrified. There was a woman in the village, and I went to ask for her advice. And she put me wise—but to a dead and not to a living soul am I speaking."

And he kept shouting through the window, "Pretty Maid Ibronka, what did you see looking through the keyhole?"

"And then my sweetheart took leave and went away. And I wished he would never come again—but to a dead and not to a living soul am I speaking. The woman said, I was to try to do the spinning at some other place, once here, once there, so that he might not find me. But wherever I went, there he came. And again I went for advice to the woman—but to a dead and not to a living soul am I speaking."

And he was shouting through the window, "Pretty Maid Ibronka, what did you see looking through the keyhole?"

"Then the woman advised me to get myself a ball of thread, which I was to fasten onto his sheepskin cape. And when he asked me and I said 'Nothing did I see,' he said, 'Tell me at once, or your sister shall die.' 'If she dies, we will bury her, but nothing did I see looking through the keyhole.' And he came again next evening and asked me what I had seen through the keyhole—but to a dead man and not to a living soul am I speaking."

And all the while he never stops shouting through the window.

"And my sister died. And next evening he came again and was calling to me through the window—but to a dead and not to a living soul am I speaking. 'Tell me what you saw, or your mother shall die.' 'If she dies, we will bury her.' Next evening he is calling to me again, 'Pretty Maid Ibronka, what did you see looking through the keyhole?'—but to a dead and not to a living soul am I speaking. 'Tell me what you saw, or your father shall die.' 'If he dies, we will bury him, but nothing did I see looking through the keyhole.' On that day I sent word to my friends, and they came and it was arranged that when I died they would not take my coffin either through the door or the window. Nor were they to take me along the road or bury me in the churchyard."

And he went on shouting through the window, "Pretty Maid Ibronka, what did you see looking through the keyhole?"

"And my friends cut a hole through the wall and went along the road when they took me to the churchyard where they buried me in the ditch—but to a dead and not to a living soul am I speaking."

And then he collapsed under the window. He uttered a shout which shook the castle to its bottom, and it was he who died then. Her mother and her father and her sister rose from their long sleep. And that is the end of it.

· 5 · The Tale of a King, a Prince, and a Horse

Once upon a time, there was an old king, living beyond the beyond. The old king had three able sons. Now, that old king never stopped weeping with one eye and laughing with the other.

Says the eldest boy to his brothers, "Let us go to our royal father and ask him what makes him weep with one eye and laugh with the other."

And so they did. The eldest goes first. "May God bless you with a happy day, sire, my royal father."

"God bless you too, my son. What is the matter? What do you wish?"

"Oh, my royal father, just this; tell me what makes you weep with one eye and laugh with the other?"

At this question the king snatches up a mighty pig-sticker from a nearby table and flings it at his son. And in truth, if the boy hadn't saved himself by a quick jump the dagger might have gone through his body. He turned and went back to his brothers.

"Well, what did our royal father tell you?" The eldest answered, "Go to him, and hear for yourselves." He never even dropped a word of what had befallen him.

So the second boy takes his turn, "God bless you with a happy day, sire, my royal father."

"God bless you too, my son. What is the matter? What do you wish?"

"Oh, my royal father, just tell me what makes you weep with one eye and laugh with the other?"

Again the king snatched up the dagger to fling it at his son; again a jump saved the boy from being pierced by the dagger. He returned to his brothers, and the youngest asks him, "Well, what did our royal father tell you?" Vexed, the two older brothers answered, "Never mind what he said to us; go and hear for yourself."

The youngest boy now take his turn: 'May God bless you with a happy day, my royal father." "God bless you too, my son. What is the matter? What do you wish?"

"Oh, my royal father, just this; tell me what makes you weep with one eye and laugh with the other?"

Whereupon the king once more snatches up his dagger and flings it at his son. But the youngest stands stock still, although the dagger stuck into the wall between his side and one arm. He takes it out of the wall and replacing it on the table steps back to where he stood before. Only then does he speak: "Oh my royal father, you must tell me now what makes you weep with one eye and laugh with the other."

"To be sure, my dearest son, you have shown yourself a real man, so I will tell you what I did not tell your brothers. In my younger days I had a dear comrade. Together we went to the great war, and side by side we fought in the battles. But since then we have lost each other, and I do not know to which part of the world he has gone. If only once I could see him again, I know both my eyes would weep first and then both would laugh."

With a bow the boy took his leave and returned to his brothers. They were hatching some evil plot against him, wondering what he had learned from their father and whether he too had saved his life by a quick jump. "Well, brother, what did our royal father tell you?"

The youngest then told them truthfully what happened. The eldest spoke first, "I say, brother, you do admit that I am the eldest of us three, don't you?" "To be sure I do, dear brother."

"So I am going to search for our father's old comrade." "That is right, dear brother, and may God guide your steps so that you can do justice to our father's wish. As true as I am your brother, I'd be the happiest fellow if you did."

The eldest boy then went to his father's stud farm—a fine one indeed, as the king took great pride in his horses—and there he chose himself the most fiery looking bolter. As soon as he managed to saddle it, he mounted the horse and set forth into the wide world. He did not bother to say good-by to his youngest brother because he still was hurt that their father had taken the youngest into his confidence.

After he had been on his way a month, he came to a copper bridge. He did not dare to go further because he was afraid to cross the bridge. Instead of crossing, he took one small copper plate so that he could show it as a proof to his father of how far he had gone. It took him another month to get home again. At once he took the copper plate to his father, so that he could show how far he had journeyed. The king said, "Oh, my son, did it really take you two full months to make this journey? When I was young, I did it in a single day."

Now the second prince goes to the stud farm. He looks for a horse and finds an even more beautiful one. "It is my turn to go now," he thinks to himself. "And I am going to find my father's old comrade, be there a hundred copper bridges to cross."

So now he sets out to try his luck in the world. He too, reaches the copper bridge, and here he remembers; this is how far my brother came. But he, too, was afraid to ride across it, so he dismounted and led his horse safely across the bridge. Then he went on and the distance he covered was once again as long as it had been to the copper bridge from the very start. Again he comes to a bridge, this time it is a silver bridge. Here he stops. The silver plates gave a sound just like the twang of a *cymbalo* [dulcimer]. "I had better not ride across this bridge here," he thought. "There might be someone to see me cross it, and there might be no end of trouble for me if he did. Surely, I have come already a long way. Let me see how far that wretch, my youngest brother, will dare to come. I wonder if he will have the guts to set out on this journey." So he took a small plate of the silver bridge to show it as proof to his father how far he had gone. It took him two months to get back to the first bridge, and another two months from there to reach home. After four months he was back again, and at once he went to report to his father how far he had gone. He showed him the silver plate so that it would bear out the truth of his words.

"Oh, my son, did it really take you four months to make this journey? When I was young I did it in a single day."

So the second boy just turned and left.

It was now the turn of the youngest boy. To him his two elder brothers say, "Hi, you little king, strongest of the strong, surely it is up to you to find our father's old comrade. Get along, boy, and try your luck. Go and find out what you are in for. Should you go as far as we did, you will never live to see your home again."

"Never mind, my good brothers, and pray, be not vexed with me. What I will do, I will do for my father's sake. And upon my word, it will not be done in wickedness or in complicity, but with the help of Almighty God."

Thus he collected himself in mind and went to the stud farm to choose a horse for the journey. As he was taking a good look around, there walks right up to him a nag, the sorriest of all sorry nags, with its coat worn bare on its poor head and neck as if it had been eaten away by mange. There was hardly enough hair left on its tail to make a small brush. One of its legs was as skinny as that of a yearling colt, while the other was as thick as the nag's stumpy neck. The miserable creature also limped on one leg and had lost the sight of one eye. In short, it offered such a spectacle that its fellows could not help jeering and laughing at it, just as people would make fun of some old hag.

Suddenly the spavined nag began to speak: "Hearken, Prince, son of the king who weeps with one eye and laughs with the other, if you want to find your father's old comrade you will have to choose me for your horse."

The boy, of course, was scared when he heard the nag talking as if it were human. The horse continued, "It will be your father's request that all the horses be driven up to his courtyard so that he can see for himself what horse you choose for the journey."

"All right, my good horse, I will choose you and no other. True, it is going to be rather a slow journey with you, but we will manage somehow. I can lead you, and you will help me with your counsel. You can trust my two strong arms and leave the rest to me. But I see you have some experience and can make good use of your brains."

It happened as the horse said. The prince returned to the palace and there he was commanded to appear before the king. "Well, son, have you chosen a colt for the journey?" "I have, my royal father." "Well, son, give order that all my horses be brought up to the courtyard so that I can see for myself what sort of a colt you have chosen."

So the boy goes back to the stud farm and orders the grooms to drive up the horses to the palace courtyard. Again the nag whispers into his ear, "When the king asks you which horse you have chosen. I will trip and you must say, 'I have chosen the one over there, the one which has just tripped.'"

So it happened. The horses were all driven up to the palace, where the king and his two elder sons were inspecting them from the window. Well, now, when the king said, "Well, son, which horse have you chosen?" the nag dropped on its skinny knees. "This one, my royal father, the one which has just tripped." At this the two older boys cupped their mouths with their hands and began to guffaw. "Let that wretch of a boy mount his sorry nag," one boy whispered to the other, "and he will not get any farther than the last house in the village before he sees his miserable nag give up the ghost. What a spectacle it will be! Just imagine him leaving on horseback and slinking back on foot, carrying along the nag's hide in a sack." "It will serve him quite right," the eldest said, "the wretch that he is. Hasn't he gone out of his head, trying to outstrip us in the eyes of our royal father!"

The old king then said to his youngest, "Well, son, take your horse and have the other horses driven back to the field."

The boy obeyed, took his horse by its ears, and led it to the stable. There he looked for a halter to tie his horse. But the nag spoke again, "Listen, dear master, you must not fasten me with the halter. Your brothers are scheming against us. Let me move freely, and they will not be able to do us any harm. And now pay heed to what I will say." And the animal continued, "Do you see that woodpile right over there, in the courtyard?"

"I do."

"Then set it on fire and let it burn down into smouldering embers. When it has burned down to smouldering embers, fill that barrel there, that stands by the well, with fresh water. I am going to eat up the smouldering embers and wash them down with a barrel of water. Tomorrow you must again make some embers; set that bigger pile on fire and fill two barrels with water. I will eat the smouldering embers and wash them down with two barrels of water. The day after tomorrow it must be the same; set that third and biggest pile on fire, and when it burns down to smouldering embers I will eat them up—and this time, fill three barrels with water for me, which I am going to drink. Then see what happens."

So it was. The first day, the boy set fire to the smallest pile of wood. When it burned down to smouldering embers, the nag devoured the whole lot, so that not so much was left as could light a pipe for his brothers. The second day the boy set fire to the bigger pile, and the horse washed it down with two barrels of water. The third day it was the same; the boy set fire to the third and biggest pile; the horse devoured it and washed it down with three barrels of water. Then he said to the prince, "Now have two pairs of shoes cut from diamonds be made for me and have me shod with them; and let an extra four pairs of diamond shoes be made for me, complete with diamond nails, all of which we are going to take with us. And now go to his majesty, your royal father, and ask him for the sword and the saddle which he used in his youth."

The prince went to his father and made his request. The king said, "My dear son, I see that you take great pains to please me. May God be with you. But not for my life could I grant your wish, as I have no idea what became of the sword and the saddle I used in my youth."

The prince left his father and returned to the stable. There he told his horse what he had learned from his father. The horse said, "Go again to his majesty the king and make him promise that he will let you have the saddle, the sword, and the bridle of his youth as soon as you find them."

So it happened. The prince went to the king and promised to go in search of the sword, the saddle, and the bridle, if his father would let them be his. The king said that he could have all three of them and that he would gladly give one of his hands in addition too, if he knew that it would help his son. "Try to find them, and then make good use of the sword," he said.

The boy left with a bow and returned to the stable, where he told his horse of his father's words. "Do not worry, dear master," the nag said. "Go at once to the cellar, and there furthest back, in the right-hand corner, if you take a good look, you will find what you are looking for, all walled up. Take them from that hiding place and bring them to me."

So it happened. The boy went to the cellar and furthest back, as the horse said, he found the saddle, the sword, and the bridle. With his findings he returned to the stable. "Did I not tell you, dear master?" the horse said. "You were right again, my dear horse." "Well, then, take heed. This very day you must let me be shod with the diamond shoes and diamond nails. And give orders that the extra four pairs of diamond shoes are also to be made, complete with diamond nails. And then bring them to me."

As soon as the prince had them ready, the horse said, "Well, dear master, we are ready now to start on our journey. The time has come for you to say good-by to your family, and we had better start this very day. We could just as well start tomorrow, but your two brothers are hatching some evil plot against us for tomorrow night. It is not really as if we wanted to leave on the run, but it is wiser to depart in peace. Go then and say good-by to your father and take leave of your brothers. This done, put the saddle on my back, the bridle on my neck, and buckle on your sword. But do not waste time with cleaning them. When you have said good-by to your people, we can set off on our journey."

So it happened. The boy went to his royal father to take leave. The old king shook his hand and gave him a parting kiss. For all his tears and weeping he could hardly utter his farewell, "God

speed you, my dear son." The boy departed with a bow and went
to take leave of his two brothers. He said, "My dear brothers,
before I leave, I want your pardon as I might not live to see you
again. Pray, bear no ill feelings toward me, as I am only doing
my duty to my royal father the king." Thus he bid farewell
to them too. In the meantime some food had been prepared for
the journey, but first he went to the stable, where he equipped
his horse with the saddle and the bridle, both shabby and musty
from age. Then he buckled on the big sword, which made him
walk like a dog with a clog, impeding both feet as he went.
But only his two brothers ridiculed him. He then took his horse
by the bridle and started to lead it. As soon as they passed the
gate, his two brothers began to jeer at him, "Hi, old man, where
are you bound for with that nag?" The boy felt deeply hurt by
their mockery, but he just clenched his fists and set his teeth,
saying to himself, "Come what may, one day I am going to
shame you, my princes, you mocking fools." And he led on his
horse, who told him not to get into the saddle as long as they
could be seen. The horse knew, of course, that they were being
watched by the two older boys, and that as soon as they got
out of sight, the boy could mount him.

After a little while the nag spoke again, "Dear master, pray
halt in front of me."

The boy stopped and with a mighty snort the horse blew his
breath toward him. Suddenly the boy stood there all in golden
apparel, his clothes, his sword changed into glittering gold—and
more than that, the horse lost its hideous thin coat and turned
into a beautiful golden-haired steed.

"Well, dear master," it said to the prince, "you can mount me
now. But first, mind your eyes and take good care that you shall
neither hear nor see nor speak to me, or you will bring down
a hundred thousand misfortunes on yourself."

"I will not speak to you, and I will bind up my eyes and ears
to that I can neither see nor hear. Only go on running, my dear
horse."

The boy bound up his eyes and his ears so that he could neither
see nor hear and promised to keep silent. But after a while—just

a couple of minutes, perhaps—the running horse suddenly tripped.

"What made you trip, my dear horse?" the boy asked.

"I would rather you had lost your voice before you spoke to me," the horse said and stopped. "Well, you may untie your eyes now." The boy did so. "What is it that you see, dear master?" "I see a copper bridge." "Well, that is how far your eldest brother came. But now dismount and then cut off my head with your sword so that it will roll away at least two yards from my body. Then look into my right ear and there you will find a small vial. Take out this vial. It contains a healing grass. After your fight you will have to apply it to my severed head so that you can stick it back onto my body. In my left ear you will find another small vial which contains an elixir. A few drops from it sprinkled over my body will do the trick, and it will revive me so that we can go ahead. And there is a strap right under this saddle here."

It looked exactly like a sword belt only it had three buckles on it. "Buckle on that belt and it will make you strong enough to move a mountain. And then you must take cover under that bridge there. Then a dragon will appear which has six heads. It will call to you, 'Crawl out from under the bridge, you wretched prince, son of the king who weeps with one eye and laughs with the other. You had not grown to the size of a plateful of millet mash in your mother's womb when I knew that I would have to fight you.' To this you shall answer, 'Just wait till I unfasten a buckle of my belt.' And then you say a prayer. Again the dragon will call, 'Crawl out from under the bridge, you wretched prince, son of the king who weeps with one eye and laughs with the other.' And you will have to answer, 'Just wait till I unfasten the second buckle of my belt.' And then you shall say a second prayer. A third time the monster will call to you, 'Crawl out from under the bridge, you wretched prince, son of the king who weeps with one eye and laughs with the other, and let us fight.' Again you will have to answer, 'Just wait till I unfasten the third buckle of my belt.' When he calls you the fourth time, step forth from under the bridge, and he will ask you, 'How do you want to fight me, you miserable

wretch?' Then answer, 'Just as you please,' and then draw your
sword and fling it at him. You can leave the rest to your sword."

It all happened that way. The boy was unhappy that he was
to cut off his horse's head and wept sadly. He was also worried
for fear of what might happen to him. But there was nothing he
could do about it but to follow his horse's orders. So he cut off
his horse's head, then buckled on his belt and took cover under
the bridge.

Lo, all of a sudden a terrible storm came up, with thunder
rolling and lightning flashing from a dreadful big black cloud,
as if it were the crack of doom. In that terrific hullabaloo there
appears a dragon with six heads. He roars at the prince, "Crawl
out from under the bridge, you wretched prince, son of the king
who weeps with one eye and laughs with the other. You had not
grown to the size of a plateful of millet mash in your mother's
womb when I knew that I would have to fight you." The boy
answered, "Just wait till I unfasten a buckle of my belt."

And he said a prayer. Again the dragon roared at him, "Crawl
out from under the bridge, you wretched prince."

The boy answered, "Just wait till I unfasten the second buckle
of my belt." And then a third time the dragon roars at him,
"Crawl out from under the bridge, you wretched prince, so that
I can tear you to pieces." The boy uttered another prayer and
said, "Just wait till I unfasten the third buckle of my belt."

For the fourth time the dragon challenged him, "Crawl out
from under the bridge, you wretched prince, so that I can fight
you."

Then the boy stepped forth. "How do you want to fight me?"
"Just as you please." "Then guard yourself!" No sooner did he
say it when the boy flung his sword at him. And lo, at one blow
the sword cut off all six heads and then chopped them into tiny
pieces near the bridge. Then the boy took the small vial which
contained the healing grass. He applied its contents to the
horse's severed head and to the body, and then sprinkled both
with the elixir, and lo, the horse rose at once as if it had only
awakened from sleep.

The boy mounted the horse and heard it say, "Well, dear
master, you had a narrow escape, saving your skin this time,

but now bind up your eyes and your ears and do not speak to me or you will bring down a hundred thousand misfortunes on yourself."

The boy did as he was told. He mounted his horse and followed his advice. But after it had made a jump or two, the horse tripped again.

"What is the matter, my dear horse, what made you trip again?" The horse stopped. "I did trip; however, I would rather you had become dumb before you spoke to me. But now untie your eyes and your ears and take a good look around. What is that you see?"

The boy took a good look around and said, "I see a silver bridge."

"Well, that is how far your second brother came. And now dismount and cut off my head again." "Not for the life of me will I cut off your head, my dear horse. I would die of sorrow if I had to do it again."

"You have to do as I command you," said the horse. "Cut off my head. The vials you will find in my ears. Only this time you will have to keep the buckles on your belt. But again, you must take cover under the bridge. This time you will have to fight a dragon with twelve heads. It too will challenge you to crawl out from under the bridge. And you must answer, 'Just wait till I fasten a buckle of my belt.' And then you say a prayer. A second time the dragon will challenge you to crawl out from under the bridge. Again you will have to answer, 'Just wait till I fasten the second buckle of my belt,' and again you say a prayer. And a third time the dragon will challenge you to crawl out from under the bridge. Again you will have to answer, 'Just wait till I fasten the third buckle of my belt.' And again you say a prayer. When the fourth time the dragon calls you to crawl out from under the bridge, do not tarry any longer, but fling your sword at him. To be sure, your sword will know its duty."

So it happened. The boy did as he was told: he cut off his horse's head, rolled it away from the body at about two yards' distance so that the dragon should think it was a dead horse and should not go at it while he was taking cover under the bridge. Then he crawled to his hiding place, and lo, a twelve-headed dragon rushes forth amidst such terrible wind and storm that it tore up the trees by their roots.

And there the dragon stands at the bridge and roars at him, "Crawl out from under the bridge, you wretched prince, son of the king who weeps with one eye and laughs with the other. You had not grown to the size of a plateful of millet mash in your mother's womb when I knew that I would have to fight you. You have killed my younger brother and you have to pay for it with your life."

The prince answers, "Just wait till I fasten a buckle of my belt." And he says a prayer. Again the monster roars at him, "Crawl out from under the bridge you wretched prince, son of the king who weeps with one eye and laughs with the other." And he answers, "Just wait till I fasten the second buckle of my belt." And a third time the monster challenges him, "Crawl out from under the bridge, you wretch, so that I can fight you." The prince says, "Just wait till I fasten the third buckle of my belt." And he says a prayer. For the fourth time the monster challenges him, "Crawl out from under the bridge, you wretch. You have killed my younger brother, but it will cost you your life."

The boy then crawled out from under the bridge and stepped forth. "How do you want to fight me?" "Just as you please." And as he said it he flung his sword at the dragon. One blow and all twelve heads rolled off and were chopped into a hundred pieces near the silver bridge. The boy did to his horse what he had been told to do, applied the healing grass and the elixir to the body and the severed head. At once the horse shook itself, and this time it was even more beautiful than ever before.

"Well, my dear master, mount me and bind up your eyes and your ears and do not speak to me, nor see, nor hear."

"Do not worry, my dear horse, I shall not speak to you."

The horse set forth and was galloping at terrific speed. They had already traveled a long distance when the boy observed that his horse's hooves were cutting hard against some stony road. With the greatest caution, so that his horse should not notice it, the boy looked around to see to which parts they had come. This was of no avail. What he saw before him was an unfamiliar place, one he had never seen before. But as he was looking around, he caught sight of a beautiful golden hair lying on the ground.

He says to his horse, "Just look, my dear horse, what a beautiful golden hair is lying there on the ground."

The horse asked, "So you have beheld it?" He says, "Yes, I have." "I would you had gone blind before you had seen it, because that may cost you your life and even mine. But now, dismount and pick it up. And tell me: do you see that golden bridge right over there?" "I do." "Well, we are passing now through the country of the three dragons. The copper bridge leads to the country of the six-headed dragon; the silver bridge leads to the country of the twelve-headed dragon; and the golden bridge leads to the country ruled by the twenty-four-headed dragon. And beyond over there begins Fairyland. But now dismount and prepare for a fight with the twenty-four-headed dragon. Again, you have to cut off my head, and again you will find the heal-alls which you must apply as before. And again you will have to crawl under the bridge and wait for the dragon with twenty-four heads. He will roar at you to crawl out from under the bridge. And you will have to answer, 'Just wait till I fasten a buckle of my belt,' and then you say a prayer. A second time he will roar at you, and you answer, 'Just wait till I fasten the second buckle of my belt'. And you say a prayer again. For a third time he will roar at you to crawl out from under the bridge. And you answer, 'Just wait till I fasten the third buckle of my belt.' And a third prayer you will say. When he roars at you for the fourth time, you must crawl out from under the bridge and step forth. He will ask you how you want to fight him. Do not give an answer, just fling your sword at him. Your sword will know its duty."

It all happened that way. The dragon with twenty-four heads roared at him, "Crawl out from under the bridge, you wretched prince, sone of the king who weeps with one eye and laughs with the other. You had not grown to the size of a plateful of millet mash in your mother's womb when I knew that I should have to fight you. If you refuse to fight me, I will devour you or tear you to pieces to take vengeance for the death of my two brothers."

The boy says, "Just wait till I fasten a buckle of my belt," and then he says a prayer. Again the monster roars at him, "Crawl out from under the bridge you miserable wretch." The prince answers, "Just wait till I fasten the second buckle of my belt." For the third time the monster calls, "Crawl out from under the bridge, you sorry wretch, so that I can take vengeance for the death of my two brothers." The boy says, "Just wait till I fasten the third buckle of my belt," and he says a third prayer. And when the dragon challenges him for the fourth time, the boy sprang forth from under the bridge, saying: "Here I am, so what?" and he flings his sword at the dragon.

As sure as if you had seen it with your own eyes, at one good swing and two turns of the sword all twenty-four heads were cut off and lay strewn all over the ground. The boy chopped them up into small bits and set to reviving his horse. He fitted the severed head to the body and applied again the healing grass and the elixir to it. And lo, the horse sprang to its feet now a hundred times stronger than ever before.

"Well, dear master, once more you have come through safe and sound. But now bind up your eyes and your ears and do not speak to me."

"Not for dear life shall I speak to you, my dear horse," said the boy and mounted. Off went the horse, galloping at terrible speed. They had left behind them a long stretch when the boy noticed that the horse's hooves cut hard against the road. "Bend your head, dear master, and lean over me." When the boy did so, the horse continued, "What do you see?"

"I see immense brightness. But tell me, what sort of road is that under your hooves?"

"We are passing through the glittering Glass Mountain of Fairyland. You see, those who want to carry off a fairy girl for wife must cut their way through the Glass Mountain. But there is no other horse except me that could do it. You know now why I have asked you for the diamond shoes. Without them we would not be able to cross the Glass Mountain. But I dare say, by to-morrow morning all Fairyland will rise against me. Just take a look back and see what havoc my diamond shoes have wrought on their beautiful mountain. But better not worry now. Bind up your eyes and let us go ahead."

So they did. The boy bound up his eyes, and they set forth on their way. The horse was going at great speed and left behind an immense stretch of road. "Now, dear master, you can untie your eyes," the horse said. "Take a look around and tell me what you see."

The boy took a good look around, but he felt the same as if his eyes were still bound up. "I cannot see a thing, dear horse," he said. "There is just darkness around me and a loud whispering."

"We are entering Devil's Land," says the horse, "but what is that you hear?"

"I hear a great rustling and swishing."

"Do not fear. Bind up your eyes and your ears and do not speak to me before I let you speak." "All right, my dear horse, not for dear life shall I speak to you." "But now we go further." The horse was running on and on when it came to a halt at last. "Well, my dear master, untie your eyes and your ears and take a look around to see to which parts I have brought you."

The boy looked around and saw around him a beautiful meadow undulating with the ripple of pure silk and with every blade of grass in it as bright as a pin. And there right in the middle of that meadow he beholds a hut and near the hut a horse. And near the horse there lay a man. As the man lay there, his sword went round and round him. "Do you see that man sleeping over there?" the horse asked. "I do." "He is the old comrade your father is yearning to see. And do you see that horse standing nearby?" "I do," he says. "That horse there is my brother. But now let us go to the hut. And when we get there, pray do not tie me to the manger. And take care that you do not waken that man, or touch him with your finger, or you can count yourself dead, cut to pieces by his sword which keeps walking round and round him and has a steel blade, twin only with yours. So if you feel tired, you can lie down and sleep, but lead me first to that other horse so that I can face him."

So it happened. The two horses stood face to face, and the boy, what does he see? The two horses greeted each other with kisses as brothers do when they recognize each other.

Around the sleeping man his sword kept watch, going round and round. The boy did not wake the sleeper but lay down for a while to wait till the other had enough sleep so that when he woke he could make his acquaintance. But he felt exhausted and went to sleep as soon as he put his head down. The old man near him was the first to wake.

"And who might be this fellow, lying here? Well, whoever he is, he must be a real good sort, since he did not disturb my sleep. So I am not going to wake him." And, beholding the boy's horse, he thought, "A real fine horse that fellow has." And what does he behold next? The stranger's sword, which kept walking round the sleeping man just like his own, went round and round the boy. "Well, since you were decent enough not to disturb my sleep, it is only fair that I let you have a quiet rest. There is plenty of time to find out later who you are," the old man thought to himself. And so it was.

Soon the boy woke up and greeted the old man: "May God bless you with a happy day, uncle." "God bless you too, my son. What has brought you here, beyond the beyond, far even for the birds to come?" The boy then sees how the old man, just like his own father, was weeping with one eye and laughing with the other. "What wind has blown you hither, and who calls you son?" the old man asked him.

"I am a prince, the youngest son of the king who weeps with one eye and laughs with the other. It was his wish that I come here to lead you to him, because you are his dear old comrade. and just like him, you weep with one eye and laugh with the other. But he feels sure that if he could see you again, both his eyes would weep first and then laugh for joy."

"Oh, son, it is the same with me. I know that if I could see your father, we would both feel young again, and weep first and then laugh away the worries of this world. But never again shall I see your father, son. You must know, I am a sort of ranger here, and I must take care of this meadow. It is the Silk Meadow, and it borders on Devil's Land. From morning to night and from night to morning, I can never get a moment's rest from the devils. They have a great spite against me. Every night they come here and bring their horses—more horses than there is grass in this meadow—and they do not leave until their horses have grazed off all the grass in the Silk Meadow. All night I have to chase them and try to drive them out from the meadow. No wonder that I feel dead tired by now, and so does my good horse."

"Do not worry, uncle," the prince said. "Tonight you are going to have a quiet sleep. I will take care of the Silk Meadow myself." "Thank you very much, son. It would be nice if you could relieve me for one night. But I am afraid not one hundred good fellows of your sort could guard it safely." "Do not worry, uncle."

When the day began to close in and it was just getting dark, the prince perceives a horde of devils rushing on their horses toward the Silk Meadow. He gets into his saddle. He knows he can trust his horse, and soon they are after the devils. With each blow of his sword, a hundred devils are killed and cut to pieces on the Silk Meadow. Off he goes in pursuit of the rest, chasing them back into their own country. And there, in the terrible darkness of Devil's Land, he kills them by the thousand. He rounds them up in their big barracks and has no fear to enter the devil factory where the devils are produced by the dozens. There in one hall he found an old and limping devil, looking exactly like an old woman. And like an old woman weaving with deft hands at a piece of rug, this old, limping devil was busily working at his loom, weaving into being one devil after another. One shuttle shot this way, and one kick with his foot, and lo! a hundred brand new devils sprang forth. One shuttle shot that way, and one kick with his foot, a hundred more devils sprang forth. And so it went. One shuttle shot this way, a hundred devils; one shuttle shot that way, another hundred devils.

And then the prince set to and with every swing of his sword he chopped off a hundred heads. He slew from right to left, and he slew from left to right, but how could he go on forever? So with a mighty blow of his sword he cut the old weaver into two pieces. With the last gasp, the devil's feet went faster and

faster, and with his last kick more devils sprang forth than
before. The boy now gripped his sword and cut the whole nasty
lot into a thousand pieces. And then, from an adjoining room,
a limping devil jumped forth and tried to escape. The boy ran
after him.

"Oh, prince, son of the king who weeps with one eye and
laughs with the other, show mercy to me, and I shall lead you
out of Devils' Land. I know you can kill me, but if you do,
you will get lost in this land and never leave it alive." "Right ho.
Then lead me out of Devil's Land. But first tell me the truth;
upon your soul, are there any more devils in this land?" "I
was their king, and all their powers dwelt in me. And now I
am the only one left alive." "Well, then, lead me out of Devils'
Land."

As soon as they were safely out of Devils' Land and back on
the Silk Meadow, the prince thought to himself, "If you are the
only devil alive, it is better if you die too, and none of you
is left", and he cut the last devil into small bits.

Well, my dear listeners, take heed of my words which serve to
testify that there are no more devils on this earth.

And when the last devil was killed, all of a sudden Silk
Meadow turned into the glittering Fairyland it had been before
when the prince crossed the Glass Mountain. You must know
that this part of Fairyland had been held unlawfully by the devils
for some time. But now that good riddance had been made of
them, the king of Fairyland gave commands that no stone be
left unturned until the person was found who had liberated the
country and freed it from the hellish crew. Wise men and
women, well versed in fairy lore, gathered from all parts of
Fairyland. The fairy ladies came riding on swans and peacocks
and big ostriches, or in their glittering glass coaches, covered
with rush matting. Scattering all over their country, they went
in search of the gallant hero who had rid Fairyland of the devils.
At last they found him on the Silk Meadow.

"Let us take you at once to our king. It is his ardent wish to
see for himself what sort of a man it is who has freed his country
from the devils." What else was there for the prince to do but
to accept so courteous an invitation which came from such a

high court. Soon he was standing before the king. "I am at your grace's service, sire, your majesty," he said. "Do with me as you please. I have come from a far-off land they call the White Country. I am the son of its king who weeps with one eye and laughs with the other. I came here to free Fairyland from the devils."

"Well done, my brave and gallant son. I speak for myself and all of us in Fairyland when I tell you that we think a great deal of your services to our country and have taken you so much to our hearts that you can have my daughter for your wife if you wish so, and if you like, you can remain here and live in this country which you have freed from the devils. In addition, you can have the Silk Meadow, and I will make you king of it."

The prince looked at the princess—and you can take my word for it that she went weak in her knees when she set eyes on the handsome young prince, and that there was no need for her to think twice before she gave him her diamond ring in exchange for his handkerchief. Inside the ring was the inscription: "Should evil befall you on your way, turn this ring once, and again, and again, and I'll come to your aid, even if you don't care for this maid." The prince thanked them for their favors and respectfully asked permission to take his leave.

"My dear and valiant son," said the king, "there is just one more favor I want you to do for me. Find me that person who cut his way through the Glass Mountain."

"I am that very man myself, sire, who cut his way through the Glass Mountain. It was the wish of my royal father that I go in search of this valiant comrade of the old days, the ruler of the Silk Meadow, who weeps with one eye and laughs with the other." "All right, son, tell me now which road you will follow on your way back?" "The same road that led me here, sire." "And now tell me where is that wonderful horse of yours that did not fear to cross Glass Mountain which is as steep as a roof?" "Here it is, sire, I am holding it by the bridle. And to be sure, we are going to cross Glass Mountain once again."

The king then stepped over to the horse and treated him to clean wheat grain and a pail of fresh filtered water, so that he should have no reason to complain. Then the king ordered a great feast in honor of the prince, who told about his adventures and how he had killed the three dragons and thus had won a rightful claim to their possessions as well as to that part of the Silk Meadow which he had freed from the devils' rule.

"And now, sire, let me have your promise that I can take your daughter for wife when I return here."

The prince's words were well received, and he took his leave in good grace. He hurried back to the old man on the Silk Meadow, being anxious to make good his promise given to his royal father.

There the old man stood waiting in front of his hut. "May God bless you with a happy day, dear uncle," the boy greeted him. "God bless you too, my son. What has kept you so long?"

The prince then gave an account of all that had befallen him.

"I see, son, God has guarded your steps. I knew for sure that your faith would bring you your just deserts. I am much relieved that there are no more devils left and that with them perished Devil's Land, and that you yourself, handsome prince, have safely escaped all perils. As for me, believe me, I have no greater wish than to see your dear father again. But I am afraid it cannot be done. Nor can you go home yourself. Just look at your horse's hooves and see how the diamond shoes have been worn away during your journey through Fairyland. How could I cross Glass Mountain when my horse has no shoes at all? And neither does yours."

"Never mind, dear uncle. We have got the shoes we need, if that is worrying you." And the prince produced the four pair of diamond shoes, taking them out from under his saddle.

Now, as the horses were properly shod, the prince and his companion set out and were soon homeward bound. To be sure, this was a much shorter journey than when he had started on his way. There was no need now to do any fighting, and it was a peaceful journey.

As soon as they arrived, the prince presented his companion to his father. There was such a great to-do that even the birds in the trees began to weep and laugh for joy. And the two kings felt as young again as in the best days of their youth and were weeping now with both eyes and then laughing merrily so that their eyes, too, became as clear and young as in the days of old.

The prince was made not only heir to Fairyland but also to Devil's Land with the Silk Meadow, and to the lands that had once belonged to the three dragons. You may have my word for it that he became a very great king. Greater than the greatest kings before him.

He then married the princess of Fairyland, and they had a big wedding feast at the old king's palace. And if they are not dead, they are still alive to this day. Believe me, I was there myself where it was told, and I came to tell you this tale as it was told to me. I loved to listen to it. This is all I have to tell you. If you think it was a silly matter, rack your brains for another that is better.

· 6 · The Tree that Reached Up to the Sky

Once upon a time there was a king. He had a beautiful castle. In front of one window there was a tree. But the king had no idea what kind of a tree it was, nor did he know whether it had any fruit or not. One day he summoned the young noblemen of his kingdom; immediately all the barons and counts and dukes gathered at his court. And it was proclaimed to them, and it was proclaimed also in every other country, that any man who could climb to the top of the tree and bring down some of its fruit would be made the king's heir and be given the princess in marriage.

There came from all parts of the world the princes and the dukes, the counts and the barons, and other fine folks, to show their mettle. Each went climbing. Each went as high as a couple of feet and then fell to the ground. One broke his arm; another broke his leg. Not one of them could climb the tree, not one of them brought down its fruit. And yet the king was loath to have the tree cut down.

One day a poor swineherd showed up at the court. He said he would climb the tree and bring some of its fruit. But he made a condition: the king must grant his requests. The king gave his promise that he could have what he wanted if only he would go and climb the tree and bring one of its fruit, or just a twig, or a leaf of it, so that he could see what kind of a tree it was.

Then the swineherd asked for fifty hooks and fifty small stools so that when he grew tired of climbing he could drive a hook into the three and fix his small stool onto the hook and sit on it for a while and take a rest. And he also asked for provisions enough to last him for fifty days. The king let him have all the things he had asked for.

One day, in the morning before the sun was up, the boy started on his way. He climbed up and up till the day was drawing to a close, but he found nothing. When night came, he drove a hook into the tree, fixed a stool onto it, and took a night's rest. In the morning he had some food and drink and when the sun rose, he set out again. He was climbing well-nigh a whole day. When night closed in, he drove a hook into the tree and fixed a stool onto it. He ate and drank and had a night's rest. In the morning he went on climbing. It was the same on the third day. When it grew dark, he drove a hook into the tree, fixed a stool onto the hook; he ate and drank and took a night's rest. When the sun was up, he went climbing. He climbed up and up till nightfall, but there was no trace of a single bough to be seen. For seven days he was climbing. On the eighth day he drove a hook into the tree, fixed a stool onto it, and ate his supper. In the morning he climbed further. On the evening of the ninth day he reached a spot where the tree branched out. But he saw only two branches. One pointed east; the other pointed west. He ate and drank and rested there. In the morning he set off on the branch which pointed eastward. It was a thick branch, and he could walk on it as safely as if he were walking on the ground. He took only his food and his stool with him. He was walking all day, and night was closing in when he came to a small cottage. He knocked at the door and then walked in. Inside the cottage he found an old woman.

"Good evening, mother."

"Good evening, son. What has brought you here?"

"I have come here at the command of his majesty the king to bring him some fruit of this tree so that he may see what sort of tree this is. For ten days I have been climbing this tree, but I have not see anything whatever. Now I've just caught sight of this cottage, so I came in to find out who is living here and to ask you if you could tell me whether the tree bears any fruit or not."

"All right, son. But you must have grown tired after a day's climbing. You had better take a rest here. In the morning I will tell you which way you should take if you want to find the fruit!"

The boy thanked her for her suggestion.

In the morning when he woke, the old woman gave him breakfast. The boy asked her, "Well, dear mother, pray tell me now, which way shall I go to find the fruit of the tree?"

"Listen, son, I've been living here for a hundred and twenty years or so, but I've never eaten of its fruit, nor have I set eyes on any. Now find your way back to the spot where you set out from. And then go straight ahead on the branch which points westward. You will come to a small cottage. Go into the cottage. There lives my aunt. She will tell you all you wish to know. And she'll take you into her service. Three days will count for a year. In the stable she keeps her horses. And you will look after her horses. After three days she'll ask you what you want for a year's service. Then tell her that in the hen coop there is a saddle and a bridle, all covered with droppings. It is these two things you want her to give you. And beside the dung pit you'll see a five-legged horse. You must ask her for that horse too. Then she will try to argue you out of your requests. She'll say that the saddle and bridle are just worthless junk and that the horse is too weak to raise its feet. And that it wouldn't be any good to you to get either. Instead of them she'll offer you gold and jewels and all the treasures of the world. But you must stick to your requests and accept nothing else. And if she sees that you are firm and won't budge, she'll give in and let you have them."

"Then the horse will take you to a beautiful castle. Opposite the castle you'll see a stable. Tie up your horse in the stable.

You'll find three horses there. With yours there will be four of them. But none of them will be five-legged like yours. You must look after the horses; feed them and water them and curry them. But don't go into the castle unless you're called for. And then a servant girl will come to the stable and ask you in. She'll say that you've deserved to get a good supper in the castle for having looked after the horses so well."

The boy went to the hen coop, took the mucky saddle and bridle from the perch, and then went to take a look at the pit which was full of dung. Then he took his small stool and went into the house.

"Good evening," he said.

"Good evening, son, What has brought you here, beyond the beyond, where no bird would fly?"

"Well, mother, this is how I've fared. This big tree stands right in front of a window of the king's castle. But never has the king seen or tasted its fruit. So one day he sent word to all barons and counts and dukes, and to the rich and the poor, all over the world, that he would give his kingdom and his daughter in marriage to any man who would bring him some fruit of the tree. And they all came and tried. And all of them have come to grief. Many of them broke their arms and legs, and many more of them broke their necks and died when they fell from the tree. I was the last to come and offer to bring the king some fruit of the tree. And the king granted all my requests. To be sure, I had a rough time getting here. But all the way I haven't seen anything except this cottage here. And I've run out of my provisions and wouldn't mind taking service with you, if you'd care to take me on."

"All right, son. There are three horses in my stable. You can look after the horses and see that they are fed and watered and curried properly. Three days count for a year here. And when your service is up, I shall give you whatever you would be asking for in payment."

"That's right, mother. I am quite used to doing a bit of work."

The boy had his supper. Then he went to feed and water the horses. But as they were covered with muck, it was close to daybreak when he finished currying and rubbing them clean. When the old woman came, she found the horses spotlessly clean, their hair gleaming as bright as the stars.

"I dare say, son, never before had I a servant boy who would have taken such good care of my horses."

"You see, mother, I had a horse of my own at home, and I always went to great pains to keep it well groomed."

"Well done, son. Now let us go into the house, and you'll have your breakfast."

The woman gave him a square meal, and when he finished his breakfast, he went back to the stable and sat down on his stool. In the evening the old woman came again. This time the horses looked seven times as beautiful as in the morning. She called the boy into the house and gave him a good supper. When he had his supper, she gave him a glass of wine. The boy then went back to the stable and sat down on his stool. Suddenly he felt very drowsy, so much so that he nearly dropped off to sleep.

One of the horses then said, "Do not go to sleep, my dear master, because if the old woman came into the stable and found you asleep she'd push you off the tree and you'd crack up on the ground and be reduced to a pulp."

The boy opened his eyes wide on hearing this warning. He drew forth his pipe and lit it. But the old woman noticed that he was smoking and made for the stable. The boy saw her and pocketed his pipe before she entered.

"I see you are looking after the horses with great care. I have come in to find out whether you could keep awake. It would have been the end of you had I found you asleep here."

The old woman went back to her cottage and went to bed. And the boy went on currying the three horses till their hair shone brighter than candlelight.

In the morning the old woman came again to have a look at her horses. When she saw how well groomed they were, she invited the boy into the cottage and gave him breakfast. Again she gave him a glass of wine. And when he had his breakfast, the boy went back to his horses to feed and water them. Then he sat down on his stool. Suddenly his eyes went heavy with sleep.

Says the second horse, "Do not go to sleep, my dear master, or it will be the end of you. If the old woman, that old hag, came in and found you asleep, she'd push you off the stool. And you'd go down, down with such a crash that your whole body would get smashed up and not a scrap of it would be left there to show that it had belonged to you."

The boy lit his pipe and began smoking it. When the old woman noticed that he was smoking, she made for the stable. The boy saw her, cupped his pipe with his hand, and slipped it quickly into his pocket.

"I see that you are taking great care of my horses. But isn't it smoke I smell in here? Don't you ever dare smoke a pipe inside the stable; it might catch fire, you know."

The boy said he would not dream of smoking his pipe inside the stable and that he would always go outside if he wanted to smoke.

The old woman left him. Anger was growing in her at the thought that the boy would have acquitted himself so well by the day his time was up that she would be compelled to give him whatever he would ask in payment.

In the evening the boy had his supper in the cottage. Again the old woman gave him a glass of wine. He drank it and then went back to the stable. He fed and watered the horses and rubbed them down. When he finished currying them, he sat down on his stool.

The third horse then said, "Do not go to sleep, my dear master, or you are done for. If the old hag found you asleep, she'd push you off the tree. And down you would go, right to the bottom of a dried-up well. And never again could you get out of it, not as long as you live."

The boy lit his pipe and began smoking it. The old woman noticed that he was smoking and in great anger rushed into the stable.

"Don't you remember that I did not give you leave to smoke while you were in the stable?"

"Oh, mother, but I did not smoke my pipe inside the stable. I went out to have a smoke."

The old woman took a look at the horses, and when she saw

that they were clean and well groomed she went back to her house, and soon she was sleeping.

The boy kept himself busy with the horses. It was the third day of his service, and in the evening his time would be up.

On the morning of the fourth day the old woman went to the stable and called the boy into the house. "Come in, son. To be sure, you've taken good care of my horses. Not one of the ninety-nine servant boys that served before you made them look so clean. Now, take your breakfast and do well for yourself. And then you must tell me what you wish in payment."

"Oh mother, you know that I have come here for one thing only: to get some fruit of this tree, to see what kind of fruit it bears."

"Well then, listen, son. I have been living in this cottage over the last two hundred years or so, but I have never eaten or set eyes on the fruit of this tree. Whatever else you may ask for, I will give it to you. Be it gold or anything else you can decide on, you shall have it."

"All right, mother. But then show me that you are as good as your word. In the hen coop there is a saddle and a bridle, all in muck. I want to have them. And on the dung heap there is lying a poor nag. I saw him there when I was carrying the dung from the stable. He was in poor shape, scarcely able to move his head. He may have given up the ghost since then. But if you give me that horse, mother, I will not bother you with any more requests."

"Oh, son, what would you gain by having a soiled saddle and bridle, and a decrepit nag which is on its last legs? He could not carry you as far as a mile. In fact, I'm quite sure it can't even get on its legs again."

"Never mind, mother. Just leave it to me. I'll manage to drag him along somehow."

The old woman was still loath to let him have his request. She offered him gold, as much as he would take; she offered him the finest castles in the world; and if he wanted a horse, she offered him the best horse from her stable, with the finest saddle and bridle to go with it. But the boy was stubborn; he would not change his mind.

"Well, son, as you are so persistent, you shall have what you want. A lot of good it will do you though."

"Never mind, mother. I'll get along with them as well as I can."

The boy then went to the hen coop; he took the mucky saddle and bridle from the perch. Then he went to the dung pit. The five-legged horse was lying there quite near the pit. It called for some effort to get the bridle on its neck. But as soon as it was there, the nag shook itself and got up on its feet. It whispered into the boy's ears, "My dear master, put the saddle on my back. But do not get into the saddle because for a while I am just going to stagger along somehow, even toppling over every now and then, until we get safely out of sight of this cottage here."

And unsteady on its legs and toppling over more than once, the nag made for the gate. The old woman came and fell to lamenting again. "Didn't I tell you, son, that the nag won't be any good to you? Just wait and see how far you get with it before it will give up the ghost. And then all your labor will have been in vain, and you'll have come off with nothing."

The boy did not budge.

"Oh, mother, there's no need to worry about it. We'll manage to drag along somehow and get somewhere."

And when there was a good distance between them and the cottage, the horse shook itself.

"Now, my dear master, get into the saddle and off we go."

The boy got on its back and the horse asked him, "Shall I go like the wind or as quick as thought?"

"Whichever you like, but neither of us must come to any harm."

Then they went flying with the wind, and soon they caught sight of a beautiful palace. When they were only a little distance from the palace, the horse came down to the ground and from there on it proceeded at a trot.

Then it said to the boy, "Listen, dear master. We are going to that palace over yonder. But before you go in, you'll have to take me into the stable. You'll find three horses there. And you must not forget to look after us. Feed us and water us and curry us properly. And when you're called into the palace, keep a

watch on your tongue. Say no more than necessary. Don't say
from where you've come and what business has brought you
here. Say that as you are here, you would like to look after the
horses and that you'll feed them and groom them with proper
care."

The boy took his horse to the stable and tied him there. The
three horses seemed to recognize their companion at once. Then
the five-legged horse said, "Now let us have our food and drink.
In the corner you'll find a rag, the remains of an old sheepskin
coat; with that rag rub us clean."

The boy fed and watered the horses and rubbed them down
with the rag. And into what beautiful horses did they turn!
There was no need to put on a light in the stable because the
hair of his five-legged horse gleamed with the brightness of a
lamp. When the day was drawing to a close and he had finished
grooming the horses, he saw a beautiful maid. She was coming
through the palace garden, making for the stable. With a leap
he was at the stable door and the maid called in, "Come along,
János! You are to have supper in the palace! It is by the order
of the king's daughter."

The boy followed her. While he was having his supper the
princess came into the kitchen and said to him, "Listen, János!
Look after the horses with great care, and when the king comes
home you'll get a rich reward."

The boy thanked her for the supper and went back to the
stable. He fed and watered the horses and then sat down on his
stool, smoking his pipe.

Three days went by and the horses were getting impatient.
How they would have enjoyed a long run!

On the third eve of the third day, János was called into the
palace to have his supper there. Again the king's daughter came
out to him. A great love she felt for him. And so did János
for her.

On the morning of the fourth day—eight o'clock it was—a
coach drawn by two horses drove up before the palace. János
could hardly take his eyes off the horses and the fine coach.
Then the king's daughter came out of the palace and rode off in

the coach. Off they went in less than a wink; you could not tell which way they went.

When she was gone János went back to the stable in deep sorrow.

Said one of the four horses, "What is eating your heart, dear master? Are you unhappy because the princess rode off in her coach? She went to church, and if you'd like to see her I will take you there. We'll be there when the priest appears. But when you go in, don't walk up to the first pew to sit there. Stay behind and take a seat in the third pew but last. And when the priest has finished reading the Gospel and got halfway through the sermon, then you must leave the church. I'll be waiting for you right at the church door. Then jump on my back because the king's daughter will be getting up by then to leave."

"All right, my dear horse, I will do as you tell me."

"But before we go, bring me a bushel of oats, and I will eat it. Bring me a bushel of embers, and I will eat that too; then give me a bucketful of water. I will drink the water, and then we can set off."

The horse shook itself, and as he did so, everything there was on both of them turned into silver. There was János standing in clothes of silver. And the saddle and the bridle on the horse, they too turned into silver; and so did the horseshoes. Then János swung into the saddle, and such a handsome fellow he was, he did not look inferior to any prince. And then the horse rode off with him. And it did not stop until it came to the church door. János dismounted, went in, and seated himself in the third pew but last. All the time he kept his eyes on the princess who was sitting in the front pew. And the princess never took her eyes off him. She kept wondering to herself who that prince might be, as she had never seen him there before. When the priest got halfway through the sermon, János quickly left the church. He jumped into the saddle, and like a shot, the horse carried him home. Then he tied his horse up in the stable, and sat down on his stool. There he was sitting at the stable door, smoking his pipe.

As he was sitting there, the coach came driving up to the

palace. The princess called out to him, "Tell me, János, haven't you seen a prince on horseback riding this way?"

"Since your royal highness left I've been sitting here tending the horses and smoking my pipe. But I didn't see anyone."

The princess stepped out of the coach, and the two horses drove off as quick as lightning. The princess went in to take off her coat. Soon János was called into the palace to have his dinner. While he was eating the princess came out into the kitchen and pressed him with questions about the prince, because she imagined that he must have seen him pass. But he said that he had not seen him. And the other servants said that they had not seen János leave the palace.

Another week went by. János was still looking after the horses, feeding them and watering them with care. When Sunday came, a coach drawn by four horses drove up before the palace. The princess got into the coach and like the wind she was driven off to church. With a heavy heart, János went to the stable.

Said the second horse to János, "What is eating your heart out, my dear master? Are you unhappy because the princess has gone to church?"

"Oh, how I wish I could be there myself!"

"Well then, bring me two bushels of oats and two bushels of embers. I will eat them up, and then I will take you after the princess."

The horse ate the two bushels of oats and then swallowed the two bushels of embers; then it shook itself. And as it did so, everything there was on it turned into glistening gold. The bridle, the saddle, and even the horseshoes were of gold. And so it was with János: his sword, his shako, and everything he had on him. Then János jumped into the saddle. And in a wink the horse dashed off with him, quick as lightning, so that there was no one to see them go. The horse took him to church. This time János took his seat in the second pew but last, and he left as soon as the priest began his sermon. He swung into the saddle and, quick as thought, the horse took him home.

And when the coach turned up with the princess, János was already smoking his pipe, sitting at the stable door. The four horses drove up before the stable, and the princess called out to

János, "Tell me, János, have you seen a prince, in such and such apparel, riding past the palace?"

"Oh, princess, I've been sitting here all the time since your royal highness drove off, and I went into the stable only every now and then to tend the horses. But I haven't seen a prince pass by."

And faster than the wind the four horses drove off with the coach; not even a trail of dust could be seen in its wake.

After a bit of time, a maid came to call János into the palace. While he was having his dinner, the princess came out to him and pressed him with questions about the prince, because she thought that János must have seen him pass the palace.

But János said that he had not seen anyone pass the palace. The princess, however, still had great confidence that she would meet the prince.

When he finished eating, János went back to the stable to feed and water the horses and to give them a currying.

Said the third horse to János, "Listen, dear master. There's still a whole week to go before Sunday next. Carry on just as usual, looking after us. But on Sunday when I take you to church, try to find yourself a seat in the last pew, so that the princess should not get near you. And there's something else. When you leave the church, take care that you should not step on the top stair as it will be smeared with pitch, and your golden boots would get stuck in it, and the princess would then get hold of you."

All this János kept well in mind. Throughout the week he was looking after the horses; he fed them and watered them and gave them a proper currying.

And on the third Sunday a coach drawn by six horses drove up before the palace to take the princess to church.

János was sitting again on his stool at the stable door. And when the princess drove off in the coach, he went into the stable with a heavy heart. He had no greater wish than to follow her.

Said the third horse to János, "Listen dear master. Bring me three bushels of oats and three bushels of embers. I will eat them up." Then the horse shook itself. And as he did so, everything there was on them turned into diamonds. The clothes on János, his sword, and the trappings on the horse, all were diamonds.

The horse then instructed János to seat himself in the very last pew in the church and to leave as soon as the priest began his sermon. And that on leaving the church he must step over the first stair or else his golden boots would get stuck on the pitch, and the princess would rush after him and get hold of him. And it happened like this.

János mounted his horse. In a wink he was carried to the church door. He went in. He sat down in the last pew, and when the priest got to the end of the mass and began his sermon, János rose and quickly left the church. The horse was waiting for him close by the church door so that when he came out he swung into the saddle at once.

They got home safely, and before long, he was sitting at the stable door smoking his pipe. And after a bit of time the coach drawn by six horses drove up to the stable. The princess asked János, "Tell me, János, have you seen such and such a prince, on such and such a horse, riding past?"

"Since your royal highness left, I've been sitting here, but I have seen no man pass the palace."

The princess did not stop to alight but drove off at such awful speed that all six horses dropped down dead on the way, one by one, and the coach was smashed to pieces.

The princess then walked back to the stable where János was sitting and said, "Well, my handsome and beloved one, whoever the gallant might have been who followed me to church, he must have come to remove the spell from me. To this day I have been living under a spell. But now that the spell is broken I am just like any other princess, and so I can declare my love to you."

János made evasions as best he could. He told her outright that he had been promised to be made a king and would get a princess in marriage when he returned to the kingdom down on the ground and brought the king some fruit of this very tree.

The princess said to him, "There is no way of getting the fruit of this tree unless you have a horse which can fly as fast as the wind. You must know that every fruit is guarded by a fairy; and only by flying past it could you snatch a piece of fruit or two."

János answered that he would go up and never stop, whatever trouble or pain it cost him, until he got some fruit of the tree.

The princess then persuaded János to stay rather than go, and to marry her. János became so enamored of her that he followed her to the palace, where they spent a couple of days together. He forgot completely about the horses in the stable. But after a while it came to his mind that the horses should be fed and watered and curried. So he made for the stable to look after them. But when he entered the stable, one horse gave him such a kick that he landed in the courtyard. But otherwise no harm came to him.

So he returned to the stable and said to the horses, "It's true, my dear horses, you had completely slipped my mind. But never again shall I forget to look after you."

Then he fed and watered them and gave them a proper curry-ing. Three or four times a day he went to look after the horses, so that the princess asked, "What keeps you so long? Why must you always bother about the horses?"

János answered, "I dare say, the horses have to be tended. Can't you understand that if I did not look after them properly, they would not be fit to take us out when we wanted to drive in the coach or go hunting?"

The princess realized how right he was and approved of his conduct. Then they went into their room and had great fun together. They made up their minds that on the following Sunday they would go to church and get married.

János was still reluctant to have it this way, but the princess had taken a very great fancy to him. And with such finesse did she use her honeyed tongue that at last he made no further objection. On Sunday they went to church and were married. There was a big wedding feast, and there was great merriment, and the princess was the happiest of all because the enchantment had gone from her.

A week went by, and a second week went by, and János was kept busy with the horses and was looking after them with great care. On the third Sunday and on the fourth, following their wedding day, János began to show signs of restlessness. He did not feel like going to church on Sunday morning. It was different with his young wife, who would not have stayed away for anything as she was used to spending her Sunday mornings in church. This being the state of affairs, the young queen took leave of her husband. But before she went, she gave eleven keys to the young king.

"Here. Take these eleven keys. True, there are twelve rooms in the palace, but there is no key to the twelfth room. I'm giving you these keys so that you may while away your time looking into the eleven rooms, as I see you have no mind to come to church with me."

Then the young queen drove off to church, and the young king took the eleven keys and made the rounds of the eleven rooms.

But how intrigued he was by the twelfth room. He was itching to have a peep into it, but he had no key to it. Then he took the eleven keys and tried every one of them to see whether he could find one to fit the lock. One of them fitted and the door flew open. He stepped into the twelfth room, but there was nothing inside the room except a big tub. And there was no opening in the tub except a small hole in the lid. As he was going round the tub for better inspection, he heard a voice calling out, "Oh, oh! I am going to perish with thirst."

"Who are you? And what are you doing inside the tub? And why must you perish with thirst?"

"I am the dragon with twelve heads," the voice said, "and I am kept prisoner in this tub with all my limbs in fetters. I am near dying with thirst. Give me a drink of water, and you will not regret it."

The young king went at once. Instead of water, he brought him a glass of wine. He poured it through the small hole in the lid so that the dragon, who kept his mouth close to it, could gulp it down. As soon as he drank the wine, three fetters burst on his limbs and three chains burst on the tub. Then the dragon asked for a second drink. The young king gave him a second glass. The dragon gulped it down and said, "One good turn deserves another," and he asked for another drink. The king brought him a third glass of wine. When he gave it to the dragon, he said, "For the third time now, I am giving you your life."

And once more the dragon asked for a drink. And again the young king gave it to him. Then all the fetters burst on the dragon, and all the chains burst on the tub. The tub fell to pieces, and the dragon stepped out of it.

"To be sure, you did a good turn to me, young king; in reward I will spare your life three times."

The young king paid little attention to these words, and the dragon went his way. As the dragon was going along he met the young queen who was on her way back from church. At once the dragon snatched her up and carried her away.

The young king was waiting for his queen. He waited for two hours, but the queen did not come.

"Where is the queen?" he asked the servants and the parlor maids.

"How should we know where the queen is?" they said. "Maybe she was carried off by the dragon your majesty let out of the tub and set free."

I should not have gone into the twelfth room, the king thought to himself, and I should not have given the dragon wine which helped to revive him. But as there was nothing he could do now about it, he went to the stable to look after the horses. And he gave them food and drink and curried them, and there was great sorrow in his heart.

Says the five-legged horse to him, "The dragon has carried off your beautiful wife the queen, hasn't he, dear master? Well, what is there to be done?"

Says one of the horses, "Listen, dear master, give me food and drink. And I will carry you, and you'll bring back the queen."

The young king fed and watered the horse. When he got into the saddle, the horse rode off with him to the castle of the dragon. When they were only a little distance from it, János dismounted and left his horse there. Then he walked up to the gate to inquire whether he would find the dragon home. He was told that the dragon was in the castle. As he was walking up to the door the young queen stepped out with a bucket to fetch water from the well.

János took her in his arms and said, "My fair and beloved queen, my horse is waiting there yonder. I have come after you to rescue you from the dragon."

"My fair and beloved one, it would be of no avail. The dragon would follow us and kill us both. You'd better go home now and look for a second wife. Before long I shall come to a miserable end here."

"Oh my fair and beloved queen, you must let me take you away."

So the queen left her bucket at the well and followed her husband. They mounted the horse and rode off. They were well on their way home when the dragon's horse began to paw furiously at the stable floor.

The dragon rose and went to the stable: "What the devil has come over you? Didn't you get enough oats and hay? Are you in want of food? Have you not a beautiful mistress?"

"I have plenty of oats and hay. I have enough to eat. But my beautiful mistress is gone."

"Tell me then if I shall have enough time to finish smoking a bushel of tobacco and to eat up a bushel of hazel nuts?"

"Indeed, you shall. And you can have a night's rest as well and yet we shall be there in good time to overtake them."

The dragon then took his time smoking the bushel of tobacco and eating up the hazel nuts. He went to sleep and when he rose he mounted his horse. The horse took three leaps, and another four leaps, and there they were, catching up with the young king and his wife. Suddenly the dragon lifted the queen from her saddle and then said to the king, "One life I have spared you. And now go about your business."

What else could he do but go home in great distress? He tied his horse up in the stable and then fed and watered the four horses. And great sorrow was eating his heart away.

Next day the second horse says to János, "Well, dear master, let me have my food and drink and off we go to bring back the young queen."

The horse was fed and watered, and the young king mounted

him. They were riding for some time and before long they drew near the dragon's castle. When they were only a little distance from it, János dismounted and tied up the horse. As he was walking up to the castle whom does he see come out of it but his young queen making for the kitchen garden to get some greens.

When she saw him, she cried out to him, "Alas! Here you are again."

"Here I am, and I am going to take you away."

She said, "Oh, but the dragon with twelve heads brought me back to make me his wife. There is nothing now you could do for me."

"Do not worry about it. I am going to take you away."

She followed him and they both mounted the horse and rode off.

The dragon's horse was pawing furiously at the stable floor, kicking up a terrible shindy.

The dragon rose and went to the stable. "What the dickens has come over you? Didn't you get enough oats and hay? Are you in want of food? Have you not a beautiful mistress?"

"I get plenty of oats and hay. I have enough to eat. But my beautiful mistress is gone."

"Tell me then if I shall have enough time to finish smoking a bushel of tobacco and to eat up a bushel of walnuts?"

"Indeed, you will. And you can have a night's rest as well, and yet we'll be there in good time to overtake them."

He took his time smoking the bushel of tobacco and eating up the walnuts. He took a night's rest, and then rested for another night, and then he mounted his horse.

The young king and his wife were not quite halfway home when the dragon caught up with them. At once he got hold of the young queen, and then he said to the king, "Only once more shall I spare your life."

János rode home in great distress. He tied up his horse in the stable and then went about feeding and watering and currying the horses. Said the third horse next morning, "Well, dear master, give me food and drink and off we go to bring back the young queen."

The horse got his food and drink, and then the king mounted him. They set off and came safely to their destination.

The young queen was just going to the orchard to pick some fruit. The king called to her, "O, my fair and beloved queen, I am going to take you away. Come and follow me."

"Alas! I cannot go with you. The dragon with twelve heads would follow us, and he might kill us both."

The king said, "I do not care what he is going to do, but I am not going to leave you here."

He led her to the horse and got into the saddle. They rode off and were well on their way when the dragon's horse began kicking up a terrible row in the stable. The dragon rose and went into the stable. He said, "Didn't you get enough oats and hay? Are you in want of food? Have you not a beautiful mistress?"

"I have plenty of oats and hay. I have enough to eat. But my beautiful mistress is gone."

"Tell me then if I shall have enough time to eat and drink?"

"Indeed you shall have time enough to eat and drink. And you can take a rest as well, and yet we shall be there in good time to overtake them."

The dragon ate and drank and had a good sleep. Then he mounted his horse and soon caught up with the pair. He got hold of the queen and then said to the king, "You shall not dare to come again. Three times I spared your life. The fourth time I shall take it."

In great distress, the young king rode home. His own horse, the five-legged nag, saw his despair and said, "Dear master, I see that your heart is full of grief. But you must not give way to despair because your beautiful queen was carried off. Bring me now five bushels of oats and five bushels of embers and also five buckets of water. I am going to swallow all of it. And when I have finished, get on my back and we shall bring back the queen."

On the morning of the following day the king mounted his horse, and they set off. Then his horse began blowing flames, blue and red and green flames, and forthwith they rose into the air and went flying. When they were only a little distance from the dragon's castle, the horse alighted in the garden before the palace. The young queen saw through the window that there was a horse in the garden. She did not recognize the king's very own horse, because she had never set eyes on it before. She went to have a look at it. As she left the room she found the young king standing at the door.

He said, "My fair and beloved queen, I will take you home. And we are going right away."

The queen said, "Alas! How could I go with you? Don't you remember the dragon's threats? Didn't he warn you that if you came again he would kill you?"

"Do not worry, my fair and beloved queen. Just let me carry you away."

And he took the young queen into his arms and carried her into the garden where the horse was waiting. They mounted the horse and rode off.

They could not have gone more than just a few miles when the dragon's horse started kicking up an infernal row.

The dragon went out to the stable. "What the hell has come over you? Didn't you get enough oats and hay? Are you in want of food or drink? Have you not a beautiful mistress?"

"I've got plenty of oats and hay. I have enough to eat and drink. But my beautiful mistress is gone."

"Tell me then if I shall have enough time to eat and drink something?"

"It is too late for that. There is not a minute to spare."

In great anger the dragon mounted his horse. When they were drawing near the royal pair, the king's horse turned his head and neighed to the other horse, "Has it never occurred to you that I am carrying on my back two noble souls while you are carrying a loathsome monster? Why don't you spill him and crush him under your feet so that not a scrap remains of him?"

The dragon's horse uttered a sharp whinny. He took a leap and then rolled over. No sooner was the dragon thrown from his saddle than his horse was all over him, trampling and crushing him under his feet. Then with one leap he shot ahead to the other horse who was waiting for him. The two horses kissed each other. The queen then mounted the dragon's horse, and the king remained on his own. Quietly, the two horses trotted along, side by side, taking their riders home.

When they arrived, the king and the queen tied the horses up in the stable. Now they had five horses there. They fed and watered them. And then they went to the palace and ate and drank and went to take a rest after the many troubles they had gone through.

On the morning of the following day the king said to the queen, "Well, my fair and beloved queen, we have come safely out of all our troubles; now let us go and find what sort of fruit this tree bears."

She said, "All right, let's go. But we can not go by daylight. We must wait till midnight."

At midnight on the following day they mounted their horses; she on the dragon's horse, and he on the five-legged horse. Their horses rose with them and flew up to the boughs where the fruit was hanging. On each bough there was a fairy sitting to keep guard. But as they were flying over the boughs both the king and the queen snatched off a pair of apples. Each time they took hold of an apple a fairy fell off the tree, and this way they always knew which bough they had already relieved of its fruit. When they had gotten the fruit, two apples each, they flew home to the palace. And for many months they went on living there, looking after their horses.

One day the young king said to the queen, "I guess I should be leaving now and go back down to my own country to show the old king the fruit of this tree."

The queen was of one mind with him. And so one day they set off together, the queen on the dragon's horse, the king on the five-legged horse, and the maid and the cook and the scullery maid, each on the back of one of the three other horses.

Their horses rose with them, and when they landed on the ground they found the old king sleeping, as it was still late at night.

Then they saw a forest. It was not very far from the king's palace, about a mile and a half off. On the outskirts of the forest they built themselves a beautiful palace. And in that palace they made their abode.

On the morning of the following day the old king was looking out of his window. His eyes fell on the magnificent palace, which towered over there, on the edge of the forest. A beautiful palace it was, indeed. It was so beautiful that he was almost blinded by its splendor. And then his eyes fell on a bridge. A bridge built of marble, spanning the air between his own palace and the beautiful new one. And around the palace there were a number of beautiful trees, some laden with fruit, vying with one another only in their excellence. And on each tree there sat a falcon. Suddenly each falcon broke forth into song.

At once the old king gave an order to his footmen to drive the coach before the door. He got into the coach to have a look at that splendid palace over there. He took his daughter with him. His heart was leaping with joy as he saw the beautiful flowers in the garden and as he heard the sweet song of the birds trilling on the trees around the gate.

The coach stopped at the entrance and they stepped out. As they were going up the flight of steps leading to the door, the doorkeeper and the footmen came to meet them and inquired politely whom they wished to see.

"Oh, we really do not know," the old king said. "We have come here to find out who is living in this fine castle. Yesterday there was nothing in this place, and when I looked out of my window this morning, the first thing I saw was this beautiful palace, fit for a king to live in."

"Will your majesty and the princess please come this way? It is a young king and a young queen who are living in this palace."

"And are they at home?"

"Yes, they are. They are having a rest."

The visitors went in and knocked at the first door. It woke the sleepers. And at once the young recognized the old king and the princess. Great joy overcame them on seeing each other, and the two men and the two women kissed each other as if they had been sisters and brothers.

The young king then invited them to sit down and gave an account of his wanderings and showed them the four apples which they had brought from the tree. Two apples he gave to the king and two he kept for himself and his queen.

The old king then asked him if he would like to marry his daughter.

The young king answered, "I cannot marry the princess because I have a lawful wife, married to me by the priest."

He thanked the old king for this great honor and said that he did not wish any reward for the fruit he had brought him. The old king had a great desire to taste the fruit and took a bite of the apple. No sooner had he swallowed the first bite than he became as young as he was at eighteen. And how great was his surprise to see himself younger than his own daughter or young János, the gallant youth who had brought him the apples.

He thanked the young king for doing him a good turn, and then he ordered a great feast in honor of the young pair. There was great merriment and a grand banquet.

I was there myself; can't you remember, we had a good time of it.

·7· *Péterke*

Once upon a time there was a poor man. He was as poor as a church mouse and had nothing to his name, not even a house in which to live. But of children he had plenty—so many, indeed, that he found no other way of counting them than to buy with his wages a hundred pounds of walnuts. He counted the nuts and gave one to each child, and yet, at the end, twelve kiddies were left crying and without a walnut.

When his wife was expecting their next baby, there was not a man he could have asked to stand as godfather, for all the men in the village had been asked before when his other kiddies were born. He went then to seek a sponsor for his coming one. So he took his bag and, equipped with a wanderer's staff, he set out and went on till he came to the outskirts of a forest. There he built a great fire and settled down to eat the food—it was only an ash cake—he had brought for the journey. As soon as he began eating, there appeared an old man with white hair, as suddenly as if he had dropped there right from the sky.

His greeting was a polite one: "Do you mind if I sit down by your fire?"

"You are welcome to it, father. Aren't we both God's children?"

And to please him he went to a juniper shrub and returned with an armful of boughs so that the old man might sit on them. He made it even more comfortable for him by placing neatly on the top the tufts of the juniper. Then he settled down again to his food and asked the stranger to share his meal. The stranger thanked him for it, and while they were eating, the poor man told him all about his many troubles and worries. He told him that he had more children than there were meshes in a sieve and that he was so poor that he had nothing to his name, not even a house in which to live. He said that his wife was soon to have another baby and that there was nobody in their village he could ask to stand sponsor for it. And that he could not even think of a name to give the new one, be it a boy or a girl.

The stranger listened to his complaints and then said, "Do not go any further, my brother of this earth. If you don't mind having an old man like me to stand godfather to your newborn, I will give it a name. You needn't tell me the day of its birth because I know it better than you do. And I'll be there to give the child a name and see it christened. Go home now, but never raise your eyes from the dust on the road while you are on your way."

They lay down then to have their night's rest. When the day was breaking, the poor man woke from his sleep. He looked right and left, but the bearded stranger was gone. His own bag was there, so chock-full of food and money that he could hardly move it. For a while he was afraid even to touch it for fear that it might have been put there to test his honesty. But suddenly his eyes fell on a slip of paper on top of it. There was written on it: "This is for your children so that they may have something to eat till I come."

The poor man took his bag and set out on his way back home. While he was on his way he never raised his eyes from the dust on the road. Suddenly he saw a small diamond egg lying in the dust. First he took it for a piece of broken mirror, but when he examined it more closely, he was sure that it was a diamond egg. When he reached home with the diamond egg, he exchanged it for money. He received such a lot of money for it that he could give each of his children a sackful.

Then he bought a fine house with a big orchard. He had clothes and shoes made for his kiddies and provided them with plenty of food.

The day came when his wife gave birth to the new baby. When it arrived he began to wonder whether the new godfather would find his way to them. They were not living in the old cottage now. But no sooner did this thought enter his head than he heard a knock at the door. "Come in," he called, and in came the stranger with the beard, wearing a pair of clogs. He recognized him at once as the sponsor. He greeted him with great politeness, and so was his greeting received.

"Pray, how on earth did you find us, father?" he asked the stranger. "Aren't we living now in a quite different kind of house? But to be sure it's you we can thank for it. May God bless you for your kindness. Since we met in the forest, none of my family has suffered hunger or seen want. If only I knew how to show you my gratitude!"

Says the old man, "There is only one way to show your gratitude: have faith in my father and in me, and I will make you rich."

"So will it be, but still I do not know who you are."

Says the stranger with the beard, "I am Jesus."

All the kiddies then ran to Jesus and hugged him and kissed him.

Next day the new sponsor took the newborn babe to be baptized. When he came back with the child, he handed it to its parents and said, "The child has been christened Péterke. I am his godfather, and I am going to give him a calf. But take good care that you do not lose the calf or else you'll have to wait till my godson grows up into a youth, since only he could find the calf."

The stranger then made the sign of the cross, and thus blessing the family he disappeared as suddenly as he had come. Only the calf was left standing there.

Next day the whole string of children marched to the field with the calf. All the time they were guarding it anxiously for it was the apple of their eye. And yet, when the bell began ringing for noon the calf was gone. There was not a single place they did not search for it. They looked into every mouse hole, but there was no calf.

The days and years went by, and Péterke came into his twentieth year. Said he, "Prepare me the things I will need for a journey because I am not going to stop until I find my calf."

They provided him with all the necessities for his journey. His brothers offered to go with him, but he did not want them to go along. He said that if he could not find his calf by himself, then a thousand men would not be of any help.

He set off and did not stop until he came to the outskirts of a big forest. He went on till he found an opening in the wood. There he sat down to have a rest. He took some food from his bag and began to appease his appetite, eating at his leisure, sitting there by himself.

Suddenly a limping and saddle-backed fox bobbed up before him. He asked for a bit of food. Péterke did not begrudge him the food and shared with the fox all he had.

When they finished eating, the fox said, "Well, dear master, one good deed certainly deserves another. Get on my back, and I will take you to the tollgate. The gatekeeper is a giant. When we get close enough to him, get off my back and walk up to the gate. The tollkeeper won't let you pass unless you promise to give him your *táltos* bull. The calf which was yours has bred one thousand and eight hundred offspring during the past twenty years. Among them you'll find a *táltos* bull and five cows. The giant is going to ask for the *táltos* bull. Just promise to give it to him. The bull will know how to get away from the giant. When you have passed through the tollgate, go right ahead, cutting across the forest, until you come to an opening. There you will find a big wooden trough. Empty the trough, and when there is no more water in it, lie down in it. When the *táltos* bull comes to have a drink, you must take hold of its horns and stroke it with your left hand. The bull will utter a loud bellow, and his roar will bring the cows there. And the bull will take up the lead, and the cows will follow him. Then when all of you come up to the tollgate, let the giant have the bull. You must drive on the cows, and then you can see to the rest of the job."

The fox stopped not far from the tollgate. Péterke dismounted and did as he was told to do. Suddenly the fox vanished. Péterke walked up to the gate. He found a giant there. He greeted him politely. To the giant this seemed like the squeak of a mouse. Standing before the giant, Péterke looked about the size of a mouse.

Said the giant, "Hey, you Hop-o-my-Thumb there! What business has brought you here?"

Péterke shouted up to him, "I'm driving my cows. Would you please let us pass the tollgate?"

"If you are the master of these cows, I won't let you pass unless I can have the one which goes first to the trough."

"Good. You shall have it. But let all the others pass."

The giant opened the big iron gate, and Péterke passed through it. He did not get much further than a mile when he came to a small opening in the wood. There he found a big trough. He emptied the trough, and when it was empty he lay in it. Suddenly he heard a great trampling, followed by a tremendous roar which seemed to have filled all the place around. But Péterke remained quietly in the trough. Then a bull came walking up to the trough to take a drink there. But there was no water. When it caught sight of Péterke lying there, the bull made for him and wanted to toss him up with his horns. But Péterke reached out with his left hand and quickly stroked the horns of the animal. All of a sudden the bull grew tame.

It began to speak and said, "Well, my dear master, it's true that you've never thought twice about selling me on the advice of a fox. But do not worry now. I'll manage somehow to get away from the giant. You just keep behind and keep driving the cows."

The bull then uttered a second roar and dug deep into the ground with his hoofs. His bellowing was a call to summon the cows. When they were all gathered around him, he took up the lead and quietly set forth again, followed by the cows. Péterke closed up the rear. All he had to do was to crack his whip every now and then till they came to the tollgate.

When they reached the gate, the giant took the *táltos* bull by its horns and led him off and locked him up in a huge iron cage. Péterke passed the tollgate with the cows.

No sooner had they reached the outskirts of the forest than Péterke heard the *táltos* bull bellow and, just in a bit of time, there it was again, joining the cows.

And again the bull walked ahead of the cows and took up the lead. And they went on till they were back at home. And now suddenly the whole place seemed to be full of cows. There were cows in the courtyard and the stables, in the orchard and in the front garden. Wherever you looked there were cows and bulls, just cows and bulls, all over the place.

Great joy came over Péterke's parents when they saw that their son had brought back the lost calf, now a cow with its offspring. Next day Péterke wanted to take them out to the fields. The *táltos* bull then said to him, "My dear master, do not turn us out to graze. Take us to the cattle market and there sell the whole herd, except me and the old cow, the one which was once the calf you got from your godfather. And when they are all sold, you will see twelve men lead up another big bull. A bull so strong that it needs the might and main of twelve men to pull it along. When at last they reach the market place, ask them how much they want for their bull. They will answer that the bull would be more than your match since the twelve of them could hardly make him move. But you must say to them that you will take the bull home by yourself if they will sell him to you. And then they will lay a wager with you that you will get the bull for half its worth should you take it home by yourself. Then walk up to the bull and stroke its horns with your left hand. When the men give it a slash to make it move, get hold of his chain and lead him up to me. And then fasten his head to mine. This done, you can leave the rest to me. And when you've paid the man the price he asked for his bull, then take us home. When we get home, I'll give you some more advice."

Péterke drove the herd to the market. The bull went ahead and was followed by the cows. When they came to the market place, the animals were quickly sold. Even the old cow would have gone with the rest, but Péterke did not want to sell her. As soon as the last of his cattle was sold, except for the bull and the old cow, Péterke heard a tremendous bellow. From the opposite direction twelve men were struggling hard with a bull, trying to pull him along. They were sweating blood and water and called down a thousand curses upon the bull, wishing that it had died before they ever set their eyes upon it.

When Péterke caught sight of them, he walked up to the twelve men and asked them to sell their bull to him. He told them that he too had a bull and wanted to get him a companion so that he should not feel lonely.

Says the owner of the bull, "You'd better think twice before you talk, young man. Can't you see that the twelve of us can hardly manage him?"

Says Péterke, "I dare say I could take him home myself, if only you sell him to me."

"It's a deal. If you can take him away by yourself, you can have the bull at half price."

Then Péterke walked up to the bull. The bull never stopped bellowing at him, but Péterke paid no heed to it and began to stroke its horns with his left hand. Suddenly the bull grew tame. It did not even mind when Péterke slipped through under its belly. Then Péterke jumped onto its back and took a firm hold on its horns. But the bull did not stir; it stood stock still as if it had turned to stone. Péterke dismounted, took hold of his chain, and led it up to his own bull. Then he tied the two bulls together by their heads. This done, he went back to the owner of the bull to ask him about the price. Such was the amazement of the man that he still found no words for dickering and gave the bull away for half of its worth. Péterke paid him off on the spot.

Then he took the two bulls and the cow and went home with them and tied them up in the stall.

His parents were just a bit angry with him for having sold the cows. Till then they had plenty of milk from the cows. They were fond of milk and were afraid now that they would have to do without it. But the old cow was holding its own, and she gave milk in such abundance that all of them could bathe in milk.

Next day Péterke went to the stable and asked the *táltos* bull, "Well, what would you advise me to do, my dear bull?"

Said the bull, "Listen, dear master, go to the king and ask him to give his daughter in marriage to you. He will say that you will not get his daughter unless you plow a thousand acres of his land in one day. Then ask him for a plow which can make a thousand furrows at one turn. And also for a suitable forecarriage for the plow. Then ask him to let you have an iron yoke, fifty meters in width, with a proper pole. When you have got all this, go to the king and tell him that you want to go to the fields and yoke the bulls but that first he must show how to use the plow. The rest of the job you can leave to me."

Péterke followed his advice, and when the plow and the fore-carriage were ready for use he took his two bulls and went with them to the fields and put them to yoke. There was a wager between Péterke and the king that he would put the plow to a thousand acres between daybreak and sundown. And if he did he would get the king's daughter in marriage. Just wait and see, my king and my lord, he thought to himself.

When Péterke and his bulls went to the field the sun was high in the sky. By noon Péterke had put the plow to half the land. The king saw it all from the window of his palace and was not at all pleased about it. Why should such an unworthy youth get the better of him? He summoned the comeliest servant girl in the palace and sent her with a midday meal for Péterke. He gave orders to the girl that she should dally with the plowman until he went to sleep. Only then could she return to the palace.

The servant girl did as she was told. When Péterke finished his meal, she began flirting with him and did not stop with the dallying until she made Péterke return her kisses. And then they had fun together until he went to sleep. Only then did the girl return to the palace. And she felt mighty pleased with herself for having humored his majesty the king.

In the afternoon Péterke awoke from his sleep. He still imagined he had the servant girl at his side and, half-asleep, he put his arms around one leg of his bull. But opening his eyes he saw that the girl had gone. And worse than that, the sun was far gone to the west. And the king's land remained unplowed.

He heaved a deep sigh. "Oh, God Almighty, what am I to do now?"

Said the *táltos* bull, "I dare say you had a long sleep, my dear master. But what about your wager? Next time you must not fall for a maid so easily. This once we are going to help you out of this fix, but next time you'd better think twice before you do something like this."

And he turned to the other bull, "Now blow with all your might, friend bull. Blow the sun back to where it stood at noontide."

And the other bull began wheezing and puffing with such might that it made the sun travel back a good distance.

Says the *táltos* bull, "I dare say if that's all you are worth, then you are not fit to wear a pair of horns on your head."

Then the *táltos* bull himself blew with such might that it made the sun shoot back to where it stood at early breakfast time. And when the sun was making toward noon again, Péterke had finished plowing the king's lands. Then he went home, singing all the way along.

Now the king almost burst in his anger that Péterke had won the hand of his daughter with such a small effort. Then he hit upon a new idea. He told Péterke that he would not give him his daughter unless Péterke succeeded in carting out in one cartload all the things, lock, stock, and barrel, that were to be found within the palace gates.

Péterke took counsel with the bull about the new task.

The bull said, "Go and tell the king that he must order a cart for you. The cart should be five hundred feet in length and one hundred feet in width. It should be made of pure iron. And the yoke and the two sides of the cart should be made of iron too. As for the rest of your task, you can leave that to me."

Before long Péterke had all the things he had asked from the king. Then he sent word to his brothers and summoned them to the king's court. As soon as they came, and a fair number of them there was too, they set to work. Each was carrying something to the big iron cart: a plow, a barrow, a harrow; then the hens, the chickens, and the geese. Whatever they caught sight of they picked up and took to the iron cart. They took the fine furniture from the palace and carried all the belongings of the king's daughter to the iron cart.

When there was not a single thing left, either in the palace or in the courtyard, said the *táltos* to Péterke, "Now go to the palace and go up into the attic, and there you'll find a box filled with money. Bring it down with the help of your brothers and put it on top of the cart. And then go and fetch the young princess and let her sit beside you on the top of the cart."

Meanwhile, the king sent for all his carters and had them fill up the courtyard with mud. The iron cart got bogged down in the clayey mud up to its axletree. There was thick mud everywhere around the cart and all the way along to the gate. Hard as they tried, the two bulls were unable to drag the cart to the gate.

Péterke was sitting on the top of the cart with the king's daughter beside him. He took his whip of twenty-four tails and began prodding his bulls. But they were stuck in the horrible mud.

The *táltos* bull then whispered to his fellow, "Blow now with all your might, brother bull. Blow so mightily that it will make the mud freeze at once."

The other bull then began to puff and blow with such strength that the mud began to harden.

Said the *táltos* bull, "If that's all you're worth, you'd better wear your horns on your hindquarters."

And he blew with such force that it made the mud freeze at once and become as hard as concrete. Then he turned to his mate, "Now blow with all your might, friend bull, and when you hear me give three little coughs, let us pull hard so that we can drag out the cart from the mud."

No sooner had the *táltos* bull given his third little cough than the cart was at the gate.

Says the king to Péterke, "Péterke, my boy, let me get back my things from the cart. I would die of shame if the people in the city saw that all that I had in my palace went bag and baggage onto a single cart. I would sooner ask you to remain here. And if you will, you can marry my daughter this day. Only do not put me to that terrible shame."

Péterke uttered a loud cry of joy and began whooping. He was hardly listening to the king and shouted that he was taking away the bride.

Said the king, "Péterke, my boy, make your bulls turn back with the cart and you shall get half of my kingdom."

Péterke was now whooping at the top of his voice.

The king went down on his knees before him and said, "You shall have my whole kingdom, only do not put me to that terrible shame."

Péterke then turned the two bulls around and made his brothers carry back everything to the palace. And on the very same day he married the king's daughter.

Then he sent for his mother and father and his sisters and his brothers. He gave them a home in the king's palace and provided for their living.

When the old king and queen died, Péterke inherited their kingdom. He made grand marshals of his brothers, and all of them lived happily ever after. And if they are not dead they are still alive to this day.

· 8 · *The Story of the Gallant Szérus*

In those far off days there was a king who had a beautiful daughter. And so proud was he of her and so jealous of her beauty that he feared lest some man might besmirch it. When the girl reached the age when the lads began casting long looks at her, the king was so afraid of losing her that he had a big barrel made, not a barrel though, but a room on a tower, and had her locked up there so that she might not communicate with a single soul.

One day two strange wanderers happened to pass by. One of them saw who was inside the tower. It roused his anger, and he turned to his companion. "Go and pull out that dry stalk yonder there and hold it up against that hole in the tower."

His companion pulled out the dry stalk and held it up against the hole. And the smell of the stalk pervaded the girl and made her pregnant. Well, it must have been a male stalk. But when the king became aware that she was with child, he sent word to the cooper and had him make a big barrel for her. And then he ordered the girl to be brought down from the tower and to be put into the big barrel. To punish her for disobedience, she was to be locked up in the barrel and turned adrift on the sea.

The waves carried the barrel, and the girl within the barrel, and both had to endure the hazards of the sea. And the girl in the barrel was rolled along by the waves and was tossed by the storms for months and months. And she knew that the day of her confinement was drawing near. And then the barrel was swept up by a great storm and hurled against a big rock. It was dashed to pieces, and the girl came ashore on an island. But there was not much time for her to waste, and she was not long about making herself a sort of shelter from the driftwood she found washed ashore on the island. She collected all these sorry pieces of wood and built herself a small hut. And in this hut she gave birth to her child. There was neither a doctor nor a midwife to help her labor, and she had to manage by herself as best as she could. She swaddled the infant in a piece of rag and fed it at her breast.

When the child grew older, she left him when hunger overcame her and went to get herself sweet roots and fed on them. Sometimes she caught fish, and she plucked the young shoots and made a fire, and then she roasted the fish and boiled seawater, and when the salt settled she used it for cooking, and in this way she provided for herself and the child. Soon the child learned to walk, and he grew into a sturdy young fellow who would jump into the sea to catch a fish. From infancy, swimming became second nature to him, and at the age of twelve he was

such a fine swimmer that his mother took him to that part of
the island which lay nearest to the mainland. He swam ashore
and found himself in a big forest. As he was looking about in
the forest in search of some food, he found wild fruit of all sorts
and a fine big apple tree. He took three apples from the tree
because they were so pretty to look at. Only when he was back
on the shore did he begin speculating as to how he could best
carry the apples back to his mother. Finally he put one apple
in his mouth and held it between his teeth; then grasping one
in each hand he went swimming back to his mother.

When the mother saw the fruit the child had brought her
from the mainland she was no end pleased, but then she began
to weep because it reminded her that she too had come from the
mainland and did not know whether she would ever get back
there.

The child made a habit of going to the mainland. He went
quite often, two or three times a week, and brought apples to
his mother. One day, when he was standing by the tree picking
apples, he saw a man pass by. It was a hussar in full attire.
Never before had he seen a hussar, and now that he had seen
one, he could not take his eyes off him. But he felt a bit scared
as well, so he plunged back into the sea and swam back to his
mother. He told her that he had seen something peculiar and his
mother wanted to hear all about it. He said that on the top it had
something red on it; then he pointed to his feet and said that
down there it was all black and shiny. His mother guessed that
he must have seen a hussar and told him that he too could get
himself such attire if he said his prayers. But he did not know
how to pray. His mother wanted to teach him to say prayers,
but it would have been of no use, as the child had not yet been
christened. So his christening soon took place. His mother took
him to the seashore, and he had to step into the sea where the
water was shallowest, and then she sprinkled seawater over his
head.

And while she was doing so she said, "I christen thee in the
name of the Father and the Son. The sun be thy father, as I
know no man, and the moon be thy godfather, and the stars be

thy brethren-in-law, and the winds be thy kin. And thy name be Gallant and Handsome Szérus."

But that was about all he had, a name for himself, because he was still without a stitch of clothing. But he never stopped swimming over to the mainland and bringing apples to his mother. And his mother taught him the short prayer she used to pray while tossed about in the barrel on the high seas. Now he too knew how to pray when he went picking the apples.

And one day, in the midst of his prayer, a complete hussar outfit fell to his feet from the top of the tree. By whom it had been put there I really couldn't say, though I was standing under the tree myself. I didn't see a soul there, I am sure. Szérus—a husky young lad he was—took the trousers into his hands and turned them round and round and propped his head against his first finger in his great effort as he tried to remember how the trousers looked when he saw them first. And then he tried, first getting one leg into them, and then the other. And a pair of tight-fitting trousers they were. Yet not all seemed right. He had got into them the wrong way, so that the back was in front and the front was at the back. He slipped out of them and then got both his legs into the right place. And now he felt as if he were clad in a suit of armor and strong enough to kick up the apple tree by its roots.

Then he tried on the pelisse [coat]. First he got one arm into it, and then the other, and then he buttoned up the shining buttons in front. But some figuring had still to be done over the boots and the cap and the sword. He started with the boots. He got his feet into them so that the spurs were facing the front. But that just wouldn't do. He couldn't even stand up that way. So he tried them the other way round, and it was all right. And he could now hear the jingling of his spurs.

There was still the cap and the sword to be dealt with. What these two were he could not guess. Not to mention the carbine which lay beside them. And while they kept him wondering, he felt something pressing hard against his breast in one of his pockets. He put his hand into it and drew forth a small mirror. And as he looked into the mirror, suddenly it flashed through his mind that when he met the hussar, there was something small and red on his head. In a wink he had his cap cocked over his eye. And there he was, as regular a hussar as you could wish.

But the sword, that loñg and gleaming thing, was still puzzling him, and so was the carbine with its long empty snout. He took up the sword and, as he was turning it in his hand, it slipped from its sheath. And then he seized the naked sword, struck out with it, and the young trees were cut in two at one blow of the gleaming blade. Then he slipped the sword back into the sheath and took in his hands the carbine. He examined it at close quarters, speculating about the purpose it might serve. He blew into its empty barrel, but no sound came out of it. And when by chance he pulled the trigger, the carbine went off with such a bang that it gave him quite a start. Now he guessed that it served to frighten things. He buckled on his sword and flung the carbine across his shoulder. As he was going back to the seashore the sword kept clanking against the spurs on his boots. He enjoyed it, and it made him step out more briskly.

But when he reached the shore, he stopped there and fell into speculation; it seemed impossible to go into the water in his fine attire. For some time he was puzzling over this problem. Suddenly he turned and went back to the apple tree. He unsheathed his sword and cut down the tree. He felt strong in his hussar outfit, able to cope with any task. Invulnerable, he would be now protected against harm. He flung the tree across his shoulder and carried it back to the shore. There he took off all his clothes, made a neat bundle of them, and tied the bundle to one of the branches. Then he pushed the tree into the sea and on the tree he went punting back to the island.

His mother was happy when he came, but she began to worry when she saw that instead of apples he had brought a tree, root and branch, and when he stood there in his new apparel, she was worried even more for fear of what might become of her. But the boy comforted her as best as he could and promised that he would take her to the mainland when they had no more apples.

And when the last of the apples was consumed, the boy made a bundle of his clothes, tied the bundle to the tree and, making a place for his mother to sit on, he went punting back with her to the mainland. When they came ashore, the boy set off toward the forest to find some shelter for himself and his mother. Leaving his mother behind on the spot where the apple tree had stood, he made for the forest of the giants, which was not far off.

When he reached the edge of the forest, a giant came running up to him. "You miserable crawler, what business has brought you to our land where no human creature ever dared to come? Should it come to the knowledge of our ruler, the king, he'd grind us both under his heels."

But a fat lot does Szérus care about the giant. Unheeding, he walks up to him. And then he draws his sword and cuts off the giant's head. As he was going further on he saw a tree, and on the top of the tree there sat a crow. At once he took off his carbine and, aiming it at the crow, pulled the trigger. There was a bang, and the crow fell from the tree. He picked up the crow, which he had almost scared to death. And there and then he found the gate of the giant's castle. He kicked it open and walked in. When the giant king caught sight of him, he gave orders to twelve giant soldiers, and they took up arms and rushed out of the castle to tear him to pieces. But tightening his grip around his sword, Szérus forced them back and walked into the palace. The king gave him a hearty welcome. Hadn't he seen just now a veritable wonder? He would be happy to have Szérus stay with them and would help him in need.

There was a cook in the castle, and a maid too. Szérus then told the king that he had a mother and that he was going to bring her along. The king said that he should do so. And Szérus brought her to the castle, and she was lodged in a fine room in the palace. As soon as she was there, her son stripped off the cook's skirt so that his mother should have a skirt. And she clad herself in the cook's clothes, and she looked indeed a fine woman in them. And in his heart of hearts the giant king fell in love with her. And the woman and the giant were now one in laying a scheme against the boy to bring about his destruction so that they might live together in the castle alone.

Said the giant, "You know what? There's a bear's lair in the forest. There lives an old bear with his two sons. Pretend that you are ill and tell your son that you won't get better unless he brings you one of the bear's sons so that you may take its heart and eat it. And your son will go for the bear, and the bear will kill him."

That was what they had concocted, but in the end the scheme went foul. When she asked the boy to bring her a cub, he left at once to do so. He found the lair, snatched up one of the cubs, and was just going to leave when he ran into the old bear. He took his carbine and leveled it at the bear.

But the bear said, "Do not shoot me, because it would be of no avail. Take the cub along. I know very well that it is not a cub your mother wants. And then just let the cub go, and it will find its way home."

And so it happened. He took the cub with him. His mother and the giant were watching for him from the window. When they saw him coming with the cub, his mother called to him, "Oh, my son, you need not bring in the cub. The mere sight of it makes me feel much better!"

Szérus now remembered the old bear's words and thought that there might have been something in what he said. However, he did not let go of the cub but took it back to the lair and put him down where he had found him. Great joy came over the bear, and he gave a whistle to Szérus so that whenever he got in trouble all he would have to do would be to blow the whistle and the bear would be there to help him.

When he went home, he found his mother ailing again. He asked what was the matter with her. She said that she had fallen ill again and that he should go to the forest. Beyond the bear's lair he would find a wolf's den, and in it the wolf's cubs, and he should bring her one of the cubs.

Szérus guessed what she was speaking about because he knew every part of the forest. He went to the wolf's den, snatched up one of the cubs, and brought it home. When his mother saw him come with the cub she said again, "Oh, do take it back. The mere sight of it makes me feel much better."

He took the cub back. The old wolf gave him a whistle so that whenever he got into trouble all he had to do was to blow the whistle and the old wolf would come to his aid.

When he reached home, he found his mother ill again. This time she sent him to fetch her a lion's cub. Her wish was nothing

new to him. He went and found the lion's den and the cubs in
the den. He took one cub home to cure his mother. But again
they did not let him bring in the cub, and his mother called out
from the window, "Oh, my son, do not bring in the cub. The
mere sight of it makes me feel much better."

This one too he took back, and again he was given a whistle.
Now he had three whistles in all, tucked away in his pocket.
And when he got home there was nothing wrong with his
mother. But cunningly she questioned him about his wonderful
strength and wherein it lay. Just to tease her he said that his
strength was in his two first fingers.

"Just put both your first fingers side by side, my son, and
let's see how strong you are."

So he did what she asked. The woman coiled round them a
spool of silk thread and asked him to pull the thread asunder.
And he pulled it asunder. And then she wound around his
fingers three spools of silk thread. But he felt his fingers fagged
out, and he could not tear the thread apart, and so his two
hands remained tied together. When his mother saw that he
could not cope with the three spools of thread, she opened the
back door and the giant dashed out, holding a huge ax in his
hand, to take the boy's life.

"What is your last wish, you dog?" the giant asked him.

Now he saw how matters stood with him and that he could
fear the worst. His last wish, he said, was that the giant should
take the three whistles from his pocket and put them into his
mouth so that he could blow his whistles before he died.

His mother, cruel as ever, would not hear of this. "What an
idea! You'd better finish with him at once."

But the giant king said, "He could have killed me if he had
wanted to, and it seems right that I should let him have his
last wish." So he took the three whistles from the boy's pocket
and put them into his mouth.

The boy blew all three whistles, and at once the three animals
appeared. The lion took hold of the giant, the wolf seized the
mother, and the bear showed himself helpful by unwinding
the silk thread from the fingers. At last Szérus had his hands
free again. He gripped his sword and, unsheathing it, took the

giant's life at one blow. The giant soldiers took to their heels, but the three animals remained with him. The lion asked what they should do next. In the backyard there stood two big vats, one of them empty, the other filled with water. He chopped up the giant's body and threw the pieces into the empty vat. Then he had the other vat, the one filled with water, placed beside it. And between the two vats he placed a small stool and thereon he seated his mother, saying that if she loved the giant in his lifetime she might love him in death as well. Then he ordered the animals to clear out everything from the castle except for the things he made them bring in. And then he left the castle, and the three animals went with him, and he made them roll two big mountains over the castle so that only the chimney stack stood there. And they left for good.

Szérus was wandering along, but loneliness began to tell on him and he wished for a companion. What if he married! But the trouble was that he did not know where he should look for a bride. One evening, when they were preparing for their night's rest, he asked the lion's advice. The lion said he should ask the wolf. The wolf said he should ask the bear. The bear grunted out in answer that he did not really know about anyone suitable, but that he would give him a piece of advice which might be found helpful.

"So if that's what's troubling you, gallant Szérus, you must ask your father, the sun. He carries the light, and he can look into all places. I dare say he is the one to find you a pretty bride."

So that was that. But how was he to find his way to the sun? The lion said that he would see to that. He said that Szérus must jump on his back, and the bear should sit on the wolf's back, and the wolf was to hold fast to the lion's tail. And thus the lion went carrying them all up to the skies.

When they reached the sun, Szérus felt a bit shy about how to begin. He greeted the sun politely, "May God bless us with a good day. It's me and the limping wolf. We've come to see you. And as you're my father, I would hear your advice."

The sun asked him what his wish was.

"I'm in quest of a bride, Father. Have you seen somewhere a suitable and comely maid?"

No, he hadn't, because he had other fish to fry. He was kept busy to provide the light and the warmth. "But wait till the night settles and your godfather, the moon, is up. He's rambling along all night. Maybe he sees more than I do."

The night fell, and the moon was up. Szérus went to see him. Couldn't he recommend a pretty maid to him?

He couldn't. "But ask your brethren-in-law, the stars. There are lots and lots of them. Maybe they could help."

But it was impossible to ask each star. Again he turned for advice to the moon. He should ask the brightest star in the sky, the morning star, the moon said, and the morning star could ask all the others for information.

Szérus waited till the morning star appeared and then asked him if he could recommend a pretty maid to him. The morning star asked his fellow stars, but none of them had seen a suitable girl. But they advised him to ask the winds who were his kin. Didn't they blow in every hole and corner? They might know more than the stars did.

The winds came whispering around his ears, and he asked them if they had not seen some pretty woman for him. The winds whispered into his ears that indeed they had seen one, a beautiful princess she was, but she lived at the very bottom of Hell, and forty-two devils kept rocking with golden strings the golden cradle in which she lay sleeping. "That maid is meant to be your wife, but how you will manage to bring her up from Hell remains to be seen."

Then the lion took him down to earth, and they found themselves on the estate of a rich count. They made the stable their shelter for the night, and putting their heads together they did a lot of speculating as to what they should do next. Szérus went to the count and told him about his intentions. The count already knew about the princess. There was a time when he had even ventured to bring her up from Hell, but he always failed at the end. So he found it very much to his liking that the princess should be brought to his estate. He offered his hospitality to Szérus and the lion, and promised to help them in every way.

Szérus thanked him for the proffered help, although he did not want to avail himself of it. He resolved to take all risk himself.

As the day came to an end he went to the lion and took counsel with him, so that he might hear the lion's advice as to how he should set about bringing the princess up from Hell. And the lion gave his advice.

"I tell you what. When night falls, all four of us, you and I and the wolf and bear, will set off. But first we have to get hold of the three golden ducks."

The first night the ducks were shot. The second night they carried off three gold mares. That took quite a long time since both the bear and the wolf had to come and help, each taking a horse. The third night they were to go for the bride. But before they left the lion said that Szérus would find a short stick in the dummy window of the stable and that stick they had to take with them.

Off they rushed down to Hell, and when they reached the gate they struck at the latch with the short stick. At once the gate flew open; facing them they saw the room in which lodged the golden princess. And there was the golden cradle swinging in the air and forty-two golden threads twined around the hands of forty-two devils and running to the cradle, and with these threads the forty-two devils kept it rocking with the princess inside it.

Sitting on the lion's back, Szérus charged into the room and threw his arms around the cradle. The bear on the wolf's back went around the room and with a sharp knife neatly cut the forty-two threads fastened to the cradle. Clasping the cradle, Szérus started toward the door, and when he got outside, he gave a kiss to the princess. The girl cried out, and her scream woke the devils, who dashed off in pursuit. They caught hold of the lion's tail and pulled at the coat of the bear. Then the lion remembered that he had a brush with him, and he flung the brush at them. At once there grew up a dense forest, and it took the devils some time to push through that thick forest. But soon they were catching up with Szérus and his companions. This time the lion threw back a handkerchief, and the handkerchief turned into the Adriatic. It took the devils some time to go

around it, but again they were overtaking the escapers. And then
the bear remembered the three pins stuck behind his ear. And
he cast the pins behind them. From the three pins grew three
mountains. And high they were, reaching right up to the sky.
And thick they were, extending from one corner of the firmament to the other. Here then was something to stop the devils
in their pursuit. They could not go around the mountains without toppling over the edge of the firmament. Nor could they
climb the mountain, for St. Peter would chase them away. So
Szérus and his companions got safely away with the princess.

But when they got back to earth, their host, the count, took
the princess from them in order to marry her. Then she made a
condition that she would marry the man who could milk the
three gold mares. Well, that called for some thinking on the part
of both wooers. Szérus then told the lion what condition the
bride-to-be had made. The lion said it was nothing to get worried about, and that Szérus shouldn't think twice about taking
up the challenge. The lion would find a way to help him.

Szérus accepted the condition of the princess in good grace.
The three animals took hold of the gold mares and held them
fast. Then they milked the mares, milking white poison into a
tub, and the milk burst into blue flames. When the count saw
this, he went to the princess and reported that the mares had
been milked and she should become his wife. But the young
miss said that she would marry only the man who would be
willing to take a bath in the mare's milk. And a horrible condition this was, since no one could step into the milk without
being burned to death.

The count at once gave orders to Szérus to take a bath in the
tub. Again, Szérus went to the lion and complained about the
count's command.

The lion said, "We'll manage somehow. Only you must ask
for the three animals to be present to pay their last honors to
you."

Then the lion dressed up as a priest, the bear as a choir master,
and the wolf was to act as their acolyte. And they were to go on
with the ceremony at length so that the lion should have time
enough to cool the milk in the great tub, and when he said

"Amen" Szérus could step into the tub safely without being burned by the milk.

And it all happened as they had fixed it up among themselves. The lion dragged on and on with the ceremony, and the bear took no less time in the singing, and the wolf performed his duties with a great deal of marking time. When "Amen" was said, Szérus stepped into the tub and took a bath in the milk. And when he stepped out of it, he looked seven times as handsome as before.

It would have pleased the count to fare the same. He too felt eager now to take a bath if only he would become as handsome as Szérus. And again the ceremony was performed, and it was the same as before, going on at great length, the oration lasting even longer, only this time the lion was not cooling the milk but kept it scalding. And when it was hot enough to burst into flames, then it came about; the count plunged into the milk and was burnt so dreadfully, that it cost him his life. (It was not in Szérus to wish him such an end.) Then Szérus went to the princess, kissed her tenderly, and asked her if she would marry him. The princess said that as he had endured so many trials for her sake, she would marry him.

But when he went out into the garden to take a short rest after the excitement of the day, he fell asleep. And then the younger brother of the count cut his throat with his own sword.

And up and at him were the three animals, aroused by the smell of blood. And at once they went in search of the elixir and the healing grass. The lion ran ahead of the other two, and he was the first to come across the serpent. He asked the serpent what he was carrying in his mouth. The serpent answered it was the elixir and the healing grass, and that he needed both, because the reaper had cut his son in two and with the help of the healing grass he would make him whole again, and bring him to life with the elixir. The lion asked the serpent to let him have some of each as his master had come to a bad end too, someone having cut his throat, and that he wished to bring him back to life. But the serpent would not give him a bit of either. Then the lion trod on the serpent's head and took both the grass and the elixir. Angrily the serpent made for him, but there was not much to be done about it. So he lashed at the lion with his tail and did it with such force that it shaved off all the lion's fur, except that part around his neck and the end of his tail.

Then the lion ran back to his companions, and the wolf uttered a terrible howl, and the bear came shuffling along. And all three of them were soon taking great pains to revive their master. The bear did the doctoring, but something went amiss, because when he stuck the decapitated head onto the body, Szérus did not come back to life. The bear had done it all wrong, putting the face the other way around as if in an about-turn. Then the bear had it coming to him; the lion did not spare the big stick, with which he whacked him soundly. Then he separated the ill-joined head from the body and set the two parts together in proper order. But it was long before Szérus came to life again, and meanwhile preparations had been going on in the castle for a grand wedding feast. The younger brother of the count was to be wedded to the princess, and a great celebration was to take place. But the princess was playing for time.

And then Szérus asked the three animals which of them felt inclined to go to the palace with the news that he was alive. He asked the lion, but the lion did not want to go. He asked the wolf, but he too refused to go. The bear asked leave to go to the palace, but they were unwilling to send him along as they knew what a silly creature he was. But finally it was the bear who went. And when he appeared it caused a great uproar among the wedding guests.

"Look, look! There's a bear coming!" they cried. "What business has he here? He's going to spoil our feast."

But the bride interrupted them, "Let him come in and see what he wants."

The bear came in, and he did no harm to them. He found himself a place at the table, took his fill of cabbage, and had a drop or two to wash it down. And then he reported to the bride that Szérus had come back to life, and the errand which had brought him to the feast was to inform her about it. But having had a glass too many, the bear felt his spirits rise, and he asked permission to perform a dance. And how eager the guests were to see the bear dance you can well imagine. Just as curious as they would feel today, but in olden times it gave even a greater thrill. The Gypsy musician struck up a lively tune. And there stood the bear, with all the food and cabbage he had gobbled up rumbling loud in his bulging belly. The women took their stand in front of the men so that they should not miss the spectacle. The bear was roaring out the tune at the top of his voice. But when he raised his tail and spun around to start a dance, the quantity of drink that had gone down his throat now forced its way out the other end, bespattering the watching crowd. So great was the consternation at his misbehavior that the princess thought it best to send him home at once.

She packed a small basket with food and at the bottom she pinned a note for Szérus, telling him that she had not been married to anyone and expected him to come, and then they would go on with the feast. The bear, still fuddled by the drink, took the basket and, while he was finding his way out, never stopped grumbling at how few cakes there were in the basket, barely enough to satisfy his master and next to nothing for his friends. So he pinched a hen and a cock and carried them in his mouth, and besides them there was the basket to be taken care of. When he came into the garden, the dogs closed in on him, barking wildly. He put down the hen and the cock and caught hold of one of the dogs and hurled it among its companions. The dogs took flight, and the bear went shuffling quietly back to his comrades. He gave the basket to his master, and the hen and the cock he gave to the lion and the wolf. Szérus read the note which the princess had sent him telling about the state of things. And no sooner had he finished it, than he rose and bade his companions go with him to the wedding feast.

When they came to the palace courtyard they wanted to send in the bear to announce that they had arrived. But the bear remembered what disgrace he had brought down on himself and was too ashamed to appear before the guests. The lion and the wolf then took hold of him and pushed him through the door. And the people began shrieking and yelling with laughter when they saw him.

"Here comes the bear again to perform his tricks."

Even the Gypsy musician was making fun of him. And the

angrier the bear's growling grew, the livelier the tunes the
musician was playing. When he felt this had gone too far, the
bear seized the double bass and hurled it at the cymbalo player.
Then the bear let out a tremendous roar. You could have heard
a pin drop in the hush that followed. And then the bear asked
permission to present his master.

The bride answered that indeed they would be pleased to see
him. And when Szérus walked into the hall, the younger brother
of the count grew as white as if he had turned into a figure of
plaster. Up and at him were the lion and the wolf, and they tore
him to pieces. What remained of him was thrown to the dogs.

And the young pair had a good time for a couple of weeks.
They enjoyed their life, except for feeling a bit lonely all by
themselves. Then Szérus remembered that he had a mother living
in the castle buried by a mountain. He wanted her to be dug
out and to live with them. So he set out for the forest of the
giants where the castle was buried under the mountain. He had
his mother dug up and found her still alive. But nothing remained of the giant, as she had been living on his flesh all that
time; and when they found her she was picking away at the
giant's shin bone, and long and sharp it was, just like a hunter's
knife. And she took that bone along with her.

For a few weeks the couple and the mother were having a
quiet time, just living an ordinary life. Szérus went hunting
with the animals. His mother was keeping house for them. And
one night the mother fixed the sharp bone in her son's bed
with a handful of straw strewn over it. When Szérus came home
in the evening and threw himself down on his bed, the sharp
bone ran through his heart and he died.

When the blood had soaked through the straw and it began
dripping down, a drop fell on the nose of the lion who lay
stretched out under the bed. He came forth and uttered a terrible
roar. The other two came running. They were gazing at their
master, but there he was stone dead, with his heart pierced
through. As they still had a little of the elixir and also some of
the healing grass left, they brought Szérus to life again. But
when he came round, his mother had already been torn to pieces
by the lion. And then the lion told Szérus that the castle of the

giants had once belonged to the three of them. They were men of great might who had lived in the castle. And they told him that if he went into the forest behind the castle, he would find the three dens—he might remember which way to go—and in front of each den he would find a stone pillar. If each stone pillar were smeared with the blood of his new-born babe, it would break the spell and they would become again the princes they had been.

The bride was already expecting their first child, and when it came it was a boy. Then Szérus asked the lion when the child would have to be sacrificed for their sake.

"If you really want to know, and are willing to help us, you may take his life in sacrifice, though I am sure you could not do it, because it would mean that when the child is seven years, seven months, seven weeks, seven days, seven hours, and seven minutes old his throat would have to be cut and his blood smeared over the three stone pillars."

The boy was in his seventh year and Szérus had great affection for him, but he was no less fond of the three animals. He remembered every good turn they had done him. And when the boy was seven years, seven months, seven weeks, seven days, seven hours, and seven minutes old, he took his carbine and his bolo knife and bade the mother say farewell to her son. And both of them were smothering the child with kisses and hugging him and shedding bitter tears over him. Then he took the child and set off with him to the stone pillar.

When the lion saw them leaving, he went to the father and said that he need not cut the child's throat; it would do if he cut into the child's left arm and let some of the blood run into a vessel so that it could be used to break the spell.

Szérus then took his bolo knife, cut into the child's arm, and let the blood run into a bottle. When this was done, he set off to the giant's castle, carrying the three lives in the bottle. He went to the stone pillars, to each in turn, and smeared them all over with the child's blood, head-high, waist-high, and knee-high. And one after the other, the three animals turned into princes again. And they clicked their heels in a courtly manner and thanked him for his noble deed. And the castle of the giants became again what it had been, the castle of the princes in the beautiful country that was bordering on his own.

And all of them are living happily to this day if they have not died.

Part II
Jokes and Anecdotes

Once there was a poor man. He had about thirty-six sons. But all of them were feeble bodied, as they had been brought into the world by threes and fours at a birth by their poor mother. Poor folks they were, indeed. One day the man said to his wife, "I'll leave you now to take service with one of the farmers. Maybe I can earn a little money to buy some food for the children. That's what they are always crying for." The poor man went away and took service with a farmer in the next village but one. The farmer promised to pay him two hundred *forints* at the end of the year. A year was three days. The poor man was working hard.

When the year was over, the farmer said to him, "I say, my poor fellow, I haven't got any money. But look here! I have a cow and it is worth more than two hundred *forints*. If you are willing to accept the cow instead of money, you can have it."

"Very well. I'll take the cow, guv'nor."

And feeling himself rather lucky, he slung a rope over the cow's neck and was going with it back to his village. When they came to the outskirts of the next village they found all the village folks gathered round the gallows. They were about to hang a young boy, not more than thirteen years old, and were waiting now for the magistrate to give the final orders for the hanging. And just as the poor man with his cow was walking up to the crowd, the magistrate arrived. The poor man stepped up to him and asked, "Why is this child to be hanged, guv'nor?" "Because he had cheated his fellow villagers out of two hundred *forints*, fleecing them in turn. It was a piece of rascality, and he must swing for it."

The boy wore a greasy white shirt and *gatya* [white linen trousers] of the peasants and as he had no other garments the name "Greasy Whiteshirt" stuck to him.

The poor man said to the magistrate, "Look here. I did a year's work for two hundred *forints*. But instead of the money

I have been given this cow. And this cow is worth more than two hundred *forints*. Here, take the cow and let me have the child."

"That's a deal," the magistrate said.

The man gave him the cow and took the child by the hand. "Come on, boy," he said to him, and the two went away together. When he arrived home, his own children, all the lot of them, came running up to him. "Well, father, have you brought us something to eat?"

"I've brought you nothing," he said.

His wife then said, "What the dickens made you bring that child home to us?"

"Leave him alone, woman. It's right that the poor wretch should go on living. They wanted to hang him. I got a cow for a year's hire, and I gave it away to save the child."

"Oh, you blithering fool!" the woman said. "Haven't you enough children already? I can hardly scrape together anything to feed our own kids."

"It's no use getting cut up, woman. It would be just as well if you put up with it, as he's going to stay with us," said the man.

They supped and went to bed. But before they went to sleep, Whiteshirt said to the poor man, "Tell me, father—I might as well call you father since you've saved my life—isn't there a rich man in this village here?"

"Of course there's one, son. Our next neighbor is the village rich man; he's a very rich farmer indeed. There's no wealthier man in the village."

"Well, have your night's rest, father," said the boy.

And soon they were sleeping. At half-past-eleven the boy went over to their neighbor's house. The rich farmer kept a couple of damned big watchdogs in the courtyard. But they let the boy pass without so much as a growl. The boy walked up to the pantry door and stuck his little finger through the keyhole. The lock burst open at once, and the boy stepped through the door into the pantry. Neatly placed on the shelves were eight big loaves, and the meat and lard of five pigs, sackfuls of beans, and sackfuls of the finest flour and bread stuffs. And soon the boy was carrying the whole lot over to the poor man's house. And he piled up that lot of food in his kitchen, and there was hardly room enough to hold all the flitches of bacon, the hams, the strings of sausage, and the plump chitterlings.

Next morning, when the poor man rose and went into the kitchen, he was beside himself with joy at the sight of such a lot of food. He ran back to the room and woke his wife, "Come, come, missus!"

And she goes into the kitchen, and there she beholds the heaps of food. And what a joy it is for her to see such plenty. And before long the children came into the kitchen too. And they fell on the food and stuffed themselves so ravenously that by noon six of them were dead.

And at their neighbor's house, in the morning, the rich farmer's wife goes into the pantry to bring some bread and sausage for their breakfast. And what a shock it is to see that all their provisions were gone. She runs back into the house, lamenting bitterly, "Oh, dear, oh, dear! All of it is gone. Oh, oh, oh! Who has robbed us of it?"

That day, the rich farmer's mother said to her son, "Oh, my son, I am very ill. Let's send for the doctor."

The doctor was called to the old woman. He said, "You'd better stay around her, because she might die this very day or tomorrow."

And toward evening the old woman died. They laid her out. At about midnight, Whiteshirt up and goes over to the rich farmer's house. There he slipped his little finger into the lock of the cellar door. He turned the lock and the door sprang open. The boy stepped into the cellar. And what he had found there, he carried over to the poor man's house. He took the wine and the potatoes and the peas, and all that was in the cellar. As he was collecting the last batch of peas, he beheld a chest stowed away under them. He opened the chest. It was filled with money. He took all the money as well to the poor man's house. Then he pulled out the tap from each cask, except one. In that one cask he left some wine. Then he went into the room where the old woman was laid out. He carried the corpse down into the cellar and there he placed her in a position just as if she were standing at the cask in which he had left a little wine. Then he drew out the bung and, fixing it in the hand of the dead woman, let the wine run through the hole in a thin stream onto the ground. This done, he left the cellar and locked the door.

In the morning when the rich farmer woke, he said to his wife, "Go and take the jug and get me some wine from the cellar."

She goes to the cellar and as she opens the door didn't she nearly drop down dead with horror, seeing her mother-in-law letting the wine run off, all over the cellar floor. Wailing desperately, she ran back to her husband, "Oh, for Heaven's sake, come at once and see what your mother's doing!"

And her husband goes back to the cellar with her and Lord! there's his mother, letting the wine run out of the cask and all over the cellar floor. With a leap he got to the cask and put the tap back into its place. Then he got hold of his dead mother and laid her on the ground in the middle of the cellar. Then he went from cask to cask to see what was left. But all of them were empty.

"I dare say, mother, you've taken it out of us," he said.

Up and he went over to his poor neighbor.

"Listen, my poor friend. You're blessed with a lot of children to help you. Get my mother buried, and I'll pay you for your trouble."

Whiteshirt leapt forth at once. "I can do that."

He went with the rich farmer back to his house. Then he looked about. At the foot of a strawstack he dug a deep hole. When he got it done, he went into the cellar and brought out the corpse. But instead of burying the old woman in the grave he had dug, he pushed her into the stack. Then he filled up the hole with earth and said to the farmer, "I'll put some stones over the grave so that she'll never be able to leave it again."

"That's right, my boy."

So he brought a cartful of big stones and dumped them over the grave, and then he covered it with earth, and on top he rolled several bulky pieces of log.

"Well, guv'nor, don't you fear. She'll never manage to get out of this." Then the boy went home, carrying a sack of wheat grain which the rich farmer had given him for his pains.

That night, at half-past-eleven, Whiteshirt went to their neighbor's house again. He went up to the loft. He could hardly get in, so full was it with the finest wheat grain. One third of the grain—or was it one quarter?—he carried over to the poor man's house. Then he went back again, and pulling out a couple of shingles, he made a hole in the roof, on the street front. Then he took hold of a wooden shovel and began shoveling the grain through the hole until some five to six tons were shoveled down onto the street. Then he came down from the loft and made for the strawstack and pulled the corpse forth from beneath the straw. And he carried the dead woman up to the loft and stuck her into the middle of a heap of grain, so that she seemed to stand there. Then he fixed the shovel into her hand to make her look as if she were shoveling the grain onto the street through the hole. All this done, he went home and said to the poor man, "Well, you aren't a poor man any longer. You have grain enough, maybe even more than your rich neighbor, as not much has been left to him. And money you have even more than he has."

And the poor man's children could have their fill now, and indeed they were doing themselves so well that each day six to eight of them died on account of overeating. And fewer and fewer they became in number.

In the morning the rich farmer looked out of the window and saw his fine grain scattered all over the street.

"Oh, Christ! What's happened again?" Calling his wife, he hurried up to the loft, and there they saw the dead woman with a shovelful of grain, standing at the hole.

"Oh, Lord! What are you up to again, mother? To be sure, you'll bring us to ruin and make us poorer than our neighbor, though he is the poorest of the poor." And immediately he went over to his poor neighbor.

Whiteshirt stepped up to him at once, "Good morning, guv'nor!"

"Good morning, my lad. I say, a poor work you've done of the burying."

"What do you mean?"

"Oh, dear Lord, isn't she shoveling the grain from the loft onto the street?"

"I'll see to this at once and get her buried again."

And again Whiteshirt went with him and dug a big hole at the foot of the strawstack. And when he got the hole ready, he fetched the corpse from the loft, but instead of burying her properly, he pushed her under the straw. Then he filled the hole with earth and covered it with stones, and on top he rolled a good many pieces of logs. "Well, guv'nor, I've got her buried safely this time."

"All right, son. Get yourself a few sacks, and you may fill them with the grain that you see scattered all over the street. That will be for your pains."

He brought a few sacks and filled them well and took them home to the poor man. "Well, father and mother," he said to the poor man and his wife, "I hope you do not regret having taken me into your house. You are well provided with food and with plenty of money. Even your children are getting fewer and fewer in number since they are not wanting for food and can stuff themselves until they burst and die."

At midnight Whiteshirt went over again to his neighbor's house. The rich farmer had a fiery colt in the stable. The boy walked to the strawstack and dragged out the corpse from under the straw. He carried the dead woman into the stable and tied her on the back of the horse as if she were riding him. Then he put the bridle on the horse and fastened the reins around the woman's wrists. And in one hand of the corpse he fixed a switch so deftly that it looked as if she had just raised it to strike at the horse. Then he let the colt loose in the stable, and he himself went out and locked the door carefully, as it had been before he opened it, then he went home. Inside the stable the colt was running up and down in a frenzy, kicking up a fearful hulla-baloo. It was neighing wildly, excited by the foul smell of the corpse fastened onto its back.

The farmer's wife was wakened first by this awful uproar, and she woke her husband. "Listen! What's that infernal racket going on in the stable? Go out and see what the colt is up to."

But he said to his wife, "You must come with me. I am afraid to go out by myself."

She got up too, and they went out together to the stable. And when they looked in through the stable window to see what was going on, good Lord! they nearly collapsed. There they beheld the old woman sitting on the back of their fiery colt, holding the switch in her raised hand ready to strike at the horse.

"Oh, my God! Oh Lord, have mercy on us!" And they ran back into their house in utter bewilderment.

"Go and call Whiteshirt over to our place," said the woman to her husband.

The young farmer hurried over to his poor neighbor, and when he saw Whiteshirt he said to him, "I say, son, would you go and call the priest who lives in the next village but one. Tell him to come at once to bless my deceased mother. Tell him that he must do something with her because there's no getting into our stable as long as my dead mother is riding the colt."

Whiteshirt set off to the next village but one to call the priest. It must have been around four o'clock in the morning when he reached the village. He greeted the priest and asked him to go with him at once and to bring along incense and holy water, as he would find a corpse riding a colt.

"All right, son. While I get ready, go into the stable and saddle the horse for me."

Whiteshirt went into the stable, saddled the priest's grey mare, and led it out of the stable. Meanwhile the priest had got into his clothes. Taking the censer and holy water sprinkler along with him, he mounted the horse. And so they set off, the priest on the horse and the boy walking behind them. And though the grey mare was going at a steady trot, Whiteshirt kept close behind her.

It was about daybreak when the priest and the boy reached the village. But when they came to the farmer's house, the boy was quicker getting to the stable and he unlocked the door. The colt with the old woman on his back leapt through the door, and when he beheld the mare in the courtyard he charged down upon her at once, crushing the priest to death. Then the boy took the dead woman and the dead priest from their horses and laid the two bodies side by side on the ground and led the colt and the mare back into the stable and tied both horses to the crib.

The rich young farmer said to the boy, "Oh, my God! What are we going to do now? I'll get locked up and be put behind bars forever and a day if it comes out how the priest has lost his life."

Whiteshirt said, "No fear! But you must pay me well."

"Well, son, I'll let you have five hectares of my best lands, only it must never come out what really happened."

And he gave Whiteshirt the five hectares. Then the boy buried the priest and the old woman. And from that day the farmer lived in peace. The boy went back to the poor farmer to give him the five hectares. In the meantime all the poor man's children had died of overeating, so only Whiteshirt was left. Time wore on, and the boy grew into an able youth and married a comely peasant girl. The poor man made a great fortune, and the rich farmer lost all his fortune and fell on evil days. As for Greasy Whiteshirt—well, he is still having a happy life if he has not died.

• *10* • *The Parson and the Poor Man*

It happened in times past. There was a poor man. He took service with the parson. He did odd jobs around the house and brought wood from the forest. One day the parson sent him again to the forest for wood. He went with two yoke of oxen, but he was going reluctantly because he knew that there were a lot of wolves in the forest and he was afraid of them. When he came into the forest he met four wolves. They asked him, "What are you doing here?"

"I am a poor man. Leave me alone this once."

The four wolves exchanged glances and were thinking for a while, "What shall we do with the poor man?" They said then, "Well, we will let you drive home with the four oxen and the cartful of wood. But we shall find out whether you've told us the truth when you said that you were poor; we shall also make sure whether the oxen belong to you or to someone else."

So the four wolves went with the poor man, back to the village, back to the parson's house. When they saw him drive into the yard pulling up at the door, they ran after the cart. And when they saw the parson coming quickly out of the house at his servant's call, the wolves exchanged glances, because they were now convinced that the poor man had not been lying to them. They turned and withdrew into the forest.

Next day the parson ordered the poor man again into the forest, to bring back a cartful of wood.

The servant said, "Oh, Father, do not send me again. Yesterday it was only by the skin of my teeth that I got away."

But the parson said, "I pay your wages, and you must go."

So the poor man had no choice but to put the four oxen to the cart again and to go for wood into the forest. As he was getting the logs onto the cart, one of the wolves stepped up to him and asked, "What are you doing here?"

He said, "I've come to take a cartful of wood to the parson."

The wolf said, "Don't think that you'll get away with it, again. We won't have any of your excuses; this time you'll have to let us have blood for the wood; it's going to be you or the four oxen. Now which way would you have it?"

The poor man said promptly, "Forgive me today. I shan't ever come again to this forest. And should the parson send me along once more, you can have his four oxen to eat."

And so it happened. On the third day the poor man was ordered again to bring wood from the forest. He tried hard to get out of this task, telling the parson that if he went again, the wolves would either kill him or eat the four oxen. But the parson said, "I pay your wages, and it is your duty to go."

So the only thing to do was to put the oxen to the cart and to obey his master. In the forest, the four wolves stepped up to him at once, "We've told you that it would cost your life if you came to this forest again. But you've paid no heed to our warning. Now, we'll eat you up or we'll have the four oxen."

The poor man said, "Let us first pile the cart with wood."

And the five of them, the poor man together with the four wolves, set to work and piled the cart with wood.

The poor man then said, "Listen! I want to make a proposal to you. Do no harm to me. But as you look very hungry, I propose that you should come here, one after another, and each of you should have an ox for himself."

The wolves said it was a good idea and they were waiting for their turn.

Then the man unharnessed the four oxen. When the first wolf came to have his ox, the poor man said to him, "The right-hand leader shall be yours." The wolf leapt at the ox and bit through its throat so that it fell on the instant. The poor man then said to the wolf, "Come here!" The wolf went to the cart, and the poor man flung the chain over his neck. "Well, have your fill now."

No sooner had he said this than the second wolf appeared.

"You too can have an ox for yourself," the poor man said to the wolf. "Take the wheeler."

The wolf said, "All right, poor man," and he bit the ox through its throat so that it fell dead on the spot.

The poor man said, "Come here, wolf! Join your mate; you'll enjoy your dinner more in company." And the second wolf walked up to the cart and got the chain over his neck.

When the third wolf appeared, the poor man said, "Take the left-hand leader and eat it up." The wolf seized the ox by the throat and killed it.

"Have your fill, wolf. But first come here to the cart. Let me fasten you to the shaft so that you may eat at leisure."

And the fourth wolf walked up to the poor man.

"All right, brother wolf. I know very well that you've been driven by hunger. So, like your companions, you too may have an ox for yourself. Here! Take the shaft ox. It's only fair that I should let you have your fill as you did no harm to me."

The fourth wolf, the oldest of the four, looked at the man, "I say, poor man, are you kidding me?"

"No, there's no kidding you. One good turn deserves another. Go and kill the ox and do yourself well on its meat."

The wolf seized the shaft ox and bit through its throat.

"Well," said the poor man, "Come here, wolf! Let me put the yoke over your neck."

Then the poor man removed the muzzle from each ox—since he had always put on their muzzles when they went to the forest —and now fastened a muzzle on the mouth of each wolf. Now the four wolves were coupled by their yokes and safely tied to the yokepins. Then the poor man went to the oxen and cut off the tail of each animal. Then he broke his whip in two and tied the two pieces together to make a strong whip-stick of them. Then he fastened the four tails well onto it, so that he had a whip with four lashes. And he started off with the cart piled with wood, and he was driving home. The four wolves were prancing, trying to break away from the cart, pulling it in all directions. But they were held by their yoke; and the poor man did not spare the whip and was lashing out at them. So there wasn't much else to do for the wolves but pull the cart with the wood back to the village. And as they went driving through the village, the people came out of their houses and stared in amazement at the cart and could not help wondering at seeing the parson's man with a cartful of wood pulled by two yoke of wolves. And the poor man brought the wolves to a halt at the parson's house and called out loudly, "Open the gate, Father, I've brought the wood." And he shouted until the parson looked out of the window. To be sure, it gave him a scare to see the four wolves before the cart. Indeed, he was so frightened that he didn't dare to leave the room and ordered one of the servants to go and open the gate. "Go and let them in," he said, "it's that raga-muffin with four wolves." The servant opened the gate, and the cart pulled up at the front door. The poor man was shouting again, "Open the door, Father."

Gripped by fear, the parson locked himself into the house and wouldn't open the door for anything. And the poor man went on shouting, "Open the door, Father!"

His master kept still and gave him no answer. The man then seized his whip and struck at the window with all his might. At that his master called out in terror, "What's the matter, János?"

"I'm here with a cartful of wood. I've brought it home with four wolves."

"Oh, bother! What the dickens shall I do with them?"

"Do as you please, Father."

"And where are the four oxen?"

"Well, the wolves have eaten the oxen and that's why I've put the wolves to the cart."

"Well, I don't care two hoots what you do with the wolves, János. All I can say is that I won't have them anywhere near the house."

János unharnessed the wolves, but he didn't take off their muzzles. Then he seized the whip with the four lashes and lashed out at the wolves. And he drove out the first wolf through the gate, and the second and the third followed. There was only one more left. Then he called again to his master, "Come out, Father, and tell me what to do with this beast."

"I've no mind to leave the room. Do what you want with it."

János then gave such a sound thrashing to the last wolf that the whip with the four lashes broke in two. And the fourth wolf, with the muzzle still on his mouth, made for the gate and went running with his companions back into the forest. But as they were running away they passed the window and saw the parson looking out of it. The parson, however, didn't bother any longer about the wolves, once they were gone. He was more interested to learn something about the oxen and about the place where they had been killed. And the poor man then told him in which part of the forest the oxen had perished, and said that if the parson went there, he might find their hides still on the spot. Driven by curiosity, the parson screwed up his courage and went to the forest. And he found the spot with the carcases of his oxen. And there was still plenty of flesh on them since the four wolves had been unable to finish all of it, having had the muzzles on their mouths.

But when the parson appeared, the four wolves recognized him at once and they said to one another, "Look! The parson has come. But in what manner should we do away with him? We couldn't even finish off the oxen because of our muzzles." And the four wolves were exchanging glances and were gazing thoughtfully at one another. Then they said that it would be best to seize the parson by his throat and kill him. And so they tried. They leapt at the parson and threw him on the ground and fought him wildly. But they could not bite him for their muzzles. The parson, more dead than alive after their attack, went dumb with fear and was unable to utter a sound. Suddenly a fox came trotting along. The fox saw the four wolves going hammer and tongs at someone and he saw also the four carcases not far from them. As he was very hungry he walked up to the carcases and was soon having his fill on them. The wolves had very nearly done away with the parson when they caught sight of the fox feeding on the oxen. Leaving the parson alone, they dashed off to chase away the fox. So the parson came through with his life. The fox is still being chased over hill and dale, and tomorrow they'll be still running after it if they have not died.

· 11 · *The Squire and his Coachman*

There was once a squire. He had a coachman. The squire noticed that his coachman never failed to raise his hat when they drove past the gallows. It roused his curiosity, and one day he asked the coachman, "Now tell me, son, why do you always raise your hat when we pass the gallows? I've seen you pass the church a good many times without so much as lifting a finger to your hat."

"Well, sir, ever so many times a good man has been condemned unjustly to hang on the gallows—whereas you'll often find a pack of ungodly rogues and hypocrites inside the walls of the church."

"You're wrong, son. The law never makes a mistake."

"I dare say that's why so many innocent people have to perish by it."

When they got home, the squire said that they would be driving out in the afternoon and the coach should be ready to take him into the town.

"All right, sir, I'll go and feed the horses now and when I come back from dinner, I'll give them water."

The coachman unharnessed the horses, fed them, and made quickly for his cottage to have dinner with his family. While he was at home, the squire struck his best horse. When the coachman came back, he found the finest of the horses, the foremost of the four, lying on the ground. When he stepped nearer to examine it, he saw that the horse was dead.

"Sir, one of the horses is dead."

"Dead? What do you mean? If so, you must have killed it."

"Do not say so, sir. I swear on the life of my children that I did not kill your horse. I went home to have my dinner, and when I came back I found it dead."

The squire rang up the magistrate, and the *pandours* [police] came promptly to take away the coachman. It was in the law that those who did harm to or killed another man's livestock should be put to death. So the coachman was marched off to the gallows.

The squire then began to feel remorse, and he could not silence his conscience. What if they really hanged the man? He jumped into the saddle and went riding full tilt to the gallows. He tied a white handkerchief to his whip and was waving it as he rode so that he might stop the execution. The hangman saw it and though he had already put the rope round the coachman's neck, he loosened it and waited for the squire.

When the squire rode up to the gallows, he called to his coachman, "Come here, Jancsi. I see now that you were right."

• 12 • *Lazybones*

There was a wealthy farmer who had a daughter. She was his only daughter. And though she was big and strong, she was a lazy girl, averse to taking the broom in her hand, and all the chores had to be done by her mother. Her laziness had soon become common talk all over the village, and there was not a young man who came to woo her, in spite of her father's wealth.

Her mother never stopped nagging. "You see, my girl, there isn't a single lad to hang around you as there are about the other girls. All of your friends are taken out to dances, while you're just sitting at home, because the young people don't want to have anything to do with you."

"Do not vex me, mother," she says. "Come Sunday, there'll be a dance, and I'll be going with the others."

And so it happened. She went to the dance. And while all the other girls had been asked by their young men, there was no one to take a single turn with her; and there she was standing like a proper wallflower, in lack of a partner.

Then a young man from a neighboring village appeared among the dancers. As soon as he entered he began to show interest in her, as she was quite a comely girl, if only she had not been so terribly lazy. And the young man was asking the others about her, and so he learned that she was the daughter of a well-to-do farmer with many possessions.

"Then why isn't she asked for a dance?"

They said, "Oh, she is no good at all at dancing. She never came to dance with us before. That's why she hasn't got a partner now."

Well, the young man thought it over and when the musicians struck up a tune, he asked her for a dance.

True, she did not excel in dancing, but as he was a superb dancer they did quite well and enjoyed it. When the dance was over, he asked her, "Whose daughter are you? What's your father's name?"

And she asked him, "And what's your name?"

"My name is András," he says, "and before you leave let me have a word with you, because I am going to visit you."

"What for?"

"Well, I intend to go to the spinning-house when you are there."

Happy she was that there was a young man who would come for her sake. The others were still teasing her and didn't think much about her success. So she left without talking to him and rapidly made for home. And then she reported to her mother,

"Mother, a young man is coming to us to make court to me." And both the girl and her mother rejoiced at this thought.

"Well, my girl, you must put your best foot forward when he comes. Show yourself quick with your hands and busy so that you may win his affection. Don't forget how ill-reputed you are because of your laziness, so try to do your best."

And one day the young man appeared accompanied by two of his comrades. The girl's mother gave him a friendly greeting, "Welcome, sit down and make yourself comfortable." And she brought a chair for him, and put a bottle of wine and a bottle of brandy on the table and a plate with cakes.

When the visitors had done well for themselves, the young man said, "Well, I don't want to take up much of your time. I've come because I've heard that you've got a marriageable daughter. I know her because we have met at the dance. All I want to know is whether you'd be willing to give me your daughter in marriage?"

"Oh dear, I am happy to give her in marriage to you. You appear to be a handsome lad whose head is screwed on the right way. And let me tell you that you won't regret marrying her. We've made a nice fortune, and we have only a son and a girl. The two will get all we have. You'll see what dowry I'm going to give her. I'll fit her up so richly with clothes that all her life she will have enough to wear and you needn't bother about buying her a single piece. And we'll divide the land between our two children. And half of our livestock will go to her too."

On that very day they went to the priest and registered for marriage. And after three weeks they had their wedding.

And the bride got a chest as long as the longest bed, and it was packed so richly with clothes that it needed some effort to clamp on the lid. And she received all she had been promised and half of the livestock, and then her husband took her to the village from where he had come.

And he was mighty pleased about the rich dowry and was looking forward to the many good things they would be getting from her parents. But the leopard does not change its spots. Once lazy, always lazy. The girl went on the same as she used

to do at home. Whitewashing and cleaning the house. Oh, no!
She fought shy of both these jobs. No wonder she was of such
ill-repute. On Sundays, when she changed her bodice and her
chemise, she never hung them on a peg or put them into a
basket, but made a bundle of the dirty clothes and threw the
whole lot into the fire. And every Sunday she followed this practice. Her husband never guessed what she was doing and when
after a year he looked into her chest, there wasn't a single bodice
or chemise left in it.

Once an invitation came for a wedding feast from a nearby
village where the relations of her husband lived. So he said to
his wife, "Well, wife, I'm going to take you to a wedding."

"Where to?"

"The son of my father's brother is going to have his wedding."

"Well, I am not going with you."

"And why not? You are still young enough. And we haven't
been going out much since we've married."

"Going to a wedding needs some decent clothes."

"Surely you've got plenty of clothes, even more than enough."

"I used to have them," says the woman.

"Oh, what are you telling me? You haven't sent them back
to your mother, have you? Didn't you get a big chest packed
with so many clothes that two men could hardly lift it?"

"Didn't you know that I've burnt all of them?"

"What did you burn? Your clothes?"

"Yes, I've thrown into the fire all my garments except the
soiled ones you see me wearing now."

"Don't tell me that you've been taught to throw your dirty
clothes into the fire? Didn't you know that what becomes dirty
by wear should be hung on a peg or put into a basket? And even
then one must not wait till it grows into a big bundle, but it
has to be washed and pressed and put neatly into a chest."

"Well, never in my life did I do any washing; how should
I have known how to go about it? I thought it would be best if
I burned what was dirty so I needn't bother about washing
them."

"Well, I've had enough of that silly talk. Whatever you've got
on you're going to wear, and I am going to take you to the

wedding. We haven't moved out of this spot for a year, and I am not going to sit at home forever for your sake."

"Well, and I am certainly not going out in my soiled garments."

The man then went out and returned with a truss of straw and reeds which he had prepared for thatching up their roofs. Then he stripped his wife to the skin and bundled her up between the wisps of straw and reed. Then he tied it up at both ends and about her waist.

"Look here, woman" he said to her. "I'll put you on the cart and throw a rug over you so that you can come with me without being seen. And first we're going to your parents' place and there you can get yourself some garments which you can wear at the wedding."

"Well let's go then" she agreed.

"And do not fear" he said. "I will ask your mother myself to let you have some of her clothes."

When they reached the place where her parents lived, he stopped at the garden and got his wife down from the cart and, bundled up as she was, he shoved her behind the haystacks. Then he went into the house. His wife's father and mother were indeed happy that the young pair had come to visit them, and eagerly the mother asked her son-in-law, "And where's our daughter?"

"She's come too; she is in the garden by the haystacks."

They asked him, "Why didn't she come in with you?"

He said to her mother, "Just go out to her; she wants to speak with you."

The mother rushed out into the garden and called out loudly, "Where are you, my dear daughter?"

"Here I am," she said, "bundled up between wisps of straw and reed. You see, I've told my husband that I couldn't go to the wedding as I haven't any decent clothes to wear. So he bundled me up between the reed and straw he had prepared for thatching and brought me along. Now, please let me have some of your clothes."

"But what did he do with that lot of clothes I had given you for your dowry?"

"Well, mother, I've burned them all."

"And why did you do that?"

"I thought it was the best way to get rid of them once they were dirty. I simply threw them into the fire and let them burn."

The young husband went out to them and hearing her words he said, "Now you can judge yourself what sort of a wife your daughter has made. In less than a year she has foolishly done away with that lot of clothes you gave her. Well, I've brought her back to you because I don't want her any more. You'll get back every penny and whatever she had brought with her. You can please yourself with your daughter and your fortune; I do not want to have either. A fat lot do I care about her relations and the wedding feast. I'm leaving her here, and I call it a good riddance."

"But look here, son, I am willing to let her have some more clothes."

"Keep your clothes, and your daughter as well. She'll never do for a wife."

And he returned to his village and left his wife at her parents' place. There she is still with them. And he married again. And if they are not dead, they are still alive to this day.

· 13 · A Stroke of Luck

He went plowing. He was a poor man. The plow cut a furrow and turned up a lot of money. When he set eyes on it, he began to speculate about what to say to his wife. He feared that she might blurt it out to the neighbors, and they would be served a summons to appear before the magistrate.

He went and bought a hare and a fish.

When she brought him his midday meal, he said to her after he had dined, "Let's fry a fish."

She said, "What do you think! How could we catch a fish here in the field?"

"Come on, woman, I've just seen a couple of them, when I

was plowing around the blackthorn shrub." He led her to the blackthorn shrub.

Says the woman, "Look, old man, there's a fish."

"Haven't I told you so?" And he flung the ox goad at the shrub so that the fish turned out at once.

Then he said, "Let's catch a hare."

"Don't be kidding me. You haven't got a gun."

"Never mind. I'll knock it off with the ox goad."

They were going along when she cried out, "Look! there's a hare on the tree yonder there."

The man flung his goad at the tree and the hare fell down.

They were working till the day drew to a close, and in the evening they made their way home. When they went past the church, they heard an ass braying.

The man said to the woman, "You know what the ass is braying? He is saying, 'The priest says in his sermon that soon a comet will appear and that will be the end of the world!' "

They went on. When they passed the city hall, the ass uttered another loud bray. The man said, "The ass says that 'The magistrate and the town clerk have just been caught embezzling public funds.' "

As time wore on they were making good use of their money.

The neighbors kept asking them, "Where did that lot of money come from?"

Then she said to one of the neighbor women, "I wouldn't mind telling you, but you mustn't pass it on to anyone." And she told her that they had found the money. Their neighbor reported it to the magistrate, and they were summoned to appear before him. And when he was questioned about the money, the man denied it. By no means did they find any money. Not a penny had been found by them.

The magistrate then said, "Your wife will tell me."

"What's the use asking her. She's just a silly woman," he said.

The woman flew into a temper and began to shout at him, "Don't you dare say that again. Didn't we find the money when we caught the fish under the blackthorn bush?"

"Now Your Honor may hear for yourself. Catching a fish in a bush. What next!"

"Can't you remember how you shot down a hare from the tree with the ox goad?"

"Well, haven't I told Your Honor? It's no use asking that fool of a woman."

"A fool you are yourself. Have you forgotten that on our way home we heard an ass braying when we passed the church, and you said that the priest was preaching that a comet would appear and that would be the end of the world."

"Now wasn't I right, Your Honor? It would be better to leave her alone, or she might give offence with her silly talk."

The woman flew into a rage and said, "Don't you remember that when we were passing the city hall and the ass uttered a loud bray you were telling me, 'that the magistrate and the town clerk have been just caught out...'" The magistrate jumped to his feet and said to the man, "Take her home, my good man, she seems to have lost her wits."

· 14 · A Hussar Stroke

In times past when men had seen regular military service for twelve years at a stretch, they were given leave. It so happened that a hussar, sent home on leave, was on his way back to his village. He was jogging along on horseback in full hussar outfit, including his arms, as in those far-off days men were expected to appear completely equipped, should they be called to serve their country in time of need. It was a fine summer day, and the hussar was making his way homeward. He had been riding for some time in the glaring sun when he came to a forest. He was about halfway through the forest when the heat began telling on him, and he was feeling terribly hot. As he was riding by a sweetly purling brook, he dismounted, tied his horse to a tree, stripped off his clothes, and stepped into the water to refresh himself with a bath. When he came out of the water he found all his clothes gone, together with his horse and arms.

"Good gracious me! What am I to do now?" And he was running about in great confusion, searching everywhere in the forest for his clothes. But he found neither horse nor clothes. So there was not much else to be done but to pursue his way and walk out of the forest. When he reached the edge of the forest, he beheld a swineherd rounding up his pigs to drive them home to the village. It struck the hussar that his only chance had come. Immediately he went down on all fours and, concealing himself as best as he could, fell in line with the pigs and trotted along with them. When they reached the village, the swineherd let the pigs take their own course, each running home to the house where it belonged. And the hussar took care to remain in the centre of the biggest herd. There was a well-to-do farmer in the village, and eighteen pigs were returning to his sties. The hussar was running in the midst of them on all fours. When they reached the farmer's house, he swiftly opened the wicket gate and the pigs ran through it and the hussar followed them. The farmer's wife was in the kitchen, putting swill in a pail for the pigs. A gate shut off the kitchen door from the farmyard. The smaller pigs managed to slip through the gate into the kitchen. The hussar pulled away the gate, and the whole herd swept into the kitchen. When the woman turned her back to the door while looking for a stick to chase the pigs out, the hussar swiftly made for the inner room and hid under the bed. The woman drove out the pigs, fed them, and got them safely in their sties. Then she went back into the house. On the big range there were a lot of pots, holding a variety of fine things, done to a turn. There was one with a baked chicken, another with a mutton chop. There was chicken broth, and there was a cock in stew, and meat roasted and grilled and baked—everything to please the palate. And she had got all these toothsome dishes ready and was impatiently casting glances through the window onto the street.

"Oh, how long it takes you today! Oh, why aren't you coming?" she kept murmuring to herself.

And before long the door opened and the parson came into the kitchen.

"Good evening, may God give you a good evening, darling!"

"Good evening, may God give you one too," said the woman. "Haven't you kept me waiting for ages? I've been on tenterhooks. I am sure all this waiting has spoilt my good dishes."

Says the parson, "Forgive me, my sweet, but I've been kept by office duties."

Going into the inner room, the woman lit the lamp, laid the table, and said, "My sweet, I'll bring in all the dishes I've prepared for you so that I won't be coming and going with them all the time but can sit down with you and we can have our supper at leisure."

The naked hussar was cautiously peeping out from under the bed. "I dare say I might do with a bit of food, hungry as I am," he muttered to himself. When the woman had brought in all the dishes and was placing the last pot on the table, the garden gate opened and the farmer was coming up to the house.

"Good gracious me!" said the parson. "What shall I do now?" And swiftly he crept under the bed. There he beheld the naked man. "Oh, what creature may you be?" the parson asked. "Are you the devil or what? Did you come to take me?"

"Exactly. I've come to take you," said the hussar, and seizing the parson, he flung him inside, against the wall. At that moment the farmer came in. His wife was standing in the center of the room. "Good evening. God has brought you home."

"Good evening, thank you."

And he looked at the table and at the food that was heaped on it. "What's the big idea?" he asked his wife.

The next thing she did was to fling her arms round his neck. And she was hugging him and giving him hearty smacks on both cheeks.

"Oh my dear husband, a solicitous and loving wife has no other thought than to please her husband." And again she smacks kisses on both his cheeks. "You see, my dear, while you have been away, I had a dream. I dreamt that you would be coming home about this time of night and therefore I've prepared all these savory things so I could serve you with your favorite dishes as soon as you came." And again she busses him on both cheeks.

And didn't she bluff him into believing all that she had said?

"Well, make yourself comfortable, old man, and let's sit down to our supper before it gets cold," she said to him.

The man took off his coat, and they sat down to have their supper. The woman was sitting nearest to the bed, and when her husband was not looking, she snatched a baked chicken from the plate and quickly reached down under the bed to give it to the parson. But it was the hussar who grabbed it from her hand, as he was lying under the bed on the side nearest the table. When the parson saw him tucking away the chicken, he whispered to him, "Oh, do let me have some of it."

"Go to hell! You've been sitting at the table. Why didn't you have your fill then?"

And he gobbled up the whole chicken. A little while later, when her husband was not looking, the woman reached down a bottle of wine to the parson. Again it was the hussar who snatched it. When the parson saw him drink, he implored again, "Oh, do let me have a spot of it."

The hussar answered, "The hell I will! Why didn't you drink while you were sitting at the table?" And he drank the wine without letting the other man have a drop of it.

The farmer and his wife finished their supper. The woman cleared away what was left of it. Then she turned down the bed, and they went to bed. When the man and his wife were sound asleep, the hussar hit upon a happy thought. He turned to the parson and said, "Slip out of your clothes, and mind that you strip to the skin."

"Not if I know it!"

"Well, if you don't, I'll cry out that you are here."

The parson fell into a blue funk. What if the lunatic should cry out and give him away? Promptly he slipped out of his clothes. The hussar made a neat bundle of his garments and put it under his head. It was toward the first gray of dawn that the parson, overcome by sleep, fell into a doze. The hussar took the bundle of clothes and stealthily crept out of the room. In the garden he dressed in the parson's garments. Then he flung himself over the fence and out into the street.

In the villages it is the saloon which is the first place to open in the morning, and the hussar saw the saloonkeeper unlocking the door. In the pocket of the parson's clothes the hussar found some money, so he made for the saloon.

"Good morning."

"Good morning, Father, what can I serve you?"

"I want something strong and good, a regular eye-opener."

When the saloonkeeper returned with the drink, he said to the hussar, "There's talk that the woman living next door has found a beautiful dapple-grey in the nearby forest and brought it home. I wonder if you might have heard about it sir?"

"Who's the woman who has found the horse?"

"The one living just around the corner. They call her Old Mother Rozi."

"Well, let me have just half a deciliter more," he said to the saloonkeeper.

The man poured the brandy into his glass, and the hussar gulped it down. Then he paid for his drink and left the saloon. He made directly for the house where Old Mother Rozi was living. It was quite early, and the sun was just about to rise. Nobody stirred in the house. The hussar rapped at the window. Old Rozi jumped out of bed and rushed to the window.

"Who's there?"

"It's me."

Mother Rozi took a look at him and said, "I'll come and let you in, Father."

When he was in the room, she said reverently, "To what do I owe the honor of seeing you under my humble roof, Father?"

The hussar snapped back at her, "To hell with you, you goddam old hag. You owe it to no other than your having stolen my horse and my clothes while I was bathing in the brook. And I want them back, but make it snappy."

The old woman got scared and produced the stolen clothes at once. The hussar threw off the garments of the priest and got into his own clothes. He left the castoff garments with the old woman and made for his horse. He mounted the dapple and setting his spurs to his sides he went riding back to the farmer's house where he had spent the night.

The farmer and his wife were still sleeping, and he rapped at their window. Heavy with sleep, the man jumped from bed and opened the window. Looking out he beheld a hussar on horseback, standing in front of the window.

The hussar said, "May God give you a good morning, farmer."

"May God give you a good morning, too, soldier."

"Look here, farmer! See that letter? It's from his majesty the king, written in recognition of my extraordinary talents because I possess such secret knowledge which I share with no other human being on this earth. And therefore I am commissioned to wander all over the world and visit every house in which trouble has taken harbor. And since I know very well which houses these are, I come to them to rid them of trouble."

"Well, soldier, it is as you say. There is trouble in my house."

"You needn't tell me," said the hussar.

"Well, soldier, I'd gladly give you three hundred *forints* if you can rid my house of this trouble."

"Let me come in then, farmer."

The farmer hastened to open the gate, and the hussar rode into the farmyard. He dismounted and left the horse in the care of a groom.

"Here! Get my horse unsaddled, and give it a bag of oats, and take it to water."

Then the hussar went into the kitchen. Immediately he made a good fire in the stove and filling a big pot with water, put it on to boil. Then he asked the farmer for some cornmeal and when the water was boiling, he poured the cornmeal into the pot. When he got the mush ready, he took the pot and placed it on the floor, in the center of the room. Then he asked for a large soup ladle and dipped it deep into the mush. Then he looked about in the room and when he found a heavy club, he gave it to the farmer and said, "Now open the door and when you behold trouble leaving the room, just do not spare the club, but deal a mighty blow on its head, so that it should not think of ever coming back to this house."

And then, taking a ladleful of the burning hot mush, the hussar threw it under the bed onto the naked man, calling out to him, "Get out of this house, trouble!"

The hot mush burned the naked body of the parson, who tried in vain to wipe it off as the hussar rapidly threw ladlefuls, one after another, under the bed. When the pain was past the point of endurance, the parson crawled out from under the bed and rushed quickly toward the open door. The farmer, seeing him emerge, dropped the club and threw up his hands in disgust. "Oh, Lord! how hideously ugly trouble looks."

Thus having got rid of trouble, the farmer counted out the three hundred *forints* to the hussar. The hussar put the money into his pocket and sat down and did himself well, eating and drinking what the farmer brought him for breakfast. Then he mounted his horse and rode away.

Toward sundown he came to a big forest, and he went riding into it. The evening was closing in on him, yet he had not found himself a shelter for the night. Toward ten o'clock he came to an inn. When he rode into the yard, the innkeeper came out.

"Good evening. God give you a good day, gov'nor."

"Good evening. And to you too, soldier."

"Well, will you bring me ten pounds of oats so that I can feed my horse?"

The innkeeper brought him the oats. The hussar took his horse, tied it in the stable, unsaddled it, and when he had the horse fed and watered well, he went into the inn. There was not a soul in the room except himself. He sat down to a round table and ordered his supper and a jug of wine.

When he had eaten enough and had drunk his wine, he said to the innkeeper, "I want a room."

The man answered, "I cannot give you accommodation here. You've had your supper, now go on your way, because every night at midnight thirteen priests come to this inn, and they won't suffer anyone else being here."

Said the hussar, "If they are priests, then I am one of their flock, and they'll have to put up with me. I am certainly not going away. You'd better get along and bring me another jugful of wine."

No sooner had he got his wine than the door opened and a house painter came into the room.

"Good evening!"

"Good evening, brother painter!"

The newcomer walked straight up to the table where the hussar was sitting.

"I say, soldier, do you mind if I sit down at your table?"

"Not at all. We can pass time better in a conversation. And there's no one else to talk with."

When the innkeeper came to their table, the painter asked him to bring him something to eat for supper and a glass of wine. While he was having his supper the hussar kept him company. When he had finished his wine he turned to the innkeeper, saying, "I want a room."

The innkeeper answered, "I cannot let you have a room. It has been the same with the other guest. I had to tell him that he must leave soon, because at midnight thirteen priests will come to this inn, and they wouldn't put up with your being there."

The hussar then said to the painter, "Do not think of going away, brother. If they are priests, we are their sheep. Just let me deal with them if they insist on showing the door to us."

The innkeeper went out. Time fled, and at midnight the thirteen priests filed into the room. The thirteenth had around his waist a bright surcingle which marked him out as the dean.

There was a long table in the middle of the room. This table had been kept for the thirteen priests. They walked up to it, unbottoned their coats, and laid their weapons on the table. Before long they took off their cassocks and hung them on their chairs. Their leader, who had the surcingle, walked to the table where the hussar was sitting with the painter. The two had already realized that the newcomers were not priests, but betyárs [outlaws] disguised as priests. And when they saw the many weapons laid on the table, the painter became so frightened that he wet his pants.

"Well, as you've stayed here, you might as well come over to our table and have supper with us because at the second cock crow both your souls will be asking St. Peter for admission into heaven."

At this talk the painter grew even more alarmed. It had set even the hussar thinking. "Dear me! There are thirteen armed men against me. That's doing it rather strong." But there was nothing they could do. So the hussar and the painter rose and went over to the outlaws' table, and they were offered seats at the middle of the table, among the robbers. The innkeeper soon appeared, bringing three big pails filled with wine. One pail he placed in the center, the other two at either end of the table. Then he brought in several jugs, putting one before each person, so that they could dip up the wine by the jugful. Both the hussar and the painter were given their jugs as well. Then the innkeeper brought in their supper. He placed it on the table, and the men set to it. When they had finished eating they sat there, drinking their wine.

Suddenly the hussar rose and said to the chief of the robbers, "Look here, sir, I have to go out."

"All right, but two of my men will give you guard."

The hussar left the room and made for the outhouse. When he got inside, he took a piece of paper and a pencil out of his pocket. He wrote on the slip: "Brother painter, keep watching me, because I'll be looking for a good opportunity to rise from the table and to deal out the six hussar blows. When you see me rise, get under the table at once, or else I might cut your head off." Then the hussar went back into the room and when the robbers were clinking glasses, he slipped the paper into the painter's hand. And when the outlaws were engaged with filling their jugs from the pails, the painter read the note. He felt just a bit relieved, though until then his heart had sunk into his boots and he was in a cold sweat.

A bit later, when the hussar saw that the robbers were making merry and were in high spirits and had risen from the table to clink glasses, he rose too and dealt the six hussar blows. Twelve heads were duly chopped off. The thirteenth robber he took by the scruff of his neck. He was the chief of the robbers, and the hussar was squeezing his neck with such force that his tongue stuck out.

The hussar said, "Brother painter, be quick and make a light," because as he had been hitting out on all sides, he had smashed the lamp too. The painter had a candle in his pocket. He drew forth the candle and lit it. But to tell the truth, it gave him the shudders when he beheld the bodies scattered around with their heads cut off.

The hussar said to him, "Quickly, quickly, brother painter. Get this gent's arms fastened behind his back." And the painter tied the robber's hand securely behind his back. Only then did the hussar loosen his grip on the man's neck. "Now stand there!" he yelled at the robber, still keeping his naked sword in his hand.

Then he said to the painter, "Go brother painter, and call in the innkeeper."

As the innkeeper stepped into the room, the hussar immediately covered him with his sword. "Put your hands behind you," he commanded the man. "Now, brother painter, get his arms pinioned behind his back." The painter did as he was told.

"Now, go and call in the innkeeper's wife."

When she entered, the hussar leveled his sword at her.

"Put your hands behind your back." As soon as she obeyed, the painter tied her hands securely behind her back.

When the chief of the rebels saw what was going on, he said, "Look here, soldier. I see now that you are a valiant fighter of great courage. Spare my life, and I shall give you treasure enough to make you the richest man on this earth."

"Well, where's that treasure?" the hussar asked him.

"It's here, down in the cellar."

"And where's the key to the cellar?"

The innkeeper said, "It's in my cupboard."

"Well, brother painter, go and look for the key and when you find it, bring it to me and get the lantern from the kitchen."

The painter went to look for the key and before long he was back with it, bringing the lantern from the kitchen.

The hussar then said to him, "You go ahead, brother painter, to give us light. The woman shall follow you, the innkeeper going after her, and the chief robber taking up the rear. And let me warn you that should any one try to fall out of line, I'll cut him in two with my sword."

When they came to the cellar, the painter took the key and unlocked the cellar door. They filed in, and in the center of the cellar they saw a big block, like a butcher uses for chopping meat. On the block lay a large cleaver.

The hussar said, "Well, where is the treasure?"

"Look," said the robber chief, "those casks over there are full of gold, and the cupboards are crammed with banknotes. You can have it all, only set us free and do not take our lives."

The hussar answered, "First tell me for what purpose you've kept this block here with that huge cleaver on it?" Both were heavily smeared with blood.

The robber chief said, "Well, if you hadn't been such a brave and valiant soldier, your head and your companion's head would have been chopped off on it, at the second crow of the cock."

The hussar said, "So you have chopped off many a good man's head on that block?"

"Well, quite a lot," agreed the robber.

The hussar snatched up the cleaver from the block and turned to the robber chief. "Well, I am going to chop off all of your heads on this block here. Put your head on it," he commanded the robber.

The robber did not want to obey him. The hussar dealt him a heavy blow on the back of his neck which sent him falling right over the block. Then he chopped off the robber's head with the cleaver.

He turned to the innkeeper. "It's your turn now."

The innkeeper did not move either, but the hussar gave him a blow at the back of his head and he fell flat over the block and his head was chopped off.

"Well, woman, you haven't been a whit better than these villains."

She walked obediently to the block, and the hussar cut off her head as well. Then he turned to the painter, "Well, brother, let's go upstairs."

They left the cellar. The hussar locked the door, and they went up into the inn. They locked all the doors from the inside. Then they went into the innkeeper's bedroom. They stretched out and slept till morning. When they got up they looked for a spade and went down into the cellar. They dug a big hole and buried the three bodies in the hole. Then they took a look around the cellar. There was such a heap of treasure in it that it would take several carts to carry it away.

The hussar then said to the painter, "Listen, brother painter,

let us take as much as we can now and come back with a couple
of carts for the rest in a fortnight. Then we'll share like brothers."

The painter took only a few handfuls, but the hussar still
had the parson's bag with him and he filled it with gold. What
he had taken was enough to make him a nabob for the rest of
his days. Then they both left the inn, and the hussar locked the
doors and took his leave of the painter. The two men parted, and
they went in opposite directions.

A couple of days later the hussar was back at home. There
was great joy when he arrived. His father and mother and all his
sisters and brothers were still alive. And how happy they were
when he produced that lot of gold he had brought in his bag.

Time fled quickly. A week after his arrival he saw a rider
riding hell-bent up to their house, his horse all of a lather from
the great speed. The rider halted in front of the house and
asked, "Is there a hussar of such and such a name who has
come home on leave?"

"Yes, there is," he said, because the rider had accosted the
hussar himself.

"Well, if you're the man, get on horseback at once and follow
me to the king, because his majesty has sent for you."

"Oh, what bad luck," he complained to his father. "The
painter will go to the inn and carry away the whole lot, as I
shan't be able to go there on the day we've fixed for meeting. But
I reckon I can't do anything about it as I have to obey the command of the king."

So he saddled his horse, took leave of his parents, mounted,
and rode away with the king's messenger. Before long they
came to Pest. They went over to Buda and up to the king's castle.
The hussar dismounted, and the other man took his horse to
the stable. Then the hussar made for the king's residence. When
he got there, he beheld the painter strolling along the corridor.

The hussar bawled out at him, "Hey, you doggone scoundrel!
So you've been telling on me to the king. That was your thanks
for my having saved your wretched life." And he drew his
sword in great anger. If the painter had not been quick enough
to jump into the nearest room and lock himself in it, the hussar
would have cut off his head. For ten minutes or so, the hussar

was kept waiting in the corridor. Then a footman appeared to call him in. He said to the hussar, "Come along. His royal majesty wants to see you."

The hussar was led into a room. The king was sitting there when he entered. The hussar gave his salute and said, "I humbly present myself at your majesty's command."

The king said, "Well, hussar, I've called you here so that I may hear your full account of what has happened to you since you've been on leave. But you must tell me the whole truth."

The hussar then told the king what had happened, and he was telling him the whole truth. When he finished, the king said, "Well, would you recognize the painter if you saw him?"

No sooner than he said this, the hussar boiled over with rage and said, 'That damn scoundrel who has denounced me, though I've saved his life?"

The king said nothing to this, but slipped out of his royal garb and put on the clothes of the painter. When the hussar recognized him, he dropped at once on his knees and clasping his hands beseeched the king to pardon him for his harsh words. The king stepped to him and said, "Get up, hussar. You have my pardon. After all, I owe you my life. That's why I've asked you here. Go back to the inn and take all the treasure you find there. It shall be yours."

The hussar thanked the king for his generosity, and taking leave of him, went home.

Then he arranged to take several carts to the inn. He loaded the treasure onto the cart and went back to his village. He became a respected and wealthy man. He married and had a wonderful life thereafter. He is still alive if he hasn't died.

· 15 · King Mátyás and the Hussars

In times past, in the days of King Mátyás, the hussars had to do twelve years at a stretch in the service of the king. It had always puzzled the king how the old hussars had managed to wet their whistles on their weekly ration, which didn't come to more than four six-*kreutzer* pieces. As he could not figure out how they were doing it, he summoned his adjutants to hear their opinion. "What do you think? How can the hussars afford to drink such a lot? Whenever I set eyes on one, I see him drunk as a fiddler." The adjutants had nothing to say to this. But the king could not get it out of his mind and puzzled over it a great deal.

One evening he again saw a tipsy hussar. It roused his anger, and he thought to himself, "Just wait. Before long I'll know how you do it." He set to thinking out a plan, then he dressed up as a hussar. When he had pocketed his ration, the four six-*kreutzer* pieces, he said to himself, "Well, now I shall see myself how far I can make it go." He walked out of the town and made for the nearest roadside inn. As he stepped up to the door, sounds of great merriment struck his ears. He went on, and whom did he find in there but four of the old hussars.

"That's a piece of good luck," he thought. "It's the very place where I shall have a good time for my four six-*kreutzer* pieces."

As soon as he got inside the door, one of the hussars seized him by the ear. "How-de-do, young fellow! Come on! You look like a damn rookie. When did you join up?"

"A week ago."

"My God! And did you get that big nose of yours by eating winter squash? Well, no need to be sorry about it." And the old hussar slapped the king's shoulder.

"It's going to be a stiff job for twelve years. Believe me, it hasn't been a bed of roses for me either. Now order a pint of brandy for me and don't worry about the twelve years. To be sure, you'll manage to pull through it somehow."

"Sorry, brother, I can't afford the drink."

"Shut up, you s.o.b.! It was only yesterday that we mooched our weekly rations. How dare you lie to my face, you young rookie?"

"Well, for the money I want to get myself a cleaning kit."

"Don't let me hear that again, you silly bastard. Didn't your folks give you some money when you left them?"

"I've only an old mother, and she's very poor."

"Damn poor she must have been if she let you go without a penny to bless you. Well, if so, we can't help it. But you must order me half a pint of brandy, and I'll let you have all the boot polish and brushes you'll ever need."

"All right, brother. I'll order half a pint for you; it will still leave me three six-*kreutzer* pieces." When he ordered the brandy, a second hussar stepped up to him. "I say, you doggone rookie, you'll have to buy me half a pint of brandy."

"No, I won't; I've only three six-*kreutzer* pieces left in my pocket."

"Pipe down. That's nothing to me. Order for me half a pint of brandy at once or I'll beat you within an inch of your life, you mutt of a rookie."

So there was nothing else to do but to order another half a pint of brandy for the second hussar.

This left the king with only two six-*kreutzer* pieces. When the two hussars finished their drinks, a third hussar stepped up to the king. "Well, and what about me? I too want half a pint of brandy."

The king ordered his drink and now he had only a single six-*kreutzer* piece in his pocket. A fourth hussar stepped up to him and said, "Look here, young fellow, you can't leave me out of it. You'd better order half a pint of brandy for me too or I'll beat you to a pulp."

What else could the king do but order him half a pint of brandy?

"Well, comrades, I haven't got a cent more in my pocket. How shall I get myself a cleaning kit?"

"Don't worry, boy," said one of the old hussars. "You'll get these things from me."

Then the first hussar said to the king, "Look here, young fellow, I'll see to it that you get in my platoon and you'll have it easy there, but now order half a pint more for me."

"Not if you get me hanged, brother. I haven't got a red cent more."

"Do you really mean that your folks didn't give you some money when you left them, you young punk?"

"That's so, brother. My mother is a poor woman. You can take a look in my pockets and see whether you can find any money in them. All I had was my ration."

Then one of the hussars called to the innkeeper, "Half a pint of brandy for us, Mr. Schwartz!"

The Jew said, "Listen, hussars! Haven't you heard the taps calling for retreat? It's high time you left the inn. Besides, I never serve drinks on credit to soldiers."

"Be damned, you doggone Jew! Let us have half a pint or I'll make mincemeat of you. Here! Take my sword, it's a regulation weapon, so you can be sure I won't let it go to the dogs."

The innkeeper took the sword from him and locked it away in the cellar. Then he brought half a pint of brandy for the hussars.

When they had finished the brandy, they said, "Let's get back to the barracks, comrades. It's close on nine o'clock. We're due for night inspection." And they lined out through the door, and the innkeeper locked the door behind them. But the hussars lingered on in the innyard and were racking their brain over some trick by which they could get hold of some more brandy.

In those days, the innkeepers kept their provisions and liquors in a deep pit dug in the ground.

Said one of the hussars to his comrades, "Listen, old Jóska, can't you remember where that pit was? I wonder if there's still that hole there leading into it."

"The deuce! I do remember that hole. It's only about a week ago that we were down there."

"That's the devil's own luck. We can shove that Johnny Raw through the hole, and he'll hand out to us all the food and drinks he finds in there. Let's hurry up, comrades!"

When they came to the pit, they said to the king, "Well, you young bastard, get in through that hole there and make a quick job of handing out to us what food and drinks you find in there."

"I'll do anything to please you, except that."

"Shut up, lad. In you go!"

The king knew that there was nothing else he could do but obey, and the hussars shoved him through the hole into the pit. And the king was handing out to them everything he found in there, as he had no other choice.

When the hussars had their fill of the food and had swilled down the brandy until they were all drunk, they wiped their mustaches contentedly—each of them being adorned with whiskers as long as two big corkscrews. "Come along, comrades. Let's leave that lad where he is. He may as well pass his time down in the pit."

King Mátyás began to implore them, "Look here, comrades. I've spent all my money on your drinks. Do not leave me in the pit. Pull me out through the hole, and I shall do my best to please you."

The oldest of the four hussars, old Jóska, took pity on the king and pulled him through the hole. Then they made their way back to the barracks. The king was trailing along behind them. As they went along, he saw how even the *pandours* [police] got out of the way when they caught sight of the hussars. The king drew a deep sigh because only now did he realize what rowdies the hussars were. He followed them to the barracks. He was very curious what the sentry on duty would do when the hussars arrived. But the sentry gave a salute and stepped aside without a word to let them pass, though it was several hours past Taps. The hussars strolled into the barracks, back to their quarters.

Then the hussar who had left his sword with the innkeeper said to the king, "Come along, brother, you can sleep with me." And he flung a rug on the floor and said, "Here! You may stretch your limbs on that rug. Don't think that you can sleep in my bed." And he threw himself on his bed.

King Mátyás stretched out on the rug, but sleep eluded him. He just could not get rid of the thought that he, the king, had been forced into stealing someone else's food and drink. "Just wait, old Jóska, and I'll make you pay for the pit and for drinking away your sword and also for your abusive language." At midnight the king rose and took a pair of scissors from his pocket. Then he stole to the bed where old Jóska was sleeping and snipped off half of his mustache. All the hussars who were sleeping in the same quarters were serving their last year, and were soon due to be discharged. All hussars had big whiskers in those days, and they set a high value on them. The king then slipped out of the room and left the barracks.

The many drinks he had drunk in the evening had their effect, and old Jóska had to relieve himself during the night. As he went to the outhouse, he passed his hands over his cheeks to end with a twirl at his mustache. But his fingers touched only bristles on one side of his mouth. "What's this? What's happened to me?" And he pulled out a pack of matches and a small mirror from his pocket. And what horror to see his image in the mirror! He's struck all of a heap. There now! half of his wonderful mustache has gone. In despair he shuffles back into the room. He looks for the young rookie, but he too has gone. Now it begins to dawn upon him that the young fellow must have had a finger in it. But what is he to do now? He opens his kit and takes out a pair of scissors. Then he walks stealthily from one bed to another and snips off half the mustache from the faces of all the sleeping hussars.

In the morning, when the bugle sounded reveille and the hussars got out of their beds, one look in the mirror was enough to make them fly at one another. Soon each was thrashing his comrade within an inch of his life. "How are we to show up at home with half our whiskers gone?"

They kicked up such a terrible row that it brought their captain to the room. And amazed he was at the spectacle of the defaced hussars.

When King Mátyás arrived back in his castle he had already made up his mind. "Not all of them, but at least old Jóska, is certainly going to have it in the neck. I'll punish him severely for drinking away his sword, and if he cannot give a good account of the missing sword, I'll have him hanged."

Next morning the hussar regiments were ordered to go on parade under arms. They were told that the king himself would be inspecting the troops.

All the hussars were buckling on their swords. Only old Jóska was running from pillar to post to borrow a sword. He even went to the cobbler and to the tailor, but there was no one with a spare sword. They sent him off, telling him that they needed theirs for the parade.

So Jóska tried the wheelwright. "Last night I left my sword in pledge with the innkeeper. This morning we're to go on parade under arms. And the king is going to inspect the troops. You must make a sword for me out of a piece of lath."

"Oh, you silly old mucker. What would you do with a wooden sword?"

"Never mind that. Just let me have a wooden sword that will slip into my sheath."

The wheelwright set to work and soon had a wooden sword ready for old Jóska. He slipped it into his sheath and went to join the hussars, who were already lining up on the parade ground. And he was just in time, because the commander had come to take over the regiment, and promptly afterward the king arrived to inspect the troops.

Then the commander gave his salute and reported to the king that the hussars were in readiness "All present and c'rect," and the men stood motionless in salute. The king had to turn his head to conceal his laughter as he set eyes on the defaced hussars. "What the dickens has happend to them? I nipped off only one mustache, that of old Jóska, and now I see the whole lot of them with only half their whiskers. Just wait, old Jóska, I'll make you smart for that." And as he inspected the hussars, he kept his eyes peeled to see whether old Jóska had his sword or not. "Well, well, hussar," he thought to himself when his eyes fell on Jóska, "I wonder what account you'll give me. But I'm certainly not going to make it very easy for you."

Then the king gave orders to one of the sergeants, "There's a hussar locked up in prison. Bring him out at once and take him over there to that grave which has been dug for him."

The hussar was brought out of the prison and led up to the grave. Then the king gave orders that he wanted to have him beheaded, and the hussar regiment had to march up before the king. The king then stepped up to old Jóska and said, "Well, as you are the most valiant of my hussars, I make it your duty to behead this man."

Jóska was shaking in his boots. "A thousand hells!" he thought. "I'd cut off his head in a wink if I had my sword, but what am I to do with a piece of lath?"

He was thinking fast, and then he turned to the king: "Sire, your majesty, I've never been one for shedding blood. I'd much rather stay in service for another six years, only do not make me cut off this man's head."

The king flew into a rage, "You've heard my order."

Jóska then said, "Sire, your majesty, if it is your order that I behead this man, would you graciously grant me some time to say a short prayer?"

Mátyás said, "Granted."

The hussar then clicked his heels and sprang to attention. With his right hand he gripped the hilt of his sword thinking that the king never guessed that it had been made of wood. He heaved a deep sigh and lifting his eyes up towards heaven, he said:

> "Almighty Lord!
> Who art in Heaven
> Cast a glance on this poor old hussar,
> Into a piece of lath his sword Thou coulds't make
> So that his comrade's life he may not take."

And he drew his sword. "Look here, sire, your majesty! The Lord has listened to my prayer."

"Well done, old Jóska. I see now that one cannot get the better of a hussar."

• 16 • *A Deal that went to the Dogs*

Maybe you have already heard the story of the dogs that were sold in Buda.

The droll event I am going to tell you about right now happened in 1460–70, and though that was a good deal back in the past, exactly 470 years ago, folks still remember and laugh over this funny story.

At the time of King Mátyás the Righteous, there lived a wealthy farmer in a village not far from Buda. He was the kind of man that could find pleasure only if he could outwit his fellows and make them look like perfect fools. It seemed that envy and trickery came to him by nature.

Once this man had just returned from Buda where he must have carried off a good bargain since he had brought home a pouch well filled with money. No sooner was he back than he was telling every Tom, Dick, and Harry what wonderful prices dogs would fetch at Buda.

There was a poor man living in the same village. He too was anxious to learn how his wealthy neighbor had come by such a lot of gold. The deceitful man then said to him, "I've come by all this money not long ago when I went to Buda. There it came to my ears that King Mátyás was in need of dogs, and that he would pay a good price to anyone who sold him dogs. So I rushed home and, of course, kept that knowledge to myself. Then I sold this and that of my possessions and when I had enough cash, I bought a pack of dogs for the money. Then I took the dogs to Buda and sold them to the king for a nice sum of money. Look here, you poor fellow. See how my pouch is filled with gold. I've got it for the dogs. Now's your chance to turn your fortune for the better, as the king still wants to have some more dogs."

The poor man fell at once for this foolish talk and became quite obsessed with the idea that he too could make a lot of money. But he was a poor man with no other possession than a sorry emaciated cow. But as he could see no other way, he decided to act according to the advice of his neighbor and sell the beast so that he might buy a pack of dogs for the price. Then he would sell them to the king, who would buy them for a pouchful of gold. And so the poor man sold his only cow, and for the price he bought a pack of dogs. He put them on a string and took them to Buda. But when he came to the castle the servants barred his way and did not want to let him in. They sent him and his dogs to the pound.

At this the poor man became distressed and went away, swearing at the wealthy farmer who had brought such misfortune upon him with his fallacious advice. And the servants laughed at him and called him a fool. They sent him packing, giving him a taste of their sticks.

The king was looking out of the window and saw the poor

man weeping desperately. He bade one of the attendants to bring the man with his dogs before him. The poor man was taken into the palace and there he told the king what business had brought him to Buda and how he had been led up the garden path by a wily neighbor who had told him that the king was in need of dogs. And how he had shown him a pouch filled with gold, saying that it was the price he had got for the dogs. And how this man advised him that he should buy a pack of dogs and sell them to the king, who would give a good price for them.

It was easy for the king to see that this poor man had been duped by a rascal. He felt sorry for him, and to make up for his loss, he gave the poor man one hundred *thalers*. Then he bade the man unleash the dogs so that they might run off unharmed. He asked him to tell him his neighbor's name so that he should know it if this scoundrel ever came his way.

Well, you can imagine the happiness of the poor man, and you can pretty well guess how thunderstruck his vicious neighbor must have been when he learned that his bluffing had not come off at all and that his poor neighbor, instead of becoming the laughingstock of the village, had the devil's own luck. His envy did not let him rest for long, and soon he was selling off all his possessions so that he might buy dogs for the money. Then he took the dogs and went to Buda. But when he reached the castle he too was stopped when he wanted to enter the palace. But he would not be shaken off easily. He raised such a hullabaloo that it brought the king to the window. Mátyás bade his servants bring the man with the dogs before him. Then the man told him what business had brought him to Buda. The king realized now that it was the same wily old bird who had bamboozled the other fellow, and that by pure chance he had walked straight into the trap.

When the man finished his story, the king said to him, "Sorry, my good man, but you've missed your chance. Only once did it happen in Buda that a deal was made over dogs."

The wicked man was sent off with nothing more than he had when he left home.

King Mátyás was traveling about the country, accompanied by his scholars. They come across a plowman. Says the king, "Good day to you, my good man."

Says the plowman, "I owe it to my wife."

"How far is far?"

Says the plowman, "Not farther now than the horns of my oxen."

"Tell me then, could you milk an old billygoat?"

"Why not, my good lord?"

"Well, do not explain the meaning of your answers until you've set eyes on the features of the king."

The king and his scholars went away. "You see, the plowman gave ready answers to my questions. Now it is up to you to find out what he meant by them."

But they could not guess the right answers. One of the scholars stole back to the plowman to seek information.

He asked him, "Listen, old man, when the king greeted you saying, 'Good day to you, my good man,' you returned in answer, 'I owe it to my wife.' Why did you say that?"

"Well, let me have a hundred *thalers*, and I will tell you." He counted out the hundred *thalers* to the plowman. "Well, when the king said, 'Good day to you, my good man,' I answered, 'I owe it to my wife.' And that is truly so, because good means also that I am in good shape, and my old woman does a lot of work to keep me in good shape."

The second scholar came to ask him, "And when the king asked you 'How far is far?' and you replied 'Not farther now than the horns of my oxen,' what did you mean by it?"

"For a hundred *thalers* I will tell you." He got the second hundred *thalers*. "Well, in my younger days when I was serving in the army, my eyes were sharp and could see far. But now I cannot see any farther than the horns of my oxen."

The third scholar came too. "What about milking an old billy-goat? How could you do that?"

"Well, for another hundred *thalers*, you may hear my answer." And he got the third hundred *thalers*. "Well, haven't I been doing it just now, milking three old billygoats?"

"Not so fast, you old scoundrel! You have been blurting out the answers to us without having set eye on the features of the king."

"Haven't I? Here are the three hundred *thalers*. And three hundred times have I set eyes on the features of the king while you were counting out the three hundred *thalers* to me." They went away, and the old man put the money in his pocket.

Once the king and his scholars were walking past a reedy swamp. A hot day it was. "A bit of rain would be just in time for these reeds," said the king though the reeds stood in water. The scholars caught each other's eye and began to laugh. What need was there of rain when the reeds stood in water? The king made no reply. When they got home, he gave orders to serve them the finest dishes generously salted and without any drink to wash the meal down. And at his order big bowls were placed under the table, at the feet of each scholar. The bowls were filled with water, and the scholars had to put their feet into the bowls. When they had finished supping, the scholars desired some drink as the good dishes made them thirsty. They asked the king to let them have some water as they were nearly dying with thirst.

Said the king: "What for? Your feet are in water. You were laughing at me when I said the reeds wanted a good rain. You said, 'Why should they want rain as they stood in water?' Well, why should you want water when your feet are in it? You will get none."

Part III
Religious Tales

Why Some Women are Grouchy and Some are Slovenly

As God was thinking out some way he should go about creating Eve out of the rib he had taken from Adam's side, a dog with a bushy tail came running up and snatched the bone from his hand. Off it dashed with the bone, and God went in pursuit, as he had no intention of taking another rib from Adam's side, lest he'd make him into a disabled cripple, good for no work at all.

This happened somewhere near Israel and Jordan, not far from the shores of the Red Sea, where the creation of the world had taken place.

So God went in pursuit of the dog and caught its tail. But the dog shot forward, and its tail remained in God's hand, The dog plunged straight into the sea and came out on shore somewhere yonder there, in Egypt. But it still had the bone. So what was God to do about it? He'd never think of taking another rib from Adam's side. He took the dog's tail, said "Hocus-pocus!" over it, and at once it turned into Eve.

You know, this is a fact. And that some women never stop grumbling and grouching whatever you do, all goes to show that it is a fact, that God had created Eve out of a dog's tail. But this is something never mentioned in the books. It was only when I happened to get around a bit in those parts of the world, I mean Jordan, that I found out the truth.

Well, you know, Adam and Eve had two sons born to them. According to the Book they were named Cain and Abel. One of them—I couldn't say for sure which, was it Abel?—sacrificed a sheep and the other—it must have been Cain—was burning grain as an offering to God. But as it had been pretty damp, the smoke didn't rise to the sky, and God wasn't much pleased by it. Uncouth folk as they were, they could never guess why the smoke of the burning grain didn't go up to the sky. But Cain begrudged

God his best grain and what he offered in sacrifice was pretty damp and already rotten. Therefore the smoke was just hanging over it. It is the same today when we burn potato stems on the field. The smoke will just linger over it and then melt away, without rising to the sky.

Well, it so happened that Cain knocked Abel off his pins, and Abel died. Then Cain had sons born to him, one of them called Seth. But there is no mention made in the Book whether he had any daughters and where his sons found girls to marry. This is again something about which we haven't been taught the facts. But when I was getting around in those parts of the world, I made inquiries and finally I've got at the truth and learned how they happened to find wives for themselves.

Cain had three sons. Adam and Eve had a daughter. But of course, one girl couldn't make three brides. So they beseeched God to help them in some way or other, as it would have been unfair if only one of their sons found a wife for himself and the two others were to go without one. So God said to Adam and Eve, "Lock up your daughter in a room with a pig and a dog, and I'll help you." Adam and Eve did as they were told and locked up their daughter in a room with a pig and a dog. There the three of them sank at once into a deep sleep. In the morning three beautiful girls came out of the room. So there was now a woman for each of the three sons. They married the girls, and Adam divided his estate among his sons. He had plenty of lands as there had been only a few people living on them at that time. The boys left, and each had become his own master.

On the first Sunday following the marriage of the new couples, Adam and Eve paid each of them a visit. This custom hasn't gone out of fashion to this day, and we call it a "small gathering" or a "small wedding feast".

So Adam and Eve went visiting the first young pair. They asked their son, "Well, son, are you satisfied with your wife?"

He said, "Well, Mother, on the whole she suits me well, as she's cleanly and good to look at. If only she wouldn't snap at me so often with unkindly words. And then she's also a grouchy sort of a woman, hard to please; and little does she do to humor me."

Adam and Eve knew at once that she was the one who had turned from a dog into a woman.

Well, that was that.

Next Sunday they went visiting the second pair. Adam asked his son, "How do you get on with your wife, son? Do you like her?"

"Well, Father and Mother, she doesn't do too badly. She is peaceable enough and not lacking patience. However, little does she care about the house and cleaning and tidying it. She's just a bit lazy and given to idleness. She spends half the day chatting with the neighbors." How could she have done so, there being no neighbors? Yet her husband said that she'd spend half her day chatting with the neighbors and that he thought it rather difficult to do all the work by himself. Adam and Eve knew at once that she was the pig turned into a woman.

Then they went visiting the third pair, their youngest son. "Well, son, are you satisfied with your little wife?"

"Oh, dear Father and Mother, I am indeed. She's such a sweet and well-spoken little lady. She always does her best to please me in every way. She's as fine a woman as you are, Mother."

And they knew at once that she was the descendant of Eve.

· 19 · How People Got a Taste of Tobacco and How They Took to Dancing

In the beginning, after the world was finished and Adam and Eve had been settled in Paradise, it so happened that they had to move out and set to tilling the soil for their living.

And in the course of time they had taken to procreation, and a hundred years later their offspring had multiplied. But not any of them had ever heard of such things as smoking a pipe or dancing. It is true that every now and then they used to come together, but the time was passed in conversation and the singing of songs by the women, while Adam was telling the people about the beauty of Paradise, of the wonderful life they had there, their expulsion from it, or about the murderous Cain and the death of his son Abel.

And sometimes he would tell the people about the things he had heard from the archangels, Gabriel and Raphael, about the bliss of Heaven, the Fall of the defiant angels, of the torments of Hell, and about the advent of Jesus Christ. And he would always find something to tell the folks, and they liked to listen to him. It's no wonder that Adam and Eve had known such a lot about these matters, since they had been told about them by the Archangel Gabriel himself. So their leisure time was passed amidst such useful conversation, or in singing, but never was there anything wrong in their amusements.

But Satan, the archenemy of all that is good and holy, would not indulge such seemly conduct on their part.

He thought to himself, "If they go on forever like this, then what is the use of Hell? If folks are going to behave in this manner, I shan't ever get a single soul into damnation. Surely I shan't gain anything by sitting tight and looking on idly. I've forfeited my right to go back to Heaven, and I can't go back to Hell unless I do something to my credit."

Satan has plenty of wits and he always finds the easiest way to entice people into folly. So he thought to himself, "I will teach them to do something which will bring them right into my net."

Once when the people came together to pass the time, as they were wont to do, conversing, praying, and singing, Satan dressed up as a gentleman and, holding a walking stick in his hand and a *chibouque* [long pipe] in his mouth, walked up to the house where the gathering was held and knocked at the door. But the people inside the house had not been used to knocking and did not know what it meant. So nobody answered the first knock, and only after the second and third knock did one of them go to open the door. Then Satan entered and greeted the people, and they returned his greeting, wondering what sort of a man this stranger might be, as never before had they seen a man with a pipe in his mouth, breathing out smoke like a chimney. They offered a seat to him, and he sat down on a bench, beside one

of the men. There he sat quietly pulling at his pipe. For a while
the conversation went on as usual, but this did not suit the
visitor. After all, he had not come here to sing with them. So
he rose and said, "I must be leaving now because I have a long
way to go. I came here to see whether you did not know a better
way to amuse yourselves than this. I think it is pretty dull."

The people said, "We do not find it dull. For us singing
hymns and praying is a good enough recreation, and besides it is
an entertainment which joins us in a friendly community."

"All right," the stranger said, "but I know something better,
and why shouldn't I teach you how to get more fun. You could
learn that sort of amusement which is the custom in my country.
I could teach you to dance, and I am sure you'd like it very
much. It's a poor sort of entertainment to go on praying and
singing forever."

The women asked him, "What is a dance? Will you please
show us what it is, since never before did we hear of such a
thing."

With an ugly grin the visitor answered, "Well, as it is your
wish I will teach you to dance, but you must listen to me atten-
tively and keep your eyes open. But before I begin teaching you
to dance you must try my pipe and take a draw at it in turn,
till all of you have got a taste of it. You'll see how delightful
you'll find its smoke, feeling better after each pull at it." And
he handed the pipe to the man sitting next to him, adjusting
the mouthpiece in the right way between his lips.

"Just hold on to it and you'll never regret it," he said, and
he thought to himself, "Now I've got you, my man. Once you've
had a taste for it, you'll never give up smoking, and you'll be
willing to pinch the egg from under the hen to get yourself a
pipeful of tobacco."

The man began pulling at the pipe and found it so much to
his liking that soon he was loud in its praises. When he had
enough of it, he gave it to his neighbor, and thus, from one man
to the other the pipe was passed along, and they found it so
much to their liking that it went around and around, and all
of them had a pull at it. And while they were having their
pleasure in the pipe, the stranger broke suddenly into a song

and began dancing a *csárdás* in the fiery way of the Magyars, shaking his feet and clapping at his bootlegs and clicking his heels in a fury.

The people stood around him and were staring in open-mouthed astonishment at this performance. Never before had they seen a dance, and now the strange gentleman was leaping to one and then to the other, taking a round with each of them in turn, until they got out of breath and the tears came into their eyes from the frantic whirl of the dance. Then he bade them sit down and have a short rest so that they would not dance themselves tired. He asked them if they didn't think it was greater fun than praying and singing for their amusement.

The people cried out, "Thank you very much indeed! We shall never forget what you've taught us."

And great was Satan's joy upon hearing them say this because he knew that many of them would now dance themselves into perdition.

"Fine!" he thought to himself. "It seems that I will reap where I have not sown. Many a bird will I catch in my snare by this dance." And he started anew with his frenzied dancing, but this time he was not dancing alone; all the others were shaking a leg.

Satan looked at the dancers with no end of pleasure. "Well, that did the trick," he said to himself. "I've got my birds in the snare."

And since that day people have taken such a fancy to dancing that they have never stopped going on with this folly. And they have grown so fond of smoking their pipes that even their children have taken to that habit.

Satan enjoined them to stick to the pleasures of smoking and dancing. Again he started dancing, and with him were dancing all the others, and they went waltzing around and around the room, and Satan knew very well that they would not think of praying as long as they were dancing.

And he gave them his pipe and plenty of tobacco for it, and also tobacco seeds so that they should never be in want of it. And he taught them to make brandy and enjoined them to make merry by smoking and drinking, as a wetted whistle will make for merrier songs.

Now we know beyond doubt that it was Satan's doing that people have taken to brandy and fallen into the habit of smoking. Confound it all! Hasn't it worked toward the undoing of many a good man!

If it had not been for the pipe and brandy there'd be less quarrelling between people. Because if a man has to do without a pipeful he'll raise hell in his own house.

• 20 • *When Jesus Became Thirsty*

In far-off days when Jesus was still going about in the world, one day he was making for the Hungarian *puszta* [prairie] to see how the herdsmen were getting on. It was a hot summer day, and Jesus became thirsty from walking in the heat. Suddenly he caught sight of a sweep-pole well and bent his steps toward it. Near the well he saw a herdsman, stretched comfortably on the grass under a big and leafy tree. All his cattle were lying scattered around him, chewing their cuds contentedly.

"Cowherd," said Jesus to the man, "will you let me have a drink of water to quench my great thirst?"

The herdsman never guessed with whom he had to deal, and sprawling lazily under the tree, he lifted one leg and pointed to the well. "There's the well there. Go and put the dipper in the water and have a drink."

So Jesus had to help himself to a drink. When he had quenched his thirst, he proceeded on his way; but to punish the cowherd he sent a swarm of gadflies to him.

And as Jesus was going on and on, again he became thirsty from walking in the great heat. When he saw another sweep-pole well not very far off, he bent his steps toward it. Near the well he found a shepherd in great trouble with his herd, as the sheep were badly plagued by flies and were running madly about in all directions, leaving the shepherd in great confusion. He hardly knew which way to turn to round them up.

"My good man, let me have a drink of water to quench my great thirst," Jesus said to him.

In no way could this shepherd have guessed by whom he had been addressed, and yet he answered with good grace, "My dear man, of course I'd be glad to bring you a drink from the well, but you can see for yourself to what trouble I am put by the herd, they being pestered badly by the flies and running about like mad."

"Just bring me a drink of water and do not worry about the sheep," said Jesus. "I'll be looking after them until you get back."

The shepherd took pity on the stranger and went with his jug to the well. He filled the jug with fresh water and brought it back to offer a drink to the stranger. When he came back he found the herd bunched together, not a single one of them missing or running about.

Jesus thanked the shepherd for his kindness, and pleased by it he proceeded on his way in good humor.

From that very day, when the summer sun is blazing down with her hottest rays, the sheep will flock together for a midday rest; and it also marks the commencement of the shepherd's noon when he can cook his meal, or have a rest, or take a short nap.

But it is different with the cowherd. When the weather turns too hot, he must be always on the run after his cattle. Then the gadflies appear, and the animals run in all directions; and the herdsmen have to do quite a bit of riding before they can round up their cattle.

• 21 • *When Jesus Grew Tired*

One day when Jesus and Peter were trudging along, going from one village to another, Jesus grew very tired.

"I wouldn't mind at all if we could ride the rest of our journey," he said to Peter.

Before long they saw a horse grazing by the roadside.

"Listen, you horse," Jesus said, "We've grown very tired. Would you carry us to the next village?"

The horse answered, "I've just been unyoked by my master. Wait till I have eaten my fill."

"Well, never shall you know how it feels to be full. You shall be forever seeking food in the litter."

And since that day the horse is always grazing and looking for food, but it never gets full. Whenever his master stops him on the road, the horse will go nibbling at the grass by the roadside.

Jesus and Peter proceeded slowly on their way until they saw a shepherd who was just getting off his donkey's back and turning it out to the pasture to graze.

Jesus went to the donkey and said, "Listen, you donkey, we've grown tired. Would you carry us to the next village?"

"Certainly," said the donkey. "Get on my back."

And they proceeded on their journey, Jesus sitting on the donkey's back and Peter legging it beside them. And the donkey, feeling great hunger, bit into a reed as they were passing along the way. You can still see a gash on every reed stalk to show the bite.

"You are hungry, aren't you?" Jesus said. "And yet you were willing to let me get on your back and carry me to the next village. In return for your kindness, I shall not let you ever feel hungry. For days on end you shall be able to carry on with your work, serving your master without having a morsel to eat; and you shall not suffer from cold or frost either."

And since that very day, no donkey has ever been seen shivering with cold or having a chill. Nor has there ever been a broken-winded one.

• 22 • St. Peter and the Horseshoe

It happened in the times when our Lord Jesus Christ was wandering the earth with St. Peter. They were traveling from one place to another, and on their way to a village they found a horse-shoe on the road.

Said the Lord to Peter, "Pick it up, Peter!"

Peter answered, "Why, it would be a waste of energy to stoop down for that."

So it was the Lord who had to pick up the horseshoe. When they reached the village, he sold it to a man and for the money he bought some cherries. As they went along, the Lord dropped a cherry or two. Now it was Peter, trailing along behind the Lord, who stooped at once to pick up the cherries to appease his hunger and thirst. When the Lord saw how busy he was picking up the cherries, he said to him, "Well, Peter, you thought it wouldn't be worth your while to stoop once for a horseshoe, yet you've been quite busy picking up the cherries. That will teach you that you should not mind taking a little trouble even if you think that it is for something of little value."

Well, as they were proceeding on their way they came to a roadside inn. Peter thought to himself that it would be nice to go into this inn, as people were having a good time in there and so might they. So he said to the Lord, "Let's go into this inn, Lord."

"It's not a decent place, Peter. There is a party of revelers in there in the midst of a drinking bout. When they get drunk, we might come to harm."

"Oh, no harm would come to us there, that is for sure," said Peter. "Let's go in."

The Lord thought that there was an opportunity to teach Peter a lesson. And in a wink, a *cymbalo* [dulcimer] had grown onto Peter's back.

In the inn a party of journeymen carpenters were having a spree. All of them were about three sheets to the wind when the two wanderers entered.

"Play up! Make music for us!" they shouted at the top of their voices to Peter when they saw the *cymbalo* on his back.

Peter looked about, for he didn't know why they were shouting. But the carousers kept bawling at him, "We want music. Play for us!"

Well, as Peter was not aware of the *cymbalo* on his back, he stood there utterly confused. But the drunken journeymen carpenters rushed at him and were hitting out at the *cymbalo*. Of course, Peter had a hard time of it as most of their blows landed on his back and shoulders. But as he was still unaware of having a *cymbalo* on his back, he didn't understand why they were manhandling him so badly.

So he said, "Let's get out of this place, Lord. To be sure, these fellows are a tough lot."

When they left the inn, Peter said, "I dare say they treated me plenty dirty. They rightly deserve some kind of punishment."

"What sort of punishment?"

"Well," he said, "I think that big iron nails should grow on the trees and that they shouldn't be able to cut them out when they make lumber."

"No, Peter, that wouldn't do at all. They couldn't even make a roof-tree then for the houses. But what about wooden nails?"

And to this day the stubs of branches on the trees are called Peter's nails in Hungary.

Well, they went along and soon they came to another inn. When Peter heard sounds of merriment coming from the inn, he said again, "Let us go in."

The Lord said then, "All right, let us take a little rest in there."

Inside the inn, the village youths were making merry, shaking their legs in a lively dance.

The two wanderers lay down by the wall to rest for a while. But Peter, who was lying nearest the dance floor, received so many kicks in his side as the dancers went dancing past him that before long he felt anything but pleased at their manners. So he thought that it would be quite a good idea to change places with the Lord.

"Let us change places, Lord," he said, "and let me lie next to the wall for a while."

"All right, Peter, let's change places."

But now the young dancers thought that for a change they should give a few kicks also to the man lying next to the wall, and it was Peter again who got all the kicks.

Thus the Lord taught Peter a second good lesson.

Peter then said, "Let's clear out of this inn. I've had enough of these rowdy knaves; when I was lying on the outside, all these brutes were kicking at me, and the same happened when I was lying next to the wall. I'm sure I don't want any more of their churlish pranks."

So they left the inn and proceeded on their journey. The Lord then said to Peter, "You see, Peter, I've told you before that no good whatever comes of visiting such places where you get mixed up with a lot of rowdies. One should seek rest in a house where there is tranquility and where the people hold their peace."

Never again did Peter suggest that they should go into a house where revelers were having a spree; he sought repose at modest and quiet places.

• 23 • *The Little Innocent*

Once upon a time there was a family. To them a child was born. But when the little one came, its parents had to administer a hasty baptism to it as it died soon after it was born. And the Little Innocent then flew up to the skies and knocked for admittance at the gate of Heaven. St. Peter called out, "Who's there?"

"It's only me, Little Innocent, who has not been christened properly except for the baptism received at my parents' hands. I've come to request admittance into Heaven."

St. Peter asked the Lord if he should grant the request. But God said he should not because the Little Innocent must be sent back to earth for seven years and spend it on the road in a rut where the wheels would roll over him incessantly. So he went back and spent seven years sitting in the rut. When his time came to an end, he went for a second time to ask admittance into Heaven. St. Peter asked the Lord again. But God said that he must send him back to earth for another seven years to suffer under the swingle. And the Little Innocent spent another seven years on earth, in the hemp beaten by the swingle. At the end of the seven years, he went again to request admittance into

Heaven. But God bade St. Peter to give a gourd to the Little Innocent, with the command that he should fill it with water which had not fallen from the sky or come seeping up through the earth. The Little Innocent had to be sent off again. And as he went flying along and was weeping bitterly, his tears dropped straight into the gourd which he was holding close to his eyes. And as he was flying and weeping bitterly, he came over a big, big forest where twelve robbers were engaged in dividing up their spoil. And suddenly they became aware of the weeping and began to wonder from where the sound had come. The chief of the robbers called out, "If you are of God's creation, come and join us; if you are from the Evil One, leave us!"

The Little Innocent then descended among the robbers and told them his story. He told the robbers about his horrible sufferings and that, in spite of them, he had not yet been granted admittance into Heaven. This set the robbers thinking: if the Little Innocent had to endure such horrible sufferings, what awful torments would be awaiting sinners like themselves? They decided then that it would be better for them to die. And they began weeping over their sins, and the tears came rolling down into their hats and into their hands held cupped right under their eyes. And when they were full they poured the contents into the gourd. When the gourd became filled to the brim, the robbers shot each other dead, then with the Little Innocent they flew up to the skies. When they came to the gate of Heaven they knocked for admittance.

St. Peter called out, "Who's there?"

"It's only me, the Little Innocent, who received baptism only by his parents' hands. Seven years I was suffering in the rut; seven years I suffered under the swingle. Now I've brought you back the gourd which you've given me. And I've filled it with water which has not fallen from the sky or come seeping up through the earth. And I've brought the twelve robbers with me; we've come to request admittance into Heaven."

St. Peter asked the Lord if they should be admitted. And God said they should be admitted now because the Little Innocent had made atonement for the sins of his twelve fellowmen.

Part IV
Animal Tales

·24· *When a Magyar Gets Really Angry*

There was once a peasant. He had a vineyard. A ditch ran along-side his vineyard. There was a fox's den in the ditch. The fox mother had six cubs. The peasant went to his vineyard every day. One day he saw that great damage had been done by the foxes. He went to the ditch and swore terrible at the foxes. "I'll get you smoked out of here, you bastards."

The fox mother was not at home then. When she came back, the cubs complained to her, "Oh, Mother, oh, Mother! let's move out of this hole! The man was swearing at us something terrible. We are in great danger."

She said, "Was that all? Didn't he do anything else besides swear? If so, it doesn't mean that he's really angry with us."

Next day, the man went again to his vineyard. The damage was even greater than the previous day. He swore the same as before.

When he stopped at the ditch on the third day, he was just laughing up his sleeve."

When the fox mother came home, the cubs said, "Well, Mother, we needn't move out from this hole. The man has made it up with us. He didn't swear at all. He was just laughing up his sleeve."

Then their mother said to them, "If the peasant was laughing up his sleeve, we'd better move out at once. You know what Magyars are like."

Because if a Magyar gets really angry he'll just start laughing.

There was a man who had two cats. One day the man went to town and sold one of the cats. The buyer wanted to know what food he should give the cat. The man said that whatever he wanted to give it would do.

The man then took the cat home. He had one of his oxen killed and fed the cat on its meat. In a year the cat had eaten up everything the man possessed. Then he went to his neighbor to seek advice as to how he could best get rid of the cat. His neighbor advised him to lock the cat in the house and then set fire to the whole thing. The man followed his advice, but when the burning house was in a fair way to collapse, the cat slipped through the smoke hole and thus made its escape.

Then his neighbors advised the man to have his horse killed and to leave it with the cat in the deepest part of the forest. He did so, and the cat was feeding on the dead horse for quite a long time. One day a fox came walking up, and he, too, wanted to eat some of the dead horse. But the cat dashed forth from behind the horse's carcass and gave the fox such a fright that it went running away and did not stop until it ran into a wolf.

"Where are you running to, brother fox?" the wolf asked him.

"I say, the gallant Cecus-Becus Berneusz has given me such a fright that it sent me running, and I haven't been able to stop. Go and have a look at him and if you can, kill him."

The wolf tried but he fared the same as the fox. Then they proceeded on their way together and before long they met a badger, a boar, and a bear. All of them took their chance in turn, but they fared the same as the fox.

Next morning they made preparations for a big feast in honor of the gallant Cecus-Becus Berneusz. It took them rather long to decide which of them should be sent to Berneusz with the invitation. The fox said that the gallant Berneusz might easily catch him by his long tail. The boar said that he would feel too exhausted before he got there. The bear said that he would be too slow for that job. So it was the wolf who went to invite the gallant Berneusz.

When Prince Cecus-Becus Berneusz arrived, the bear wanted to seize him and eat him with his mates. But the gallant Berneusz was quick in climbing up a tree. The animals went in pursuit; each jumped on the shoulders of his mate so that they might reach up to Berneusz. The wolf was on top and when he reached out to seize him, the gallant Berneusz sneezed and the wind of his sneeze swept the wolf off the tree. It gave a mighty scare to the others as well, and they tried, helter-skelter, to get down from the tree. In their great haste, one broke its neck, another broke its legs.

Prince Cecus-Becus Berneusz ran home to his master and then led him back to that same tree. There they packed the animals onto a cart and drove home with them. For a long time they were well provided with food.

•26• *Mányó is Dead*

A shepherd was grazing his sheep along the roadside. A cat came walking down the road and another cat was approaching from the opposite direction. When they met, one of the cats said, "May God give you a good day, brother!"

The other replied, "May God give you a good day. Where are you going?"

"I'm going to a funeral," he said. "And where are you going?"

"I'm going to a wedding feast. Tell me, who has died?"

"Mányó."

"Oh, don't tell me. Is he really dead?"

"To be sure, he is."

"Well, then I'd better go with you to his funeral." And they went along.

The shepherd went home and said to his wife, "Say, did you ever? A cat was going along the road. Another was coming from the opposite direction. They greeted each other. One of them asked, 'Where are you going?' 'I'm going to a wedding, and you? Where are you going?' 'I'm going to a funeral.' 'Who died?' 'Mányó.' 'Is that so? Is Mányó dead?' 'Yes, Mányó is dead.' 'Well, then I'd better go with you to the funeral.' And they went together.''

The shepherd had a cat. As soon as he finished his story the cat jumped on top of the oven and said, "Is that so? Is Mányó dead?''

The shepherd said, "He is, to be sure.''

The cat took a leap and smashed through the window and was gone. He hasn't come back yet.

• 27 •   The Dogs and the Wolves Converse

A shepherd was on his way to the market. He went along deep in thought. There was neither a herdboy nor a good neighbor he could have asked to look after his herd.

On the road he met a fellow shepherd. The man asked him, "Where are you going?''

He said, "I'm going to the market.''

"Who's taking care of the sheep?''

"God's taking care of them.''

"God?''

"Yes.''

And he went to the market. While he was away, the other fellow picked twenty-five choice sheep out of the flock. "Well, let's see,'' he said to himself, "whether your God can take care of your sheep.''

The shepherd comes back from the market. He counts his sheep; twenty-five are missing. He says, "I guess it's no use leaving things to God.''

There were always a lot of wolves that came to visit those parts, and each morning a couple of sheep disappeared. Three giant dogs this shepherd had, each as big as a donkey. These dogs had seen the wolves coming on, but they drew back from the herd and let the wolves carry off the sheep. And when the wolves had got far enough, they stopped and stuffed themselves till they were ready to burst. What remained of their prey was finished off by the dogs. This had gone on every night or every other night. The shepherd gave way to despair; not only had he lost twenty-five of his choice sheep, but the wolves were coming night after night to carry off some more. Not one would be left by Spring. The shepherd began weeping in despair.

A white-bearded old man came passing by. "God give you a good day, my friend!"

"Why are you weeping, brother?"

"Sure, I've good reason to weep," he says, "what with the wolves coming night after night to carry off my sheep."

"But you've got a couple of big sheep dogs, haven't you?"

"A fat lot of good they are to me," he said.

"Well, what's the food they are kept on?"

The shepherd said, "Half a pound of meat a day."

"What do you mean, half a pound?"

"Well," he says, "I give a mouse a day to each dog."

He always gave a mouse to each dog, and that was what he meant by half a pound of meat.

"I dare say, comrade, that's what's wrong. Surely you must have some sickly sheep that is on its last legs. Kill it and cut it up and throw it to your dogs to feed on."

The shepherd followed this advice and on that same day when he let his dogs have their fill, the wolves couldn't carry off a single sheep. On the following day he again gave his dogs plenty of meat. Just before dusk two wolves appeared. The oldest dog barked to the wolves, "Get along with you! We have a good master who feeds us well. We don't want any of your prey."

The shepherd heard what the dog was barking to the wolves. But he also heard the youngest dog barking to them, "Come on! Take what you want and let me have some of it."

The old dog then leaped at the young dog and threw him on his back. "May the wolves have their fill of you," the old dog said. "Haven't you got a good master? Doesn't he keep you well?"

The wolves wouldn't really believe that the dogs had turned against them. But when they drew nearer to the sheep, the three dogs closed around them and before long the wolves were torn to pieces.

Thus the shepherd learned how to feed his dogs. And since that day the wolves have never taken a single sheep of his flock. If you do not believe me, go and ask the old shepherd himself.

· 28 · Three Kids, the Billy Goat, and the Wolf

There was once a goat family: the billy goat, three kids, and their mother. The three kids used to visit the nearby thicket because there were plenty of berries there and they were fond of nibbling away at them. Every day the three kids went to the thicket, one after the other.

One day the smallest of the three went to the thicket and met a wolf.

"Where are you bound for, kid?"

"I'm going to the thicket."

"Aren't you afraid that I'll eat you?"

"To be sure, I am."

"Why are you speaking in such a reedy voice?"

"Because I am scared. You'd better take my brother, he's much fatter than me."

The second kid came walking up.

"Where are you bound for, kid?"

"I am going to the thicket."

"Aren't you afraid that I'll eat you?"

"To be sure, I am."

"Why do you speak in such a reedy voice?"

"Because I am scared. Why don't you take my brother? He's much fatter than me."

The third and biggest of the kids came walking up.

"Where are you bound for?"

"To the thicket."

"Aren't you afraid that I'll eat you?"

"To be sure, I am."

"Why do you speak in such a reedy voice?"

"Because I am scared. But take the next one who'll come along, he's the billy goat."

The billy goat came walking up.

"Where are you bound for, billy goat?"

"To the thicket."

"Aren't you afraid that I'll eat you?"

"Why should I be afraid: I carry a pair of pistols over my head, and I've got a pouch between my legs."

Gee willikers! The wolf got scared and took to his heels.

And that's the end of it.

· 29 · *The Goat That Lost Half His Skin*

A man had a wife and three daughters. He said to his eldest daughter, "Go and take the goat and let him pasture on grass neck-high and water knee-deep."

When she returns with the goat, he says, "Well, my dear goat, have you had your fill?"

"No, I haven't," says the goat, "because your daughter kept me tethered to a stake while she was dallying with the village lads."

Well, next day, he gave orders to his second daughter to take the goat to pasture. He said to her, "Take the goat and let him pasture on grass neck-high and in water knee-deep."

When she came back with the goat, the farmer said, "Well, my own little kid, have you had your fill?"

And the goat gave the same answer as before.

Then the farmer ordered his youngest daughter to take out the goat, but when they came back the goat said she hadn't done any better than her sisters.

Well, as he saw that he couldn't leave the goat to the care of his daughters, he said to his wife, "Now, you will go with the goat."

She went with the goat, but when they were back, the goat said the same about her as he had of her daughters.

So next time the farmer himself took out the goat. When they were back, the farmer's wife said, "Well, my little kid, have you had your fill?"

"Not I," he said, "it was much worse with the master than with you. When I went with you, it was only being tethered to a stake. But the master was making love to a woman and before we came home he gave me a sound hiding."

At this talk the farmer flew into a rage and decided to flay the goat. Promptly, he set to this task and when he had got half the skin off, the goat ran away.

As he was running, he ran straight into a fox. But he kept running for dear life; he passed the fox and slipped into a hole. It was the den of the very same fox. Of course, the fox was afraid to go back into the hole and called in, "Who's there, in my house?"

"It's me, the goat with half its skin flayed, and I'm going to stamp with one foot, and I'll butt you with one horn, and you had better run away or I'll eat you."

Of course, the fox got terribly frightened and ran away. As he was running, he met the wolf. The wolf asked him, "What put you on the run, brother fox?"

"Oh, dear me, what a horror! Do come to my house and see for yourself."

The wolf then went with the fox back to his home and called into the hole, asking who was inside. He got the same answer as the fox. "It's me, the goat with half its skin flayed. I'm going to stamp with one foot, and I'm going to butt you with one horn. You had better run away, or I'll eat you."

So he, too, ran away.

As the fox and the wolf were going on together they met a hedgehog. The hedgehog asked them, "Where are you running?"

They told him what was hiding in the fox's house. So the hedgehog returned with them to see for himself. When he asked who was inside, he got the same answer as the other two, "It's me, the goat with half its skin flayed. I'm going to stamp with one foot, and I'm going to butt you with one horn. You'd better run away, or I'll eat you."

Well, by no account did the hedgehog run away. He rolled up into a ball and rolled straight into the hole. As he was rolling along, his sharp spines prickled badly against the flayed side of the goat, so much so that the goat went flying out of the fox's hole. As soon as the fox and the wolf caught sight of him, they cried out, "How then! Was it this one who scared hell out of us?" And they were terribly put out about it and ate up the goat.

• 30 • The Yellow Bird

Beyond the seas, on the yonder edge of the wide world, there was once a hunter who went in pursuit of a bird for seven years, trying to shoot it down. But he never shot it down.

The hunter had a wife and a daughter. They lived in the forest. One day, the hunter sent his wife to the well. But a violent storm came on, and the woman was struck dead by a stroke of lightning. Well, they buried her, and he was left alone with his daughter. But he never gave up his pursuit of the yellow bird.

Time wore on, and a year passed by. The hunter sent his daughter to the well. But again a violent storm came on, and she too was struck by a stroke of lightning. He was left all alone. And for seven years he lived in grief in the forest. He went about in the forest and got along somehow. One day he fell ill and he died. There wasn't anyone to bury him. The carrion beetles and the blow flies finished off his unburied corpse. His skull split up, and the rains filled it with water. Then the yellow bird flew there to take a sip of water. But as it alighted on the brim of the skull, the split up parts closed over the bird. Then the bird broke into a song: "In all your life you never ceased to pursue me. Now that you are dead, you've caught me. But of what use it that to you?"

So both were dead, and there was nobody to bury them.

That's all of it.

Part V
Tales of Lying

In 1848, when my grandfather hadn't yet been born and my father was just a small kid, I was myself a miller, and it all happened in those days.

I had two big oxen, both for the left-hand side of the cart. Around Christmas time the snow was knee-high. But I had to go with the cart to collect grain for milling. Well, I went to the fore and turned to the back and managed to turn over the cart, so that I should be ready to start at once. I put the oxen into the cart and harnessed the milled corn sacks to the cart.

When I reached the market place, the sacks left the cart and went home, each to the place where it belonged. Then I collected some more grain and putting the sacks again on the cart, I drove homeward.

When I reached the end of the street, I brought the sacks to a halt to let them relieve nature. I stuck up my whip in front of them so that they shouldn't move on. I too had to relieve myself. While I was doing this, the sacks strayed away and went picking strawberries on the hillside. I followed to retrieve them. But since both the snow and the sacks were white, I was not able to trace them. Well, it couldn't be helped, so I strolled back to the cart. But there was neither cart nor oxen. There was only my whip, and out of its handle there had grown a tree so high that its top was brushing the sky. I thought to myself that I was quite fed up with toiling on this earth, what with my cutting the ice forever around the mill. Here I go, straight up to Heaven.

So I went climbing the tree till I reached the gate of Heaven. And it was so chilly thereabouts that the flies gave me no bother at all. The top of the tree was brushing against the gate. I knocked at it because I beheld there a trapdoor, right in front of me.

Some superior party called out from the inside, "Who's there?"

'It's me, St. András," I said.

St. Péter—he was the party in charge of the keys to the gate of Heaven—then said, "I won't let you in, unless your head is as bald as an egg."

"Good gracious me!" I thought. I had such long hair that it had to be coiled round my neck three times, and yet it reached down right to my heels. What could I, or what should I, do with so much hair? I tried to put it up this way and that, but either way it seemed wrong. Then I coiled it on top of my head and pulled my cap over it.

St. Péter said to me, "Step in, buddy." Then I slipped through the trapdoor, and next thing I was having the time of my life with the angels. You should have heard the things I told them. I made them nearly split with laughter. But then some great saint admonished me to behave more decently or "We'll throw you down from Heaven so that you break your neck." What a pity, I thought, that neither my brother-in-law nor my stick were around, as the two of them would surely send them flying. But as I was on my own, there was nothing I could do. So they led me back to the trapdoor, and I was ordered to get out and start on my way down.

But meanwhile the stump of the tree had rotted away, and the wind had laid the tree low. What else was there to be done but to stay where I was? St. Elijah then said, "On no account can you remain here. But over there, on the top of a white cloud, there's a bundle of straw. We can braid it into a rope and make a sling of the rope and pull it tight under your arms; then we can let you down by it safely enough."

I thought it was a good idea; at least I didn't need to worry about how to get down. Then St. John gave me a *chibouque* pipe, and St. Nicholas presented me with a packet of tobacco. They filled my bag with a lot of good things and then fastened the rope under my arms. And then I took my leave of them. I gave a kiss to Archangel Gabriel that left a blue spot on both cheeks. And I said that being a miller down on earth I would be able to provide for a wife, and why not marry me?

Then I crawled out through the trapdoor, and I was lowered down by means of the rope. The only trouble was that the rope had not been made of braided strands of straw; it was a twisted rope. And when I got halfway down, my pipe went out. Then I drew forth my tinder box with the flint and steel my grandfather's grandfather used in his days. I tried to strike fire, but the tinder was moist and it didn't take fire at first. And as I went on jerking at the tinder, the rope became frayed and snapped. I went hurtling down and crashed at the end of our street, right into the centre of the road, with such force that I sank seven meters deep below the ground. I was struggling hard, wriggling left and right, to get out of there, but I didn't have one chance in a hundred of getting out. I was driven mad to think of it, in fact I was boiling over with rage. I got myself into such a temper that it made me leap out of the hole. I rushed home and snatching up a spade and a pickax, I went back to dig myself out of the hole.

When I had dug down deep enough to reach my hand to myself, I took a firm grasp of my hand and pulled myself out of the hole. But there was such a fog that I just couldn't see properly, and so it happened that I hacked off my head with the ax as I was digging away to get myself out of the hole. And as I was shovelling away the earth my head must have rolled away with the clods of earth. I took my pickax and flung the spade over my shoulder and made for home. When I reached the bottom of the street, I came across the doctor, who said that in all his born days he hadn't seen a man without his head but certainly he was seeing one now.

"What do you mean, doctor?," I asked him. "I've got my head on." And immediately, as I wanted to make sure of it, I passed my hand down along my backbone down to my heels. But there was no head. Then I went back to the hole from which I had dug myself out. I walked around and searched for my head. And there it was, all muddied up with the freshly dug earth. I snatched up my head and put it back on my neck, but I got it back all wrong, just the other way round, with my nose looking down on my heels and with the nape of my neck to the front.

Again, I went home. On my way back I came across the parson. When I greeted him, he said that in all his born days he had never seen a man like me, who had his head the other way round on his neck.

"Come now, parson, what do you mean? My head is certainly in its right place." All the same, I wanted to make sure. And didn't I find my eyes staring in the direction from which I was coming? Then I seized both my ears and screwed my head around until I got it almost back in the right direction. And when the summer season came—it must have been around St. John's Day or thereabouts, and there was a spell of frost with sixty degrees below zero—that great cold turned my head at last to the right place.

I went home and arrived on the very day that my grandfather was born. When I came in he was just being bathed in a tub. The midwife was administering to my grandfather's mother. When she saw me, she said, "Go and chop some wood and make a fire, or your grandfather will freeze to death in the tub." So I went out to the barn. I found there a pile of wood, partly chopped up, partly in big logs. In one of them there was a woodpecker's nest. In and out of the hole slipped a flock of chirping sparrows. I thought to myself, "I just could do with a couple of them. Soon people will be coming to visit the newborn babe, and I could get ready a nice stew for them."

So I propped the ladder against the pile of logs and went up to the top to reach the nest. But the ladder broke under my weight. Then I propped a fishing rod against the pile and climbed up once more to reach the nest. When I tried to put my hand through the hole, I found it too small to let my hand pass through. In my sudden anger I slipped through the hole, body and limbs. I snatched up the sparrows and tucked them under my vest. Then I slipped out and came down. I pushed down the log, and with the help of my ax I wedged my stick into it. I split the tree and chopped it up. I went back into the house, carrying a cord of wood on my back. I let it drop in front of the hearth with such a bang that it made my grandfather skip out of the tub. And as he dashed out of it, he bumped his hand so hard against the bedpost that since that day he has been called "maim handed" János Albert.

Just then I woke up, and that's all I've seen.

When I was a kid of ten, there wasn't a single soul in this world.
I took service with a peasant. I became his servant boy. He gave
me two pounds of cart grease and bid me grease the cart with it.
I greased both sides of the cart, and the forage rack, and the
shaft, and the stake brace. I ran out of the grease before I could
get to the axle. The peasant was swearing angrily because I should
have begun with the axletree. So I took out the axletree, went
over it with the grease, and reported to the peasant that I'd
finished my task. Then the peasant ordered me to put the plow
and some tools into the cart and to bring out the four horses
from the stable and put a yoke of horses in front and a yoke
behind. And there he comes swearing and laughing when he sees
that I had harnessed a pair of horses in front and the second pair
to the back of the cart. He put them right and we set off. As we
were driving, he turned his head and saw at once that the forecarriage of the plow had not been put in the cart. He asked
me, "Where is it?"

"Left it at home. I wasn't able to lift it into the cart."

He made me go back for it. He unharnessed a horse so that I
could put it to the forecarriage. As I didn't know how this was
to be done, I slung the forecarriage over the horse's neck. And
then I whipped the horse so that we could catch up with the cart.
The forecarriage kept knocking against the horse's leg and
bruised it badly. As I was afraid of getting hauled over the
coals by the peasant, I let the horse loose and took to my heels.

The night was descending on me, and it was pitch dark in the
village. I went into a house and asked if I could stay there overnight. The farmer wasn't at home. Only his wife was there, and
she said she couldn't put me up. She was thinking of leaving
home herself as her husband had gone drinking in the village
pub. But I pleaded with her until she took pity on me and let
me stay for the night in the nook between the wall and the
chimney corner. There I curled up. Before long, the swineherd

came home. The woman's husband was a swineherd. He was swearing horribly as he came in, and he sang out wildly,

> Wife! get thee out! get thee out!
> I'm coming from a drinking bout.

As he came in, he tripped over my foot and fell sprawling on the ground. He began to swear terribly and pulled me forth by my leg in order to find out what was it that made him fall. The woman tried to speak up for me, saying that I was only a poor boy and that she had taken pity on me because I was cold and hungry and had nowhere else to go. So I stayed there for the night. The swineherd asked his wife to bring him his supper and invited me to have supper with them. In a big pot the woman brought us beans, and we did ourselves well on them. Then she brought in a plateful of cheese curd noodles. The swineherd gazed at it open-eyed, because he had already stuffed himself with beans. In a temper he snatched up a hatchet and said, "Well, kid, damn you, gobble up that plateful of noodles or I'll cut your throat."

Scared to death, I made as if I was gobbling up the noodles, but I managed to tuck them away under my shirt. Soon my belly seemed to be swelled up by the lot of noodles. The swineherd didn't take his eyes off me until I had finished the plateful, and only then did he put down the hatchet. He took up his bagpipe and began piping up a tune. Then he ordered his wife to have a dance with me lest I should burst of having stuffed myself with the noodles. The woman took hold of me, but at the first swift turn, my shirt came loose and all the noodles lay strewn around us. The swineherd got a proper scare because he thought that I must have burst. He bawled at his wife, "Let him go at once!"

As she let me go, I bolted through the door and continued on my way. At the farther end of the village I found another house. I saw that the light was still on so I went in to ask for shelter. They let me stay for the night. It happened to be the wheelwright's house, and the wheel hubs were neatly piled up in one corner. On top of them the woman made up a pallet for me where I could stretch out. When the wheelwright came home, he didn't swear at his wife, indeed, he appeared quite amorous and complained that though they had been married for quite a long time, she had never let him see her bottom; now he wants to take a look at it. The woman made evasions, but he grew insistent and tried to pull off her garments. Of course I was burning with curiosity and stuck out my head to have a peep. As I stirred, the hubs rolled off, and there was nothing to conceal me from the wheelwright's eyes. The man became furious when he caught sight of me and bawled at the woman to slip into her skirt at once. "How's this," he thought, bewildered, "I was only looking at her, and there's the child as soon as all that."

Well, there I was taking to my heels again. I found abode this time at the opposite end of the village. I hid in a stack of straw. It was nice and warm in there, and I hoped to have a good rest till morning. But before long a young pair came walking up to the stack. Very likely they came for a bundle of straw because they had brought a piece of rope. But when they reached the stack, the young lad made passes at the girl and pinched her backside and so on, and behaved in quite a naughty way with her. The girl then asked him who'd be looking after the child if she'd be with one. The lad said that the one who was up above would take care of the child. I became scared indeed, because I was up there above them. I called down that it was a pretty hard job for me to look after myself and they shouldn't expect me to look after their child.

They were so terrified that they ran away. As I was afraid that they might come back and discover me, I jumped down from the stack and went running. Before long I came up to a big tumbledown mill. I was a bit afraid, and so I hid in the mill hopper. Then some folks came in—whether to have their grain milled or for other purposes, I couldn't say—but when they stepped up to the hopper, a big brawny man grabbed at me and brought me out of it.

Then he turned to his companions, "I dare say, that's where we're being watched from." And he threw me down. I broke my head and lost my hair. Then I made a run for it, and I never stopped until I got home.

And since then I've often told about these things to my folks.

Part VI
Historic Legends

In days of yore when there were vast forests and marshy reed banks and rush beds all along the river Karcsa, the fairies lived in Lake Karcsa. Their palace was deep down in the waters. But only half of the lake was inhabited by the fairies; in other parts of the water lived the witches, who'd have liked an alliance with the fairy folk, but the fairies wouldn't hear of it. In the course of time, the number of witches grew and grew until there were lots more of them than fairies. So there was nothing much left to the fairies but to think out a way of escape.

One day, the fairy queen left her palace in the lake and came out of the water to take a good look around the upper world. She was looking for a suitable spot where they could build a palace and a church for themselves. Well, you know, the place where you'll find the Presbyterian church today in Karcsa—which is said to have been built by the fairies—was the very spot the fairy queen found to her liking. It took the fairies two nights and a day to build their fine castle. When the castle was finished, they brought up heaps of polished marble and built a church, right there where you can see it to this day.

And then they decided to bring up their old bell from the lake and put it in the church tower. They thought that the ringing of the bell would stave off the witches and make them retreat if they came after them in pursuit. Two fairy maids then dived for the bell and brought it up from the lake. They were struggling along with the bell when they were spotted by the witches, who went in pursuit of them. The fairies had already flown as far as the centre of the lake—fairies never walk, they fly from one place to the other—when the witches nearly caught up with them. But suddenly a cock began to crow, and the startled fairies dropped the bell. As it fell it rang out a chime, and its sound scared off the witches. The fairies had made their escape, but their church had to remain without a bell as they were too scared of the witches to risk flying back to the lake to bring up another bell from under the water.

In the course of time, when there were no more fairies living on the earth, a man was strolling along the shore of Lake Karcsa. Suddenly, he heard sounds coming from the depths of the water. It seemed to him as if he had heard the chiming of a bell. He went to the magistrate and told him about it. He said that he had often heard folks telling him how there was a certain spot in the lake where in times of yore the fairies had dropped their bell into the water. So the magistrate sent men to that spot, and they started digging right away. (Owing to years of drought, certain parts of the lake had dried up.) The people got busy with picks and spades and dug away until they found the bell. They fastened a long rope to it and tied strong chains to the bell hanger. At the end of the chains twelve yoke of oxen were pulling hard. They were on the point of pulling it up to the surface when there came a cry from the depth, "Ouch! It's my little finger."

Then the rope and chains with which the oxen held the bell snapped asunder. The oxen fell to their knees, and the bell has remained forever in the lake. Rumor has it that every hundred years you can hear it chime. However, since that day when they tried to get it out, no living man has ever heard its sound.

And here's something else that belongs to my story: when the fairies built the church, they made the bell tower very high. The enraged witches raised a violent storm to pull down the tower. And it came down, and there's still a stone to mark the spot, about half a mile distant from the church, where it fell. You can still hear old folks telling about that church. They will tell you of its wonderful walls, built of polished marble, so clear that the people who lived near the church took their brushes and razors and soap along to do their Sunday shaving in front of these walls, which were as bright as a mirror. But this is a thing of the past; the walls are no longer so bright. In the course of time, the church has twice been destroyed by fire. During one of these fires the roof collapsed. Some of it crashed down inside the church, but another part came down outside, just along the walls so that the smooth and shining surface has been chipped and scratched by the falling roof, as well as marred by the fire and heat.

· 34 · When the Tartars Came

I've heard quite a lot about bygone times. Our town of Balmaz-újváros, for instance, hasn't always been there where we know it to be now. It was some ways farther off, nearer to the Cuca. But it was laid waste by the Tartars. At that time this place where we have the town now used to be barren land, inclosed by reed banks and rush beds. It became a good hideout for the local people when the Tartars came. Old people often told about how the Tartars, at least those who knew a little Hungarian used to go around the reed banks shouting:

> Sári! Mári! Come on! Come on!
> The dog-faced Tartars are all gone.

And all those who were lured out by these shouts were either killed or carried off by the Tartars. It was after these times that the people settled where we have the town today. But that was long before 1848.

· 35 · The Valiant Fish Trapper

There's a village by the name of Luka. There's a lake there, named Lake Varjános after a certain János Var. In the days of Turkish rule, the villagers of Luka woke one day to find some one hundred and fifty Turks holding a nearby hill. Wailing and lamenting, the people of the village gathered on the opposite hill, where the church stood.

"What's to become of us! The Turks will kill us all. We'll surely perish if we fall into their hands."

There was an old man named János Var. He made his living by trapping fish in weirs set up in the lake. Also, he used to go to a nearby wood and collect the eggs from the nests of the birds, and sometimes he went to help the fishermen.

When he heard the wailing and lamenting of his fellow villagers, he stepped up to the magistrate and asked him, "What's wrong with the people, sir? Why are they lamenting?"

"Sure, there's reason enough. Just look at that hill over there. The Turks will be here in no time to cut off our heads."

Old János Var said, "No need to worry about that, sir. Just let me deal with the Turks."

The others waited to see how he would be going about it. They saw him row over to the opposite side of the lake. When he got ashore he made for the hill and walked straight up to the Turks. From his gestures they could guess that he was trying to persuade them to get into his punt. But it was a very small boat, only able to hold one person, besides himself. The Turks thought that he was offering to take them over to the village, and so one Turk got into the boat. When János got to that part of the lake where the water turns into a reed-filled swamp, old János just tilted the boat. The Turk fell into the water, and when he bobbed up again old János hit him on the head with the punt pole and pushed him down, keeping him under water with the pole until he saw the last bubbles coming up. When he had finished with one Turk, he went back for the next one. Since the Turks could not see what was happening in the reed-filled swamp, they had no idea of what had happened to their comrades. They thought that the old man had taken their companions to the village where they would be waiting for the rest to come. But old János did away with the whole lot of them, drowning one after the other in the lake.

When he had finished off the hundred and fifty to the last man, János went back to the magistrate and said, "Well, sir, I've saved the village from the Turks. There was no need to make such a fuss about them."

Before then uncle János had been a poor cotter, but after this piece of gallantry he was raised to noble rank and was given a large estate.

·36· *The Kidnapped Child*

A Turk robbed a woman of her child and carried the little boy off to Turkey. The mother went in search of her son, wandering from village to village. After a long time she came to Turkey. She took service with a rich Turk and became the nanny of his son. When she put the little boy to bed she always sang him the same lullaby:

> Sleep, sleep, you little babe in Turkey,
> I, too, once had a babe in Hungary.
> But when the Turks besieged the city,
> One of them carried off my darling kiddie.
> Oh, I'd know him at a single glance,
> Oh, I'd recognize him at once.
> There was a plum-stone mark on his right
>   shoulder and thigh,
> A peach pit marked his left shoulder and thigh.

One day the Turk heard her singing to the child. He went into the room and said, "Will you sing that song once more?" She began singing, weeping all the while she sang, "Sleep, sleep, you little babe in Turkey, ..."

When she finished her song, the Turk asked her, "Would you recognize your son if you saw him?" Then he took off his clothes and said, "I'm the Hungarian child who was kidnapped by a Turk." The two fell into an embrace, and the young man then told his aged parents that the nanny had to be given all due respect as she was his real mother.

When she found him her son was a rich man of high standing. To be sure, God had guided her steps as she was wandering from village to village, from one city to another, urged on by her great affection for her son. And so it happened that she came to find him.

It happened in the days when the insurrectionist [kuruc] armies were laying siege to the fortress of Szatmár. Rákóczi encamped his troops under the fortress, but the besiegers seemed to be in no hurry at all to beset it and the civilians kept going in and out of the castle and carrying pieces of information to the insurrectionist army.

Prince Rákóczi was extremely fond of hunting. One day, escorted by eight bodyguards and two huntsmen and his hunting dog Leo, he set off to the woods of Csenger and Tatárfalu.

The whole afternoon they were beating the woods for boars. They were still a couple of hours walk from their hunting camp when it began to rain. Passing a farmstead on their way the prince stopped and said that they would stay there overnight. But as they had nothing to eat the bodyguards went off in search of some food. Meanwhile the two huntsmen prepared a bed for the prince. They carried into the house a big bundle of straw and spread a horse blanket over it. For a cushion they brought in the prince's saddle. Rákóczi put it under his head and wrapped himself in his cloak.

It became stuffy in the room and the prince opened the window to get some fresh air. His dog then began to growl; it had gotten wind of a stranger approaching through the farmyard. It was not the farmer, because the dog would have recognized him. The prince cocked the trigger of his pistol which he carried in his pocket and stepped to the window. The moon had just come out from behind the clouds, and by its light the prince beheld an Austrian officer in a plumed helmet. The enemy soldier aimed his pistol at the heart of the prince and with an ugly sneer called to him, "Surrender!"

This officer had been spying upon the prince for some time

and thought that if he captured the prince the Kaiser would, as a reward, raise him to the rank of baron.

Rákóczi asked him, "What will happen to me if I surrender?" The officer answered, "Since you'd be a prisoner of war, you'd get decent treatment."

While he was speaking, Rákóczi drew forth the pistol from his pocket and sent a bullet through the officer's head.

But the house had been surrounded by enemy soldiers. They forced the door to the prince's room, although Rákóczi and his two huntsmen were firing at the intruders. When some of the enemy were hit, their commander ordered a retreat into the farmyard. They decided to set the house on fire because they hoped for a good reward even if they should bring the prince in dead.

The roof of the house was all afire when the bodyguards, who had gone in search of food, came riding back at great speed, alarmed by the sound of shooting. Then they dashed at the Austrian soldiers and such was their anger they killed them to a man, including even those who wanted to surrender. And sparing neither trouble nor pains they succeeded in putting out the fire. In the morning they all rode back to their camp, and the prince rewarded his brave soldiers.

• 37b • Rákóczi Legends: Rákóczi and his Táltos Daughter

Ferenc Rákóczi was attacked once by enemy troops, partly Austrian, partly *labanc* [quisling] soldiers. But they were defeated by Rákóczi's insurrectionist [*kuruc*] troops. The Austrians were now at a loss because they realized that their opponents were more than their match. Rákóczi was, indeed, too much for them; he was holding thirteen fortresses.

Then the Austrians approached the captain of the insurrectionist army. "Desert Rákóczi, your leader, and you'll get a third of all the lands in Hungary."

The captain thought it over and then disbanded the most valiant soldiers of his troops. "There's no immediate danger, my sons; you may go home on leave."

When the *kuruc* soldiers were gone, the captain sent word to the Austrians: "You can do it now; only the guards are left in the fortress."

The Austrians prepared for the attack. But Ferenc Rákóczi had a daughter who was a *táltos*. He bid her go to the House of Parliament. He said to her, "Go, my daughter, and find out what actions they are going to take against me."

In the shape of a fly, his daughter flew into the Assembly Hall. When she had finished listening to the talk there, she flew back to her father to report to him what she had learned.

Rákóczi asked her, "Well, daughter, what are they going to do about me?"

"Father, Your Grace! Three days hence, the enemy will attack you."

But what could he do, since the captain of his forces had betrayed him and there were no soldiers there? So he sought the advice of his *táltos* daughter. She said, "Have the horseshoes reversed on your horses' hooves, and the enemy will never be able to find you."

When the enemy stormed the fortress, Rákóczi made his escape by riding away. And, save for the guards, the Austrians found not a soul in the castle. Of course they went looking for Rákóczi, but it was only the trail of his horse that they could find. And misled by the reversed horseshoes, they went in pursuit in the wrong direction.

• 38 •   How We Saw the Last of Forced Labor

I've heard it from my grandfather. He was just a small kid at that time. One day he took dinner to his father who was working in the field. He and the others were digging a canal. It was in marshy land, covered with reedy plots. In order to make some use of it, the manor gave orders for the digging of a canal so that the water could be carried into the River Kapos. Men from all over the county had been marched out as forced labor to do this piece of work. All the people were grumbling in great discontent to one another, wondering when they should ever see the end of their terrible drudgery.

When they were having their midday meal, a wanderer came up to them and said he would tell them when their forced labor would come to an end, if he got a *kreutzer* from each of them. The workers collected the money and gave it to him.

The man said, "This isn't enough for me; you must give me another *kreutzer*."

They gave it to him, and he said, "It's still not enough; let me have one more from each of you."

Some of the folks refused to give him another *kreutzer*, saying that it was all a piece of bluff. But many of them were curious to learn what he was getting at, and they gave him another *kreutzer*. But when he asked to be given a fourth *kreutzer*, they didn't want to hear of it. They said to one another, "Let's teach him a lesson with our shovels. He's just leading us up the garden path."

Then the wanderer said to them, "Leave me alone! I'll give back your money. And let me tell you that your drudgery will come to an end when you take up your hoe or your scythe and 'up and at them'; to show that you won't do any more forced labor."

The chance for "up and at them" came in 1848; it brought an end to serfdom and forced labor.

· 39 · *Captain Lenkey's Company*

In those days Hungarian soldiers were, as often as not, stationed outside their motherland. So when the Revolution of 1848 broke out, a hussar was reading a letter his folks had sent him from home. He said to his comrades, "Listen to what it says; there's a war going on in Hungary while we're kept stationed here."

And another man comes running up to listen, and a second and a third and a fourth, all of them soldiers doing service abroad. And they are reading the letters to one another written by their fathers and mothers. Their sergeant was listening to them and said, "What's up, boys?"

"Oh, sergeant, there is trouble indeed. There's a war in Hungary, and we're wasting time here all for nothing. Come along with us, sergeant, we're going to clear out tonight."

The sergeant says after some consideration, "Look here, boys, I'd be in on it, but I do not count for enough. Let's talk it over with the first lieutenant."

And there is the first lieutenant walking up to them, because he too, had overheard their talk. The soldiers gather round him and say, "This is how matters stand with us, sir."

"Believe me, boys, this is a pretty kettle of fish! But you know what? Swear that you'll obey me, and I'll lead you, and we'll go home."

The whole company took the oath.

"Well, boys," he said, "I'm going to lead you. But first every hussar shall pull out his saddle blanket from under the saddle. Cut the blankets in four and tie the pieces round your horses' hooves. They must not be heard clattering along when we make our getaway."

They did as they were told, and the first lieutenant then took the lead, and the company set off.

The commander of that hussar company was a certain captain János Lenkey of Tarcal.

Seizing the very first opportunity, the hussars took their chance and set off on their way home. It began raining. From a trot they broke into a gallop and then proceeded at a slow pace. When the day was breaking, they heard loud shouting coming from behind.

The first lieutenant said, "Someone must be coming after us." He brings the company to a halt. "Well, men, just keep your wits about you. Let us fight to the bitter end rather than surrender."

The sergeant then exclaimed, "It's the captain, coming after us." And they hear him shouting, "Listen, men! Wait for me! Have you taken leave of your senses? Where are you going?

Turn back, before it's too late to get out of trouble. So far, I am the only one who knows what you're after."

The hussars gathered round him. "Do join us, sir! There's trouble in the home country. Let's do our bit to save our country."

"Listen, men! We're bound by our oath of allegiance and cannot leave here."

But they would not listen to him and urged him the more, "Take the lead! Take us home!"

"Very well, men, let it be."

The company then swore him allegiance.

"Well, men, tie me up so that no one might say that I've joined you on my own accord if they were to surprise us."

The hussars then tied him up and took away his sword. Thus they carried their captain with them, but only until they had crossed the frontier.

"Well, boys, here we are back in our own country."

The hussars jumped from their horses and kissed the boundary stone on the border of Hungary. And from there they proceeded at a lively trot.

They rode straight up to Pest, to report to General Görgey, who was camping there with his troops. Things were getting very hot when they arrived. When the Serbs launched their attack, the Hungarian *Honvéds* [revolutionary fighting forces] marched against them. First lieutenant Pompejus was their commanding officer. He was hit by the first bullet.

"What's the matter, sir? Let me help you to your feet."

"The bullet went through my heart, son. But you, my sons, must carry on!"

· 40 · *Lajos Kossuth and Sándor Rózsa*

When people all over the world had been stirred into rebellion, Lajos Kossuth betook himself to Sándor Rózsa and his gang of outlaws. He said to them, "Look here! I want your help."

It was in the company of the chief justice of Szeged that Kossuth went to the haunts of Sándor Rózsa. All along the way, the chief justice was trembling in every limb, in such deadly fear was he of Sándor Rózsa and his gang.

On their arrival, the outlaws closed up around them and began shouting, "Out with your money! We want your money!"

But when Sándor Rózsa drew closer and recognized Lajos Kossuth, he stepped up to his men and slapped their faces. Then he led Kossuth into his hideout. Heaps of treasure were there, as may be imagined, and from it he gave an amount to Kossuth.

Then Kossuth made a round of the villages to warn the villagers of the harm which would be brought upon them by the Austrians. He said to them, "Beware! Lend us your assistance in as many ways as you can or it will be all up with us." As soon as the people became aware of the danger threatening their country, they did not need to be told twice to join forces with the Hungarian soldiers.

· 41 · Kossuth Wanders Through the Countryside

Laborers were felling trees in the forest. Kossuth struck up a conversation with them, asking the men about this and that, but without disclosing who he was. Only when he was leaving the forest did he post a notice on a tree: "Lajos Kossuth passed through this forest."

The squire, a man of great influence and wealth, had given orders that the workers were to do the hoeing in his vineyard, working downhill, so that the blood should rush to their head and cause their death. Kossuth walked up to them and said, "Listen, folks, do the hoeing working uphill."

Then he hid behind a bush. After a little while the squire appeared and began whipping the men. "Is that what I've told you to do? Didn't I tell you that you must do the hoeing working downhill?"

Kossuth stepped forth from behind the bush and snatched the whip from his hand. And at his orders the squire was to receive, right then and there, forty strokes on his buttocks. When they got through half of them, the squire began to beseech Kossuth for forgiveness. Kossuth then asked him, "What wages do you give these laborers for their daily work?"

The squire gave an account of it, but Kossuth said that it was not enough and that a certain amount of tobacco should be added to the wages. And he warned the squire, "If you're not willing to grant it, you'll receive a thousand more strokes."

The squire asked him, "Who are you?"

"I was your king, Lajos Kossuth."

And the squire passed on the news to the other noblemen to look out, as Kossuth was wandering through the countryside in order to look into the state of affairs.

•42• *A Piece of Roguery*

Pista Sisa's folks were all serfs and he himself was a serf, working in the squire's service in one of the nearby villages. It happened once that on some account he was soundly drubbed by the squire. Then and there he swore to himself that one day he would pay him back in his own coin. The War of Independence furthered his schemes. After a battle, when the Austrian troops came off victorious, a festival was arranged in the village to celebrate their victory. Pista Sisa, who had joined the Insurgents of 1848, was fighting against the Austrians. After that lost battle, he boldly made up his mind to break up the party of the merry-making officers and to take it out of the squire who entertained them. So he dressed himself up as an Austrian officer and walked into the squire's house with the other guests. Then he figured out some pretext to coax the squire into coming out with him, and as soon as he got him outside the house, he gave him something to sing for. By the time the others found out what had happened, Sisa had already made his getaway.

As the story goes, he had walked up to the squire and by way of introduction said to him, "Oh, my dear godfather, it's been a long time since I saw you last."

The squire did not recognize him and said so.

"Oh, I'll make you remember me," Sisa said, and when he had beaten him to his heart's content, he added, "To be sure, you aren't my godfather. And this was for the confirmation [drubbing] I had at your hand."

Pista Sisa never did any harm to the poor; it was only the rich who got it in the neck from him. And it should be said for him that he never stole a thing in all his life. But here goes the story of how he played a trick on a stingy man.

There was a saloonkeeper in the village. One evening a peasant hadn't the money to pay for a drink, and the saloonkeeper would not serve him on credit. Sisa stepped into the saloon just as the saloonkeeper refused the peasant a drink. Sisa walked up to the counter and filled the peasant's jug with wine. Then he went to the saloonkeeper and said, "Say! What a fine coat you've got. Just let me try it on. I'd like to see how it fits me."

The saloonkeeper helped him on with the coat.

Sisa then asked him, "Do you think it fits me well?"

"Fits you like a glove," the man said, fearing to contradict Sisa.

"Well, if it fits me, it will do for me." And he walked away with the coat.

·43· Outlaw Jóska Gesztén Goes His Own Way

Here's something about Jóska Gesztén. As people were going to the market, Jóska withdrew into the woods and hid behind a tree. He was lying in wait for those who had to pass through the woods on their way to the market.

A young orphan girl came first. She was a servantmaid and

had saved up a little money and now was going to buy a dress for herself.

When she came to the tree, Jóska stepped forth and stopped her. "Say, girlie, where are you going?"

"I'm going to the market."

"I say, aren't you afraid of meeting Jóska, the outlaw?"

She said, "Why should I be afraid of him? Haven't got anything he'd wish to take from me. I am only a poor orphan."

Jóska said, "Tell me, girlie, how much money have you got?" And she told him right away how much money she had.

"What will that paltry sum buy you, girlie? But I'm going to give you some money," he said, "and then you can buy yourself a nice silk dress. And on your way back, I want to see what you've bought for yourself."

The girl did as she was told. She bought some things for herself. When she passed the wood on her way back, Jóska was waiting for her at the tree.

"Now let me have a look at your dress," he said to her. "I want to see what you've bought for yourself."

The girl showed Jóska her new dress, and he said, "Well, my girl, when you marry, you must ask me to be your best man at the wedding."

And the girl asked him to her wedding, and he gave a rich present to the young pair.

Then a Gypsy woman was passing through the wood. She too was on her way to the market. She carried a big bundle on her back and a baking tin in her hand. When she came to the tree, Jóska stepped forth from behind it and said, "Say! Aren't you afraid of meeting Jóska Gesztén, the outlaw?"

"Why should I be afraid of that s.o.b.?" she said.

Jóska then said, "What's that you're going to sell at the market?"

"Quilting needles and all sorts of things," she said.

"Well, let me have half a dozen of the needles," and when he got them, he tied her up and stuck the needles into her bottom. Thus he was taking it out of her for having called him a s.o.b. That's all of it. It was his way to give as good as he got.

·44· Jóska Gesztén Makes His Getaway

This happened as far back as the sixties [1860]. There was a fellow called Murányi. He was the bailiff on Count Károlyi's estate near Nagykároly in County Szatmár.

On a winter day, the bailiff and his little son of seven took a sleigh ride to the fields. The farmhands were busily dressing the snow covered fields, raking the dung from the manure carts. A lot of hands were doing the raking as there were some twenty or so carts there. Suddenly a man came walking up to them, clad in a finely embroidered *szűr* [felt cloak worn by herdsmen]. Throwing off his cloak, he snatched the pitchfork from the hands of the nearest man and set at once to working the dung assiduously over the field.

As I've told you, this happened in the early sixties [in the days of oppression] during the Bach epoch.

Well, before long a couple of gendarmes on patrol came riding up to them. They were Austrian soldiers with the large double-headed eagle on the front of their brass helmets. The patrol leader; very likely an officer, must have known the bailiff because he rode up to him and greeted him. He asked the bailiff if he or his men had seen anyone loafing around thereabouts, as they had good reason to think that the man they were after had come this way. Of course the bailiff said, "No, we haven't seen anyone." The patrol then rode off in the opposite direction. The man was still busily forking the dung from the cart. The bailiff had seen him indeed, but being a good patriot he would not give him away to the gendarmes. When the soldiers disappeared out of sight, Jóska Gesztén walked over to the bailiff and thanked him for his great kindness.

The bailiff asked him, "Say, Jóska, why don't you clear out of these parts? Things are getting too hot here for you."

"It wouldn't be much help, sir. Wherever I turned up, whether it be this side of the River Tisza or the other side of the Duna, I'd be recognized at once." And slinging his cape over his shoulder, he took leave of the bailiff and walked away.

Part VII
Local Legends

SECTION A

The Herdsmen Legend Cycle

· 45 · The Two Herdsmen Who Used Black Magic

I was thirteen then. The cowherd was in his seventy-fifth year. He had seventy animals on his hands. In the evening he left the pasture and went to have his supper at home, as he lived only about half a mile from the place where we had been night herding.

Says the old man to me, "You keep to that spot, sonny. I'll be back soon with the two dogs, the two *pumis* [sheep dogs]. They'll take care of you and the cattle too."

It must have been around ten or eleven o'clock when suddenly the whole herd went jumping over the fence, following their belled leader. But I wasn't one to lose my presence of mind. I went after them and before long I had them corralled. No sooner was I back in the hut, not more than ten minutes later, when the animals went off again. I penned them in, but soon the same thing happened all over again the third time. That gave me such a scare that I took to my heels and ran home. At dawn, when the old man came back, he did not find me in the hut.

When he got back to the ranch, he said to me, "Come along, boy, I'm going to show you who it was that gave trouble to the herd."

Some fifty steps away from the corral, there was an old dried-up well with walls of stone. When we reached the well, the old man said to me, "Look into it, my son!" And what do you think I saw in the well? The neighboring cowherd, who kept his cattle on C. *puszta*. Then we went back to the corral, and the old man got hold of the young bullock which had the bell. He seized his tail and pulled out of it a handful of hair to make into three lashes for the whip. And he put the lashes onto my whip so that it should give a sharp crack. Then he let his sheepskin cape slip to the ground, put his staff into my hand, and bade me strike his cape with it. While I was beating fast and hard with the stick I heard the cowherd in the well utter cries of pain. When finally I had grown too exhausted to go on, the old man put a stop to this devil exorcising and the cowherd was permitted to come out of the well and go on his way. It must have been about six or half-past six in the morning.

The old man said, "Let's have our lunch before we let the cattle out of the corral." Then he bade me go on cracking the whip all day long—which indeed I loved to do—until the three lashes gave out. It must have been an hour past noon when the cowherd of C. *puszta* came over to us while his cattle were having their midday rest. He came to beseech me to stop cracking the whip, and he promised that he would never again try his tricks on our cattle.

The old man then said to him, "There's one more lash to the whip, and it's sharp enough to knock your eyes out should you put us to trouble again. Let me warn you that there are fourteen devils at my service while you can only count on seven." Then the other man asked forgiveness and took his leave. Never again did we have any trouble with him.

• 46 •   The Herdsmen and the Wolves

I have heard it from my grandfather. It happened when he was a young kid and served as herdboy with a cowherder. It was at noon on a certain day. The cattle had been watered and were having their midday rest, chewing the cud at leisure. They lay scattered near a small wood. My grandfather was still a young child, a boy of thirteen or fourteen years. He was not sleeping, though the cowherd usually took a nap at noon when he felt tired. My grandfather was awake, and suddenly he saw two wolves coming out of the wood. Christ! he got scared. He ran to his boss and shook him awake, "Get up, get up! Look! The wolves are coming."

The cowherd rose lazily on one elbow. "Let them come," he said. But my grandfather was shaking with fear when he saw the wolves getting nearer and nearer. Soon they reached the herd and were running to and fro among the animals. Grandfather was terribly worried and asked the cowherd to do something about it because he knew that his boss could use magic art. But the cowherd only snapped at him, "Keep quiet, son. Mind your own business and leave the rest to me." The wolves seemed to take their choice. There was a fine, two-summer bullock in the herd. A fine specimen it was, already fat and plump. The two wolves seized the bullock, each getting hold of one of its ears. Slashing at the bullock with their tails, they led it out of the herd. My grandfather despaired at the thought that the wolves should carry off their best bullock.

"Do not worry, they're not going to get away with the bullock. You can go and take a rest," his boss said to him.

My grandfather told me that the cowherd kept an old shoddy file in his bag. It was a poor thing, of no use at all since its edge was so blunt.

The cowherd watched the wolves and the bullock until they reached the edge of the wood. Then he sat up and stuck his file straight into the back of his cape which was spread under him so he could lie on it. The file stood upright in the cape.

That very moment the wolves let go the bullock and fell on their haunches. The old cowherd walked up to them. So did my grandfather, but he was a bit scared and kept behind the old man. And when they got near enough, he saw that the two wolves were weeping, shedding tears as big as beans while their mouths kept twitching as if they wanted to say something. But of course they could not speak. The old man then said to them, "What do you think I am going to do to you? If I wished to, I could make you remain forever in the shape of wolves." The two wolves clasped their front paws together and implored him for mercy. They knew that the old man was wearing round his waist a hoop made of a shoot of a year-old birch. He fastened it with the tape of his linen trousers. My grandfather then took off this hoop and bade the wolves slip through it. And then the wolves ran away. But as they were running they kept looking back at my grandfather and waved to him happily because if he had not made them slip through the hoop they could not have changed back into human beings.

· 47 · *The Herdsman's Magic Cape*

It happened at Karcsa in far-off days. There was a horseherd in constant trouble with his horses, for they were always going astray. He was a hired man, and his wages were hardly enough to cover the losses.

One day he said to his friend, "Look here! It has got around hereabouts that your father is a knowing man. Go and ask him if he couldn't help me."

His friend said, "Listen! Take the old man to the inn and pay for his brandy. Let him have as much as he wants and you'll never lose a horse again." And he added that though there wasn't a single horse left in the pasture, his father could make them all return, even though they had been corralled behind an iron fence.

The horseherd followed his advice and spoke to his friend's father, "I say, Uncle Terjék, wouldn't you help me?"

At first the old man seemed reluctant and said he could not do anything. But three pints of brandy did the trick, and he said, "Look here! I spread my cape over the table, and you'll have to go on striking at it until I stop you."

After he had struck seven or eight times, the old man said to him, "Look out of the window!"

He looked out of the window and said, "I see the horses coming."

"Count them!"

When they reached the inn, the horseherd counted the horses and said, "Six are missing."

The old man then rose and turned out his cape. "Now, go on striking at it."

After he had struck at it three or four times, old Terjék said to him, "Look out of the window. Are the horses coming?"

"Yes, they are."

"How many?"

"Six," he said, "but one of them is carrying a man on its back."

"All right! Let him come."

And the old man sent the horses back to the pasture.

"Now go," he said, "and strike three times at the man sitting on the horse."

"Surely he wouldn't wait till I get there?"

"Do not worry. He won't be able to dismount until you strike at him three times."

So the horseherd went to the pasture and found the man still sitting on one of the horses. He was the ranger on duty at Tiszakarád. He had found the horseherd's horses running loose and had rounded them up in the corral at Tiszakarád. The last six had been tied up in a stable. The others escaped when they were let out to be watered; this was at the very moment when the horseherd began striking at the old man's cape at the inn.

The horseherd then gripped his staff and struck three times at the ranger.

"Do not blame me," the man said. "As a ranger I had to carry out my orders, and drive in the stray horses. And now, as much as I've tried, I cannot get off this horse."

But after the third stroke he was able to dismount and he went away. From that day on not one single horse ever went astray. Whenever the horseherd had to go into the village, he never missed going to the inn first, where he bought some brandy. He took the brandy to the old man who had grown weak with age and could not manage to walk to the inn, which was a good way off from his home. And the old man always helped him to keep the horses from going astray.

· 48 · The Cowherder's Bull

The village bosses took Uncle Tomori, the old cowherd, to the cattle market at Ricse, to buy a bull for their cattle. They bought one and then went home, leaving the bull to the care of the old man. But the old man felt like having a day of it and began whiling away his time at the inn. He sent the bull off by itself to make his own way home. And the beast went home. The old man intended to go home after evening came. When the bull got home, it stopped at the stable door and did not go into the stable until the cowherd got there in the evening and said to it, "Heigh! Get in with you!"

The bull rose and walked into the stable, and the old man tied him up. For a week everything went on as usual. Then one day, when the old man was driving the bull to the well, the bull began to chase him. The old man couldn't guess what to make of it and wondered why the bull was all of a sudden going at him and wanted to toss him. He ran away and when he reached the window, he called in to his wife, "Be quick! Get me the thinnest switch."

He had fifteen of them, and his wife looked for the thinnest and gave it to him through the window. When the bull came up to him, he struck at its nose three times. The beast turned at once and stopped chasing. It walked quietly back into the stable, and the old man tied him up.

Then the old man made for a nearby thicket to look for the thorniest bushes he could find. From the very thorniest he cut off a bundleful of twigs to bind into a broom. When he had the broom ready, he started sweeping some five or six yards away from the stable. When he got quite close to the stable, he pressed the broom against the ground with such force that it cut into the earth. Suddenly the cowherd who kept his cattle in the pasture next to the old man's came walking up to him and said, "I say, brother, stop that sweeping. Look, the blood is running all over my back, for your broom is cutting into my flesh."

And truly it was so. Though Uncle Tomori was going over the ground with his broom, actually the thorny broom was scratching the back of the cowherd who had set the bull against him. The old man then said, "Never dare you do your trick with the bull again, since I am more skilled in magic art than you are, and I shall certainly destroy you if you try once more to set the bull against me."

· 49 · *Uncle Gyuri's Bulls*

In far-off days there lived an old cowherd at Karcsa. They called him Uncle Gyuri. When he got a bit tired of herding and felt like having a drink, he left the herd to itself on the pasture and came into the village to visit Nátán's inn. There he would have a few drinks in the company of his comrades and the village bosses.

"Well, Uncle Gyuri," one of them said to him, "who's looking after the herd now?"

And he said, "Do not worry. Good care is being taken of them."

They were laughing at this answer and made fun of the old man. So he said, "Well, you may laugh at me, but I can make two of my bulls walk straight up to the pub and look in at you through the door."

"Sure, we'd love to see that," said the magistrate.

The old man began singing a tune, and as the others were looking out of the window, they saw two bulls coming from the direction of the pasture. Soon they came up to the door and popped their heads through it, bellowing to their herdsman.

"Well, now you can see for yourselves that they aren't left without care," he said.

"Well, well, but how are they going to find their way back to the others?" they asked him.

The old man started the two bulls off, back to the pasture, and he remained with the others in the pub. His comrades warned him that the bulls might go astray and cause damage.

"Never fear," he said.

They could not believe him and thought it best to follow the bulls. But the bulls did not go astray; they went straight back to the grazing herd. And whenever the cows happened to stray on to forbidden land, the people who were watching could hardly trust their own eyes, for they saw one of the bulls get up and go round up the straying cows, just as if it had been their herdsman.

· 50 · *The Herdsman's Dog*

I have heard it from my grandfather. The cowboys' foremen were having a spree at a wayside inn called the Villogó Csárda. Toward sundown they went out to relieve themselves. Suddenly they saw a dog come trotting along the road from the direction of Karcag. They stood there, waiting for the dog to pass the inn. It was going straight ahead, keeping to the road, looking neither left nor right.

When the dog passed them, one of the cowherds said, "Must be on marching orders, this dog."

"What do you mean?" they asked him.

"This dog has got to get to Mezőtúr before the sun goes down."

No one believed that he knew what he was talking about. But he went on, "It has been sent this way."

"How could one send a dog alone to go so far by itself?" they asked him.

"Well, the dog has been sent. And if you want me to make him go back where he has been sent from, I can do it."

"That is impossible."

"Well, let me bet you a hundred *itce* [twenty gallons] of wine that I can make the dog so back where it came from."

The dog was already nearly out of sight. The cowboys accepted the wager, and the man who had offered the bet stepped out on the road and crossing his arms, stood there stock still, following the dog with his eyes. He neither whistled nor uttered a word, just stood there, fixing his eyes on the dog. After he had done so for a few moments, the dog turned back and sat down on its hindquarters and looked back in the direction of the inn. Suddenly it rose and set off, retracing its way to Karcag.

When the cowboys went into the inn to square the bet and drink off the wine, the man who had sent the dog back to Karcag said, "In less than an hour the master of that dog will be here."

The others did not believe him. They were drinking the wine, but were not through half of the hundred *itce* when they saw a man on a grey horse, riding hell bent toward the inn, coming from the direction of Karcag. From the pommel of his saddle hung a brass *fokos* [halberd].

The man dismounted, walked straight up to them, and said, "Who's the interfering fellow who's butting into things which are none of his concern?" But he did not reach for his *fokos*, as the others had theirs at hand and would not have thought twice of making use of them.

The cowboy who had sent the dog back to Karcag then said, "Believe me, no harm was meant on our part. After all, we are all the same kind of men, we are all cowboys and herdsmen." So the newcomer sat down with them and together they tossed off what remained of the wine.

That man was endowed with secret knowledge. He was called Sándor Nagy. In those days there was no medicine to use against rabies in dogs. Sándor Nagy trained his dogs to act as if they had gone mad. He would send them to this or that pasture. The dogs would run into a herd of cattle, sheep, or horses, where they would frighten the animals and bite some of them. The herdsman was, of course, frightened when he beheld a stray dog, probably a mad one—as no decent dog would leave his master— which might infect the herd. So he would go at once to report to his boss that a mad dog had been seen among the herd and had bitten an animal. The boss would send at once for the veterinary, and Dr. Nagy from Karcag would be called to the pasture. He would give orders for the cleaning of the drinking troughs and pour some harmless drug into the water, and for a couple of days the animals would have to be watered with this. Natur-

ally, not a single animal came to harm, and everybody thought a
great deal of the vet and how well he understood his job. Of
course his services were generously paid for because the land-
owners set great store by their livestock and were always willing
to make a sacrifice for their sake. In this way a clever man could
make a lot of money.

SECTION B

THE COACHMAN LEGEND CYCLE

• 51 • *The Magic Whip*

It happened in olden times. There was a manor called Györgytarló. It belonged to the College of Sárospatak, and all that was
needed for the college kitchen was provided by this farm. There
was János, the cartman. He always went with two greys. A pair
of regular sloths these two horses were. One day János went to
Sárospatak to haul coal from the station to the manor. All the
other carts were already loaded when he arrived at the station
with his two greys.

His fellow carters said to him, "Why don't you urge your
horses along, János? You won't get back before tomorrow morning if they crawl along like that."

"What the hell can I do," he said, "if they won't pull? It's
no use to whip them."

By the time he finished loading the coal onto his cart, the
others were already halfway home. As he was feeling a bit chilly
he decided to have a swig of brandy before going home. He
made for the nearest saloon and went in. There was a man in
the saloon, holding a whip. It was a smartly got up whip, with

its handle embellished in fine ornamentation and with a gaudy
tassel to add to its quality.

When the man with the whip saw János swilling down his
brandy, he said to him, "Look here, partner, buy me a drink,
half a decilitre [about one-fourth of a cup], and you can have
this fine whip for it."

"What for? I've got a whip."

"Don't refuse me," the other man said. "Half a decilitre
wouldn't ruin you."

So János ordered two more drinks, one for himself and one
for the other man. They drank the brandy, and the man gave
him the whip.

Then János left the saloon. No sooner had he stepped onto
the singletree, than the two greys set off, and what's more, they
were pulling fast. János didn't know what to make of this. Had
he used a pitchfork to prod his horses they would never have
run like that before. And now he hadn't even touched the driving reins, and fast as the wind the two greys were going. And
just to think, some ten quintals [one metric ton] of coal had
been loaded onto the cart, so that all in all, taking into account
the heavy cart itself, it was a good fourteen quintals for the
greys to pull along. And all the way they were going at a brisk
trot.

So he sat there, loosely holding the reins, not so much as touch-
ing the whip which he kept stuck in the whipholder at his side.
By the time the others got back to the manor, János had already
unloaded his coal, for he had soon overtaken the other carters,
though they had been more than halfway home before he
started. Having finished the unloading, he unharnessed the
horses and took them into the stable to tie them up. Then he
made for the ladder to bring fodder from the loft. As he put his
foot on the first rung, the horses pushed him off. He looked
down and saw that his new whip was already in its place, hung
on a hook. Then he turned to look at the horses and saw that
the manger had been filled with hay and the two greys were
feeding quietly on it. When they had had enough, János took the
pail to give them water, but the horses knocked the pail out of

his hand. When he looked about, he beheld a pail of water before each horse.

Yet it never occurred to him that there might be some black magic in all this, and that it had been the doing of his new whip.

Next morning, when he went into the stable to curry the horses, they kicked the currycomb out of his hand and did not let him come near them. And yet, even before the others had gotten ready to curry their horses, his two greys looked all spick and span, their coats gleaming and spotless.

When the bailiff of the manor saw the two greys, he said to János, "Look here, Uncle János! From today, you're going to drive the coach, and you're going to drive in the chief coachman's livery."

There weren't any horses on the farm now that could run like the two greys, which before had been the slowest moving beasts in the neighborhood. But after serving two years as the head coachman, Uncle János was getting tired of it. Besides, he was growing old, and it was not easy to rein in the two fiery horses. They always carried the coach at full speed, though he never so much as touched them with the whip, which he had kept at his side, stuck in its holder.

One day, when he went with the coach, carrying the bailiff to Sárospatak to report on the farm accounts to the college, Uncle János paid a visit to the saloon. There he stepped up to an old carter and said to him, "Don't you want to have that whip, brother? I wouldn't mind selling it to you." János had realized that there was some magic in his whip.

"Well, what would you want for it? I might pay you two pints of brandy, if you'd call it a deal."

János gave his whip away for two pints of brandy. When he got home and took the harness into the stable, he found the whip in its place, hung on the hook. "Well," he said to himself, "I'm not going to worry over it. I'll try next time to get rid of it."

After a lapse of time, it happened that some business called János to Sárospatak. He went to the saloon and sold his whip, this time for just one pint of brandy. When he came home, the whip was again on the hook. He could not account for the way it always got back after he had sold it at the saloon.

The third time, he sold it for only one decilitre. But again the whip hung on the hook when he got back. "Well," he said to himself, "confound it all. I'm going to sell that darned whip for as little as I gave for it."

It was after quite a long time, a couple of years or so, that János had to go to Sárospatak again. He went to the saloon and when he saw that one of the cartmen had taken a fancy to the whip, he sold it to him for half a decilitre of brandy. The man offered to pay more, but he did not want to accept more than that.

But when he was driving the bailiff back to the manor, the two greys went at a snail's pace, because the whip was no longer there to make them run. Only as long as János possessed the whip did the horses pull fast, trotting along briskly. But when he sold the whip for a dram of brandy, it never again came back to him, and the two greys became as slow as ever they used to be.

• 52 • *The Magic Calk*

There was a head coachman in the service of the count living at Berkesz Manor. Some thirty good horses, to be used only for the count's coach, were under his care. But he never even so much as touched any of them because there were a lot of grooms whose duty it was to look after the horses. They fed and curried the horses and harnessed them to the coach when the count drove out. The coachman had nothing else to do but get on the box and drive the horses. Now the coachman was a man possessed of secret knowledge.

There was a man once who was working on the roof of his shed. He was covering the roof with thatch. One day when out driving the count, the coachman—called Mihály Dajka—had to pass this shed on his way, and the four horses suddenly stopped dead and stood as if nailed to the spot. The coachman tried everything to get his horses to move on, but they wouldn't stir.

Wondering what was the matter, the coachman looked up at the man working on the roof of the shed. He called up to him, "I say, my friend, let us pass on our way."

But the man up there pretended not to hear him.

Again the coachman called up to him, "I say, my friend, let us pass on our way."

The man then looked down and said, "What's that? What's the matter with me? To be sure, I'm not holding your horses to keep them from going on. Or do you mean, perhaps, that I should be pushing on your coach?"

"Not at all. You needn't push my coach. Just let us pass on our way."

"Well, go on, if you can."

The coachman listened to him without saying a word. He always carried in his pocket a spare calk so that he might fix it onto one of the horseshoes, to prevent the horse from slipping. He drew forth the calk from his pocket and fixed it to the end of one of the four lashes of his whip. Cracking his whip, he lashed out at the horses. At once the horses began to pull, going off at a steady trot. The very minute that he lashed out with the whip, the man fell from the roof. The calk had knocked out one of his eyes, though the coachman had not touched him with his whip. The count was in the coach, and he saw it all with his own eyes.

Here is another story about Mihály.

This happened on a Saturday in Easter week. The count was called away by a telegram. The telegram had been delivered late, so he gave orders to Miska Dajka, the head coachman, to drive up to the manor house at once as he wanted to catch the eight o'clock train at the station of Kisvárda. It was a good eight miles' distance from the manor house at Gégény to Kis-várda. The count rang up the stationmaster to ask him about the train.

"Well, sir, it has just pulled out," the stationmaster told him.

The count got into the coach. "Well, Miska, we've just missed the morning train."

"Never mind, sir! We can catch up with it at the next flag station which is at Demecser."

So they drove off at once, and the count arrived in time to get a ticket and get on the train. Miska drove back, but halfway to the manor one of the horses nearly collapsed. When later he led the horses into their stable, one of them went in, but the other dropped dead. As soon as the count came back home, the coachman reported to him that Lancsi, the dapple horse, was dead.

"Well, Miska," the count said to him, "let's not worry about it more than we can help, but you must tell me how it happened. One of them had been all of a sweat, but not the other horse. Could you tell me the reason why?"

"Well, sir, there's no denying it that Lancsi was as good as dead when we'd got halfway home, but I managed to bring him home."

"You brought him home, didn't you?"

"Yes, sir, I did."

"Well," the count said, "so that's that. Now listen! We're still in the early part of the year, my son; you'll get your year's wages, but mind that you keep out of the stable."

"All right, sir. It can't be helped, I must do as you wish. To-morrow, as soon as my portion of life [wheat paid in kind to farmhands] has been measured out to me, I'll move home, and I shall never set foot on the manor again. All my life I've been a coachman, and that's the only job I mean to do. It's for you now to find somebody to drive the coach."

And so it happened. The count paid Miska a year's wages, and Miska left the manor. But what next? The count had a lot of horses. Twelve grooms had been looking after the horses, feeding and currying them. But after Miska's departure, not one of the grooms could go near the horses. Whenever the grooms appeared with hay and water, the horses would jump so that you'd think they'd hit the ceiling, and then they would bite and paw the ground and kick out in a frenzy. There was no way to get them under control, neither by using a halter nor by any other means. Finally, the steward of the manor had to be sent for, so that he could see for himself what was going on in the stable. The grooms reported to him that for the past three days the horses had taken neither a bit of fodder nor a drink of water, and that all of them would soon perish if this went on for long. They said that there was nothing else to do but to send for Miska and call him back.

Next day a man was sent for Miska. "Uncle Miska, you must come back at once."

"At whose order?"

"At the count's order."

"Well, boy, I won't take any notice of it. Go back and tell the count that you haven't found me at home."

In the afternoon a second messenger came to Miska. He fared the same as the first since Miska took no heed of the count's message. "Go back, son, and tell the count that I shan't return until I hear the same voice calling me back that ordered me to leave. Should the count take the trouble to come here in person to call me back, I might return and see what could be done with the horses."

Then the count himself went to call him back and said, "Come back, Miska, and you shall have your old job as long as you live; and when you get old, you'll get a pension, and I shall always see after your needs. Only come back at once, because all my horses will perish if you don't."

So Miska went with the count and together they drove back to the manor. Miska made for the stable. It was a mighty big stable, kept clean and in order, with the name of each horse written over his stall. When he went in he found the horses in a frenzy.

"Get me that whip, the one with the snapper." And promptly he made use of it, lashing at the horses sideways. "The plague on you! What the dickens has come over you? Here! Now let them have their feed and drink. I dare say they're not going to refuse it. It's only that you haven't been looking after them in the proper way."

And for another three years Miska was looking after the horses. When he grew old, the count gave him a pension, and there was no disgrace in his going away, and it was right to take on another man in his place. All the same, if at that time he had not been called back, all the count's horses would have perished.

That's a fact, and there's no lying about it. True, I haven't been there myself, but I've heard it from men who wouldn't tell a lie.

I was there myself once when a man said to Sanyi, Miska's son, "You owe your fine horses to the magic of your father."

"There wasn't any black magic about the old man," Sanyi said. "Maybe your horses can turn out just as good."

"Then tell me the secret of your old man."

"Well, in spring when the flies and butterflies begin to try their wings and flit over the fields, go out and look for one with a red wing and try to catch it, even if you have to follow it across seven boundaries. And when you've got hold of it, cut your ax into the tongue of your cart, and push that butterfly into the split."

As a matter of fact, I have never tried it myself, because I have a fear of such things.

·53· *The Count's Horses*

When my father and his brothers were just little kids, they used to gather round my grandfather, and they often heard him telling about men who could use black magic. Nothing was impossible for such men. They could turn any man into a horse, just by sheer witchcraft.

There was, for instance, a coachman in the service of a count. He had seen long service on the manor and was possessed of secret knowledge. It was by means of his magic powers that he once played a trick on the count.

One day he sold the count's horses. Then he went into the stable and filled some sacks with straw, so that they looked like horses. Then he did something to the sacks, and they turned into horses. He harnessed them to the carriage and used them just as if they had been horses when he drove out with the count in the coach.

It happened once that the count became angry with him about

something and fired him. He took his belongings and left the manor. Next morning the count went to the stable. There wasn't a horse in the stable. What on earth had happened to his horses? He looked about, but he saw only four sacks there. He kicked them; there was only straw in the sacks.

"What did he do to my horses?"

The count sent for the *pandours* [soldiers serving as police], and with them he went to the coachman's cottage. When the coachman came out, the count said that he would send him to the gallows if he didn't tell him at once what he had done with the horses.

"What horses? There they are in the stable."

"They aren't there. There are only four sacks filled with straw."

"Well, four sacks and four horses."

"I've told you, there are no horses there, just four sacks."

"Well, we'll see. Let's go there right now, and if we find the horses in the stable, then I'll be asking for your head," he said to the count. "Well, how about it? Will you send me to the gallows, or do you want to take me back into your service?"

"I'd rather have you back," the count said.

"You can count me out. And I am not going back to the stable either. I'll stay here, and that's that."

But the count and his wife wouldn't leave it at that, and they were after him until they persuaded him to have a look at the sacks.

He drove back with them and at once made for the stable. Inside the stable he gave a kick to each sack, one after another. As he kicked them a shiver went through the sacks, and they changed back into horses.

"Well, sir, are these sacks or horses in your stable?"

Such wizardry gave the count the creeps, and a cold shiver went down his spine. He was more dead than alive when they carried him back to the manor house. They sent at once for the doctor who had to do a great deal of doctoring to revive him. When he felt better, he took counsel with his wife as to what they should do about their coachman. Would it be better to have him hanged, or should they take him back into their service?

The count's wife said, "Don't let him be hanged, because you couldn't kill him. He's a devil, and you can't take a devil's life. He might do some terrible harm to us or might turn us into heaven knows what. Otherwise he is not a bad fellow, so do not take his life. Pay him more than before and let him come back."

When he recovered the count sent word to the coachman by his house steward that he was willing to take him back into his service and would send a carriage for him, so that he could move back at once.

The coachman replied to the count's offer, "If the count is willing to double the sum he paid me before, I will go back into his service. If not, then the answer is no."

The steward went back and reported to the count that if he wanted to have the coachman back, he must pay him double as much as before.

"Go at once with a carriage and bring him back."

A cart was sent for the coachman, and he came back to the manor. And they lived happily ever after; nothing ever went wrong, neither in the manor house nor with the livestock. And the count increased in wealth and became so rich that he could hardly take stock of his many possessions. True, he wondered quite a lot why all this should have come about through the devil.

• 54 • The Carter and His Wheel

It was the practice on the farm for farmhands to have their quarterly wages measured out for them in kind. But there were only two mills at Nagyvázsony, and these two were not capable of coping with all the milling to be done. Some of the wheat, therefore, had to be carted as far as Veszprém and Füred. Once it was my turn to go with the carters. All in all, six carts, well packed with grain, started off to the mill at Veszprém. Some carts had women as well as men on them, but it was mostly men that went along.

Coachmen are wont to stop at every inn on their way, and when we came to Tótvázsony six of the carters went into the inn, known as the Highwaymen's Inn. One of the carters hadn't any money on him, but he ordered drinks for himself when the others were drinking. And when the innkeeper asked him to pay for his drinks, he said, "Just wait till I come back and I'll pay you from the money I get for my wheat." But the innkeeper wouldn't hear of it and asked him for a sack of wheat. The man refused to give him wheat. So the innkeeper went outside to the man's cart and, raising the back of the cart with a big log, removed a back wheel and took it away. When the carter came out, he saw that one of the wheels was missing. However, he didn't say anything about it, but thought to himself, "If you've taken it, you can just as well have it. I'll see to it that you return it to me."

The women soon came out with the other carters, to proceed on their way. They saw that a wheel had been removed from the man's cart. The innkeeper was watching them from the door. The man with the missing wheel still didn't utter a single word, but his companions wanted to give the innkeeper a sound thrashing unless he returned the wheel. But the carter said they should not do this as he would find his wheel, and urged the others to set off without him as he would soon be following them.

They left, and the man was soon following them. Though he set off without the fourth wheel, the axle stayed in its place, and the cart rolled along on three wheels. I know it, because I was sitting on that cart. After a while the man said to me, "Take a look back. Can you see something?" I looked back, but I didn't see anything at all. After a quarter of a mile, he said again, "Take a look back. Can you see something?" And then I really saw something coming after us, kicking up the dust on the road, but still too far off for me to see what it was.

"Well, that's the wheel, coming after us," the carter said.

After a while he said again, "Take a look back. Can you see something now?"

And then I saw quite clearly that the wheel was rolling after us in a cloud of dust. But strangely enough there was nobody with the wheel. It came faster and faster, and with a noise as if it were being blown by a whirlwind. As soon as it had caught up with us, it clicked into its place and the cart rolled quietly along till we came to Veszprém.

The others didn't know how to account for this strange occurrence and were no end astonished about it. As soon as they had unloaded the grain they set out for home. They went as fast as they could until they got back to the inn. There they found that the cellar door had been smashed to pieces. People were standing around the door wondering what had happened and what the innkeeper would be doing with all his wine lost.

It turned out that when the innkeeper had removed the wheel he had locked it away in the cellar. The wheel had begun revolving by itself and had gone rolling against the door. The first time it failed to break through, and, as it rolled back to dash again and again at the door, it had smashed into the casks and tore them open. Soon the cellar floor was flooded with wine, so that you could see a proper wine pond in it and wade in wine ankle-deep. At the great noise the innkeeper came running down into the cellar. When he tried to go inside, the wheel made a final effort, dashing at the door with such force that it broke through; then it went rolling down the road after the cart.

So when the carters came back, the innkeeper demanded that the carter pay him the damages done by his wheel. But the man said, "It's my duty to pay you for my drinks," and paid him for the five pints, declaring that it was all he owed him and that the innkeeper had no rightful claim for more. The innkeeper broke into abusive language and raised his fist to hit the carter. But a powerful blow to his ear sent him sprawling on the floor. He rose and went at the man, but two more blows to his face brought him once more flat on the floor. But it was not the carter nor anyone of his companions who dealt out this punishment. The innkeeper rose heavily to his feet and left them without a word.

The carters went home, but I was burning with curiosity to learn how it happened that the innkeeper had been struck, though I heard only the sound of it and hadn't seen anyone do it. On our way home, I kept on asking the carter what he knew about it and begged him to give me the explanation.

"I cannot tell you, son," he said. "It's a secret which must not be revealed."

However, I was itching to find out the truth and never missed asking him about it whenever I had a chance to talk to him.

Finally, hearing certain rumors, I began to think that he had a devil and said so.

"Well, son," he said, "I shan't have it for very much longer; I'm going to get rid of it."

One day, it was on a Sunday—being a farmhand it was his free day—he up and goes to the woods, taking a hand drill with him. He made for the forest, which lay a mile and a half across the boundary of our village. When he reached the thickest part of the wood, he took his drill and began boring a deep hole into a birch tree—a black birch it was. I was still a young boy at that time, and I was trailing him with one of my buddies, though we kept a good distance between him and ourselves. When we saw him working on the tree, we drew back so that he would not see us. When the hole was deep enough, we saw him draw forth a small box from his pocket. He pushed the box into the hole and then from another pocket he pulled forth a sort of plug which he fitted tightly into the hole. This done, he took to his heels and ran for dear life back to his village. An infernal din and racket came from the tree as he was running away from it. As soon as he got across the boundary and reached the edge of his village he collapsed on the ground. "Thank God! I'm safe now!"

From the tree a voice called after him, "You doggone skunk! You can call yourself lucky to have escaped me by running away, or I'd have fixed you."

But the carter had crossed the village boundary and was safe. The devil had no power over him beyond the edge of the woods. That's how he got rid of the devil.

Knowledge Obtained at the
Crossroads

I've heard this from János. He served on the squire's manor.
There was a carter on this manor. He always drove a fine big
horse. János slept in the stable, together with this carter, and had
noticed that the man had never once fed or curried the horse.

He thought it was odd and asked the carter about it. "How is
it that you never curry the horse?"

All the carter did to the horse was to pass his hand over its
back, and that very minute the horse would go off like the wind
or pitch off its rider. The carter used this horse to carry water
to the threshers. János used to go with him and help with the
casks.

One day there was a quarrel between the bailiff and the carter.
The dispute arose just before they got ready to go to the threshers.
Until that day they had always taken five casks of water. This
time, the carter said that they would take only two. János wondered why and asked the carter about it.

"Never mind, Jancsi. The two casks will do."

When they went to the stable to harness the horse, they found
it in such poor state that they could hardly manage to get him out
of the stable.

"What's the matter with the horse? What the dickens has
come over this doggone beast?"

Well, when they had filled the two casks with water and
wanted to set off, the horse was not able to pull the cart. The
bailiff saw that and stepped to the carter and said he was sorry
for his harsh words.

János saw that the carter had a piece of rag in his hand and
that he passed it along the sides of the horse. And when he led
the horse back into the stable, and passed the rag once more along
its back, suddenly it seemed to come to life and it looked as fiery
as a *táltos* horse.

János would have liked to obtain such secret knowledge as the carter possessed and asked the man to let him in on it, so that he too could make use of it at home with his horses.

"Well, I can tell you how to go about it, but I'm sure you'd back out before you had gotten through with it."

"I don't think so. Just let me hear it!"

"Well, then go out to the crossroads, and there you will learn what you want to know. But mind that you go three nights in succession."

And János had made up his mind that he would go to the crossroads. He knew the place, it was where a crucifix stood by the roadside. But before going he wanted to talk it over with the old shepherd, a wise old man, who served on a nearby farm.

When the shepherd heard what János had in mind to do, he said to him, "I see, old boy, you've already made up your mind to go. But be careful and do not bring yourself to ruin. If you really want to go, you must take along a piece of blessed chalk, and when you come to the crossroads, you must draw a big circle around yourself. And should you drop terror-stricken on the ground, take care that you remain inside the circle. And then you'll see who it is that comes to meet you."

János took leave of the shepherd and went to see his foster mother. He told her about his intention of going out to the crossroads. She was all against it at first, but finally she gave him a piece of blessed chalk and a bunch of protective grass (being the village midwife and medicine woman, she possessed these things).

So János set off one night, and when he came to the crossroads, he drew a big circle with the chalk around himself.

The first night he did not see anything in particular. Nor on the second night. On the third night—it was about midnight— he beheld a big snarling dog running straight up to him from the direction of Olaszi. But the dog dashed past the circle. Then, suddenly, the sound of trampling reached his ears; a herd of fillies came running up to where he stood. He thought that they would run him down. But when they reached the circle, they turned and took off in another direction. Then he saw a big, vicious bull making for him, with his horns ready to butt him.

"The beast will toss me up and send me flying straight out of this circle," he thought to himself. But when the bull reached the circle, it gave an angry roar and then turned and ran away. Soon he beheld a regiment of soldiers drawing closer and closer. A whole army it was, with the artillery, the infantry, and the hussars marching straight in the direction where he stood. But they too passed by. And then a fine glass coach came driving up, pulled by six fiery horses. There were gentlemen sitting inside the coach, and what fine looking gents they were.

"Hullo, Jancsi!" And they reached their hands out to him when the coach stopped at the circle.

"Come on, friend! Step out of the circle and come nearer to us, as you were so eager to make our acquaintance."

"I won't step out of the circle, because I know very well what you're after."

"Oh, do not fear us, Jancsi. Come here and let's make friends."

But when their time was up, they bawled at him, "Just wait and see, you doggone scoundrel! We'll fix you for having bluffed us."

János went home and went to bed. But every night thereafter he was taken by them and carried to the Mancsalka (a hill at the edge of the village, known as the Evils' Haunt). There they had their midnight merriment. They pressed János to repudiate God and the Blessed Virgin, and to give up going to church.

"I wouldn't do it for any horse," he said.

And he went to his foster mother to seek her advice, because he felt terribly ill. And finally he made a clean breast of it all and told the old woman how he had been dragged away to Mancsalka Hill night after night, and how he had been tortured there and make to suffer such agonies that now he had come to the end of his rope.

After that she went to see him as often as she could and, sitting at his bedside, she prayed for him. But as soon as she went away, he was dragged again and again to the hill.

"Oh, you good-for-nothing lad. So that's why you've asked me for a piece of blessed chalk," she said scornfully.

And as she couldn't think of any other way to help him, she

went to the priest and told him about János' trouble. The priest was horrified to hear about it and said he should confess his sins, as that was the only thing that might help him. So János confessed to the priest, and after that the devils tortured him no more, and he was left in peace.

János died last year. He told me himself about these things and said that every word of it was true, and that it had all happened in his lifetime. He also said that he wouldn't swear to its verity, but it was up to anyone to try it for himself, if he thought it wasn't true.

SECTION C

WITCHES

· 56 · The Witch that Came with the Whirlwind

There might be a witch in the whirlwind. My grandfather told me about it. They were harvesting wheat. He and his partner were having their midday meal, sitting under a shock of wheat. Well, to make it short, as he was sitting there and eating, a nasty whirlwind came sweeping along, knocking over a group of shocks. When it reached the shock under which he was eating, my grandfather threw his knife straight into the center of the whirlwind. And immediately he made a search for his knife. But there was no knife. What had happened to it? Where had it gone? For all he knew, it had vanished into thin air. It was no use wasting his time looking for it.

When winter came, he went to the village one day to visit his friend with whom he had harvested wheat. His friend offered him a snack. "Try this cold bacon, partner."

"Thanks, partner, I'll try it."

"Well, help yourself."

He pulled the plate to him. "Would you like a knife?," his friend's wife asked him, and gave him a knife.

He takes a good look at the knife. "I say, missus, this is my very own knife."

"To be sure, it isn't yours."

"Why, certainly it's mine."

"Well, how did you lose it?"

He said, "When we were out harvesting the wheat at this and that field, a terrible whirlwind came on. I was nearly swept away by it. So I threw my knife into the whirlwind. And since then it has been lost."

"Well," she said, "I tell you what. Never do it again. See! Here's the mark of your knife on my heel. I took your knife away on that day."

That's why I say that there's a witch in the whirlwind.

·57· The Man Who Understood the Language of Animals

There was an old woman. There was a young man called Jancsi. He was in her service. The old woman had a daughter. She had land and jewelry, and plenty of both.

The old woman said to Jancsi, "Go, my son, and plow the fields on the day before St. George's Day. After you have plowed a while, bring me a frog. But it must be the first frog turned up by the plow. And take care that you do not lose it."

Jancsi brought her the frog. Then he kept watching her because he wanted to learn what she'd do with it. She tore the frog asunder. She swallowed one half immediately, and cast the other half under her bed.

At noon when the old woman went out to milk the cows, the boy went into her room. He pulled forth the other half of the frog and ate it. Soon he heard the horse neighing in the stable. Suddenly he understood what the horse said. And from that day he understood the language of every animal.

The old woman came in and looked around for the other half of the frog. She wanted to give it to her daughter the next day. But in the meantime the girl fell ill and died. The old woman was weeping and wailing, but the girl was dead and they buried her.

Jancsi knew that she had been buried with her jewels. He wanted to get hold of those jewels. During the night he dug up her coffin. When the coffin was open, he tried to raise her into a sitting position, so that he would be able to unclasp her diamond necklace, which was fastened at the nape of her neck. But he didn't succeed in getting at it. "Damn you, woman, why won't you sit up?"

At that moment a bone popped out of her mouth. She rose at once. "My! I must have been in a dead sleep."

"I dare say you were."

"Where am I now?"

"In the grave. You've been buried."

Then he took her home, and the two of them fell in love. She told him that her mother had made her eat a piece of uncooked shank bone, so that she might obtain certain knowledge through it.

Jancsi married the girl. Before long the old woman gave up the ghost. But after her death she still visited their house. She appeared in the form of a horse and frightened them with her neighing. She wanted the young woman to die so that she might go with her.

"So that's what you're after, old witch!," said Jancsi, and he drubbed her soundly.

Then, one of the horses—they, too, had been tortured by the ghost—said to Jancsi, "Do not worry, master. Take that piece of dirty rag from that hook over there. It was used by the old woman to wipe the teats of the cow after milking. When she returns, just strike at her head with that rag."

And he did so. When she appeared next time and began neighing, he struck at her head with that piece of rag. She died on the spot and changed back into her human shape; there she was a dead old woman again. He buried her and rolled a big stone over the grave so that she could not leave again through the hole by which she formerly slipped out. And she never returned again to trouble them. Thus Jancsi got the better of the old hag.

·58· *The Witch's Doughnuts*

Well, young folks, come here and sit down around me and listen to my tale. One of these days I'll turn eighty-seven, so you must not blame me for the many slips in my story. Now I will tell you of things which happened a long, long time ago. I was just a small kid at that time, four or five years old. One day a lot of us kids were listening to a story that passed between the elder folks. It was about an old woman who lived at Szerdahely. Well, perhaps not so very old: in her late fifties, but not yet on the wrong side of sixty she must have been. I still remember her name; she was Ma Gurnyicki, and the talk was about the way she could do black magic. Why so? Oh well, even we little kiddies knew about it. We used to say that Ma Gurnyicki was such a one that she could even turn cow dung into curd cheese doughnuts.

Well, Ma Gurnyicki was a wealthy farmer's wife. They had a big farm and everything that goes with it. Where and how she had learned her evil arts, no one could tell. But a great witch she was, who certainly knew how to bake into a cake such disgusting things as I've just mentioned to you.

Well, harvest time had come on. The harvesters went to the fields. The younger folks, as usual, would stay outdoors and sleep around the barns. They found it easier that way to get ready for their early morning tasks.

Well then, Ma Gurnyicki had always got her curd cheese doughnuts ready for her folks when they rose in the morning and set off to the fields. It was quite a long way off from the village to the fields, and the harvesters used to take their dinner with them, bacon and bread, or whatever their means allowed them. Some even had their dinner brought to them from their village homes, that is, if their folks found time to take it to them.

From the Gurnyickis two young couples went, Ma Gurnyicki's two sons with their wives, and her husband, a man in his sixties.

And every morning when they went to the fields they took curd cheese doughnuts with them. It was good food and made a tasty midday meal. In the evening, when they came home, the old woman used to prepare them a nice stew and some other dishes to follow it. But in the morning, it was always the curd cheese doughnuts which the woman gave them for dinner.

One day, one of the two young women—as I've said, there were two young couples, and all of them were living on common bread with their in-laws—thought to herself, "Well, when we come back in the evening, there's never so much as a pinch of curd cheese in the cheese cloth." And truly, she hadn't seen any. And yet, in the morning when they started off, the curd cheese doughnuts, fresh from the oven, were prepared for them. "To be sure, that makes one wonder," she mused. "Not a sight of curd cheese, and yet there are the doughnuts as sure as eggs is eggs."

One evening when the others had gone to sleep that young woman said to herself, "I'll be blowed if I don't catch you out tonight. I'll find out when and how the doughnuts are made."

She kept awake and watched. After a little while, there goes the old woman, lighting up the floating wick (back in those days, folks used to press the gourd seeds for oil and use the oil for lighting) and out she goes into the stable. The young woman was watching her all the while. She saw the old woman walk to the cows and make them get on their legs. She had a large wooden bowl in her hand; this she was holding up to the beasts and gathering their droppings as she went from one to the other. By the time she had finished with the gathering, the oven had gotten hot enough for baking. Then the old woman placed the droppings on the oven shovel and, flattening them neatly into shape, thrust the shovel into the oven. And before long she was ready with a batch of doughnuts for the morning.

The young woman had been a witness to all that her mother-in-law was doing. "So that's what she makes us eat, cow dung! She can turn it into curd cheese doughnuts. But how on earth does she do it?"

In the morning they rose as usual and when they were ready to start off, the plateful of doughnuts was already prepared for them.

When they had their midday meal, the young woman didn't touch the doughnuts. Her husband said, "What's the matter with you. Don't you want to eat any of them?"

"Nor would you, if you knew what they were made of." But that was all she said to him then. In the evening, when they got home and went to bed, she said to her husband, "Just stay awake tonight and you'll learn how your mother prepares the curd cheese doughnuts for us."

They did their evening chores as usual before going to bed. Then they lay in their beds, and the daughter-in-law let her husband sleep for a while. But when she saw the old woman go out to the stable, she woke him and said, "Get up and see for yourself what the curd cheese doughnuts are made of."

He rose and watched his mother. He saw her go to the stable and make the cows rise to their legs. Three milking cows there were in the stable. He saw her leave the stable with the bowl in which she was carrying the droppings of the cows.

"Now follow her and see what she'll do with it."

He went along behind her. She placed the droppings on the oven shovel and flattened them into shape. Then she thrust them into the oven. Soon a batch of doughnuts were ready to take from the oven.

When she had finished with the baking, the old woman went back into the house and lay down to sleep. Only her son and his wife had seen what she had been doing; the others knew nothing about it.

In the morning, as usual, the old woman served them a plateful of curd cheese doughnuts. Her husband was not there when she brought in the plate, only her two sons and their wives were in the room. Her son said, "Why don't you treat yourself to these, Mother."

"What's wrong with them? There are people, and a good many of them, who'd be only too glad to have their fill of doughnuts."

"Indeed, they'd be glad, but not if the doughnuts were made of cow droppings. How do you dare to feed us such stuff?" And he threw the plate with the doughnuts at her feet.

And no sooner had he done this than the curd cheese doughnuts changed back into cow droppings. Whoops! Then what a terrible row they all kicked up! There seemed to be no end to their quarreling. But they took care that no one should hear what was going on inside the house.

Then they sent the old woman packing because they wouldn't have any more of her cooking. They said that the elder daughter-in-law should stay at home and do the cooking for them while they were away working in the fields. But the younger woman knew that her sister-in-law wasn't any better than the old woman because she had already passed on to her some of her evil knowledge. The elder daughter-in-law was a quarrelsome woman, and it put her back up to hear that she should stay at home. She began reproaching the younger woman and said that she was lazy with the milking; that was why she did so poorly with the butter, next to nothing, compared with her own results. The younger woman guessed that her sister-in-law must have worked on the two men, so that they would ask her to take up the daily chores.

So the younger stayed at home and did the cooking. At midday she took their dinner to the field. Next day the elder woman said to the younger, "Well, Sister, tomorrow I'll take you to Bak Hill. And I'll show you where and how these things are done." So next day they went together, and the older woman took a slab of butter with her. There was a well there on Bak Hill, and to that well the two women went. It was called Devil's Well, and when they came to it, the woman threw the butter into the well.

"Come here and look into the well and see what's going to happen to that slab of butter."

For a while, I should say for a quarter of an hour or so, the butter went circling round and round in the well. Suddenly it was all covered up with filth and mess, and overrun by a swarm of nasty little creatures, frogs and water salamanders and lizards, and crawlers and creepers of the most hideous kinds seething around it. All these loathsome creatures were pulling and tearing at the butter and having their fill of it.

"Now this is for you to see," she said to the younger woman. "When I die and our mother-in-law dies, our souls will be dragged away and torn to pieces by the devils, just like that."

"Well if you know it, why did you set up for this kind of thing?"

"Because it helps me to make plenty of milk and butter. But what about you? Do you want me to teach you my knowledge?"

"Well, I must ask my husband what he thinks about it."

"Well, let's be going home then," the older woman said. "And let's pass through your garden first and then we can pass through mine."

A deep furrow running through the center of the big garden divided it into two separate parts. One side belonged to the elder, the other side to the younger brother. The two women went through the part which belonged to the younger couple. Her garden was beautiful, like Eden, all in flower and blossom.

"Well, let's pass through my garden," the older woman said. And as they cut across her garden, whichever way they looked it was a hopeless mess. Infested with moles and mice and hungry gophers, burrowing their way into the earth, and the trees with their maggoty fruit and worm-eaten leaves—indeed, it was a sickening sight.

"You see," she said to the younger woman, "the same will happen to our souls when the devils take possession of them. The Evil One will worm his way into our souls until they are torn to bits. Well, do you want me to teach you my knowledge?"

"Not for the life of me! I'd sooner starve to death before I'd think of getting anything at this cost. And that is what I will say to my husband."

But when they got back to the house, the two men were in a bad state indeed. As sick as a dog one husband, and as sick as a cat the other, and both jaundiced by some terrible ailment.

"What's the matter with you?"

"Oh, those hideous doughnuts have done this to us. If you don't help us we'll be soon dying."

And for a long time they were ailing and suffering from the effects of that loathsome and disgusting food. They grew so feeble that they were not able to go on with their work and finish harvesting. A couple of farmhands had to be sent for to do the rest of the work.

Well young folks, you've heard my story; it's for you to pass it on to others.

SECTION D

OTHER PERSONS ENDOWED WITH EXTRAORDINARY KNOWLEDGE

• *59* • *Three Funny Stories About Magic*

I

Well, then, I'll tell you about Uncle Szabó. Not just because I want to make you laugh. Oh no! They are true stories. At least, that's what folks say. Anyway, who would doubt the words of such an honest and godly man.

Well, here goes his story.

When I was young, I spent most of my time fishing on the Túr. One night, it must have been around eleven or half an hour past it, strains of merry music struck my ears as I was fishing near the bank of the river, under a weeping willow. I had just taken a dip in the water and was taking some rest on the bank, near the foot of the bridge. When I looked about, I beheld a wedding party walking up behind me. They were making merry and dancing to the tunes of the musicians. When they caught sight of me they asked, "Shall we tie it or untie it?"

I was afraid that if I said, "Tie it," they would tie me to the tree under which I was sitting. So I said, "Untie it!" And in less than a wink they had finished undoing the meshing of my net. But that was not all. They insisted that I should join in their dance. And no sooner did I get on my pins than a buxom brunette was thrown into my arms. The musicians were playing tunes which tickled our feet, and soon we were all shaking our legs in a lively dance. As soon as midnight came they suddenly stopped and the whole party made off. But that comely female was left with me. So I called after the others to ask what I should do with her. They called back to me, "Just push her away if you have had enough of her." I pushed her away, and in a wink she turned into a piece of flotsam wood.

But there's something else I want to tell you. While we were enjoying ourselves at the feast, platefuls of doughnuts were brought to the guests. I too had some of them and thought that it would be nice if I took a few home for my wife.

So when I got home I gave her an account of the things that had happened during the night, but when I reached into my pocket for the doughnuts, there were none; there was just a ball of horsedung in it. "Now you see, wife, what sort of wedding feast that was."

And what's more, I had to make a new net for myself.

II

There's another one about Uncle Szabó. Apart from fishing, he had a great passion for hunting, too. It happened once that he was invited to Halmi by some gentlemen, to go hunting with them. Well, I want you to remember, because it's important for this story, that there was plenty of game thereabouts: fox and wolf and rabbit, and as many as you could wish, and even a bear would sometimes turn up. In those days, game bred rapidly in the nearby wood; and so Uncle Szabó accepted the invitation and went to Halmi.

When he was walking into his host's house, he found the guns side by side, set up in neat order, in the anteroom. As he went past them he stopped at each and blew into their barrels.

Well, then. He entered the room, and his hosts gave him a hearty welcome indeed, though he was only a simple man, cloaked in a *guba* [peasant's cloak]. Well, they sat down to eat and drink, and then the coaches took them to Kökönyösd where the hunt was to be held. Before long the game was beaten up and came dashing out of the woods. There was soon such a cracking of guns that it sounded as if a war were going on. But in spite of all the shooting not a single animal was shot. They just ran off, and the hunters had no bag at all. Uncle Szabó stood there without so much as raising his gun. He just stood and watched the others. They said to him, "What a shame that we have to go home without a single kill. Why don't you knock off at least a rabbit for us so that we can have it cooked for dinner?"

"Well, I heard you boast at the table what crack shots you are, but it seems to me you were all just bragging. I've been watching you, and all I see is that there's no bag. Well then, I see it's up to me to get you one."

No sooner had he said this than a big rabbit came running up. "Get it! Get it!," the hunters were shouting. But this, too, was gone before they could hit it. Uncle Szabó then turned his back to the running rabbit and with his gun pointing backwards he took aim and shot it. And no mistake, folks, there's no lying in that, that's what he did. But there's something else I must tell you. Just listen to me. Soon the game which had escaped their guns came running up toward them. It was Uncle Szabó's doing, he must have done something to make them return. And now the hunters were able to shoot them. And such was their bag, indeed, that it filled two carts. When they had loaded their kill on the carts, they went home. A great banquet was arranged for them, and they sat down to a fine supper.

But that's not all of the story. While they were doing themselves well at the table, the hunters were boasting about their kills. (Shut up there, Marika, and listen to my story!) And Uncle Szabó had to listen to their big talk.

"Well, if you're really so deft with your guns, which of you could pot a hare if there was one in this room?"

"Me" and "Me" and "Me," the hunters were all shouting.

Well, there was a smallish stack of straw in the garden, quite near the house. Uncle Szabó went out and walked to that stack; he took a handful of the straw and made it into a little bundle. Then he tucked it under his cloak and went back to the house. When he stepped through the door, he flung the straw into the room. And there! it turned into a big rabbit. It jumped on the table and stood there moving its ears back and forth. The hunters raised their guns and took aim at the rabbit. But damnation! All their shots went wide. And the big rabbit went jumping from one place to another, from the table onto the bed and back and forth, so that there was no way of getting at it.

"Look here, Uncle! Why don't you pot that damn rabbit?"

Uncle Szabó fired off his gun, and the wisp of straw blazed up in flames. But that's not the end of it all. To be sure it isn't. The best is yet to come.

Well, with the rabbit shot, they finished their supper and went on with their drinking. Soon their spirits rose, and they felt their feet itching to dance. They stood up for a dance, taking hold of each other's hands. "What we need is a couple of musicians to play for us," they said.

Then Uncle Szabó snatched up a piece of charcoal from the fireplace—it might have been some charred oak wood, but I couldn't tell for sure. Meanwhile, the hunters felt more and more like having a dance and were jumping and spinning around the room.

"I'll make you dance, all right," said Uncle Szabó, and with the piece of charcoal he drew a complete Gypsy band on the wall, to the right of the doorpost. "Strike up a tune!," he commanded the band, and the Gypsies broke into such a lively tune that the windowpanes fell out and the doorpost almost popped out of its place. And the band went on playing livelier and livelier tunes, and the gentlemen continued to dance to it. But the dance seemed to have no end, and they began to grow tired. "Send them away, uncle! Make them go!"

"Why so? I've got them here in order to please you. You wanted to dance, didn't you? Now you can go on dancing." And he didn't let them stop. But after a long time, toward morning, he wiped the drawing off the wall. "Be off with you! You're not wanted here any longer."

III

My father knew that man. He was a godly man. And you shouldn't think that all this happened somewhere beyond the beyond.

Well, this man had more cares than you could imagine. The folks used to call him Uncle Szabó. One day he went out to the fields, near the village boundary. From there he called over to the villagers of Turca, "I won't have your bees feeding on my pasture."

But the folks of Turca laughed him to scorn.

"Listen, folks! I'm telling you, I won't have your bees feeding on my pasture."

But they called back in mockery, "Drive them in if you won't have them on your pasture."

"Well, to be sure, I will."

Next day, the people of Turca looked in vain for their bees. The hives were empty; not a single bee was to be found in them. Looking around for them, they saw their bees in Uncle Szabó's farmyard. A cluster of bees was sitting on each picket of the fence. No doubt about it, Uncle Szabó had meant what he said; he had driven the bees in.

"Let our bees come home," the villagers of Turca begged him.

"Not me! Unless you pay me for the use of my pasture."

And after some haggling the people of Turca struck a bargain. Whether it meant that Uncle Szabó would return a couple of bees for a penny, or ten for a farthing, I'm sure I can't remember now. But he asked them for a certain sum, saying that such and such a number of bees were in each swarm. The people of Turca just wouldn't believe that he had got the figures right. Uncle Szabó then counted the bees and flicked them off with his two fingers. And when he had sent off the last bee, it turned out that he had been right; there were exactly as many bees as he had said. And not one of them had stung him. Of course, the villagers of Turca were pretty surprised that he should have guessed right. So now they were willing to pay him ten *forints* a year for the use of his pasture.

Then Uncle Szabó said to the bees, "You may go now." And
the bees flew back to Turca. They couldn't have gone if he
hadn't sent them back home.

• 60 • *The Miller and the Rats*

In the days of old when the mill at Zsáró (also known as the
mill of Borosérhát) was still going, there used to be millers who
ran that mill who were possessed of extraordinary knowledge.

Suppose some fellow who came on business to the mill pinched
some trifling thing which belonged to the miller; well, he'd
soon grow to regret it. I've heard about a man who walked home
with something from the mill. Until that day, there had never
been a rat in his house, nor a single one anywhere near it. But
next morning he could hardly move about because his house
was overrun by rats. This was due to the ability of the miller
who, as soon as he became aware of something being missing,
could send along a horde of rats to the thief's house. "Go now,"
he would say to the rats, "and you shall do damage to that man
not only equal to the value of the thing he has taken, but a
hundredfold its worth."

And that man just could not get rid of the rats until he
returned to the miller what he had taken from the mill. But then
I have also heard of a man in our village of Karcsa who could
deal with the rats. He just kneaded some dough into a ball, and
when he got the paste ready, he grated some of the dough and
then placed the gratings and the dough into a big tureen. At
sundown he took the tureen with the dough and went to the
man whose house had been overrun with rats. He stopped in
the farmyard, but neither on his way to the house, nor when
he got there, did he give or return a greeting to anybody. When
he got into the farmyard, he turned his back to the house and
threw the dough with his left hand behind his head, while he
called out loudly, "This way, my dear guests, please come this
way!"

And he walked out of the yard and as he went, he was throwing the grating behind his head. The rats followed him, unseen to human eye. And he said to them, "Well, my dear guests, let's go from here to some other place."

And when he got them well out of the village, he said to the other fellow that he possessed greater magic than the miller who had sent along the rats to his house.

Then he called to the rats, "Well, my dear guests, I'm going to take leave of you, but not before I throw these gratings to you, so that you may have your fill of them. But when you've finished eating, you must go back to the mill at Borosérhát, and during the night you must knaw into the pillows under the miller's head and into the eiderdown under which he sleeps."

And in the morning the miller woke and found himself lying in a sea of down, as the rats had gnawed through his pillows and his eiderdown.

This sort of sorcery used to happen in times past.

· *61* · *Why Men Grow Old*

There was once a man possessed of such extraordinary knowledge as no other man in this world has ever had. Well, he hadn't done much work throughout his life. One day as usual he got up in the morning, washed, had his breakfast with his coachman, and then said to him, "Hitch the horses to the coach. I want to drive out."

The coachman pulled up before the house and his master took his seat at the back and the coachman took his on the box, in front. They drove off, but they didn't follow the roads; they went cross-country through the pastures and fields. It was always this way when they were out driving. Well, after a long time it happened that when they were driving out again and were crossing over the meadows they passed a nice grassy patch in a hay field.

The man then said to his coachman, "Let's stop here!"

The coachman brought the horses to a halt. His master said, "Here, take this small box. Get off the coach and put that big frog which is there on the road inside the box."

The coachman said, "Oh, guv'nor, I'm scared of it."

"There's no need to be scared of it. Move on and get it into the box."

There was nothing to do but obey, and with the help of the handle of his whip the coachman managed to push the frog into the box. It was a toad, and so big a one that there wasn't anything like it under the sun. When he got the toad safely into the box, his master said, "Well, get in your seat and let's drive home."

They were coming up the road, driving homeward. Before long they came to a roadside inn to the right of the road. The master called to his coachman, "Let's stop here!"

The coachman brought the horses to a halt.

"Well, you can unharness the horses and feed them, and when you're done with them, you can come in and have something for yourself."

He did as he was told and then went into the inn. His master had already cut out a piece of the toad, a nice big piece it was, about palm-size. And two slices of toasted bread were lying beside it on a plate before him.

"What will you drink?" he asked the coachman.

"Well," he said, "I could do with a swig of brandy."

When he drank his brandy, his master said, "I want you to roast that bit of frog meat on a spit for me. And there are two slices of bread for the drippings. But mind you that you do not taste it or you'll die."

The coachman went out to roast the frog on the spit, and as he was turning it over the fire and holding the slices of bread to catch the drippings, he thought to himself, "If my master can eat it without coming to any harm, why should I die of it?" And he took a taste of it. But his master knew that the coachman had tasted his food.

When the man got the meat, he went in and placed the roasted frog and the bread on the table. His master ate it with great relish, and then they set off to drive home. On their way back, as they were driving through the fields, they heard the grass talking to them. One of the blades was saying, "You can make such and such medicine of me;" and the other blades were all talking as well, saying, "You could make of us this and that sort of medicine." And thus, while they were driving home, his master obtained secret knowledge which would enable him to prepare drugs that would turn him into a youth of eighteen again, though he was well on in his fifties.

When they were back at home, the master said to the coachman, "Well, Pista my son, listen to me; you must cut me up into pieces, make them as tiny as you can. Then cram them all into that big twelve-liter jar which we use for pickling cucumbers. Then tie up the mouth of the jar. When you've done that, take it to the dung heap and dig a big hole there, then leave the jar in the hole. After nine days you must take it out of the hole."

Well, the coachman did all that his master ordered. But when he went on the ninth day to take out the jar, it was gone. Someone must have stolen it.

Now you see, that's why we have to grow old: it's because we've been robbed of the extraordinary knowledge contained in that jar. If it had come in our possession, not a man would have ever grown old.

And was there any good in all this for the coachman? Nothing at all. Never again did he hear the grass talk to him. And what a pity that he did not come into the possession of that secret knowledge. He might have passed it on to others, and then instead of being seventy-five I'd still be eighteen and I'd be dancing and sowing my wild oats.

· 62 · The Black Bull and the Garabonciás

My grandfather used to tell us about a family who lived in our village. A child was born to them, a boy who was born with his teeth already showing through. It was common knowledge among the people that if it could be kept secret that a child was born with teeth then he would survive, but if they let it out, then he'd die before his twelfth year. So they took great care of the boy, and no one heard about his teeth while he was a child. The boy then reached his twelfth year.

One morning he went out to the pasture where the herdsman, Uncle Peter, was herding the cattle of the villagers. Uncle Peter knew the boy very well.

"Well, sonny, what business has brought you out here?"

"I've just come along to see you, Uncle Peter. It's such fun just to be looking about and hanging around."

"Well, sit down, sonny, and enjoy yourself."

But the boy didn't stay long. "I say, Uncle Peter," he said, "I'd like to ask you to do something for me."

"Let me hear it, sonny."

"Would you back me up in a fight?"

"In a fight?"

"Yes, Uncle Peter. But don't be afraid. Just fill that trough with water. I'll drink up all the water from it. And then you'll see a big black cloud coming from the east. But don't get scared; as I've already told you, there's no reason for you to be afraid. When that big black cloud comes down, you'll see a bull step out of it. The bull will roar and paw at the ground and will kick up earth sky-high. And then you'll see me turn into a bull. I'll take the shape of a white bull. And then I shall have to fight the other one. Now I know that you're a brave man and that you've got a strong cudgel. What I want to ask you is that when we start fighting, go with your cudgel at the other bull's hoofs. And don't spare him, go slogging at its hoofs with all your might. And have no fear of that bull; it wouldn't risk letting me out of its hold. He won't be able to hurt you."

"Righto, sonny. You needn't worry about me; I won't stop short of a hundred and one blows, just to help you pull through."

Well, the boy drank the water that was in the trough, and then he shook himself, and all at once he turned into a bull. A bull of leaden-white color. Uncle Peter walked round him in great amazement. "Oh, sonny, what a strange thing to happen."

Suddenly he sees a big cloud coming on. And next thing, it comes down, right in front of them. And as soon as it comes down, a black, sooty-necked bull steps out of it. And it is roaring, and it is pawing the ground. And in a rage it goes kicking up earth with its hoofs and tossing it sky-high with its horns. And there it goes, straight for the white bull. And they charge against each other, and in what fury they butt against each other! Not under the sun has there ever been such a fight between two bulls. Then Uncle Peter takes hold of his cudgel and up at the black bull he goes, hitting out as hard as he can. And suddenly the big cloud appears again and descends over the two bulls. And in a wink they were carried off in the cloud.

Well, Uncle Peter kept silent about what he had seen. He would not dare to tell anybody about such matters. Anyway, the boy had warned him that on no account should he talk about it to anyone, not even to his parents. And if they came to look for him, Uncle Peter should let them go on with their search and say nothing to them about their son. "After six years I'll come back to you," the boy had said, "and then I'll tell you all about myself."

And it all happened as the boy had foretold. The two bulls were carried off in the cloud. The boy's parents came and searched for him everywhere.

Six years passed, and Uncle Peter was standing at the well one day when a young wanderer, with his satchel slung over his shoulders, came walking up to him. "May God give you a good day, Uncle Peter."

"May God give you a good day, my dear son. I dare say, you've grown into an able lad."

"Well, can't help growing up when one's eighteen."

"Sit down, sonny, and let me offer you a little snack. Here's some bacon and bread. Help yourself!"

"No, thanks, Uncle Peter. But I want to tell you something. I just now passed that house over there on that farmstead. The people living there have a cow; they call her Flossy. I'd have liked to drink some of her milk. I've asked them to let me have a liter or two in a jug, but the woman refused. She swore that she hadn't a drop of milk in the house. I know that she has plenty of milk. She keeps it in a bench chest, and the jugs fill two shelves. And yet she begrudged me that little milk. Now, I want you to witness how I'll pay her back in her own coin. Soon a black cloud will be coming on. And then you'll see what's going to happen."

The boy then left Uncle Peter and withdrew to a nearby reed bank. And in about half an hour the black cloud came on, bringing along a cloud of dust and breaking into a thunderstorm which cast darkness over sky and earth. But on that very spot where Uncle Peter was standing, not a single blade of grass was seen to stir, nor was he touched by that terrible storm. The storm raged over that house on the farmstead. Suddenly, as if seized by a giant hand, the roof was carried off and smashed to pieces at the back of the garden. Then the storm ended.

And then the boy came back to Uncle Peter and said, "Well, have you seen that, Uncle Peter? I have such great power that I can punish the wicked and I can help the just, though it is not my right to do so. But I am a wandering student, a *garabonciás*. My mother has brought me up, and no one knew that I was born with my teeth. And when I turned twelve, I had to slip away from my home without telling even my parents. You see, this is my mission. I go wandering over the mountains and make my way into the most perilous caves. And on the mountains and in the caves, I find such evil ones that if there wasn't a power to destroy them they would do terrible harm and bring the country to ruin. And when I see the evil one gather force, then —look at this book here. I read out of this book, and it will drive him out of the cave. And when he comes out, I get the halter over his neck and I ride him to the top of Szengellő Hill. And there I go on torturing him till he is destroyed. Do you remember that black bull? He was one of them; a sort of a dragon, the offspring of a serpent. Only instead of me going to get him, he had to come after me. Now you know what sort of things I do.

"Well, shall I tell you what happened the other day? As I was going on my way along the road, a cart pulled up beside me. A man was carting grain from the threshers to the neighboring village. I was rather tired, and the driver said, 'Climb on, brother!' So I seated myself on top of the sacks. I was so tired that before long I fell asleep. When I woke, we were driving some five kilometers above the earth. I looked about and saw that the driver was reading my book. And he seemed so utterly lost in it that we might have gone up right to the stars. So I snatched the book from his hand and began reading it myself. And so we landed safely on earth. I said then to the driver, 'I say, brother, never let your curiosity make you look in someone else's book. You see, if I hadn't become aware of it, we would have gone beyond the stars.'"

This is what happened in our village, Berkesz, in Szabolcs County.

•63• *The Dragon Rider*

It happened in a village called Bakonybél. My mother had a yellow-legged, black brood hen. The hen began laying. But not in the nest box. So mother said to the apprentice boy, "Go and look for that hen; to be sure, she's hiding her eggs somewhere."

At the back of our house there was a ramshackle lean-to. At

one corner the wall had tumbled in. There the hen had made a nest to lay her eggs in. But it took us quite a long time to find it. When we discovered that the hen was laying in the tumbled-in shed, mother said, "Let's see if there are eggs or hatchlings there. I want you to bring them in."

My brother took a ladder because the lean-to had a high wall. He went up the ladder and cautiously popped his head through the hole in the wall. There was the hen, cackling and clucking, sitting over its brood. "Come here, mother," my brother called.

"What's up, son?"

"Bring the basket, mother; there's a clutch of chicks under the hen."

"Are you sure there are chicks?"

My brother went a step higher up so that he might get a better look. He reached in his hand and took hold of the hen. Suddenly five small lizards slid off from the nest.

"Come on, hurry up! Let's kill them!" Three of them they managed to destroy, but two escaped and disappeared in the alfalfa field which bordered on our garden.

A week or so later, a young boy came to my mother to inquire about the lizards.

"Why are you bothering your head about them?"

"Because when they grow up they'll be my horses."

"Your horses?"

"Well, not now, they are just my chicks now; but when they grow up they'll become my horses."

"Well, sonny, you must look for them in the hay field. That's where they are hiding."

The boy began weeping and lamenting that the lizards had been driven off to the alfalfa field. A little while later he grew hungry and begged my mother to give him a little milk, "I say, Ma Cartwright [fictive relationship plus vocation as children's term of address], could you let me have a drink of milk?"

"Why, of course, sonny, I've just milked the cow. There's milk enough. But won't you have anything else?"

"No, I must not take anything else but milk and a little bread."

Now this answer made us realize what the boy was, though

there had been already some talk of his being a *garabonciás*. After the boy had eaten, he gathered a heap of shavings in one corner of the workshop and lay down on it. "This will do fine for me. Let me take a good rest, and then I'll be going to look for my chicks." Next day the boy said that after seven years he would come back. Then he took his leave and was gone.

And after seven years—though who on earth would have thought that he really meant it—the boy came back to us. He had grown into a fine lad. Father recognized him at once. "Well, son, have you come back for your hatchlings?"

"To be sure, I have, Uncle Cartwright." Then he stayed with us for three or four days; all this time he would be out and back, or say his prayers, or just wander about the house. One day mother was soaping the linen.

"What are you doing, Ma Cartwright?"

"I want to get the linen soaped today so that I can boil it tomorrow and do the washing the day after tomorrow."

"You'd better hurry up with it, Ma Cartwright. The day after tomorrow, in the afternoon, there will be a storm; you'd better finish your washing before it comes on. The linen laid out to dry might be swept away by the storm."

My mother laughed off his warning. "Young scapegrace, how could you know that a storm will be coming on? [Though mother knew that the boy was a *garabonciás*.] But all the same, I'll hurry up."

"You'd better get on with your washing," my father said; "the boy might be right after all."

Mother then finished the washing during the night so that she could hang out the linen in the morning and get it dried in good time. The boy left us and made his way to the mill at Gerence. There's a bottomless spring there, and people say that a man once sank there with his cart and his horse. Only his hat was seen swimming on the surface to show the spot where he went down in the water.

Well, the boy walked into the mill. The miller's wife was washing linen and drying a lot of hemp spread on the grass.

"I say, you'd better take in your linen and the hemp, Ma Miller, or it might be carried off by the storm."

"How do you know, child?"

"To be sure, there's going to be a storm at four this afternoon. And when it comes it will be so terrible that you won't know where you are."

There was a poor old man, close to seventy, who lived with us. He was called József Sánta [lame], probably because one of his legs was shorter than the other. Father said to him, "Go and follow that boy, Uncle József, and find out where he goes." Both the miller's wife and my parents were getting curious about the boy, though they had only half a mind to believe his words. Well, the boy left the mill, and the old man was following him from a distance. There's a big forest there, some way from the mill. The boy made for the forest. Now the forest grew up the side of a big mountain. I still remember the giant trees and the snowdrops with their double cups that grew there on that mountain. The boy went on and on, and the old man followed him. When he arrived on the top of the mountain, the boy found himself on a level ridge. It was covered with fine silky grass. There was a big rock somewhere near the center of the ridge. The boy stopped and, leaning against a tree, began praying. Then he sank to his knees. He took out a book from his pocket and was praying now from the book. Then he took out of his pocket a piece of leather strap. And as he was praying over the strap, it turned into a pair of reins. By then the sky grew dark, and peals of thunder came rolling by, and the lightning was flashing. The old man was still watching the boy from a distance. "Whatever storm may come, I'm going to stick it out and see what's going to happen," he said to himself. Suddenly the boy walked up to the rock, and a horrible animal stuck its head out from a biggish cleft. In a flash, the boy threw the halter over its neck. But all the while he never ceased praying. Then he pulled out of his pocket a second rein, all the while holding fast to that horrible beast with one hand. Then a second, even more hideous animal came out of the rock. The boy got the bit in his mouth and now he was holding both animals. As they were prancing and trying to break loose, the boy got on the back of one of them.

It was still raining in buckets, and the storm carried off all the linen and hemp which the miller's wife had spread out on the grass. On the mountain, one of the monsters suddenly rose on its hind legs, and then both animals took a leap into the air and like a shot they were off.

Never had there been such a storm in Bakonybél as on the day the *garabonciás* was carried off by the two dragons.

•64• *The Man Who Lodged With Serpents*

One day an old man set forth to his vineyard. On his way there he had to pass a pit—a very deep pit, indeed. This was in wintertime when there was a sharp frost and everything was frozen. When he reached the vineyard, the snow began to fall. It came down in big flakes, as big as your sandals, and it became thicker and thicker as it went on snowing. The man braced himself with a glass or two of wine and decided to wait until the snow stopped falling so that he could go back home. In his shoulderbag he put three bottles of wine which he wanted to take home to his folks. Meanwhile it began to grow dark. The snow reached now to his knees, so he did not want to wait any longer and started to make his way homeward. He had to pass by the edge of the pit, but missing his step on the untrodden snow, he slipped right into the pit. Perhaps he had had a drop too much of the wine; and we must remember that he was not a young man either, and that the snow was slippery and the pit had a sloping wall. No matter how he tried, he went deeper and deeper down into the hole instead of getting out of it. When he got to the bottom, he felt as if he had come to a nice warm place. He looked around and found himself in a small room. Curled up in one corner there was a big snake, as thick as a man's body. There was another snake, just as thick and big as the first one, curled up in the opposite corner. In front of each snake there was a big stone, but it was not really stone, it was salt, a big chunk of rock salt. For a while the man gazed at the snakes, and the snakes stared back at him. He was in a blue funk, then and there, but he could not get out of the pit as the walls were too steep for him to climb.

After he had been there for two days, one of the snakes wriggled up close to him. It did not want to do him any harm, it even rubbed itself against his side. The man took heart at this and when the snake began licking the salt as if it wanted to encourage him to follow its example, the man took a lick at it too. He was hungry, and the snakes seemed to expect him to, so he fed himself on the salt; and as long as the three bottles lasted, he took a good swig at them. As he was not able to get out of the pit, and as he had nothing else to eat, he lived on the salt for the whole winter.

His folks at home made a wide search for him, here and there, but all in vain. There was no trace of him. The short of it was that they could not find him. So what! He was gone for good. And that was that. For a few years they still hoped for his return, but as he did not come back they divided his land and whatever he possessed among themselves. After all, they had lost their father; he had vanished into thin air, and there was nothing to do about it.

One day a *garabonciás* came to the pit to have a look at his snakes. They belonged to him, and he wanted to use them for horses. The pit the old man had fallen into was the very one the *garabonciás* used to rear his snakes. But this time he did not find them strong enough. "You'll have to stay here for another seven years," he said. "And after that perhaps I will find you good enough." Hearing this, the man implored the *garabonciás* to take him out of the pit. But he refused. "Here you stay. This is a good place for you. After seven years you can leave with the snakes. Until then you can give me a hand with these beasts."

So the man had to spend seven years in the pit. Seven years after the day of his first visit, the *garabonciás* came again. This time he brought a pair of bridles. The heads of the snakes were like the heads of horses, so the *garabonciás* had brought two red bridles and two matching reins for them. One bridle and one rein he gave to the man; one bridle and one rein he kept for himself. "Now take this bridle and put it on this snake here, and I am going to bridle the other snake myself," he said to the man, "but take care that you do not miss at the first try when you fix the curb bit into its mouth, or you are a dead man. The beasts will tear you to pieces. But if you are clever enough when you fix the bit, no harm will come to you. When you have done that, you can jump on its back and it will fly out with you from this pit. That's your only chance of ever getting out of this hole."

So it happened. The man fixed the bit and the rein on to one snake, and the *garabonciás* did the same with his own. Riding their snakes, they were soon carried out of the pit. Then the old man got off the snake's back and gave the reins to the *garabonciás*. And off went the *garabonciás* and his two snakes. But all along their way they were followed by a terrific storm with hail which destroyed crops and fruit and all.

So after seven years, the old man got out of the pit. Seven years, you know, is quite a long time, and there were all sorts of changes so that the place seemed just a bit strange to the man, but he still remembered the way to his village and soon he was bound for home.

When he arrived in the village, they recognized him at once in spite of the fact that his beard had grown quite white. But superstition still had a strong hold on people, and they were afraid of him and kept out of his way. He called after them, "Do not be afraid of me. I am a living creature"; but they were scared of him. When he came to his own place, he found it changed too. His sons had divided among themselves what once belonged to him, and nothing was the same as when he had seen it last. Even his own children fled from the house when they caught sight of him. They feared that he had come back to right some wrong which they might have done. So it was only after some time that he was able to make them stop and listen to him. "Don't be afraid of me. I fell into a pit. I can show you which one. And that is where I have been all that time."

So his sons lost their fear and asked their father to live with them. But he had not long to live. He had lived too long on air spoiled by natural gas during the seven years he was kept in the pit. He was no longer able to live on fresh air. It made him die.

·65· *The Grateful* Garabonciás

There was once a *garabonciás*. He looked just the same as any other man. No one really knew exactly what a *garabonciás* was. He was very much like his fellow creatures. But it was common knowledge that a *garabonciás* would be born with his teeth already showing through. If the midwife kept still about it, he'd remain an ordinary human being; but if the midwife let it out that he was born with teeth, the child would leave its home when it turned seven. This happened with the fellow I'm going to tell you about. When he turned seven, he left his parents' house. And from that day he would never have any other food except curdled milk. And not even a slice of bread to go with it.

In those days it was not as things are today, with every drop of milk being carried to the market. What milk people had from their cows in those days was strained, and some of it was made into curdled cheese or put to other use. Six to seven jugs of curdled milk used to be kept in the storage boxes. Of course, owing to his secret knowledge, the *garabonciás* knew about many a thing. Especially about milk; about the houses where people had plenty of milk and where people had none. He would go and ask for a jug of milk, and while he drank the milk he would converse with the folks, and after he drank it he would take his leave. Where his home was, if he had any, heaven only knew. No one had ever asked him, and anyway he wouldn't have told them if they did. But there was a house in the village where he appeared most frequently. In winter and in summer he used to visit these folks because there was always plenty of curdled milk in store.

Then it happened that the *garabonciás* made up his mind to move off to some other parts. So one day he said to the farmer, "I say, guv'nor, for years I've been living on your curdled milk. It is only fair that I should settle my debt. But you must do as I tell you."

Well then, he told them that at such and such a spot—and he told them exactly where it was—they would find a small iron box filled with money. And they needn't worry about the digging, as it was only about a meter and a half under the ground. But the digging must be done at midnight. "And," he said, "there will be a big millstone or a mill wheel, circling above your heads, hanging only by a single hair. But do not be afraid, it will not fall. That single hair will not snap. Just go ahead with your digging. But remember that while you are at it you must not stop to think what you are going to buy or do with the money."

So the three of them, two men from the house and their next-door neighbor, a poor doltish sort of fellow, set off together. "We'd better take him along," one of the two men had said. "For just a spot of money we can make him do the digging for us." So they went together to ask their neighbor to dig up the box for them.

When the poor man had dug down deep enough and the box became visible, they saw that it had three handles; one on each side and one on the top. The poor man kept on digging until he was able to lift the box, pushing it upward so that the two men could take hold of it by the top handle. As soon as they got hold of it, they said, "He can wait till he sees a cent of it." No sooner said than the box seemed to jump from their hands and went hurtling back into the hole. The poor man who was holding on to the side handles couldn't let go of it, and as the box went down deeper and deeper, he went with it. The box crashed along through the earth, breaking a hole through the ground so that the poor man was able to go with it. How long the man and the box went on and on, I could not tell you. Suddenly, the box came to a halt. And the poor man found himself in a roomy spot where he could move around a bit. As he was groping around, his hands touched a wall. A brick wall it was.

"Bless my soul, where on earth have I got to? How am I to get out of here?" And as he was pondering over this and that—he might have spent an hour or so in speculation—suddenly he became aware of sounds. Sounds of conversation, of clinking glasses, and of "here's to you", and of kindly invitations to take more drinks.

"God! This must be a wine cellar," he thought and went for the wall and started banging on it with all his might.

Two men were drinking in the cellar on the opposite side of the wall. Hearing the banging they became silent. In fact, they felt mightily scared. When the banging stopped, they took courage and went on with their drinking. And as they took more and more glasses their courage returned. Suddenly they heard someone calling to them, "Hey, brothers, help a fellow creature! Make a breach in the wall. You won't regret it if you help me. All of us will be the better for it."

It took the drinkers some time till they screwed up their courage to make a hole in the wall. Then they pulled the man and the box into their cellar. And then each of the three took a share of the money that was in the box. The poor man gave a part of it to them instead of to his first partners who wanted to cheat him out of his due share.

That's all of it.

SECTION F

Supernatural Beings

· 66 · *The Lover Who Came as a Star*

In Gajcsána, the village where I was born, there lived a man with his wife and daughter. It was my mother, and she was no longer young. I've heard her telling about these people to some of our neighbors.

Well, the man was the village bell ringer. In the evening when he came home after having rung the church bells, he often saw a star coming down, just above his stable. I might as well say his barn, because it had a thatched roof. And then the star came to earth exactly at his barn.

When he got home, he said to his wife, "I say wife, can you make this out? There's a light coming down right on our barn."

Now their daughter always spent the night in the barn. They had put up a bed for her in the barn, and there she slept throughout the summer.

"It seems to me that our daughter is getting thinner and thinner," the woman said. "And she has got sort of a dizzy look too."

"Well," he said, "we'd better get to the bottom of this and find out what's the matter with her."

Next day they called her in. "Well, Daughter, what about you? Is there anyone who has caught your fancy?"

The girl just hemmed and hawed.

"Well, then, are you going out with someone?"

"I am not."

"So there's someone coming to see you, is there?"

"Yes, there is, a young lad; he comes in the evening."

"I see, he comes to you in the evening. And it's that lad you're in love with?"

"Yes, I love him."

"All right, Daughter."

As he was anxious to find out the whole truth, the man decided to be on the lookout for the girl's lover.

When he had done with the bell ringing and returned in the evening, he again saw the same star coming down right at their barn. So he ran to the barn to see what was going on there. Spitting fire, the star came down from the sky. As soon as it touched the earth it took on human form and went into the barn.

Next day, the man called in his daughter again. "Well, Daughter, tonight we'll change places. You'll come in and sleep in the house, and I'll stay for the night in the barn."

"Oh, no, Father, that wouldn't do." And she kept on protesting and protesting. But her father said, "You'll do just as I tell you. Here, you stay in the house, and I'll go out and sleep in your bed."

And he went out, and no sooner had he stretched out in her bed than the visitor came. Of course the father had dressed himself in his daughter's garments before he lay down in her bed. And when the visitor came, he thought it was the girl lying there in the bed and he lay down beside him. And then the girl's father ran his hand along the fellow's leg and discovered that one of his legs was a goose leg. He jumped from the bed and ran out of the barn. The other went in pursuit. But the father ran into the house and locked the door from the inside.

Next evening they made up a dummy woman of straw and dressed her in the garments of the girl. They took the dummy into the barn and laid it on the bed. Then they soiled the dummy's clothes with all sorts of filthy stuff. That night the *lidérc* came again. But when it saw that the girl wasn't there, it started spitting fire in such a fury that the whole barn was covered with a rain of sparks. Three or four nights the *lidérc* came back to the barn. But since the girl now slept in the house, he never again got to her. That was the only way of keeping the girl safe from the *lidérc*, otherwise they couldn't have gotten rid of him.

So that's what I've heard my mother telling to her cronies.

•67• *The Witches' Piper*

My elder brother was piping for some people at a certain place, while another fellow, a man from Etes, was playing for the children at the same house. It must have been on a day before Ash Wednesday. At eleven o'clock or so, the children were taken home. The man who had been playing for them, Uncle Matyi, was paid for his piping. He took leave of my brother and left for home.

On his way home, three women stepped up to him and said, "Come along, Uncle Matyi! We want you to play for us. Let's go to that house over there, at the end of the street. And have no fear, we're going to pay for your piping."

When he went in, they took him by the arms (by the way, the man is still living in the village) and made him stand on the bench near the wall. And there he was piping for them. Money came in showers at his feet. "Gee! I'm not doing badly at all!" he said to himself.

At about midnight, there came a terrible crash, and in a wink he found himself standing right in the top of the white poplar, at the end of the village.

"Damn it! How the dickens can I get down from this tree?"

Suddenly a cart came up the road. When it reached the tree, he called down, "Oh, brother, do help me!" But the man drove on taking no heed of Uncle Matyi. Before long another cart drove up towards the tree. On the cart was Péter Barta, a fellow from Karancsság. "I say, brother, stop your horses and help me get down." The man brought his horses to a halt and said, "Is that you, Uncle Matyi?"

"Damn it, to be sure it's me."

"What on earth are you doing up there?"

"Well, brother, three women stopped me on my way home. They asked me to follow them to a house at the end of the street. When I went in, they made me stand on a bench and there I was to pipe for them. And they've given me a lot of money for it."

When the man got him down from the tree, Uncle Matyi began looking for the money he had tucked into the hem of his *szür* [shepherd's cloak]. But there was no money. There was only a lot of broken crockery and little chips of glass.

Such strange things sometimes still happen.

· 68 · *The Man Who Lost His Shinbones*

There's a family by the name of Pap which lived at Kenézlő. The man's name was Lajos Pap. During the day he went out to work with his horse, and in the evening he took it to pasture. If luck was in his way, he managed to get the horse into the alfalfa field of some farmer. When it had its fill, he took it home. Once he happened to turn out the horse onto a pasture which was reserved for studhorses only. "I might as well let it have its fill and then take it home," he said to himself. So he settled down on the roadside while the horse was grazing. About midnight he fell asleep. The grassy sand of the roadside made a pleasant rest for his head while the rest of his body was stretched out on the road, right across the track. He was half asleep when he heard someone shouting, "Quickly, get up there! Do not lie on the road!"

A cart was driving up with such a strange jingling as he had never heard before. It had never occurred to him that the shouts were meant for him, but indeed they were shouting to him and when the cart drove past, he clearly heard them say, "Stop! Stop! We've lost the stake braces. Both of them."

And they stopped and cut out the shin bones from both his legs, right from the knee to the ankle. That's the honest truth. That man is still alive. You may ask the people at Kenézlő; they all know about him.

Well, when he awoke on the road, he had no shinbones. He crawled home on what was left of his legs. But there was neither a doctor, nor any other man of learning, who could cure him. There was, however, a fortuneteller, a woman, who said that a year to the night when he lost his shinbones, he should go out on the road and lie on exactly the same spot where he was lying then and he'd get back his legs. But he said that he'd much rather live to the end of his life without his legs; he wouldn't go back to that place for anything.

• 69 • The Unquiet Surveyor

I've heard this from János Gyóni of Pácin. He was a cowherd and was out night-herding with his cattle. As he was sitting in front of his hut one night, he suddenly became aware of the rattling of chains and the approaching steps of someone carrying a lamp. Soon he saw a figure near the well, putting down a small table and a three-legged chair. Then he saw him put a big book on the table and settle down to write something. The cowherd walked over to the well to find out who the fellow was. But before he reached the well, the other had already taken off. The herdsman saw him bang shut the book and snatch it up with the table and the chair. And with the lamp in his other hand he ran away. The herdsman chased him the whole night, but he was not able to get near enough to see who it was.

On the edge of our village pasture there is a big pond of water. It is deeper than a full grown man. The herdsman remembered that he had often seen a surveyor around these parts a good many years ago. Now when he saw that fellow crisscrossing the water three or four times, he guessed that it must have been the same surveyor who used to work there. It was the belief of the folks hereabouts that those persons who had gotten their calculations wrong and made bad mistakes in surveying had to return from the grave. So this surveyor fellow was said to have found no rest in his grave, and rumour had it that he came back to the fields to do his measurings all over again. He used to be seen thereabouts quite a lot, some thirty years ago, and one could hear the rattling of his chains and see the light of his lamp.

One day I came across him myself, only he was too far off to be seen. I was on my way home, walking along the road when suddenly I beheld the flickering light of a lamp some one to two hundred meters ahead of me, advancing in the direction of Karcsa. I could make out the rattling of the chains even from such a distance.

When I got home I told my father that I had seen the flickering light of a lamp and heard the rattling of chains and the retreating steps of someone running ahead of me. But I could see no human being whatever.

"I say, it must have been the surveyor," my father said. "It's lucky for you that you didn't get in his way." People still remembered that once a man came across him and the ghost smashed his lamp into this man and afterward he became so ill that he could not leave his bed for a couple of weeks. But such things do not frequently happen in our days. Even if the surveyor were to walk around a bit, it wouldn't give rise to much talk. People would just laugh it off and say, "Our modern world is no place for a haunting surveyor."

SECTION G

LEGENDS THAT HAVE ASSUMED THE FORM OF TALES

·70· *A Dead Husband Returns to Reveal Hidden Treasure*

There was a squire; he was the village boss. He had three daughters. One day the squire said, "I want to go out with the coach, János." János, the coachman put the horses to the coach, and the squire said, "Take me to town."

He drove the squire to the town and then he drove him back. While having his dinner the squire dropped dead. He died without a will. He was buried in the family vault.

One night he appears in his wife's room, lifts her bed, and throws it down. He walks up to the cupboard. He smashes the cupboard to pieces. He thumps on the piano. He drums in the oven. He sweeps off everything he finds in his way. He does the things a ghost is wont to do. There wasn't a moment's rest for the folks during the night.

It was the same for another week or so. The squire's wife gave way to despair. János the coachman had been in the squire's service for a long time, so one day he screwed up his courage to speak openly to his mistress.

"I say, ma'am, would you please tell me what is the reason for your dejection?"

"Look here, Jancsi, it's no use telling you about it as you could not help me."

"Just let me hear it; maybe I can help you. I eat your bread, and I'm going to stick up for you."

"You see, János, since my husband died while having his dinner, I've never had a moment's rest. He's always wandering about, dashing and shattering to pieces everything in the house."

"Pray, ma'am, just let me stay in the house for one night. I'll keep watch in your room and in the squire's. Only let me have a liter of wine."

"That's all right, son, you'll get it." And indeed, she was rather relieved to have someone around who would comfort her and brace her up a bit.

The coachman said, "I'll get hold of him, or I'll talk to him."

Evening came; János watered the horses and then went into the squire's house. He whiled away his time playing cards and, before going to bed, the squire's daughters played the piano for him. When the women retired, he put out the lights and it was quite still in the house. Then he went into the squire's room and sat there, drinking quietly by himself.

Midnight came. The double doors flew open. There the ghost went, straight up to the cupboard, sweeping off everything there was on the shelves. János staring with his eyes wide open, but he just could not see anyone there. When all that was in the room had been swept to the floor, the ghost went from one bed to the other and lifted them and banged them down. Then he began thumping on the piano.

When he had enough of it, he went into his study where János was keeping vigilance. He sat down at the table where János was sitting. János was scribbling away at something, but the ghost just snatched it away. It gave János the creeps.

"Darn you, what are you up to?"

But no answer came. János rose and locked the door. When the ghost's time was up, he left and all was quiet in the house. János stretched out on the sofa and slept till morning. Then he rose and went back into the stable. After a little while, the squire's wife came out to see if the horses had been properly looked after.

János said to her, "Pray, ma'am listen to what I will tell you. Give me a hundred crowns. I will pay them all back to you."

"All right, son. When you come in this morning, I'll give it to you."

When he went to have his breakfast in the house, he told her what he had on his mind. "I say, ma'am, I'm going to show you that I can stop the master visiting the house. But you must do as I tell you."

"Let me hear you, son." The young misses and their mother were indeed anxious to hear him. "Go ahead, János. Let's hear it!"

And he said, "I shall die, ma'am, and you must bury me in the family vault. But take care that my coffin be placed just opposite the master's coffin. And you must not nail down the lid."

They agreed to it and did as he had told them. Word was sent to the bell ringer to toll the knells for János. And the bells were pealing. And the people asked each other, "For whom are the bells tolling?" And they were told that the squire's coachman had died and the bells were being tolled for him. János was laid out for thirty-six hours, and the doctor came to confirm that he was dead. He certified his death, and then preparations were made for the burial.

Well, they buried him, and the villagers said to one another, "Why, who would have thought that a coachman should be laid to rest in the family vault?"

The squire's wife heard it and said "That's what he deserved for having been a good and faithful servant."

But before he was placed within the vault, he said to the squire's wife, "I, too, am going to smash the things which are in the cupboard and on the tables, but I'll take care to do as little damage as possible."

So he was buried, and the villagers didn't bother any longer about him. As the saying goes, "There's no wonder that lasts longer than three days."

Midnight came, it was the hour for ghosts to wander about. The squire stepped out of his coffin and started off. Promptly, János jumped out of his coffin and followed him.

"Who's that?" the squire asked.

"It's me, János, the coachman."

The squire then said, "What are you going to the house for?"

"Well, sir, speaking in all sincerity, I've come by a hundred crowns. I put the money in my pocket and later I hid it in a hole that I dug under the manger. As it is, I cannot find rest here, and I want to visit that place."

"Well, then, let's get along, son."

The squire stepped out of his vault, but János remained behind in his. The squire asked him, "I say, János, you aren't really dead, are you?"

"To be sure, I am. But as I am still new in this job hereabouts, I do not know how the tricks are done."

"Well, then, you'd better wait here for me till I get your keys."

He went to fetch the keys and was soon back with them. Then he opened the lock on the vault and called in, "Well, come along, János."

They left together for the house. They went into the bedroom where the women were sleeping. They lifted the beds up high and banged them to the floor. The squire swept everything off the shelves and cupboards. But these things bounced back to their places, whereas those swept off by János lay smashed to pieces on the floor.

"Sorry, sir, but I'm still fresh at this business."

They continued thus for a while, and then the squire began playing the piano.

János said, "Sorry, I can't play the piano."

"Don't worry about it, just pitch into the keys and go hard at them."

János didn't need to be told twice, and in no time he was thumping the keys of the piano.

The squire said, "Look here, János, tell me in all honesty, are you dead or not? Just tell me, what brings you back here?"

"Well, then! Come along, sir." And as they drew near the stable, the horses started snorting and pawed excitely at the manger, gripped by fear.

When the two got inside, the squire said, "Well, János, where did you put that money?"

Then János went to the manger and dug out the money from the hole where he had hidden it. It was the hundred crowns in bank notes which the squire's wife had neatly packed up in paper before she gave it to him.

"Well, that settles it! I see now that you are dead. Put that money back, János. Now, it's my turn to show you what brings me back on my nightly visits. Take that key there."

"I say, I won't."

"Well, then, I'll take it myself. Come along, János."

János followed, taking a piece of chalk in his hand. When they came down into the cellar, the squire said, "Lift that stone there, my boy. See what's beneath it. A big pot filled with gold. And lift that other stone, over there. You'll find a pot of silver under it."

And János made a chalk mark on the stones.

"Look! What heaps of treasure!"

And, indeed, the pots were filled to the brim. I still seem to see it in my mind's eye.

Then the squire said, "Now you know, my son, what makes me come back. I died without leaving a will, and my folks know nothing about these pots. Now I will rest in peace because I've revealed my secret to you. But let's get back because our time will soon be up." And then he suggested, "Let's go at it all over again." And they lifted the beds and thumped the piano. "Well, it's time to push on my son; our time is up."

Well, they set off to leave the house. The squire opened the door. "Go ahead, my son!"

"Why should I go first?"

"To be sure there's no such thing as holding ranks now. You're as dead as I am."

Then they stepped through the door and when János was outside, the squire locked the door. "Come on, János."

"I dare say, I won't."

"Damn it all! If I'd known that you weren't really dead, I'd have torn you to pieces. But now I can rest in peace. And you can tell my wife that I will leave her in peace."

In the morning, the squire's wife rose and went to János. "Well, what's up?"

"Well, ma'am, I did a bit of damage, but I couldn't help it."

Then they went together to the cellar. "Look at these three stones, ma'am. I've marked them with a piece of chalk." And he lifted the stones. "Here's a pot filled with gold. And there's another one, filled with silver. And in the third pot you'll find wads and wads of hundred crown notes."

"Well done, János. You've saved us. What reward would you like to have?"

János had been sweet on the squire's youngest daughter.

"I want your daughter Marika."

"Well, my little girl, what do you say to it?"

"Nothing. If you give your consent, it's all right with me."

•71• *The Midwife and the Frog*

My grandmother's mother was a midwife—the queen's midwife, as we used to say, because she drew her pay from the parish, which in our eyes meant the whole country.

One night she was called away to assist at a childbirth. It was about midnight. It was pitch dark on the road and it was raining. When the woman was delivered of her babe—God let her have a good one—my great-grandmother started off homeward. On the road she came across a big frog. It was hopping along right in front of her. My great-grandmother had always had a holy fear of frogs, and she cried out in terror, "Get out of my way, you hideous creature! Why on earth are you hopping around me? Is it a midwife you may be wanting?"

And thus she was conversing with the frog as she proceeded on her way, and the frog jumped closer and closer to her. Once it got right under her feet, and she stepped on it. It gave such a shriek that my great-grandmother almost jumped out of her shoes. Well, she went home leaving the frog on the road, and the frog hopped off to some place, wherever it had its abode.

Back at home, my great-grandmother went to bed. Suddenly

she heard a cart driving into the yard. She thought there was
another childbirth where her assistance would be needed. Soon
she saw the door open. Two men came in; both were very
dark-skinned. They were both spindleshanks; their legs looked
like a pair of pipestems, and their heads were as big as a bushel.
They greeted her with, "Good evening," and then said, "We
want to take you along, mother; you must come and help with a
birth."

She said, "Who is it?" as it is the custom of a midwife to
inquire where her assistance is wanted.

One of the men said, "On the road you promised my wife
to help her with the child when her time came."

And this gave my great-grandmother something to think of,
because she had not met a single soul on her way back, except
the frog. "It's true " she thought to herself, "I asked her by way
of a joke 'Is it a midwife you're looking for? I might come and
help you too'."

The two men said to her, "Do not tarry, mother."

But she said to them, "I'm not going with you because I've
met no human creature and I've promised nothing."

But they were so insistent that she should keep her promise that
finally she said, "Well, as you are so keen on taking me along,
I'll go with you."

She thought to herself that in any case she'd take her rosary
with her, and that if she would pray, God would not forsake her,
wherever she'd be taken by the two men. And then the men left
her alone, and she began to dress. She dressed herself quite neatly,
and when she was ready she asked the men, "Is it a long journey?
Shall I put on more warm clothes?"

"We aren't going far. It will take us an hour and a half or so
to get back. But hurry up, mother, because my wife was in a bad
state when I left her."

Then she finished dressing and went out with the two men.
They put her in their black coach and soon were driving up a big
mountain. It was Magyarós Mountain, not far from the banks
of the Szucsáva. As they were driving along, suddenly the mountain opened up before them, and they drove straight through the

split, right into the center of the mountain. They pulled up before a house and one of the men opened the door for her.

"Well, you go in to her," he said. "You'll find my wife there. She's lying on the floor."

And as she stepped through the door, she beheld a small woman lying on the floor. She, too, had a head as big as a bushel. She looked ill and was groaning terribly.

My great-grandmother said to her. "You're in a bad state, daughter, aren't you? But have no fear, God will deliver you of your burden, and then you'll feel well again."

The woman then said to my great-grandmother, "Don't say that God will help me. My husband must not hear you saying it."

The midwife asked, "What else could I say?"

"Say the *gyivák* [a type of devil] will help you."

Then my great-grandmother—we had it from her own mouth —felt as if the words had frozen on her lips, so alarmed did she grow at the thought of what place she had been brought to. No sooner than she thought about it, the child was born, a spindle-shanks, with legs as thin as pipestems and a head as big as a stewpot. My great-grandmother thought to herself, "Well, I was brought here, but how am I to get back? So she turned to the woman "Well, your men have brought me to your place, but how can I get back? It's pitch dark outside. I couldn't find my way back home alone."

The sick woman then said, " Do not worry about that. My husband will take you back to the same place he brought you from." And then she asked my great-grandmother, "Well, mother, do you know who I am?"

"I couldn't say I do. I've asked your husband a few questions about you, but he didn't tell me a thing. He said I should go with them and I'd learn in time who you were."

"Well, you know who I am? I am the frog you kicked about on the road and trod under your feet. Now, this should serve as a lesson that if you happen to come across some creature like me at about midnight or an hour past it, do not speak to it, nor take heed of what you see. Just pass along on your way. You see, you stopped to talk to me and made a promise to me. So you had to be brought here, because I was that frog you met on the road."

Then my great-grandmother said, "I've done my job here; now get me back to my home."

Then the man came in and asked her, "Well, what would you want me to pay for your troubles?"

Then the old midwife said, "I don't want you to pay me anything. Get me right back to the place you brought me from."

The man said, "Do not worry. We still have half an hour or so to get you back. But now let me take you to our larder so that you may see for yourself that we are doing well. You needn't fear that we haven't the wherewithal to pay for your services."

And my great-grandmother followed him to the larder. In the larder she beheld all sorts of food heaped on the shelves: flour and bacon and firkins of lard here, and loaves of bread and cream there and a lot of other things, all arranged in neat order, to say nothing of veritable mounds of gold and silver.

"Now you can see for yourself what plenty there is. Whatever the rich men and the wealthy farmers deny to the poor in their greed becomes ours and goes into our storeroom." And he turned to my great-grandmother and said, "Well, mother, let's get along. There isn't much time left for us to get you back to your home. Take of this gold an apronful, as I see you have on your Sunday apron."

And he insisted on her taking an apronful of gold. He wouldn't let her leave the larder until she had filled her apron with it.

When she had put the gold in her apron, she was taken to the top of Magyarós Mountain by the same coach in which she had first come. But dawn was already coming on, and soon the cock uttered its first crow. Then the men pushed her from the black coach—though they were still near the top—and said to her, "Trot along, mother, you can find your way home from here."

And when she took a look at her apron to make sure that she had the gold, there was nothing whatever in her apron; that heap of gold had vanished into thin air.

And that is all there is to the story; you can take it from me.

The Devil's Best Man

There was once a man who was always asked in his village to go as best man when there was a wedding and who never said no to an invitation if he was called. One day this man was cutting the grass on the meadow when a young man walked up to him.

"It is you, Uncle," he said, "that I want to speak to."

"The sooner you begin, the better I like it."

"Only this," the young man says, "I want to have you as my best man."

"Well, that's all right with me. But as I have never seen you before, you must tell me first who you are."

"Now, here is information about me," and he says a few things, "and my name is János B."

"Good. But where do you live; what village do you come from?"

"Never mind. At four this afternoon a coach drawn by four horses will stop here to fetch you. You will get into the coach and drive off with it."

"Just like that? All in a hurry?"

"It must be. I am going to have my wedding," he says "and I've been looking for a best man for quite a time. That's why I've picked upon you because I know that you have been called so often, and you have never refused when you were asked. Now, go on working on your meadow till four o'clock this afternoon when the coach comes to fetch you."

So it happened. At four in the afternoon the coach arrived, the man got into the coach and drove away. After a little time he takes a look around, and what does he perceive? He cannot see the ground any more; they were driving right through the air. "What's this?" he asks, "where are we going?"

"Never mind. Let us drive on. We'll soon reach our destination."

There was still a long way to go when sounds of gay music and merriment reached the man's ears. "Are we still far off?"

"Not very far off. We'll be there right away."

And soon they arrived. Then they walked into a house. The tables were laid, and the people around them were feasting heartily. Says the man, "And where is the bridegroom? Lead me to him."

"So you have come, Uncle," the bridegroom said to him.

"To be sure I have, and it wasn't an easy journey to make."

"Not with four horses bringing you two here," the bridegroom said.

"Right you are. What bothers me is that I'd like to know where I am right now."

The bridegroom said, "You'll know it in good time. But first, let us go and have the wedding over."

So they all set out for the ceremony. The man looks round and what does he see? All along the way they are marching beneath the houses. At last they come to a house where the wedding was to take place. All at once the bell was rung for the wedding. The bridegroom and the bride, followed by the best man, go in while the guests are waiting outside. The man now looks closely at the priest while he's performing the marriage ceremony. And lo, what does he see? The priest has no shoes on because instead of feet he is standing on hooves. The man makes no remark and waits till the ceremony is over. Then he turns to the bridegroom and says, "Well, then, young man, will you tell me now where we are?"

"We are in Hell, Uncle," he says, "but do not worry, you'll get your due for having come." And he promised to reward him with a lot of money, as much as a cauldron full. "That's what I am giving to you for having come. Now go and take it."

"Look here, young fellow," the man said, "you'd better get me back the same way you've brought me here. I've no use for your money. To be sure, I'd never get home toting along a cauldron full of it."

In the meanwhile, his folks at home began to worry about him as he had been away quite a long time. It must have been three weeks ago when he was called away to go to the wedding. The

man walked up to the bridegroom as soon as the wedding feast
was over and said, "You must let me be taken back to the very
place you brought me from."

So they brought the coach, and the man was taken back and
put down on the very spot in the meadow where he had been
cutting grass before he left. Even his scythe was lying there as he
had left it, three weeks before. Soon he was on his way homeward, and when he arrived his folks gathered around him and
asked "Where have you been? What have you been doing since
you left us three weeks ago?"

"Do you mean it was as long as that? To me it seemed only
three days." So he gave an account of all that happened to him:
how he had been asked to go as best man and had then been taken
to Hell. And how he had been promised a cauldron full of
money and instead of taking it, how he had asked to be brought
home.

"I guess you could have brought some of it," his wife re-
marked.

"What do you think!" he said. "I can bless my stars to have
gotten home at all."

Notes
To the Tales

The following notes are intended to help the reader in a better understanding of the texts and to point out interrelations with other texts in the international body of folktales. The notes will also throw light on the specifically Hungarian features of our material.

In relating the texts to international tale types, I have followed, in general, the latest revised edition of the Aarne-Thompson Type Index and Thompson's Motif-Index. Where no international types were found to suit the Hungarian text, I have referred to type numbers from Berze Nagy's Hungarian Folktale Types (BN) *and Ágnes Kovács's* Type Catalogue of Hungarian Animal Tales (KÁ) *and from the same author's* Folktale Catalogue *manuscript under preparation in the Ethnographical Museum.*

PART I

MÄRCHEN

· *1* · *The Son of the Cow with a Broken Horn*

Type 301B, *The Strong Man and his Companions.*

Narrator, Imre Tákos, Sr., aged 64, member of the agricultural producers' co-operative of Kisujszállás, Szolnok County. Collected in 1952 by Sándor Makra, a Presbyterian minister.

Ten variants of this specifically Hungarian tale have been recorded in widely different quarters of the country. The development of the tale suggests contamination with Type 301, *The Three Stolen Princesses,* and Type 511A, *The Little Red Ox.* Parallels do not appear to be much known except in the Balkans, where it is found in a few Greek, Rumanian, and southern Slav variants.

The text is incomplete, as the subterranean episode and the rescue of the three princesses are missing. However, thanks to the excellent rendering of the narrator, it gives the impression of a well-rounded and complete whole. The relationship between the boy and the cow is made unmistakably clear. Although the narrator does not put it into words, it is evident that the cow represents the boy's deceased mother whose soul, after her death, entered into the body of the cow. After their separation, the cow and her son are still united by the life token (Motif E761, "Life Token"), and it is through this bond that the cow mother comes to the rescue of her son and his companions in the moment of extreme danger. Also in the more complete variants it is the life token through which the mother is made aware of the impending danger, and it is the cow mother who saves the imperiled persons by breathing her soul into them at the cost of her life. The etiological feature of the conclusion is apparently an individual invention added by the narrator.

· 2 · *Csucskári*

Type 328A*, *Three Brothers Steal Back the Sun, Moon, and Star.*

Narrator, Sándor Farkas, aged 48, Gypsy adobe maker of Garbolc, Szatmár County. Collected in 1948 by László Kovács, a teacher.

Up to this date only thirty-five variants of this tale in which the release of heavenly bodies forms the principal subject have been recorded. They have been collected in different parts of the country. To the best of our knowledge, parallels have been found in Rumania, and some elements of the tale appear to be common to Russians, to the Ural-Altaic Turks, and to our kindred nations of north Asia.

Although the ethos and scenery of "Csucskári" conform to the stereotyped Hungarian peasant tale, it also displays some marked features which connect it with the heroic myths. It belongs to that specific class of Hungarian tales which contain elements of the shamanistic religion of the ancient Magyars of pre-conquest days. The supernatural knowledge of the hero has been already pointed out by folklorists as a characteristic feature of a good many Hungarian tales and of some folk legends. In contrast to European folktales in which the hero's triumph depends mainly on the assistance of his associates, in this Hungarian tale the hero, as seen in the figure of Csucskári, is endowed with supernatural power; he is a *táltos* who uses his finger to write letters of gold and can predict future events. According to Hungarian mythology, the *táltos* or *garabonciás* was born with a full set of teeth. Frequently he has to turn either into a flame or into the shape of some animal (see No. 62) to fight his *táltos* opponents, and he must endure all sorts of difficult tests, reminiscent of those required of the shamans of our Asiatic kin. Some ethnologists would even connect the *táltos* hero of the folktales with the shaman and regard his adventures as shaman tests, in the course of which the fledgling shaman has to show his mettle. Since its first recording in the eighteenth century, the structure of this tale, in which the release of heavenly bodies forms the main topic, has not shown many deviations from the original. There is only one other variant known with a female figure as a leading character. This type scarcely ever becomes contaminated with motifs taken from other tale types. The mythical figure of the smith, in other variants called also the smith of God or the smith of the world, appears in this tale as an equal to the *táltos* hero. Episode II of Type 302, *The Ogre's (Devil's) Heart in the Egg*, occurs in two other variants of this tale as well as the one recorded here. Variants of this tale have been found in which the episode of the release of the heavenly bodies does not occur.

The narrator of our story, as well as its hero, is a Gypsy. It should be noted that the archaic form of the Hungarian folktale which has been for some time gradually falling into oblivion is still flourishing among Hungarian-speaking Gypsies, inhabiting mainly the northeast counties of Hungary.

· 3 · Handsome András

Type 400, *The Man on a Quest for his Lost Wife*, plus Type 313, *The Girl as Helper in the Hero's Flight*, Motif H1102, "Task: cleaning Augean stable," and Type 314, *The Youth Transformed to a Horse*.

Narrator, András Albert, aged 36, lumberman of Csikszentdomokos (Transylvania—Autonomous Hungarian Territory in Rumania). Collected by Olga Belatini-Braun, 1942.

András Albert is one of the most genuinely creative storytellers in Hungarian oral literature. He has a great talent for constructing traditional subjects and motifs into a seemingly new story, but remodels the old form in so ingenious a manner that instead of turning the tale into an individual literary composition, he abides by the accepted pattern of folk narrative. He is a man of many talents, endowed with a remarkably vivid and creative imagination which has been fertilized by the wonderful scenery of his beautiful homeland with its impressive pine forests, rugged and craggy snow-capped mountains, golden-green meadows, its rapid rivulets, its wild torrents, and its rich fauna. Such a picturesque environment certainly lends itself to living in a world of tales and fantasy. When he tells his own life story, his words recall a world of tales, with miraculous beings and strange images. And he refers to it frequently, telling how in the course of his wanderings he passed through endless and dark forests where he saw the figures of his tales come to life. At the same time, he is a man of great resourcefulness, a proper Jack-of-all-trades. And he also likes to give an accurate description of the airplane he built for himself, and which took to the air, be there no doubt about it— only to be caught in a tree and go to pieces. And since then he has not found time to build another one. He finds great pleasure in making colored drawings. In them, he can bring to life not only the hut where he lived during the lumbering season but a nearby lake, with a dragon on its shore, as he "saw it" with his own eyes.

The representation of a world of tales of his own fanciful imagination contrasts strongly with the narrative manner of other Hungarian storytellers, the majority of whom are possessed of a more realistic turn of mind. For Albert, however, this world of fantasy has been also an escape from reality. In the small village where he lived, some 3,500 feet high on a mountain slope, the villagers had to strive hard to make both ends meet. Sheepherding and lumbering afforded only a meager existence to the village poor. Some fifteen miles from the nearest settlement, the makeshift hut where the lumbermen had to spend the long winter season, cut off from the world around them, was where these stories were told. That was the way they lived in the recent past. Today there are roomy houses, offering healthy accommodations, and the lumberjacks do not lack such modern conveniences as a bathroom, electricity, and a radio set. But in olden days, by the flickering light of a floating wick, what other form of amusement could have been found but to pass the time telling their tales in turn, from dusk until they went to sleep? And if any of them refused to tell a tale, he was dragged out by his companions and left in the snow, until he thought better of it.

"Handsome András" is a good example of the narrative art of a gifted storyteller who can build a complete story around an incomplete episode. The main topic turns on the hero's wanderings. Well-known tale elements are skilfully interwoven to thicken the plot before the final entanglement. Thus a new story evolves: about the fairy who lures the hero to her castle, and about the hero who has to endure superhuman privation. The time element and the wanderings of the hero both belong to a world beyond reality. Three times the hero has to grow old and to rejuvenate. He is tossed about between hope and despair, and he is constantly coming up against the most extraordinary situations. But ever lured on by a magic spell, he pursues his journey, which ever holds new difficulties for him. And when he almost seems to have succeeded, there comes one more test to put him on his mettle again. Then the *táltos* horse, a well-known figure in Hungarian tales, takes pity on him, and with his assistance the hero takes up the fight with the fairy. In the concluding part of the story, the narrator made use of the "male Cinderella" episode, i.e., in order to get even with the fairy, the hero pretends to be a bumpkin before his final triumph. This same motif is used in tale No. 6.

The long wandering of the hero is described with such dramatic sense that never for a moment does it become uninteresting. The plot is cleverly intricate; a dazzlingly picturesque world unfolds itself before us, and in a fascinating manner the changing moods, the worries and anxieties of the hero are poignantly described. As if he were thinking aloud, the hero gives an account of the vicissitudes he meets with in the course of his wanderings. It sounds almost like a nightmarish dream, an exaggerated image of reality, a symbolic representation of man in the grip of all human misery.

· 4 · *Pretty-Maid Ibronka*

Type 407B, *The Devil's (Dead Man's) Mistress.*

Narrator, Mihály Fedics, aged 86, illiterate day-laborer of Bátorliget, Szabolcs County. Collected by Gyula Ortutay in 1938 and printed in Ortutay, 1940, I, pp. 278–85.

Berze Nagy's comprehensive type catalogue of Hungarian Tales lists only ten complete variants of this tale, but owing to recent recordings this number has increased to over a hundred, for the tale belongs to one of the most popular stories in Hungarian oral literature. It has been narrated in almost every village all over the country, in a fairly consistent form. It is also known in Lithuania and Yugoslavia. The variants show frequent blendings with the Lenore tale (Type 365, *The Dead Bridegroom Carries off his Bride*), the analogy becoming fully apparent in the first part of "Ibronka" in its identical setting with the Lenore story. The peculiarity may be found in the topic itself expressing the dread of a revived corpse, a feeling still very much alive in Hungarian popular belief. Possibly, this may account for the flexibility of the many variants, suited always to the local belief of the given village in matters concerning revenants, necromancy, and protective measures against them.

Fedics is one of the best narrators in folk literature. During his long life he worked as an agricultural day-laborer. He was tossed about from one big manor farm to the other as a casual jobber. With the first great wave of emigration about the time of the First World War, he emigrated with many of his fellow peasants to the United States. During the few years he spent there he found jobs on farms or worked with road builders or in factories. Although his earnings were satisfactory, homesickness soon brought him back to his native country.

He had picked up his tales in his youth during the long winter seasons in the village spinning houses. Later, he himself became a great teller of stories when he was working as a lumberjack and had to pass much of his time in the big forest barrack which served as an abode for seventy lumbermen. It was his custom to interrupt his own story, by calling out "bones" to his listeners, to see whether they had gone to sleep; if the encouraging answer "tiles" came, he went on with the story, but if there was no answer, he knew that his companions had dropped off, and the tale was to be continued on the following day.

It was toward the close of his life when Fedics first met the collector. At that time the old storyteller was living a secluded life in unfamiliar surroundings, and he kept his stories only for the collector's ear.

Unfortunately, the bulk of his tales went into the grave with his death. Only some forty stories have been recorded. Each of them is a gem of epic narrative, told in a dramatic style all his own. His suggestive diction, with its curiously abrupt sentences, expresses his sense of intuition and reveals his emotional identification with his own characters.

· *5* · *The Tale of a Prince, a King, and a Horse*

Type 463A*, *Quest for Father's Friend*, with elements of Type 550, *Search for the Golden Bird*, Type 300A, *The Fight on the Bridge*, and Type 531, *Ferdinand the True and Ferdinand the False*.

Narrated by János Nagy, aged 76, a fisherman of Sára, Zemplén County. Collected by Linda Dégh, 1959.

This is one of the tales which has appeared in a fairly consistent form all over the Hungarian language territory since its first recording at the beginning of the nineteenth century. So far only Hungarian variants have been found, some twenty in number. Although the narrative contains many conventional elements of European folktale material such as the king who laughs with one eye and weeps with the other, the talking horse, the defeat of the dragons at the bridge (cf. No. 2), and the toppling over of magic objects, it makes a unique story of its own. The main topic turns on the wandering of the hero and his victories over his enemies. His wandering takes him to domains beyond this world according to folklore topography: beyond the Glass Mountain on the very edge of the world, beyond which lie two countries, the Land of Darkness and the Land of Light (in Christian phraseology, Fairyland and Devils' Land), with the Silk Meadow between them. Certain elements brought into the second part of the tale—for instance, the tests of championship, the meeting between the young hero and the old man, the defeat of the witch who wove the enemy soldiers into being—recall the world of the heroic epics. And it seems quite justifiable to trace certain threads of the story to far-off times, linking them with the ancient heroic epic of the Siberian nomads.

Mention should be made of the *táltos* horse, an important figure in Hungarian folk literature and particularly so in our present tale. I am not referring now to its historical implication, as will be pointed out in connection with the following tale, but it should be made clear that the *táltos* horse appears as the companion of the *táltos* hero and represents his second ego. From this tale, as well as from others, we learn that the hero has to look after his horse with great care, he has to curry it and feed it, sometimes with embers, because only then will it turn into a *táltos* who can fly with his master all over the earth or carry him beyond this world. These traits which originate in the Hungarian *táltos* myth may be rightly assumed to be symbolic reminiscences of the magic drum used by the shamans. At the same time, the *táltos* horse, representing the hero's second self, can at will turn into a human being, or can take the shape of some other animal. A typical episode appears with the incident of the thrice repeated cutting off of the horse's head, followed by his revival and his reappearing each time in a finer shape than before. It is frequent in Hungarian folktales that the hero himself is cut into pieces by his enemy or by his instructor, in order to be revived by the means of an elixir (water of life) so that when he is brought to life again, he is possessed of magic powers. Traces of this can also be found in Hungarian folk legends (see tale No. 61), as well as in the initiation rites of the Asiatic shamans.

In 1959 the narrator of this tale was awarded the title of Master of Popular Arts in recognition of his great narrative talent. All his life he lived in a small fishing village, inhabited by some two hundred people who, like himself, earned their daily bread on the water and during the summer season as part-time harvest hands. The manner of their life seemed to favor storytelling, and the members of the fisher gangs spent the long evenings in their common hut, telling stories in turn. Some of the narrators could spin out a story lasting three weeks. In 1947 the villagers of Sára were allotted plots of land. They gave up fishing and with their abandoned careers, time and opportunity for storytelling came to an end. The marshy tracts, offering a romantic background for the world of legend, have been drained and turned into fertile soil. And the aged storytellers, like Nagy and his companions, tell their tales now to the collector only.

Nagy is possessed of an unusual dramatic sense, and his diction is marked by a strange pulsating rhythm. He shows sure artistry in elaborating certain episodes. When he describes how the hero obtained his horse, and what befell him during his long wanderings, he displays narrative craftmanship at its best.

· 6 ·   The Tree that Reached up to the Sky

Type 468, *The Princess on the Sky Tree*, with elements of Type 554, *The Grateful Animals*, Type 314, *The Youth Transformed to a Horse*, and Type 552A, *Three Animals as Brothers-in-law*.

Narrated by József Fejes, aged 62, town crier of Sára, Zemplén County. Collected by Linda Dégh in 1949.

"The Tree that Reached up to the Sky" is one of the most widely spread ethnic types. Forty-five variants have been recorded to date. Taking into account the fact that outside the Hungarian language territory this type seems to appear only in the folktale body of our neighbors, e.g., the Ukrainians, Rumanians, and Saxons of Transylvania, the Yugoslavs, the Slovenes, the Austrians, and the German minority living in Hungary, we may be justified in assuming that in its original form the story must have been born on Hungarian soil and only through transmission did it get into the folk literature of other nations. Probably the adoption was greatly furthered by the fact that the sky-high tree motif has been linked up with such popular tale elements as Type 301, *The Three Stolen Princesses*; Type 302, *The Ogre's (Devil's) Heart in the Egg*; Type 400, *The Man on a Quest for his Lost Wife*; Type 531, *Ferdinand the True and Ferdinand the False*; Type 532, *I Don't Know*; and Type 556F*, *The Shepherd in the Service of a Witch*. Characteristically, the number of episodes surrounding the basic plot are of such diversity that the resulting tales will vary from three to sixty pages in length. Often the basic theme of the sky-high tree shrinks into a single episode within a tale. The original story, however, which appears most frequently in the form of a skeleton story for other tales, shows a solid composition. The hero has to climb a tree which reaches up to the sky. He goes up the tree either to bring its fruit to the sick king who will be rejuvenated by tasting it or to rescue the princess who has been carried up the tree by some enchantment. To climb the sky-high tree, however, requires superhuman effort, and of the many who try, only the hero of the tale, a youth of humble birth, is equal to the task.

For lack of space I must refrain from going into the reasons which would explain the solid frame of the tale, and the absorption of the most popular elements within this frame. Suffice it to say that the sky-high tree of the folktale appears also in Hungarian folk cosmogony and has its roots in the *táltos* myth. The *táltos* tests include the climbing of a sky-high tree. Only after climbing it will the *táltos* obtain superhuman knowledge. Parallels with the Asiatic shamanists and with our linguistically kindred nations will bear evidence that the climbing of the sky-high tree by the shaman, in order to meet the dwellers of the sky, is a test imperative for the initiates into shamanhood. In our tale, the climbing of the tree by the hero is a test of similar kind, and the ladderlike representation of the tree, with iron hooks serving as rungs, could be easily identified with the tree ladder of the Hungarian *táltos* and of the shamans of Asia.

Throughout the tale, the parts which deal with the relation between the hero and his horse are carefully elaborated. The hero's loving care for his horse and the manner he looks after it are emphasized throughout the story and are characteristic features of the Hungarian folktale (See No. 3 and No. 5). Frequently the hero takes up service as a coachman. For the successful outcome of events, his treatment of his horses may become a decisive issue. The fact that it is the horse who usually helps the hero in his predicament (I am referring not only to the *táltos* horse), certainly has interesting implications from the historical aspect. It suggests a hint of the nomadic life of our ancestors in pre-conquest times, when they were roaming about on horseback. The warfare of the Magyars throughout their history had been inseparable from horses. The hussars, for many centuries the typical fighting forces of the Hungarians, were soldiers of light cavalry regiments. And it should also be remembered that until the recent past, horses played an important role in peasant farming. It is also worth mentioning, as typical of feudal Hungary, that magic powers have often been attributed to a coachman serving on a manor farm, if he has shown himself a fine hand with horses. See notes to the Coachman Legend Cycle, Nos. 51–55.

It should be noted that this tale includes an episode, in abbreviated form, which has developed into a well-rounded motif in Hungarian folktale tradition, and though this motif has not yet been listed in the international type index, it will appear under Type 554B*, *The Boy in the Eagle's Nest*, in the Hungarian Type Catalogue now in preparation. It tells of the services the hero has to perform as a groom in the household of a witch in order to obtain a *táltos* horse.

The narrator of this story, J. Fejes, has been in constant rivalry with his fellow narrator J. Nagy, whose tale we have discussed previously. It often happens that they tell their tales to the same audience in turn, and at such occasions they never miss the opportunity to crack the ending phrases at each other's expense, as a sort of challenge, thus inviting the other party to a friendly contest.

· 7 · *Péterke*

Type 532*, *Son of the Cow (God's godson)*.

Narrator, András Albert (see the note to No. 3). Collector, Olga Belatini-Braun, 1942.

Apart from the Hungarian versions, I have found this type telling the story of God's godson in Rumanian folklore. So far only five Hungarian variants have been discovered, and since all of them have been traced to secluded regions of more homogeneous language groups, it seems justified to seek for their origin in the eastern and archaic strata of our folktale material rather than in Rumanian folklore. To show that it is a justified assumption, it is enough to call attention to such elements as, e.g., the mythical relationship between the *táltos* bull and the hero, the acquisition of the bull, the manner in which the bull is treated, and reversion of the sun on her course. This latter is strikingly reminiscent of other Hungarian tales in which three personified sections of the day are retarded (Type 723*, *Hero Binds Midnight, Dawn, and Midday*). All of these elements can be easily associated with certain concepts, already pointed out in the foregoing, as characteristic traits of shamanism.

· 8 ·   *The Story of the Gallant Szerus*

Motif T381, "Imprisoned virgin to prevent knowledge of men (marriage, impregnation)," with elements of Type 590, *The Prince and the Arm Bands*; Type 400, *The Man on a Quest for his Lost Wife* (see Part V, d and f, of Christiansen's outline in particular); Type 328, *The Boy Steals the Giant's Treasure*; Type 313, *The Girl as Helper in the Hero's Flight*; Type 531, *Ferdinand the True and Ferdinand the False*; and Type 300, *The Dragon-Slayer*.

Narrator, József Minárcsik, aged 62, a miner of Kishartyán, Nógrád County. Collected by Linda Dégh, 1951.

The classification itself is suggestive of the peculiar composition of this story. Motifs of many tales, uncurtailed episodes, even complete tales, make up the narrative which accounts for the unevenness of the structure. There are episodes on which the narrator dwells at length; again there are others which are presented quite succinctly. Yet, seen as a whole, the story reflects not only the narrator's talent for inventing a story, but it is also illustrative of the free associative manner of composition characteristic of contemporary oral folk literature. The kernel of the narrative is based on Type 590, *The Prince and the Arm Bands*, which is a well-rounded whole in itself, but within this framework episodes borrowed from other tales are cleverly interwoven without disrupting the basic structure of the story. This conglomerate, made up of the most variegated tale elements, is followed by a fairly brief outline of Type 531, *Ferdinand the True and Ferdinand the False*, and from it the narrator passes on to Type 300, *The Dragon-Slayer*, which being augmented by additional humorous elements, is turned into the leading motif (the animals belonging to the hero) of our tale. The main motif then, blends with a new episode, the enchanted land, adopted from another tale, then recurs to the original story. The helping animals, an element of the tale of the unfaithful mother, are made to play a prolonged role throughout the story, and they appear as the animals of the dragon-killer hero. Before the conclusion of the tale they are transformed again so that the narrator may take up the original thread of the story. It turns out that the animals are enchanted human beings, living under the spell cast over them by the giant lover of the hero's mother. And the hero must break the spell to show his gratitude for their good services.

With regard to the inserted tale, Type 531, *Ferdinand the True and Ferdinand the False*, I should like to call attention to the episode which deals with bathing in mare's milk. In every Hungarian variant of our story we will come across the incident in which the hero's *táltos* horse accepts the challenge of the chief *táltos* horse. Their fight ends with the victory of the former, and so the hero is able to drive the horses of the stud to the palace courtyard where the mare is milked and the hero takes a bath in her milk. In Solymossy's opinion this episode should be traced back to the ancient cultural relics of our forefathers who had brought it from the east, in times dating back to the past, when they were living a nomadic life and, like their neighbors the Turks, were roaming on their horses from steppe to steppe (*Ethnographia*, 1922, pp. 32–38).

Since a hussar's outfit is mentioned in our tale, it seems quite in place to note that the full dress of the hussar was a lavishly trimmed and richly braided red and blue uniform. In popular decorative art and in folk literature (tales and legends) the hussar appears as the ideal hero, admired for his swordmanship and his horsemanship.

It should be also noted here that the two related tale types, Type 590, *The Prince and the Arm Bands*, and Type 315, *The Faithless Sister*, belong to the most popular tales in Hungarian folk literature. So far some seventy variants have been recorded.

An excellent Norwegian variant of *The Prince and the Arm Bands* is found in *Folktales of Norway*, a companion volume in this series. It appears as tale No. 75, "The Blue Band."

In days past, when the narrator had to walk eight miles to the mine and after a day's work eight miles back to his home, he used to shorten this daily walk by telling tales to his fellow miners. Today his audience consists mainly of the children of his neighbors, who like to listen to him although he has forgotten the better part of his tales. Only seventeen could he remember, and these have been recorded by the collector.

PART II

JOKES AND ANECDOTES

· *9* ·   *Whiteshirt*

Type 1536A, *The Woman in the Chest*.
  Narrated by Péter Pandur, aged 58, day-laborer of Bag, Pest County. Collected by Linda Dégh (Dégh, 1942, II, pp. 178–85).

In this narrative the righting of wrong appears in one of the most brutal and harsh forms to be found in the body of Hungarian folktales. It could not be a more outright expression of the attitude characteristic of the poor peasant against the social inequality under which he suffers. It has nothing of that simple and banal conception of justice of the tale world where the good are rewarded and the wicked are made to pay the penalty for their wickedness. The interest is not in a conflict between the good and the wicked, but between the rich and the poor, and in what way the maldistribution of material wealth is being corrected. It is about a poor lad who shows his gratitude to a poor man to whom he owes his life by robbing the richest man in the village of all his possessions and by giving it to the poor man who had saved him from the gallows. The lad thinks up a way to give his robberies the appearance of having been committed by a revenant (a figure still generally abhorred in Hungarian folk tradition); he also succeeds in making it look as if the death of the parson had been brought about by the same revenant. The young lad bears all the characteristic features of the "master thief," a popular folktale hero. He can open locks with his finger, much like the *betyár* (outlaw) heroes, who went about carrying the magic vervain plant in their hands. With the ruination of the rich farmer, the poor peasant's life takes a turn for the better. Death rids him of his numerous children, a good thing, as prolific breeding has always been considered a curse upon the poor. Thus the tale ends with the moral that "... the poor man made a great fortune, and the rich farmer lost all his fortune and fell on evil days."

P. Pandur, the narrator of this tale, died in 1956. From his earliest days he tried his hand at many things to make a living. During his varied life he served as a count's footman, a baker's apprentice, a gooseherd, a seasonal worker on farms, a road builder, a gatherer of medicinal herbs, a coachman, and an unskilled helper for builders in town. He has been all over the country seeking work. Most of his tales were told to his fellow workers in workingmen's hostels. In 1920, when he was imprisoned for having served with the former Red Army of the Hungarian Soviet Republic, he told tales to fellow prisoners. Owing to an injury sustained in World War I, he lost his eyesight in his old age, and from then on he became the most popular storyteller in the village, being frequently found in the village taverns, telling his stories to entertain the guests. I recorded some 120 of his tales and, after a lapse of thirteen years, shortly before his death, I succeeded in re-recording his tales and his life story, this time on tape.

Péter Pandur was certainly a versatile storyteller, with a rich repertory of all kinds of tales, ranging from the fairy tale to the anecdote. His weak points showed only in his language and his style which bear the stamp of trashy literature and slang that he must have picked up during the spells of his town life.

· *10* · *The Parson and the Poor Man*

Type 650A, *Strong John*, plus Type 156, *Thorn Removed from Lion's Paw* (*Androcles and the Lion*).

Narrator, István Mogyorósi, aged 38, farmhand of Sára, Zemplén County. Collected by Linda Dégh, 1951.

One of the most popular topics of Hungarian folktales involves the controversy between the poor servant and his arrogant, foolish, and close-fisted master. These tales, in which elements of Types 650A (*Strong John*) and 1000 (*Bargain Not to Become Angry*) are usually amalgamated, reflect quite clearly the wishful thinking of three million poor peasants in the recent past in Hungary. In that world the squire, the judge, the parson, and the rich farmer had always been looked upon by the landless cottar as the representatives of a power opposed to him, and therefore they usually appear as the villains in Hungarian folk tradition.

In the rich material of variants which may contain a single motif, or link a considerable number of incidents into a picaresque-like story, this narrative broadens one single episode into a tale. In order to save his life, the poor servant sacrifices his master's oxen to the wolves and, when they have had their fill of the oxen, they are put under harness and are made to drive the poor man home with a cartful of chopped wood. The only additional element appears with the insertion of an incident telling of the servant coming to terms with the wolves, who take pity on him and spare his life on account of his being a poor man. It is a fair deal between the man and the animals; the wolves get the oxen, but in return they have to take the poor man home to the parson's house. In this episode the part played by the wolves gains further significance by assuming the role of serving justice in showing mercy to the poor servant because of his poverty and by making the parson smart for his avarice when he goes in search of his dead oxen. By inserting a skilfully adapted wolves *vs.* fox episode, the storyteller avoids ending his tale on a tragic note.

· 11 · The Squire and his Coachman

Narrator, Ferenc Eördögh, aged 69, living in a state-sponsored home for the aged, at Bodrogkeresztur. Collected by Ilona Dobos, 1961.

So far this anecdote has been recorded only in Berze Nagy's collection of Baranya County folk traditions (1940, II, p. 560). The narrative offers an exceptionally realistic presentation of earlier Hungarian conditions, telling of a controversy arising between the squire and his coachman. The patriarchal relations between master and manor servants are cleverly reflected in the story. The narrator, too, once served as a coachman on manor farms. Having no one to look after him in his old age, he lives now in a state-sponsored home for the aged.

· 12 · Lazybones

Type 902*, *The Lazy Woman is Cured.*

Narrator, Mrs. József Palkó, aged 74, an illiterate peasant of Kakasd, Tolna County. Collected by Linda Dégh, 1950 (Dégh, 1955, No. 35).

Characteristic of this type of humorous story is a tendency to point a moral concerning the proper conduct of the village girl. These amusing jests aim to show that such failings as untidiness, laziness, foolishness, and slovenliness impair the poor peasant girl's chance of getting married. In our peasant society of old, industry used to be the most highly appreciated quality of a peasant girl; she was praised for her ability to work. In the village or on the farm, a woman who has no love for work will prove a disastrous choice, and in a peasant community no lazy girl will ever find herself a husband. In her story, Mrs. Palkó emphasizes the moral or proper conduct by pointing out the place of women in a rural community.

There is evidence that our tale has some connections with similar topics in Rumanian folk-literature. Variants have been collected in Estonia, Lithuania, Yugoslavia, Russia, and Japan.

Mrs. Palkó belongs with our most eminent storytellers. She came to Hungary in 1946 with a small group of Székelys who had been living in Bukovina for over two hundred years, forming a Hungarian linguistic community in the midst of people of different languages. In the course of her strenuous life, Mrs. Palkó brought up thirteen children. She learned her stories in worker's hostels, during spells of work as a seasonal laborer in agriculture. Both her father and her brother used to be famed storytellers. Only after their death did she take up storytelling for the entertainment of others. In my collection, *Folktales of Kakasd*, I published seventy-two of her tales. For the present, her storytelling is mainly reserved for winter occasions, usually when people gather to perform some work in common, or at family meetings, especially when they gather to keep vigil at a wake. On such occasions Mrs. Palkó starts telling her tales at 6 P.M. and goes on till the next morning. Her easy-flowing style reveals an unusual depth of emotion and a fine lyric sense in the fairy tales and displays her keen sense of humor in the dramatic recital of the jests. In recognition of her storytelling talent, she was awarded the title of Master of Popular Arts in 1954.

· *13* ·   *A Stroke of Luck*

Type 1381, *The Talkative Wife and the Discovered Treasure.*

Narrator, Mrs. Lajos Balázsi, widow, aged 79, a peasant woman of Kisujszállás, Szolnok County. Collected by Sándor Makra, 1950.

This tale is known throughout Europe—from Ireland to Russia, from Greece to Lapland. It has also been collected in Turkey and India.

· *14* ·   *A Hussar Stroke*

Type 1358A, *Hidden Paramour Buys Freedom from Discoverer*, with elements of Type 1725, *The Foolish Parson in the Trunk*, and Type 952, *The King and the Soldier.*

Narrator, Péter Pandur (see note to No. 9). Collected by Linda Dégh, 1942, II, No. 51.

Our narrative, telling of the adventures of a discharged soldier, combines two tales complete in themselves, bearing no relation whatever to each other. These stories represent two different types, each of which is popular. The discharged soldier is a typical folktale hero, but at the same time he is a real figure of our everyday life. For centuries, the soldier, rambling all over Europe, was one of the main disseminators of tales. As a man who had seen a great deal of the world and grown seasoned in its ways as well as in battle, the soldier was a welcome guest wherever he turned up, and he paid for the hospitality shown him with his tales. The Hungarian soldier became especially popular both as a hero and as a disseminator of tales, the more so, as right up to the fall of the Austro-Hungarian

Monarchy in 1920, the Hungarian soldiers, mostly peasant lads, had been transferred to all parts of the monarchy to perform their military service outside their homeland. And if a war broke out, they were the first to be called into action. Thus it was usual for a young village lad, doing his service far away from his home, to return only after twelve or more years, as a seasoned veteran, who would naturally have many tales to tell.

In the first part of our narrative, the discharged soldier relates an adventure of his homeland journey. This is the popular jest of the unfaithful wife and the parson. The narrator's rabid anticlericalism comes into full play in his humorous tales in which the parson's figure is always held up to ridicule. There is hardly any story told by Péter Pandur in which the parson is not bested for some reason or other. In this tale the hussar is portrayed as serving justice, quite in opposition to the parson. The parson takes him for the devil, and his guilty conscience makes him think that the devil has come to fetch him. In the second part of our narrative, the narrator has the outlaws (*betyárs*) appear disguised as clergymen. This second narrative is the genuine stuff from which to make a story of the discharged soldier, telling of the daring bravado of a hussar. The story assumes a legend-like feature by an addition of the narrator after he has finished his story: "The discharged hussar was an ancestor of Count Esterházy. It was in this way that he came by his money and estates under King Mátyás."

· 15 · *King Mátyás and the Hussars*

Type 951C, *The Disguised King Joins the Thieves*, plus Type 1736A, *Sword Turns to Wood*.

Narrator Péter Szergenyi, aged 69, a farmer of Kisvárda, Szabolcs County. Collected by Bálint Bodnár, an individual collector of folk traditions working at the District Council 1957.

King Mátyás (1440–1490), the great Renaissance king of Hungary, has become one of the most popular figures in Hungarian folk tradition. Around his name clusters a rich accumulation of legends and tales. As a king, he was known for his just rule. He curbed the impetuous oligarchs and concentrated ruling power in the hands of the king. He became popular among the common people during his lifetime for his humane measures in alleviating the hard life of the serfs. Immediately after his death, his figure gave rise to vigorous legends, as evinced by records dating from the sixteenth century.

Well-known elements of international folk tradition from almost the entire legend, tale, and anecdote cycles attached to such names as King Arthur, Solomon, Barbarossa, Frederick the Great, and Emperor Joseph II have continued to be told, substituting the name of the Hungarian king, although many of these Mátyás legends have sprung up on Hungarian soil. Indeed, for many centuries the poor Hungarian peasants firmly believed and hoped that King Mátyás would appear one day and their life would take a turn for the better. A well-known proverb has kept its popular use to this day: "King Mátyás is dead; justice has passed with him." Up to our day, oral folk tradition—apart from literary influences—connected with the figure of King Mátyás has remained very much alive.

The narrator picked up his stories in 1909, during his military service. In the past as it is today, when the light was put out in the barracks, each soldier had to tell a tale at the command of the barracks sergeant. Usually, it was in the barrack room where the young peasant lad picked up new tales from his mates in exchange for his own. Thus a specific genre, known as soldier tales, has evolved, of which our narrative provides a good example. In our days, however, the short anecdote and the obscene joke have become prevalent in the barracks, and it takes an outstanding narrator to hold the attention of his mates with a tale of some length.

· *16* ·   *A Deal that Went to the Dogs*

Narrator, László Márton, a farmhand resettled from Bukovina. The tale was written down by the narrator himself. (Published in Dégh, 1960, No. 103.)

This is a popular anecdote attached to the figure of King Mátyás; an old Hungarian proverb, still very much in use, alludes to this incident: "Only once did dogs go into the bargain at Buda," said if luck has left a person. It is closely associated with Type 1689A, *Two Presents to the King*.

L. Márton, who died in 1949, was an outstanding narrator in his day. He was particularly popular with his tales told while keeping vigil at a wake. He was the only Hungarian storyteller who put down his tales on paper, and his manuscripts, which amount to several hundred pages, are still circulating in several copies.

Buda is the most ancient part of our capital Budapest, on the right embankment of the Danube. The ancient Castle of Buda was built under King Béla IV, in 1242.

· *17* · *King Mátyás and His Scholars*

Type 921, *The King and the Peasant's Son*, plus Type 922B, *The King's Face on the Coin*. See also Type 927** in Berze Nagy's *Hungarian Folktale Types*.

Narrator, István Magyar, aged 64, a member of the agricultural producers' co-operative of Kéthely, Somogy County. Collected by Linda Dégh, 1961.

Two of the four elements contained in this narrative are not as yet known in international folk tradition. Of these two, the incident telling of the milked goats appears in several versions, the central figure changing from a young maid to a young lad or an old peasant. It is also included in Berze Nagy's Type Index. For further treatment see Bernát Heller, *Ethnographia*, 1936, pp. 290–93. The second incident, telling the anecdote of the reed plots and the courtiers, has been recorded in six variants since Kálmány's first recording in 1890.

PART III

RELIGIOUS TALES

· *18* · *Why Some Women are Grouchy and Some are Slovenly*

Motif A1224.3, "Woman created from dog's tail."

Narrator, Ferenc Kecskés, aged 65, a member of the agricultural producers' co-operative of Kéthely, Somogy County. Collected by Linda Dégh, 1961.

Collecting of myths and legends concerning Hungarian folk cosmogony and the creation was begun by Arnold Ipolyi in the first half of the past century. His *Hungarian Mythology* (1858) provides little of scientific value owing to its overromanticized character. Toward the turn of the century, Lajos Kálmány collected a considerable amount of useful material, but since then hardly any interest has been extended to that side of folk literature. Chance specimens which crop up suggest, in spite of their demythicized form, that there must have once been a rich tradition of this kind. The tenor of these tales is markedly profane and satirical, and that is the prevailing tone of our story here.

· *19* · How People Got a Taste of Tobacco and How They Took to Dancing

From László Márton's manuscript. See note to No. 16 (Dégh, 1960, No. 101).

Legends about creation, based on biblical tradition, are known in a considerable number of variants. Satan appears frequently in our folk tradition in the figure of a teacher, to acquaint people with some new form of pleasure such as smoking and growing tobacco, dancing, distillation of spirits, and card games. Our narrative, although almost medieval in its naïve conception, is well-rounded and wittily told. Particularly skilful in the description, through their manners and amusements, of the social intercourse of the first people on earth with the presentation of their idealistically peaceful community life. This idyllic existence is disturbed by the appearance of the Devil, dressed up as a gentleman. Very likely, our narrator has picked up his notions of gentlemanly ways of living while he was working in a town. His vivid and amusing style depicts the scenes with lifelike plasticity.

· *20* · When Jesus Became Thirsty

Narrator, Mihály Csonka, herdsman of Kishúnság (Nagy-Czirok, p. 297).

This and the following text belongs to a group of explanatory legends concerning natural phenomena. The central figure of this legend is Christ, and the topic illustrates how the principal cares of the Hungarian herdsman of the Great Plain are keeping his herd together and finding ways to ease his hard and tiring tasks.

· *21* · When Jesus Grew Tired

Narrator, Ferenc Molnár, herdsman of Kiskúnság (Nagy-Czirok, p. 299).

· *22* · St. Peter and the Horseshoe

Type 774, *Jests about Christ and Peter*, plus Type 791, *The Savior and Peter in Night-Lodgings*.

Narrator, József Korcz, aged 69, a farmhand of Nyőgér, Vas County. Collected by Gabriella Kiss, 1961.

This amusing legend, one of a number of similar stories, has become very popular among Hungarian peasants. It tells of the adventures of St. Peter while wandering through the countryside in the company of the Lord Jesus Christ.

In this narrative four elements are integrated into one story: Christ makes Peter pick up the cherries from the road; Christ makes a *cymbalo* grow on Peter's back; an explanatory incident: how stubs of branches ("Peter nails") were made to grow on trees; and wanderers looking for lodging at the inn where Peter is maltreated by boorish guests.

· 23 · The Little Innocent

Motif E412.2.1, "Unchristened person cannot rest in grave nor enter heaven," and Motif E754.1.3, "Condemned soul saved by penance."

Narrator, Mrs. Sándor Somogyi, aged 46, of Sümeg, Veszprém County. Collected by Linda Dégh. 1947.

This is the first Hungarian recording of a legend which tells of the superhuman tribulations of a babe who died unbaptized. The two motifs have been previously reported only in Ireland and Scotland. The composition assumes a form differing little from a tale. The infant is doomed to perform penance in the course of three successive tests, before it is granted entrance into heaven. The third act of penance, which involves the redemption of a gang of robbers, belongs to Type 756, *The Three Green Twigs*.

PART IV

ANIMAL TALES

The animal tales represented in our present selection are all characteristic specimens of the Hungarian folktale corpus. Excepting Nos. 25 and 29, animal tales are designed exclusively for the ears of the very young and are told mostly by mothers to their little ones, or by grandfathers to grandchildren left to their care while the parents are away at work. As a rule, storytelling is a man's pastime, but whenever the audience includes women as well, as often happens during wintertime when people gather

*in the spinning room, children are sent about their business, be-
cause the stories are not meant for young ears and their fidgetings
would disturb both the listeners and the storytellers. Many of our
narrators still remember how in their childhood days they concealed themselves in some hidden niche of the room where they
could listen undetected to the stories of the grownups. Perhaps
the fact that the storytellers have always been more eager to please
adult rather than juvenile audiences explains the meager quantity
of Hungarian animal tales.*

· 24 · *When a Magyar Gets Really Angry*

Type 93, *The Master Taken Seriously.*
   Narrator, József Ács, aged 66, farmer of Gerényes, Baranya County.
Collected by Istvan Banó (Banó, p. 268).

· 25 · *Cecus-Becus Berneusz*

Type 103A*, *Cat Claims to be King and Receives Food from other
Animals.*
   Narrator, György Makó, aged 55, of Alsócsernáton, Transylvania.
Collected by Dénes Jákó, 1938 (Konsza, 1958, p. 16).

· 26 · *Mányó is Dead*

Type 113A, *King of the Cats is Dead*; Christiansen, 6070 B.
   Narrator, Lajos Batári, aged 80, herdsman of Ujdombárd, Szabolcs
County. Collected by Vilmost Voigt, 1959.
   The cat king which figures in the northern European legend
tradition appears also in a Hungarian variant, but in a demythicized
form.

· 27 · *The Dogs and the Wolves Converse*

Narrator, János Nagy, aged 76, fisherman of Sára, Zemplén County.
Collected by Linda Dégh, 1959.
   J. Nagy, an excellent storyteller (see note to No. 5), told this tale
to illustrate that work should always be paid for adequately.

· 28 · Three Kids, the Billy Goat, and the Wolf

Type 122E, *Wait for the Fat Goat* (*Three Billy Goats Gruff*).
Narrator, Mrs. István Gál, aged 25, peasant woman of Egyházas-kozár, Baranya County. Collected by Ágnes Kovács, 1952.

Our narrator, a young mother, told the tale of the three kids to amuse her children, and indeed she succeeded, as the little ones, in spite of having heard this story dozens and dozens of times, responded with fits of laughter as she imitated the various animals, changing her voice from a reedy squeak to a gruff rumble.

· 29 · The Goat that Lost Half His Skin

Type 212, *The Lying Goat*.
Narrator, József Korcz, aged 69, member of the agricultural producers' co-operative of Nyőgér, Vas County. Collected by Gabriella Kiss, 1961.

This is a popular and widely spread folktale for children's audiences, deviating from the internationally known variants only in its concluding part with the adopted motifs of the goat taking cover in a fox's hole and frightening away animals stronger than himself.

· 30 · The Yellow Bird

Type 244D*, *The Bird and the Hunter's Skull*.
Narrator, András Ferencz, aged 69, herdsman of Csikmenaság, Transylvania. Collected by Linda Dégh, 1942.

PART V

TALES OF LYING

· 31 · When I was a Miller

Type 1962, *My Father's Baptism* (*Wedding*).
Narrator, András Albert. Collected by Olga Belatini-Braun, 1942.

In the Hungarian folk literature, tales of lying form an important part of our folktale repertoire, although they are meager enough in variety. The absurd element hardly amounts to much more than such incidents as the going to the mill, climbing up to heaven, being carried off by birds, and the birth of a father or a grandfather. The narrator is expected to give a high-speed recital of his story, thus heightening the dramatic effect of the rhyme-like prose of the narrative. Some parts of these tales sound, indeed, like poetry and appear frequently as opening and concluding phrases. These are more often than not apt to become personal, and the narrator draws into his tale his audience as well as his rival storytellers, thus achieving his purpose in guiding his listeners from their everyday existence into the marvelous world of fiction. The greater the skill of the narrator, the taller his stories will be, as with the tale given here and the one following. The first tale was told only by way of introduction to one of the narrator's fairy tales.

· *32* · *When I was a Kid of Ten*

Type 1962, *My Father's Baptism* (*Wedding*), followed by Type 1355, *The Man Hidden under the Bed*, and Type 1355C, *The Lord Above Will Provide*.

Narrator, József Minárcsik, aged 62, miner of Kishartyán, Nógrád County. Collected by Linda Dégh, 1951.

Some tales of lying tell of adventures encountered in childhood. They are like bad dreams, in the course of which the child has to face a series of mishaps and is on a constant run from one place to another until he comes back home and, after having collapsed from sheer exhausion, awakes next morning in the certain knowledge that he will always remember his nightmarish adventures. In our present tale, two well-known anecdotes are blended with another incident which frequently occurs in Type 900, *King Thrushbeard*: the principal female character of the story, after she has suffered humiliation, tucks some food under her apron and, when she is made to dance, the food scatters around her on the floor and she is put to shame.

PART VI

HISTORIC LEGENDS

· *33* · *The Fairies of Karcsa*

Motif V232.10, "Angels build church," and Motif V115.1.3.1, "Churchbell cannot be raised because silence is broken."

Narrator, László Lénárt, aged 44, farmhand of Karcsa, Zemplén County. Collected by Iván Balassa, 1959.

This legend, first recorded in 1851 and attached to the ancient Romanesque church of Karcsa, has become well known throughout the surrounding area. Since the twelfth century, the church has been destroyed by fire more than once, but its tower has not been rebuilt. Our present narrative has been made up of a number of elements current around the country, such as the fight between the fairies and the witches, the building of a church by the fairy folk, and the incident of the sunken bell.

Our text provides a complete variant of the legend. The narrator, an experienced storyteller, has told more than two hundred legends to the collector. Legends have kept on being repeated by the people of Karcsa up to the present time, and any social gathering or friendly meeting serves as an occasion to pass time in that generally favoured manner. The collector has recorded more than four hundred legends, an annotated edition of which is just now in press.

· 34 · *When the Tartars Came*

Narrator, Imre Sajtos, aged 86, farmhand of Balmazújváros, Hajdu County. Collected by Antal Varga, schoolteacher, 1947.

This is one of the most widely found legends in our folk literature. Its first recording dates from the seventeenth century, when an English traveler visited Hungary. The topic concerns an incident which occurred during the Tartar invasions, frequent between the second half of the sixteenth century and the beginning of the eighteenth century. The later variants of the legend are adapted to suit historical events, replacing Tartars by Turkish invaders and then by Serbians after the Serb incursion in 1848. The "dog-faced Tartars" has become an idiomatic expression in our language to denote a devastating enemy who carries people into captivity. Evidently, "dog-faced" must have been originally an allusion to the tribal emblem worn on their headgear by Tartar warriors.

· 35 · *The Valiant Fish Trapper*

Narrator, László Lénárt, aged 44, of Karcsa, Zemplén County. Collected by Iván Balassa, 1959.

The story of the drowning of the oncoming enemy troops has become one of the most widely told legends which developed during the years of the Turkish occupation of Hungary (1526–1686). Our present variant attached to Lake Varjános has become popular all over the neighborhood of Karcsa.

· *36* ·   The Kidnapped Child

Narrator, Mrs. József Török, a widow of Tornya, Temesköz. Collected by Lajos Kálmány, 1916 (Kálmány, 1952, p. 143).
So far, seven variants of this legend are known. Some texts of the inserted song have assumed an almost balladlike form. Very likely we are dealing here with a corrupted (*zersungen*) ballad, deteriorated in the course of time. (For a comprehensive analysis see Zs. Szendrey, *Ethnographia*, 1927, pp. 193–94.)

· *37* ·   Rákóczi Legends

a. A Hunting Adventure

Narrator, András Balázs, aged 63, of Cégénydányád, Szatmár County. Collected by Imre Ferenczi, 1962.

b. Rákóczi and His Táltos Daughter

Narrator, Dániel Szücs, aged 87, of Nagyecsed, Szatmár County. Collected by Imre Ferenczi, 1962.
Prince Rákóczi (Ferenc II, 1676–1735) instigated an armed insurrection in Hungary in open resistance to the oppressive rule of the Austrians. In 1703 he called the people in armed revolt, *pro patria et pro libertate*, and before long the better part of the country was held by the insurrectionist *kuruc* armies. Owing to the betrayal of the *kuruc* leader by his captains, the uprising was quelled, and in 1711 Prince Rákóczi fled from the country. For the rest of his life he lived in exile and met his death in Turkey.
Rákóczi is one of the most popular heroes in our national history. An extremely rich folk tradition arose around this figure, especially in the eastern part of the country where the insurrection started and where the *kuruc* armies had won their victories. The secret underground passages leading out of the castle of Sárospatak and the footmarks of Rákóczi's horse are shown to this day to visitors, and many stories are told about his fights and about his valiant followers. His captivity and his escape are still a living tradition in our folk literature. Legends are still told that Prince Rákóczi has not really died, that he is waiting until foals are born with teeth and the crucifix turns by itself as a sign that the time has come for his return to lead his people in their time of need (Ferenczi, pp. 389–436).

· *38* · *How We Saw the Last of Forced Labor*

Narrator, Imre Hetesi, aged 55, day-laborer of Döbrököz, Tolna County. Collected by István Bánó (Archives of the Folklore Institute, Archives of 1848, VII 2), 1947.

This story, together with the following three narratives, deals with incidents of the Hungarian War of Independence (1848–49), as a result of which the Hungarian people attained their national independence, bringing an end to serfdom in Hungary. Reminiscences of incidents connected with the War of Independence are still alive in the memory of our peasantry. It is enough to recall the fact that, when in the course of a nationwide collecting campaign a questionnaire to mark the centenary of 1848 was issued by the various bodies engaged in scientific folklore investigations, the data returned amounted to some 20,000 texts. This is ample evidence of the rich folk tradition attached to that period of our history. Immediately after the end of the War of Independence, a considerable number of legends grew up around Lajos Kossuth and his followers. As becomes clear from these family traditions, it was the abolishment of serfdom which became the most significant event for the peasantry. This well-rounded short narrative is only one of the many stories illustrating this fact.

· *39* · *Captain Lenkey's Company*

Narrator, János Halász, aged 82, fisherman of Sára, Zemplén County. Collected by Linda Dégh, 1947.

This legend gives a true account of an incident which took place on May 28, 1848, when the Württemberg hussars, stationed in Galicia, made their getaway from their barracks and, headed by their commander Captain Lenkey, went back to Hungary. In the homeland the company of hussars, 131 strong, were thrown into action in the battles taking place in the south. In the course of these engagements, First Lieutenant Pompejus Fiáth met his death on the battlefield. This incident has found literary adaptation in the work of several Hungarian poets and prose writers.

· *40* ·   *Sándor Rózsa and Lajos Kossuth*

Narrator, Sándor Gergely, aged 90, of Diósviszló, Baranya County.
Collected by Klára Csilléry, 1947.

It is interesting to note that the idea of our national independence
and that of the freedom of our people has become strangely linked
up with the romantic figure of the outlaw (*betyár*). Toward the end
of the eighteenth century, with the coming of the Hungarian national
movement, the *betyárs*, those fearless sons of the *puszta* (prairies)
and of the vast forests of the Bakony, began to appear as popular
heroes. From this time their popularity increased, particularly during
the period when the Parliament convened for the Reform Sessions
preceding the outbreak of the War of Independence. It was then that
the outlaws were known for "raiding the mighty and the rich and
aiding the poor." The War of Independence turned the outlaws into
fighting patriots, but after the defeat of the freedom fighters, with
the Hapsburg rule once again re-established in Hungary, the *betyárs*
reverted to their former way of life. Persecuted by the law, the
betyárs were put on the run, but they were willingly assisted by the
Hungarian peasants and herdsmen whenever they were in need of
food or a safe hiding place. The outstanding figure among these
outlaws was Sándor Rózsa of Szeged, whose legendary name was
well-known all over the country. It is a historical fact that Rózsa and
his men fought heroically during the War of Independence when they
were thrown into action against the Serbs in southern Hungary. But
the intractable sons of the *puszta* soon grew tired of military discipline and returned to their old haunts on the Hungarian plain and in
the forests of Bakony. Legends and ballads telling of Rózsa and his
men are still very popular in our oral literature.

· *41* ·   *Kossuth Wanders through the Countryside*

Narrator, András Urfin, aged 66, farmhand of Felső-Zsolca, Borsod
County. Collected by Mária Igaz, 1947.

Lajos Kossuth (1802–1894), the leading figure in the War of
Independence, became the Minister of Finance in the cabinet of the
first independent national government and then became governor of
Hungary. Following the collapse of the struggle for national in-
dependence, he had to flee the country. He died in exile. To the
Hungarian people Kossuth has become a symbol of freedom, and the

peasants who had pinned all their hopes on him, expecting him to bring about the betterment of their hard lot, had for a long time cherished hopes of seeing him return from exile. Like two other popular figures in Hungarian history, King Mátyás and prince Rákóczi, Kossuth has become a hero of deeds which have been, in the course of time, linked up with various elements originating in international legend tradition (Ortutay, 1952, pp. 263–307). Our present narrative is made up of two incidents known from the King Mátyás legends (i.e., chopping wood in disguise; the squire ordered to do the hoeing) and a third element which has been borrowed from a Rákóczi legend. Perhaps it is not out of place to note that a peasant was reported to have said in October, 1848, when Kossuth's followers were recruiting soldiers for the War of Independence, "Rákóczi has returned to us, only he has come back under a different name."

· 42 · A Piece of Roguery

Narrator, József Szenográdi, aged 32, of Csitár, Nógrád County. Collected 1947.

Sisa, the well-known *betyár* of the Hungarian highlands, raided the great manor stud farms as late as the seventies of the past century. There are a number of versions of the same story, with different famous *betyárs* as their central hero.

· 43 · Outlaw Jóska Gesztén Goes His Own Way

Narrator, Mrs. László Páskuly of Rozsály, Szatmár County. Collected by András Béres, 1952.

This is one of the most popular legends in which figure a variety of *betyár* heroes, the choice depending upon the locality of the tale. The legend is well-known also among our northeastern neighbors; there we find the same story attached to such popular heroes as the Slovakian Jánošík, the Czech Ondráš, and the Ukrainian Babinskij.

· 44 · Jóska Gesztén Makes His Getaway

Narrator, Gábor Kórik, aged 74, a small land holder of Tiszalök, Szabolcs County. Collected by András Béres, 1952.

This well-known outlaw of the Nyír region in northeastern Hungary, who took part in the battles of the War of Independence, has become a popular figure in folk literature because of his daredevil bravery. His popularity was due not only to his unparalleled horsemanship, his riotous drinking bouts, and his raids on the rich and mighty, but also for the great courage he showed on the battlefield. There are, indeed, a considerable number of similar legends telling of the incidents which occurred during the years of oppression known as the "Bach period" (1850–67), which followed defeat in the War of Independence, when the country was ruled by highhanded officials and policed by Austrian authorities. It is no wonder that under such circumstances the *betyárs*, who never missed an opportunity to attack the occupying forces, found the people on their side.

PART VII

LOCAL LEGENDS

To make a survey easier, I have divided the local legends into three distinct categories. The first group, comprising sections A, B, C, and D, concerns persons with supernatural knowledge. The second group, sections E and F, revolves around superhuman beings and tempters. It is not possible here to give an example of every type within these groups; therefore stories have been selected which are either typical Hungarian representatives of certain types or have their source in European folk tradition. It was deemed best to omit from our selection a number of variants of legends which have become commonplace through their wide distribution both in Hungary and in all parts of Europe. Among these are legends dealing with witches who steal milk and can turn into animals; the witches' Sabbath; revenants; sleepers suffocated by an incubus; changelings; serpents; and treasure hunts.

The third group, section G, contains a number of legends which have assumed the formal elements of tales. I am referring here to an overlapping between two genres; their characteristic elements appear alternately, so that the same narrative may have variants both in the bodies of legends and of folktales, and a strict demarcation between the two would be difficult to draw.

SECTION A

The Herdsmen Legend Cycle

There are two factors which have undoubtedly played an important role in the development of the herdsmen legend cycle. The first factor which must have had a bearing on it relates to the large-scale keeping of livestock by our nomadic ancestors, an inheritance prevailing through two or three centuries following their conquest of Hungary. The second factor points toward the extensive husbandry of the Magyars, based predominantly on livestock breeding, a practice which has continued until the beginning of this century.

Not till the end of the last century was extensive draining of the boggy marshland undertaken on the Hungarian plains, followed by canalization and river control, which has turned vast but useless areas into flourishing, cultivated land.

The life of the herdsman was hard and not without its dangers. In the course of pasturing his herd, he wandered with the animals through wild and desolate regions, and only now and then did he have an opportunity to pay a short visit to a market town where he might be hired for the care of the common livestock. Occasionally he would turn up at the manor farm to give account of losses which occurred during the winter season and of the increase in the stock under his care.

In the course of time, the herdsmen formed a distinct class of their own, proudly distinguishing themselves from the peasantry and forming a group based on a rigid system; in the order of precedence the horseherder came first, followed by the cattleherder, the sheepherder, and the swineherder. But even within these guildlike groupings the strictest discipline prevailed in the relations between the head herdsman and the herdboys.

The chief attraction of the herdsman's life was undoubtedly that it brought with it a certain independence, as the herdsman was free of the burdens inescapably borne by the peasants working as serfs in the manors and on the farms. Since the livestock were regarded as goods of the greatest value, the herdsman who took care of this valuable asset was respected by his master. He would trust him to drive whole herds to some faraway country where international livestock markets were held. In the eyes of the common people the herdsman became a popular hero, a greatly idealized figure, who owed much of his popularity to the fact that he was always ready to protect the *betyárs* and lead them to some safe hideout on the tractless bogs. He might even become an outlaw himself, if he refused to serve in the army of the oppressors of his country, or if something went wrong when it came time to give account of the squire's livestock under his care. And indeed, the herdsman was an extraordinary being, a Jack-of-all-trades; he could cure the sick, whether human or animal, turn his everyday tools into pieces of art by his fine carving, and when it came to dancing or fighting he was second to none. Hence the village young of both sexes looked upon him as their idol.

The legends which grew up around the herdsmen tell us about their supernatural knowledge and magic feats. They protected their herds against the evil designs of others, kept the herd together without the least effort, and punished their adversaries who tried to disperse their flocks. A herdsman's job was passed from father to son. Descendants of famous herdsman-dynasties still find pleasure in telling extraordinary tales of the marvelous power of their ancestors as it has survived in family tradition—although today the herders working on modern large-scale farms will hardly give credence to this kind of talk.

· *45* · *The Two Herdsmen Who Used Black Magic*

Motif G225.1, "Insect as witch's familiar."

Narrator, N. N., aged 48, inhabitant of Csót, Veszprém County. Collected by Aurél Vajkai (Vajkai, 1959, pp. 144–46).

The helping "devils" of herdsmen and coachmen, mostly in the shape of some beetle, are concealed in a matchbox and carried about in the pocket of their owners. Rivalry between persons endowed with secret knowledge was of frequent occurrence, ending with the victory of the one who possessed the more powerful magic.

· *46* · *The Herdsmen and the Wolves*

Narrator, Ferenc Vecsei, aged 54, herdsman of Sármellék, Veszprém County. Collector, Linda Dégh, 1960.

In Hungarian folk tradition, reincarnation symbolized by slipping through a birch-rod hoop appears only in connection with the transformation of wolves.

· 47 · The Herdsman's Magic Cape

Motif D2074.1, "Animals magically called."
Narrator, László Lénárt, aged 44, of Karcsa, Zemplén County. Collected by Iván Balassa, 1960.

· 48 · The Cowherder's Bull

Motif G265.6.2, "Witch causes cattle to behave unnaturally."
Narrator and collector as above. Collected in 1959.

· 49 · Uncle Gyuri's Bulls

Narrator and collector as for No. 47.

· 50 · The Herdsman's Dog

Narrator, Lajos Papi, aged 73, railwayman of Kisújszállás. Collected by Sándor Makra, 1952.

The locality of the story is a wayside inn (csárda) on the puszta near Nagykúnság (Great Cumania in eastern Hungary, called so after its ancient settlers). These out-of-the-way inns, far from every human settlement, offered accommodation to travelers and served as places of entertainment for the outlaws (betyárs), who would carouse there and pit their strength against each other, showing off their mettle in their masterly use of the fokos (halberd or axe). And to the inn would come the herdsmen too, to match their magic powers against each other. Thus the wayside inn has become the scene of many of our herdsman legends.

Section B

The Coachman Legend Cycle

The legend cycle which developed around the figure of the coachman endowed with supernatural knowledge is a specific type of Hungarian folk tradition. As far as I know, no analogies have been found in the oral literature of our neighbors or anywhere else in Europe. The central hero of these legends is the head coachman, in the service of the squire, proudly sitting on the box of the coach in his richly corded and silver-buttoned black livery. A small round hat with a cockade adorned his head. The head coachman was counted among the house

servants; he lived with his family in the servants' quarters attached to
the manor house. The coachman took the squire wherever he went
and enjoyed his master's confidence. The squire would always use his
coach if he was called into the town on some business or if he went
there to amuse himself. There was ceaseless competition between one
squire and another as to which could boast a finer coach, better horses,
and a more adroit coachman. The liveried coachman and coach were
indispensable for stylish living, so much so that up to the 1930's
coaches were preferred to automobiles on most estates. The coachman
who was good at driving and took good care of the horses was held
in esteem by his master, and for the same reason he won the respect
of the simple folk.

The coachman legend cycle, which includes a considerable number
of well-constructed legends and has become very popular all over
Hungary, is chiefly attached to the figure of a manor coachman famed
for some extraordinary quality. It tells of a series of adventures connected with these coachmen. These legends, while having become
popular in the villages around the manor estates, have been reported
only sporadically from villages where the majority of the villagers
belong to a small freeholder peasantry, and they are unknown among
the descendants of the lower peasants.

Evidently the factors which played a decisive role in giving rise to
the coachman legends must be sought in the feudal land system. But
we must look back for even more far-reaching motifs which may be
considered as cultural survivals from the pre-conquest times of the
ancient Magyars. On the other hand, there are also some features
reminiscent of figures endowed with supernatural powers, borrowed
from European myths. Attention should be called to a particular
feature of these legends which appears in the relation between the
coachman possessed of secret knowledge and his horse, recalling a
similar relationship characteristic of the Hungarian folktale (cf. tales
Nos. 3, 5, 6, particularly notes to No. 6). It frequently occurs in the
legends that the coachman feeds his horse on a piece of log and then
the horse asks him, "Shall we go as swift as the wind or as thought?"
This is the same question the *táltos* horse puts to his master in the
tales.

Generally there are two main themes around which the coachman
legends are built: how the coachman obtains his extraordinary knowledge and what marvelous deeds he performs in possession of this
knowledge.

Usually the interest of a young and inexperienced coachman is awakened when he sees that his older mate is possessed of some secret knowledge, a knowledge which enables him to keep the horses perfectly groomed without work and perfectly fit for driving without their being fed and watered. He obtains this secret knowledge in any number of ways; he may go to the crossroads; he may be carried off; he may learn it while in deep sleep; or he may acquire his knowledge through the aid of some helping spirits who live in ordinary objects, e.g., a brush, a scraper, a whip, or the like. Sometimes he obtains possession of magic power by paying half a deciliter of brandy to an older coachman who wishes to get rid of his secret knowledge. Incidents occurring most frequently are: driving home with a dead horse; flying with the horses over the river; or making an artisan fall from the roof of a house for having stopped the coachman's horses. But the coachman has to pay dearly for his extraordinary knowledge; he cannot die unless he passes this knowledge onto someone else, and even then the evil spirit with whom he had associated himself will not let him go and keeps tormenting him until his death. For a comprehensive analysis of the coachman legends see Ferenczi, 1957.

· *51* · *The Magic Whip*

Motif D1208, "Magic whip."
 Narrator, László Lénárt, aged 44, farmhand of Karcsa, Zemplén County. Collected by Iván Balassa, 1959.

· *52* · *The Magic Calk*

Motif D1209, "Miscellaneous utensils and implements," Motif D1654.12, "Horse magically becomes immovable," and Motif D2072.0.2.1, "Horse enchanted so that he stands still."
 Narrator, János Nagy, fisherman of Sára, Zemplén County. Collected by Linda Dégh, 1959.
 The two legends linked together in this narrative have been found in a considerable number of variants attached to various figures, all coachmen, but interestingly enough, in most of them dialogue has been found totally almost word for word. The stopping of the horse is a frequent magic feat, but the figure of the artisan (usually a carpenter or a mason) endowed with superhuman knowledge has not been found in any other connection save as an adversary of the coachman, who overcomes him by his superior magic power. The second story emphasizes the fact that by means of his magic knowledge the

coachman has his master in his power and could have taken his revenge on him by destroying his fine horses. Such a story explains how the coachman could win the sympathy and respect of the common people. It is characteristic that while the coachman's son denies that the extraordinary knowledge of his father may have come from the devil or from evil spirits, he willingly admits to magic practices of a different kind.

· *53* · The Count's Horses

Motif D1523.3, "Bundle of wood magically acts as riding horse."

Narrator, Mrs. János Kovács, widow, aged 87, of Karcsa, Zemplén County. Collected by Iván Balassa, 1959.

In this story as in the previous one, a coachman endowed with secret knowledge teaches his master a lesson. Here too the master is at the mercy of his coachman, against whose magic he finds himself utterly helpless. There is no earthly power which could harm the coachman. Persuasive comparative data suggest that the turning of straw sacks into horses—an incident similar to the resuscitation of the horse in tale No. 52—should be traced back to elements having their source in Asian shamanism. The transformation into a shaman involves his being cut to pieces by the ancestor spirit; his leather drum, signifying his horse, is horse-shaped and could be turned into a living animal by the mere touch of the shaman. Flayed horses and their stuffed skins have been found in the graves of the ancient Magyars. According to their belief, horses buried in their master's grave came to life in the other world. In the opinion of our folklorists, the coachman who by his extraordinary power could transform sacks into horses by whipping and kicking at them is a late successor of the ancient Hungarian shaman. Such expressions as "black magic" or "a piece of sorcery" as used in our peasant idiom should be regarded as allusions to supernatural knowledge.

The narrator of this story can certainly be ranked among the most skilful of storytellers (see also tale No. 58).

· *54* · The Carter and His Wheel

Motif D1385.10, "Wheel buried in doorstep to prevent deviltry."

Narrator, Károly Fülöp, aged 56, engine fitter of Szentgál. Collected by Aurél Vajkai, 1942 (Vajkai, 1959, pp. 153–57).

Like the herdsman in tale No. 45, there were coachmen who could enlist the aid of helpful devils. Their activities, and accounts of their escape, show certain affinities with the well-known legend of the cobold hatched out of the egg of a black hen.

· 55 ·   Knowledge Obtained at the Crossroads

Narrator, Gábor Kecskeméty, aged 60, fisherman of Bodrogzsadány, Zemplén County. Collected by Linda Dégh, 1948.

This narrative should be regarded as a variant of Nos. 51 and 52, since it tells of a coachman who revenges himself on his superior. The magic object in this story is a piece of rag, an ordinary enough thing, just like the other miraculous objects in other stories. The acquisition of magic knowledge at the crossroads always happens in an identical manner, whether it is a coachman or a person of some other occupation who wishes to obtain this knowledge in order to use it to ease his toilsome work. Even the witches have to learn their knowledge in this manner. As is apparent from our story, both the shepherd and the midwife possess certain "knowledge," but they are benevolently concerned about the fate of the young man and in order to protect him they supply him with a piece of consecrated chalk and protective grass. It should be noted here that though such elements as the disavowing of God and the witches' Sabbath could be traced back to the European witchcraft trials, other elements, like the incidents with the stallion and the bull, are undoubtedly associated with concepts related to the fighting *táltos*.

Section C

Witches

Hungarian popular belief in witches is, in its general lines, very much akin to European folk tradition concerning witches and is only slightly reminiscent of ancient cultural elements going back to the pre-conquest days of our forefathers. Indeed, picking up material attached to witches has been considered to this day the most rewarding and the easiest task of the folklore collector, as there is hardly any village in Hungary where in the course of conversation the activities of a recently deceased or still living witch will not crop up. About ten years ago, a woman believed to be a witch because of her ability to market an extraordinary amount of curd cheese and butter, brought a charge of libel against her fellow villagers. However, no witnesses came forward, for the villagers were afraid of the witch's revenge if they spoke against her.

The village witch acquires her secret knowledge in very much the same way as do the persons already mentioned as being endowed with supernatural powers; that is, either at a crossroads, or by inheritance, or it may also be passed on to her by means of a handshake. In possession of this knowledge she can transform herself into an animal, she can ride her servant, having changed him into a horse, or she can fly through the air by applying a magic unguent. She can bring illness on her enemies or cast evil spells on lovers. She can exercise all sorts of evil practices in her own interest, such as affecting the yields of animals of her neighbors in order to increase those of her own. The witch has to die a terrible death, but she cannot die unless she finds someone to whom she can pass on her evil knowledge.

It was at about the beginning of the eighteenth century, evidently as a result of the European witch trials, that some new features were added to the figure of the witch, e.g., repudiating God and the saints, the forming of witch sects, alliance with devils, and revelries in the company of devils. As the rich material of the witch legends is strikingly similar in character all over central Europe, it seemed best to pick out for our present selection only three tales, markedly characteristic of the Hungarian tradition. For tales of witches in Norway see Nos. 12 through 20 in *Folktales of Norway*, a companion volume in this series.

· 56 · *The Witch that Came with the Whirlwind*

Motif F411.1, "Demon travels in whirlwind."
   Narrator, András Berkó, aged 50, cobbler of Sára, Zemplén County. Collected by Linda Dégh, 1951.

· 57 · *The Man Who Understood the Language of Animals*

Motif E423.1.3, "Revenant as horse," and Motif G211.1.1, "Witch in form of horse."
   Narrator and collector as above.
   In this narrative several elements have been amalgamated: the witch taking revenge on her daughter because she refuses to be initiated into witchcraft; the servant boy accidentally obtaining secret knowledge (there is a popular belief in the magic power of a butterfly or a frog caught before St. George's Day, i.e., April 24, and the ability

to obtain secret knowledge by eating such a frog; cf. tale No. 61); the incident telling of the death trance of the girl, unusual in its märchen-like composition; the witch returning after her death in the image of a horse. The activities of the young lad, acting on the advice of the horses in the stable, make our narrative assume a form differing little from a wonder tale (cf. tales Nos. 5 and 6).

· 58 · *The Witch's Doughnuts*

Narrator, Mrs. János Kovács, aged 87, of Karcsa, Zemplén County. Collected by Iván Balassa, 1959.

The realistic, vivid, free recital of legend telling appears at its best in the exceptional performances of our narrator. Here we have an unusually forceful and dramatic account of the witch who could turn cattle dung into curd cheese doughnuts. The incident of a witch forcing someone—in this story her eldest daughter-in-law—to learn her evil arts appears here as it did in the previous tale. The possession of such secret knowledge may have its advantages for some time, but eventually it leads to disaster and brings eternal damnation to the person who volunteers to acquire it. It is interesting that the elder sister-in-law uses two similes, which probably have their origin in the teachings of the Christian Church, to serve as a warning to the younger woman against learning witchcraft.

Section D

Other Figures Endowed With Extraordinary Knowledge

Beside herdsmen and coachmen, there are a number of other figures in Hungarian folk tradition known to have been endowed with super-natural powers. Generally they were persons of no particular occupa-tion, but men living a free life in the reedy swamps of the Hungarian plains or in the vast forests. Occasionally they visited the villages, and there they spent most of their time in the spinning houses, telling tales of their marvelous adventures. Every now and then there would be a herdsman, forester, ranger, or traveler who would come across these strange individuals who lived by hunting, fishing, trapping fish in weirs, or keeping bees, and who seemed to know everything about animals and also about the healing power of certain plants, beside possessing supernatural knowledge. According to popular belief, there were, as well, gardeners who possessed some extraordinary knowledge which enabled them to grow flowers and fruit in wintertime. Secret powers also used to be attributed to rangers who in the course of their nightly ramblings saw many strange things; and further to servant boys, who came by their knowledge quite accidentally, overhearing the talk of persons endowed with such knowledge.

There are two specific character types, widely accepted in European folk tradition, which have become popular in Hungarian folk literature as well—the miller who by his magic power can entice rats into following his orders, and the Faustian scholar. Motifs attached to these two characters are mingled with each other and with other legendary elements. In illustration of the first, I have included in this section one variant of a miller legend. On the other hand, incidents attached to Professor Hatvani of Debrecen (1718–1786, an enlightened physician and philosopher whose experiments gained him the ill repute of black magic and who is the Hungarian counterpart of the Faustian type) have failed to find wide acceptance on Hungarian soil, and whatever material there is available indicates semiliterary origins.

· 59 ·   Three Funny Stories About Magic

Narrator, Sándor Nagy, farmhand of Rozsály, Szatmár County. Collected by András Béres, 1949.

Three quite unrelated and widely scattered stories are linked to a single figure whose name has acquired legendary fame in his village. In the first legend two narratives of the fisherman-ferryman group are cleverly blended. While the wedding guests are transferred to the opposite side of the river or lake, the question, "Shall I undo, or shall I bind?" is posed by the evil adversary caught up in the fisherman's net. In the form of a blinking fish, he wishes to play a malevolent trick on the fisherman. The second legend (Motif D2096, "Magic putrefaction") belongs to a less widely scattered group of hunting stories. Here the transformation appears in a skilful adaptation in which a bundle of straw is transformed into a living animal (cf. tale No. 53).

In other connections, the magic trick by which the Gypsy musicians are conjured up has been found elsewhere in our legend material. Several variants of the third narrative have been collected; in one of them the beekeeper uses his magic power to punish a young lad who comes in the night to steal his honey by making his hand stick to the hive; it is not until morning that the beekeeper releases the boy.

· 60 ·   *The Miller and the Rats*

Narrator, László Lénárt, aged 44, of Karcsa, Zemplén County. Collected by Iván Balassa, 1959.

In addition to their magic ability to order rats about, other marvelous skills are sometimes attributed to millers. They may enlist the aid of devils who are inclosed in a small box. Millers are said to vie with one another as to which of them possesses greater magic. They fly through the air on a broomstick, they can make a mill stop working, they can recall by their magic power any object that has been stolen from them. Their marvelous deeds are analogous to those attached to the name of the legendary Professor Hatvani. We have already pointed out that these elements originate in foreign sources and may have been influenced by the performances of wandering showmen. For a comprehensive analysis of the subject see Vajkai, 1947, pp. 55–69.

· 61 ·   *Why Men Grow Old*

Motif B217.1, "Animal languages learned from eating animals," and Motif D1884, "Rejuvenation by dismemberment."

Narrator, István Illyés, aged 75, herdsman of Győrtelek, Szatmár County. Collected by Linda Dégh, 1961.

Our story, a notable specimen of the Hatvani legend group, contains two important incidents: plants reveal their healing power to persons who have learned to understand their language by having eaten of a frog (acquiring magic power by eating a frog is a well-known element); by dissecting a body, the secret of eternal youth is obtained (cf. note to tale No. 5). Thus an incident which has its source in ancient shamanistic belief has become, by blending with elements of later European myths, the central motif of a well-rounded story.

SECTION E

The *Garabonciás* Legend Cycle

One of the most interesting figures in Hungarian tradition appears in our legends either as the *táltos* or the *garabonciás*. In Hungarian codices of the Middle Ages, the word *táltos* is used to denote such concepts as the "magus," "magician," "wise man," or "physician." Comparative data have already supplied ample and convincing proof that the ancestry of the *táltos* should be sought for in the pre-conquest days of the ancient Magyars, in the figure of the shaman. The word *táltos* is now only sporadically applied to the legend hero. It is much more frequently used in reference to the *märchen* hero who possesses supernatural powers, or to his horse or other helpful animals (cf. tales Nos. 2, 5, and 6). Evidently, *táltos* used as a denotation for the hero in the legends has been superseded by the appellation *garabonciás*. This term has its origins in the Italian word *necromanzia* (black magic), shortened to *gramanzia*, from which, through the south Slav *grabancijas*, it has found its way into the Hungarian language as *garabonciás*.

Some of the older elements most frequently associated with the *garabonciás* legends follow: the child is born with his teeth or with extra fingers; in his seventh or fourteenth year the child fights his adversary in the form of a bull and then turns into a flame; he obtains his magic powers during a magic trance while poised in the air; in a pit he rears serpents which later turn into dragons; he uses them as horses to ride through the air; by means of his magic rod or a mirror he comes upon a treasure trove.

Evidently, the *táltos* has turned out to be a late successor of the priest of the ancient shamanistic religion. The legends circulating around his person converged during the Middle Ages with other legendary incidents attached to the figure of the vagrant student (*goliardus, clerci vagantes*). The vagrant student who pursued his studies far away from his country at a foreign university, usually in Italy, has been a well-known figure in Hungary since the twelfth century. These students were well-versed in poetry, writing letters, predicting future events, astrology, and the art of healing. After thirteen years of schooling they would set off for home in the old, tattered black cape which they had worn all during their student years. In the course of their journey, they went from one house to the other, asking for a drink of milk and a few eggs. To those who denied them hospitality they retaliated by bringing a disastrous hail on the fields. They carried along a magic black book; by reading it they could forecast a storm and bring on rains and also fly through the air.

Legends telling of the *garabonciás* are still current among our peasants and can be heard in all parts of the country.

· 62 · The Black Bull and the Garabonciás

Narrator, János Nagy, aged 76, of Sára, Zemplén County. Collected by Linda Dégh, 1959.

The double origin of the *garabonciás* legend cycle shows distinctly in the first and the second parts of our narrative. The first episode, telling of the boy born with teeth and fighting his adversary in the shape of a bull, points to a shamanistic origin and belongs to the ethnic elements of Hungarian folk tradition as convincingly verified by Diószegi's comparative analysis (1958, pp. 122–33, 342–95). According to ancient rites, the soul of the shaman in the shape of an animal had to fight its adversaries, who were shamans in other animal shapes. If he were overcome, his body had to perish as well as his soul (cf. tale No. 2).

In the second part of our narrative, the second and third episodes tell of the activities of the *garabonciás* according to the concepts attached to the figure of the vagrant student of the Middle Ages as it has become widely known in all parts of Europe (Christiansen, Nos. 3000–3025). It should be noted that a recording dating back to the middle of the past century is identical almost word for word with the third episode of our present text (Ipolyi, II, 216).

· 63 · The Dragon Rider

Narrator, Mrs. Károly Fülöp, aged 53, of Csehbánya, Veszprém County. Collected by Aurél Vajkai (Vajkai, 1959, pp. 161–63).

The relations between the *garabonciás* and the serpent or dragon are well-known concepts in Hungarian popular belief. The *garabonciás* rears the serpents at some well-concealed place and later uses them as his horses, riding through the air, raising terrible storms and hail. These episodes have been found also in the folk tradition of other peoples, especially in that of our neighbors, the south Slavs; but there are two specific Hungarian references deserving of mention, one of them contained in an exemplum from the fifteenth century and another from the seventeenth century, according to which Erzse Tátos when tried for witchcraft admits being a *táltos* and having intercourse with dragons.

· *64* ·   The Man Who Lodged with Serpents

Narrator, Ferenc Vecsei, aged 54, of Sármellék, Veszprém County.
Collected by Linda Dégh, 1960.

A few weeks following our first recording of this legend, our
excellent narrator retold the story with a slight change, according to
which the *garabonciás* asks a herdboy to help him in bringing out the
serpents with his second halter from the pit where he had reared
them. Both variants are narrated in a vivid manner.

· *65* ·   The *Grateful* Garabonciás

Narrator and collector as above.

Popular belief that a Hungarian *táltos* can always spot a treasure
trove hidden in the earth has become so general that even at the end
of the eighteenth century it was possible for an imposter, a penniless
beggar called Ferenc Csuba posing as a *táltos*, to swindle his way
across the Hungarian plain, as evinced by contemporary court pro-
ceedings. He duped his numerous victims with tall tales about his
fights with dragons to make them reveal the site of hidden treasure,
and about the wild bulls which came charging against him while he
was digging for it. The second part of the legend given here contains
a well-known legend about a treasure trove (Motif N553.2, "Unlucky
encounter causes treasure-seekers to talk and thus lose treasure"
(Christiansen, No. 8010).

SECTION F

Supernatural Beings

We have dealt above with magic activities ascribed to real people
known to everybody in the villages. The present section on supernatural beings includes legends about spirits who are not real people
but who sometimes assume human form. This type of legend is less
characteristic of Hungarian folk tradition than is the former group.
Most of the supernatural beings are parallels of the well-known European types and are more closely related to the South Slav and
Rumanian forms. Among the well-known international legend forms,
it is worth while to point out two groups as specifically Hungarian.
One of these is about the evil ones, that is, demons appearing in the
form of animals, monsters, shadows, and objects, that lead astray

people who are about at night. "Witches" included in this group are demons who have assumed the shape of known persons (tale No. 66) or beautiful young women (No. 67). The demons are never tamed, they are mostly referred to as "the evil ones," "they," or "it"; in fact, it is forbidden to pronounce their names. People who enter their grounds are punished (tale No. 68). A carriage of spirits may fly through the air loaded with gay spirits and a band of Gypsy musicians. They may carry off intruders, forcing them to take part in the spirits' wedding feast.

As I have already pointed out, horror of the living dead is a very common belief with the Hungarian peasantry. So it is only natural that the most popular legend types deal with revenants. Stories told in a very simple form as personal experiences, as dreams about encounters with spectres, and as highly developed and well polished legends are equally in abundance. Many are approaching the well rounded form of the folktale, as shown below in tale No. 70.

· 66 · The Lover Who Came as a Star

Narrator, József Jankó, aged 57, of Egyházaskozár, Baranya County. Collected by Mária Vámos, 1961.

A well-known figure in the spirit world of Hungarian myths is the *lidérc* or *ludvérc*, a nightmarish creature which might appear in either sex. It comes flying through air in the form of a star or a firebrand. The apparition will then visit a boy or a girl or a widow, taking on the image of his or her absent or dead lover. In this form it overcomes its victims. The *lidérc* is not unlike the vampire, a well-known creature in popular tradition all over the Balkans, though their characteristic features are not identical. The widely accepted belief in the existence of these malevolent creatures becomes evident if we recall that what appears as a demon or revenant in Type 365, *The Dead Bridegroom Carries off his Bride (Lenore)*, and Type 407, *The Girl as Flower*, finds its equivalent in the Hungarian legends in the figure of the *lidérc*.

· 67 · The Witches' Piper

Motif D785, "Disenchantment by magic contest."

Narrator, Mihály Bertók, aged 67, herdsman of Kishartyán, Nógrád County. Collected by Linda Dégh, 1951.

In olden days the bagpiper was called to provide music for the

Shrove Tuesday dance of young folk. This legend concerns an episode with the "beautiful women" (witches) who would wake the piper from his sleep to make him play for them and then pay for the music in their usual way by playing some foul trick upon him.

· 68 · The Man Who Lost His Shinbones

Motif E535, "Ghostlike conveyance (wagon, etc.)."

Narrator, János Nagy, aged 76, fisherman of Sára, Zemplén County. Collected by Linda Dégh, 1959.

According to popular belief, to lie in the road or in a furrow at noon or at midnight will have disastrous effects because at that time evil spirits are abroad; they will cast their evil spell on any person they find in their way. The legend given here telling of such a meeting is widely known.

· 69 · The Unquiet Surveyor

Narrator, László Lénárt, aged 44, of Karcsa, Zemplén County. Collected by Iván Balassa, 1959.

The spectral figure, well-known all over Europe as "Jack-o-lantern" or "the lantern," who with his light leads travelers and men on the road astray, has blended in Hungarian folk tradition with the figure of the unquiet revenant, usually referred to as the "surveyor" or "the land-chain inspector." In the second half of the nineteenth century, large-scale road building and river control schemes were undertaken all over the country together with the regrouping of the small plots of the peasants. This involved the appropriation of land holdings, and the peasants blamed the surveyors, mostly experts from abroad, for the loss of their meager land.

Section G

Legends that Have Assumed the Form of Tales

· 70 · A Dead Husband Returns to Reveal Hidden Treasure

Motif E371, "Return from dead to reveal hidden treasure"; Motif E415, "Dead cannot rest until certain work is finished"; and Motif E463, "Living man in dead man's shroud."

Narrator, Ferenc Eördögh of Bodrogkeresztur, Zemplén County. Collected by Ilona Dobos, 1960.

In Berze Nagy's tale type catalogue this legend is listed under No. 322. So far ten variants have been collected, all with consistent elements, such as the wandering ghost who scatters everything he finds in his way, the revenant who returns from the grave to settle some matters which had remained undone, and the person who associates with the revenant in order to spy on his secret. These elements still form a part of popular belief and appear separately or linked together in more or less regular form in a considerable number of variants.

· 71 · *The Midwife and the Frog*

Type 476*, *In the Frog's House*.

Narrator, Mrs. Gergely Tamás, aged 33, of Bácsjózseffalva. Collected by Gyula Ortutay, 1943.

Our text and its twelve variants, all similar, belong rather to the legend corpus than to the tales. They are illustrative of popular beliefs kept alive to this day.

A Norwegian variant of this legend, strikingly similar to the one given here, appears as No. 49b in *Folktales of Norway*, a companion volume in this series.

· 72 · *The Devil's Best Man*

Narrator, Ferenc Lippai, aged 60, farmhand of Ujdombrád, Szabolcs County. Collected by Linda Dégh, 1959.

This is another variant of the legend given just above.

Glossary

betyár   A highwayman or outlaw (archaic).

chibouque (Hungarian *csibuk*)   A long Turkish pipe.

csárda   A wayside or village inn; a country tavern.

csárdás   A lively Hungarian folk dance.

cymbalo (Hungarian *cimbalom*)   A Hungarian musical instrument closely related to the dulcimer.

fokos   A small axe on a long helve or at the end of a walking stick. It was formerly used in Hungary as a weapon against both the enemy and wild beasts.

forint   Since 1946, the standard Hungarian monetary unit, now worth about nine cents. It has, however, been used since feudal times with various valuations.

garabonciás   From the Italian *necromanzia* (black magic). A supernatural being believed to be born as an extraordinary child which acquires magic powers through a trance. During the Middle Ages, beliefs about the unusual attributes of vagrant students merged with those about the *garabonciás*, so that at present the *garabonciás* is usually thought to wander about with a magic black book, begging for milk. He uses his powers to reward kindness and punish evil. He has many of the attributes of the *táltos* but generally appears in legends while the *táltos* is usually found in *märchen*. (See notes to tales Nos. 2 and 59 to 62.)

gatya   Wide, white linen trousers.

guba   Long sleeveless cloak worn by peasants and herdsmen.

gyivák   A type of devil. The term is probably from Rumania.

Honvéd   A member of the *Honvédség*, the Hungarian army created in connection with the revolution of 1848; a Hungarian soldier.

itce   An old liquid measure; 0·88 litre or about one-fifth of a gallon.

kreutzer (Hungarian *krajcár*)   A small coin of silver or copper used in Hungary until the end of the nineteenth century.

Kuruc   A soldier in the insurrectionist armies of Imre Thököly and Ferenc Rákóczi which fought against Hapsburg oppression in the seventeenth and eighteenth centuries.

Labanc   The nickname of the pro-Austrian Hungarian soldiers during the eighteenth century Hungarian wars of independence, derisively so called for their loyalty to the Hapsburgs. The word is a perverted form of the German *Landsknecht*.

lidérc (or *ludvérc*)   A vampire-like creature which might appear in either sex. It comes flying through the air in the form of a star or a firebrand. It then overcomes its victims by taking on the guise of an absent or dead lover. It may visit a boy, a girl, or a widow.

pandúr   An armed person doing police service in Hungary in former times; a policeman.

pumi   A small Hungarian sheep dog.

puszta   A steppe or prairie.

sánta   Lame or limping.

szür   A long, embroidered felt cloak, worn by Hungarian shepherds.

táltos   A person possessing supernatural powers. He is the apparent successor of the Asiatic shaman. Beliefs about his birth as an extraordinary child are similar to those surrounding the *garabonciás*. The tests he must endure in the acquisition of magic powers are reminiscent of those undergone by shamans. The *táltos* generally appears in *märchen*, while the *garabonciás* is more often found in legends. See notes to tales Nos. 2 and 59 to 62.

táltos horse   A horse possessing supernatural powers. It is generally associated with the táltos hero. See note to tale No. 5.

thaler   The major coin of the Austro-Hungarian Empire. It bore the image of Maria Theresa and was widely used in southeastern Europe.

Bibliography

WORKS IN ENGLISH AND GERMAN

AARNE, ANTTI, and THOMPSON, STITH. *The Types of the Folktale.* ("Folklore Fellows Communications," No. 184.) Helsinki, 1961.

ASADOWSKIJ, MARK. *Eine Sibirische Märchenerzählerin.* ("Folklore Fellows Communications," No. 68.) Helsinki, 1926.

CHRISTIANSEN, REIDAR TH. *The Migratory Legends.* ("Folklore Fellows Communications," No. 175.) Helsinki, 1958.

DÉGH, LINDA. "Latenz und Aufleben des Märchengutes einer Gemeinschaft," *Rheinisches Jahrbuch für Volkskunde,* V (1959), 23–39.

———. *Märchen, Erzähler und Erzählgemeinschaft. Dargestellt an der ungarischen Volksüberlieferung.* Berlin, 1962.

———. "Die schöpferische Tätigkeit des Erzählers," in *Internationaler Kongress der Volkserzählungsforscher in Kiel u. Kopenhagen. Vorträge u. Referate* (Berlin, 1961), pp. 63–73.

———. "Some Questions of the Social Function of Storytelling," *Acta Ethnographica,* VI (1957), 91–147.

DÖMÖTÖR, TEKLA. "Ethnographische Forschung in Ungarn 1950–62," *Hessische Blätter für Volkskunde,* LIV (1963), 665–74.

———. "Principal Problems of the Investigation on the Ethnography of the Industrial Working Class in Hungary," *Acta Ethnographica,* V (1956), 331–49.

ERDÉSZ, SÁNDOR. "The Cosmogonical Conceptions of Lajos Ámi, Storyteller," *Acta Ethnographica,* XII (1963), 57–64.

———. "The World Conception of Lajos Ámi, Storyteller," *Acta Ethnographica,* X (1961), 372–44.

FALNES, OSCAR J. *National Romanticism in Norway.* New York, 1933.

HONTI, JÁNOS. "Celtic Studies and European Folk-Tale Research," *Béaloideas*, VI (1936), 33–39.

——. *Verzeichnis der publizierten ungarischen Volksmärchen*. ("Folklore Fellows Communications," No. 83.) Helsinki, 1928.

——. *Volksmärchen und Heldensage*. ("Folklore Fellows Communications," No. 95.) Helsinki, 1931.

JONES, W. HENRY, and KROPF, LEWIS L. *The Folk-Tales of the Magyars*. Publications of the Folk-Lore Society, XIII, London, 1889.

KOVÁCS, ÁGNES. "The Hungarian Folktale-Catalogue in Preparation," *Acta Ethnographica*, IV (1955), 443–77.

——. "Die ungarische Märchenforschung der letzten Jahrzehnte," *Deutsches Jahrbuch für Volkskunde*, IV (1958), 453–65.

MALINOWSKI, BRONISLAW. *Myth in Primitive Psychology*. London, 1926.

MARÓT, KÁROLY. Review of *Kálmány Lajos Népköltési Hagyatéka*, Vol. I (*Lajos Kálmány's Posthumous Collection of Folk-Poetry*: Part I, *Historical Lays and Soldiers' Songs*). *Acta Ethnographica*, III (1953), 469–72.

ORTUTAY, GYULA. *Hungarian Folk Tales*. Budapest, 1962.

——. "Principles of Oral Transmission in Folk Culture. (Variations, Affinity)," *Acta Ethnographica*, VIII (1959), 175–221.

——. "The Science of Folklore in Hungary between the Two World Wars and during the Period Subsequent to the Liberation," *Acta Ethnographica*, IV (1955), 5–89.

——. *Ungarische Volksmärchen*. Berlin, 1957.

THOMPSON, STITH. *Motif-Index of Folk Literature*. 6 vols. Rev. ed. Copenhagen, and Bloomington, Ind., 1955–58.

VOIGT, VILMOS. Review-essay of *Selected Studies of János Honti*. *Acta Ethnographica*, XII (1963), 195–201.

WORKS IN HUNGARIAN AND RUMANIAN

ARANY, LÁSZLO. *Magyar népmese-gyüjtemény* (Hungarian Folktale Collection). Pest, 1862.

BALASSA, IVÁN. *Karcsai Mondák* ("Legends of Karcsa"). Vol. XI in *New Collection of Hungarian Folk Literature*. Budapest, 1963.

BANÓ, I. *Baranyai népmesék* ("Folktales of Baranya"). Budapest, 1941.

BERZE NAGY, J. *Baranyai magyar néphagyományok* ("Hungarian Folk Traditions in Baranya"). 3 vols. Pécs, 1940. Vol. II includes folk narratives.

————. *Magyar népmesetipusok* ("Hungarian Folktale Types"). 2 vols. Pécs, 1957.

DÉGH, LINDA. "Cinele Ţarului (Type 449A*) in tradiţia populăra maghiara," *Revista de Folclor*, IV (1959), 205–26.

————. *Kakasdi népmesék* ("Folktales of Kakasd"). 2 vols. Budapest, 1955–60. Vol. I includes narratives by Mrs. József Palkó; Vol. II, by Mrs. József Palkó, György Andrásfalvi, Mrs. Lajos Sebestyén, and Márton László.

DIÓSZEGI, V. *A sámánhit emlékei a magyar népi müveltségben* ("Survivals of the Shaman Religion in Hungarian Folk Culture"). Budapest, 1958.

DOBOS, I. *Szegény ember vizzel főz. "Igaz történetek"* ("A Poor Man Cooks with Water. True Stories"). Budapest, 1958.

ERDÉLYI, J. (ed.). *Népdalok és mondák* ("*Folksongs and Legends*"). 3 vols. 1846–48.

ERDÉSZ, S. *Ámi Lajos meséi* ("Tales of L. Ámi"). Budapest, 1962. Manuscript.

FERENCZI, I. "Az ördöngős kocsis alakjának néhány kérdése" ("Characteristic Features of the Coachman Endowed with Supernatural Knowledge"), *Ethnographia*, LXVIII (1957), 56–86.

————. "Rákóczi alakja az abaúj-zempléni néphagyományban" ("Rákóczi in the Folk Tradition of Abaúj-Zemplén"), *Ethnographia*, LXXI (1960), 389–436.

HELLER, B. "King Mátyás and His Scholars," *Ethnographia* (1936), pp. 290–93.

IPOLYI, A. *Magyar Mythologia* ("Hungarian Mythology"). Budapest, 1929.

KATONA, L. *Irodalmi tanulmányok* ("Literary Studies"). 2 vols. Budapest, 1912.

KÁLMÁNY, L. *Népköltési hagyatéka I. Történeti énekek és katonadalok.* ("Historical Lays and Soldiers' Songs.") *Szerk. sajtó alá rend.* Edited and prepared for the press by L. DÉGH, I. KATONA, and L. PÉTER. Budapest, 1952.

———. *Hagyományok* ("Traditions"). 2 vols., Vác, 1914–15.

KONSZA, S. *Háromszéki magyar népköltészet* ("Hungarian Folk Literature of Háromszék"). Marosvásárhely, 1958.

KOVÁCS, Á. *Magyar állatmesék tipusmutatója* ("Type-Index of Hungarian Animal Tales"). Budapest, 1958.

———. "Magyar népmesekatalógus" ("Catalogue of Hungarian Folktales"). Kézirat a Néprajzi Muzeum Ethnológiai Adattárában, Budapest.

KRIZA, J. *Vadrózsák* ("Wild Roses"). 1863.

MARÓT, K. "Mi a 'népköltészet'?" ("What is 'Folk Literature'?"). *Ethnographia*, LVIII (1947), 162–73.

———. *A népköltészet elmélete és magyar problémái* ("The Theory of Folklore and Its Hungarian Problems"). Budapest, 1949.

MERÉNYI, L. *Eredeti népmesék* ("Original Folktales"). Pest, 1861.

———. *Sajóvölgyi eredeti népmesék* ("Original Folktales from Sajóvölgy"). 2 vols. Pest, 1862.

———. *Dunamelléki eredeti népmesék* ("Original Folktales from the Danube Region"). 2 vols. Pest, 1863–4.

NAGY-CZIROK, L. *Pásztorélet a Kiskúnságon* ("Herdsmen's Life on Kiskunság"). Budapest, 1959.

ORTUTAY, GY. *Fedics Mihály mesél* ("Mihály Fedics Tells His Tales"). Budapest, 1940.

———. "Kossuth Lajos a magyar nép hagyományaiban" ("Lajos Kossuth in Hungarian Folk Tradition"), *Ethnographia*, LXIII (1952), 263–307.

———. *Nyírés rétközi parasztmesék* ("Peasant Stories of the Nyír and Rétköz"). Budapest, 1935.

SOLYMOSSY, S. "Keleti elemek népmeséinkben" ("Elements Borrowed from the East in our Folktales"), *Ethnographia*, XXXIII (1922), 30–44.

———. "Magyar ősvallási elemek népmeséinkben" ("Relics of Ancient Hungarian Religion in our Folktales"), *Ethnographia*, XL (1929), 133–52.

SZENDREY, Zs. "Történeti népmondáink" ("Historical Legends"),
    Ethnographia, XXXVIII (1927), 193–98.
VAJKAI, A. *A Bakony néprajza* ("Folklore of the Bakony").
    Budapest, 1959.
———. "Az ördöngős molnárlegény" ("The Miller Who Knew
    Witchcraft"), *Ethnographia*, LVIII (1947), 55–69.

Index of Motifs

(Motif numbers are from Stith Thompson, *Motif-Index of Folk-Literature*
[6 vols.; Copenhagen and Bloomington, Ind., 1955–58])

A. MYTHOLOGICAL MOTIFS

Motif No.		Page No.
A1224.3	Woman created from dog's tail	323, 350

B. ANIMALS

B217.1	Animal languages learned from eating animals	345

D. MAGIC

D785	Disenchantment by magic contest	349
D1208	Magic whip	339
D1209	Miscellaneous utensils and implements	339
D1385.10	Wheel buried in doorstep to prevent deviltry	340
D1523.3	Bundle of wood magically acts as riding horse	340
D1654.12	Horse magically becomes immovable	339
D1884	Rejuvenation by dismemberment	345
D2072.0.2.1	Horse enchanted so that he stands still	339
D2074.1	Animals magically called	337
D2096	Magic putrefaction	344

E. THE DEAD

E371	Return from dead to reveal hidden treasure	350
E412.2.1	Unchristened person cannot rest in grave or enter heaven	325
E415	Dead cannot rest until certain work is finished	350
E423.1.3	Revenant as horse	342
E463	Living man in dead man's shroud	350
E535	Ghostlike conveyance (wagon, etc.)	350
E754.1.3	Condemned soul saved by penance	325
E76	Life token	306

F. MARVELS

F411.1	Demon travels in whirlwind	342

G. OGRES

Motif No.		*Page No.*
G211.1.1	Witch in form of horse	342
G225.1	Insect as witch's familiar	336
G265.6.2	Witch causes cattle to behave unnaturally	337

H. TESTS

H1102	Task: cleaning Augean stable	307

N. CHANCE AND FATE

N553.2	Unlucky encounter causes treasure-seekers to talk and thus lose treasure	348

T. SEX

T381	Imprisoned virgin to prevent knowledge of men (marriage, impregnation)	315

V. RELIGION

V115.1.3.1	Church bell cannot be raised because silence is broken	328
V232.10	Angels build church	328

Index of Tale Types

(Type numbers are from Antti Aarne and Stith Thompson, *The Types of the Folktale* [Helsinki, 1961])

I. ANIMAL TALES (1–299)

Type No.		Page No.
93	The Master Taken Seriously	326
103A*	Cat Claims to be King and Receives Food from other Animals	326
113A	King of the Cats is Dead	326
122E	Wait for the Fat Goat (Three Billy Goats Gruff)	327
156	Thorn Removed from Lion's Paw (Androcles and the Lion)	318
212	The Lying Goat	327
244D*	The Bird and the Hunter's Skull	327

II. ORDINARY FOLKTALES

A. Tales of Magic (300–749)

300	The Dragon-Slayer	315
300A	The Fight on the Bridge	310
301	The Three Stolen Princesses	305, 312
301B	The Strong Man and his Companions	305
302	The Ogre's (Devil's) Heart in the Egg	307, 312
313	The Girl as Helper in the Hero's Flight	307, 315
314	The Youth Transformed to a Horse	307, 312
315	The Faithless Sister	316
328	The Boy Steals the Giant's Treasure	315
328A	Three Brothers Steal Back the Sun, Moon, and Star	306
365	The Dead Bridegroom Carries off his Bride (Lenore)	309, 349
400	The Man on a Quest for his Lost Wife	307, 312, 315
407	The Girl as Flower	349
407B	The Devil's (Dead Man's) Mistress	309
463A*	Quest for Father's Friend	310
468	The Princess on the Sky Tree	312
476*	In the Frog's House	351
506	The Rescued Princess	xxvi

Type No.   *Page No.*

511A   The Little Red Ox   305
531   Ferdinand the True and Ferdinand the False   310, 312, 315
532   I Don't Know   312
532*   Son of the Cow (God's godson)   314
550   Search for the Golden Bird   310
552A   Three Animals as Brothers-in-law   312
554   The Grateful Animals   312
554B*   The Boy in the Eagle's Nest   314
556F*   The Shepherd in the Service of a Witch   312
590   The Prince and the Arm Bands   315, 316
650A   Strong John   318
706   The Maiden Without Hands   xxxii
723*   Hero Binds Midnight, Dawn, and Midday   314

B. Religious Tales (750–849)

774   Jests about Christ and Peter   324
756   The Three Green Twigs   325
791   The Savior and Peter in Night-Lodgings   324

C. Novelle (Romantic Tales 850–999)

900   King Thrushbeard   328
902*   The Lazy Woman is Cured   319
921   The King and the Peasant's Son   323
922B   The King's Face on the Coin   323
951C   The Disguised King Joins the Thieves   321
952   The King and the Soldier   320

D. Tales of the Stupid Ogre (1000–1199)

1000   Bargain Not to Become Angry   318

III. JOKES AND ANECDOTES (1200–1999)

1355   The Man Hidden under the Bed   328
1355C   The Lord Above Will Provide   328
1358A   Hidden Paramour Buys Freedom from Dis-
        coverer   320
1381   The Talkative Wife and the Discovered Treasure   320
1536A   The Woman in the Chest   316
1689A   Two Presents to the King   322
1725   The Foolish Parson in the Trunk   320
1736A   Sword Turns to Wood   321
1962   My Father's Baptism (Wedding)   327, 328

General Index

Aarne, Antti (Finnish folklorist), xxi, 305

Abandoning children: at children's request, 15

Abduction: of child by Turk, 217

Acolyte: wolf as, 120

Ács, József (narrator), 326

Adam: rib of, stolen by dog, 175

Adam and Eve: how created, 175; sons of, 175; expelled from Paradise, 177–78; mentioned, 43

Albert, András (narrator), 307, 314, 327

Alsócsernáton, 326

Altaic-Turkish relationships, xli,

Ámi, Lajos (narrator), xviii, xxxiv

Andersen, Hans Christian (Norwegian author), xxxi

Anecdotes: increasing popularity of, xxiv; percentage of, in tale corpus, xxxvi

Angels: teased by miller, 204

Anger: at being deceived by lover, 42; toward children, 57; at success of opponent, 82; at hero for accomplishing task, 107; of king at drunken hussar, 161; shown by laughing, 191; of farmer at goat's deception, 198; causes miller to leap from hole, 205

Animals: helpful. See specific animal

Animal tales: usually for children, xxxvii, 325–26; scarcity of, in Hungary, 325–26

Animism: traces of, in tales, xli

Anticlericalism: displayed in tales, 321

Arany, László (Hungarian folklorist), xxvi

Archangel: Gabriel and Raphael, 178; kissed by miller, 204

Asadowskij, Mark (Russian folklorist), xiii, xxix

Asian tradition, 306

Austrians: attempt to kill Rákóczi, 218; as enemies, 218–19; attack Rákóczi, 220; celebrate victory, 225; search for Gesztén, 228; threaten Hungary, 224; oppression of, 334

Babinskij (Ukrainian folk hero) 333

Bach period of oppression, 334

Bácsjózseffalva, 351

Badger: afraid of cat, 192

Bag, village of, 316

Bakonybél, 276, 280

Balassa, Iván (Hungarian folklorist), xiii; as collector, 328, 329, 337, 339, 340, 343, 345, 350

Balázs, András (narrator), 330

Balázsi, Mrs. Lajos (narrator), 320

Balkan tradition, 305, 312

Ballads, 330

Balmazujváros, 329

Banishment. See Punishment

Banó, István (Hungarian folklorist), xiii; as collector, 326, 331

Baptism. See Religious rites

Baranya County, xiii, xxviii, 319, 326, 327, 332, 349

Bartók, Bela (Hungarian composer and music-folklorist), viii, xv

Batári, Lajos (narrator), 326

Bátorliget, 309

Bear: aids helpful hero, 115; sets master's head on backward, 122; as messenger, makes fool of self, 122; afraid of cat, 192; as game, 265

Bees: pasture of, charged for, 268

Béla, King, 322

Belatini-Braun, Olga (collector), 307, 314, 327

Benedek, Elek (Hungarian author), xxxi

Béres, András (collector), 333, 344

Berkesz, 276

Berkesz Manor, 243

Berkó, András (narrator), 342

Bertók, Mihály (narrator), 349

Berze Nagy, János (Hungarian folklorist), xiii, xvii, xxvii, 305, 309, 319, 323, 351

Besenyőtelek, xxvii

Betrayal. See treachery

Betyárs) legends about, xxxvii; disguised as priests, 156; carry magic plant, 317; as popular heroes, 332; linked with idea of freedom, 332; take from rich, give to poor, 332; as tale heroes, 333; relationship with herdsmen, 335–36

Bird: trapped in skull, 199–200

Black magic: performed by woman, 259

Blacksmith: aids hero, 24–26

Boar: advises hero, 18; fears cat, 192

Bodnár, Bálint (collector), 321

Bodrogkeresztur, 319, 350

Bodrogzsadány, 341

Borbély, Mihály (narrator), xi, xxvii

Borosérhát, 269

Borsod County, 332

Buda, 322

Budapest, 322

Bukovina, xvii, xl, 319, 322

Bulls: bewitched, 236; act as herdsmen, 238; sent from devil, 254; devil appears as, 274–76

Burials, xvi

Cain and Abel: make offerings, 175; mentioned, 178

Calf: received from godfather, 101

Cannibalism: hero's mother eats giant's flesh, 124

Carpenters: punished for having beaten St. Peter, 185

Carter: possesses magic power, 250–53 passim; exorcizes devil, 252; possessed of devil, 252

Castle: built by fairies, 213

Cat: as great eater, 192; predicts death, 193

Cégénydányád, 330

Charms: spoken to ward off devil, 55, 56

Chauvinism: as folklore heresy, vii; displayed by Kriza, vii

Choir master: bear as, 120

Christening. See Religious rites

Church: as scene of devil's activity, 49–54 passim; fear of attending, 54; non-attendance brings suspicion, 54, 90; as scene of marriage, 90; full of hypocrites, 141; built by fairies, 213; man asked to renounce, 255; legends of, 329; teachings of, as elements in legend, 343; mentioned, 86, 87, 89

Cinderella: male, motif of, 309

Cleverness. See Deceptions

Coachman: raises hat to gallows, 141; purchases magic whip, 241; possesses magic powers, 243, 247–49, 314, 339; said to be devil, 249; disobeys master, 271; quiets poltergeist, 291–96; in Hungarian tradition, 337–38; ways of obtaining magic powers, 338–39

Cockcrow: causes supernatural beings to disappear, 299
Collecting: methods of, xxi
Colt: ridden by corpse, 134
Comparativism, ix
Contest to choose the stronger: wrestling, 7–8; fist fighting, 19; sword fighting, 20–21; transformation into flames, 21
Co-operative farming: effect on storytelling, xxiii
Corpse: reviving of, dreaded, 309
Cowardice: fear of admitting defeat, 9; fear of thrown dagger, 57; fear of crossing bridge, 59; wetting pants from fear, 156
Cowherd: receives food from cow's horn, 3; commands devils, 231; possesses magic powers, 231, 233, 237, 238; use witchery to steal cattle, 236–37; controls bulls from distance, 237; helps fight devil, 273–74; sees ghostly surveyor, 289–90
Cows: provides food through horn, 3–4; laments hero's defeat, 14; as year's wages, 129; sold in order to buy dogs, 169; bewitched, 231–32; carried off by wolves, 233; milk of, refused to boy, 275; embodies soul of boy's deceased mother, 306; mentioned, 102–5
Creation: prior to, 16; of Eve, from dog's tail, 175
Cross, sign of. *See* Religious symbols
Csárdás dance: learned from devil, 179–80
Csehbánya, 347
Csenger: Rákóczi hunts in woods of, 218
Csikmenaság, 327
Csikszentidomokos, 307
Csilléry, Klára (collector), 332

Csitár, 333
Csokonai Vitéz, Mihály (Hungarian playwright), xxvi
Csonka, Mihály (narrator), 324
Csót, 336
Cumania, Great, 337
Curiosity: about charms is disastrous, 276
Curses. *See* Punishment

Dances, xvi
Dancing: taught by devil, 179–80; as road to perdition, 180–81
Danube River, xxxviii, 228, 322
Deceptions: spying to discover food consumer, 5, 52; revealing secret of strength, 25; misleading pursuer, 53; thread tied to lover reveals route, 48, 56; pitch spread as trap, 88; milk heated rather than cooled, 121; wolves tricked into pulling load, 138; wife hoodwinked, 148; wife made to appear insane, 149; wife conceals parson, 151; mustache of sleeping hussar cut off, 165; prayer used as cover-up, 168; money received for meaningless answers, 171; reversed horses' shoes foil enemy, 220; fishing net unraveled, 265; attempt to deprive of treasure, 284; bewitched piper finds self in tree, 288; witch's money is shards, 288; gold from supernatural beings vanishes, 299
 disguises: putting on catskin, 22; to overhear plot, 22; hero hides armor, dresses in rags, 40–44 *passim*; of devil, imperfect, 46; devil as lover, 46; hussar impersonates devil, 151; hussar impersonates parson, 152; king dresses as hussar, 161–62; devil appears as gentleman, 178; outlaw

pretends to be fieldhand, 228; to catch daughter's lover, 286

fatal: drinking molten lead, 25; sharpened bone in bed kills, 124; Tartars lure and kill people, 215; Turks drowned by fishermen, 216

lying: attack not revealed, 9; church attendance denied, 40–42, 87–89; spying denied, 49–51, 56; disobedience denied, 81, 82; murderer claims to have rescued princess, 122; squire kills horse, accuses coachman, 142; worthless dogs said valuable, 169; goat calls horns pistols, 197; goat denies having been fed, 197

shams: feigning illness, 114; shamming church service, 120–21; hussar pretends parson embodies trouble, 154; wooden sword replaces steel, 168; sham infection easily cured, 239; rabies shammed, 239; straw dummy catches lover, 287; coachman feigns death, 293

stealing: wife takes strength token, 26; hussar's clothes stolen, 149; fellow shepherd steals sheep, 194; from miller, 269. *See also* Treachery; Trickery

Deity. *See* God *or* Jesus

Demecser, 245

Devil: as lover, 46–49 *passim*, 55; as ghoul, 47; in church, 47; wears out iron shoes, 55; owns horses, 73; earth freed of, 74; keeps princess, 118; impersonated by hussar, 151; cleverness of, 178; as tempter, 178; teaches vices, 178–80; exorcized, 232, 252; coachman accused of being, 249; kept in box, 252; possesses carter, 252; powerless beyond

village boundary, 252; power obtained from, 254–56; carries off man, 255; forces man to renounce God, 255; quits man who confesses, 256; helpful, 263, 340; tortures witches, 263; help of, requested, 298; wedding of, 300; hooves for feet, 301; land of, 311; in insect form, 336; times abroad, 350

Dialectical folklorists, vii

Diósviszló, 332

Disguise. *See* Deception

Divorce: because of laziness and stupidity, 147

Dobos, Ilona (collector), 319, 350

Döbrököz, 331

Dogs: purchased by foolish man, 169; steal Adam's rib, 175; eat master's sheep, 195; kill wolves, 196; when well fed protect sheep, 196; travel alone, 238; trained to act rabid, 239; sent from devils, 254; mentioned, 64

Dömötör, Tekla (Hungarian folklorist), xiv

Donkey: gives Jesus a ride, 183

Dowry: half parent's possessions, 144

Dragon: many-headed, slain by hero, 18, 20, 65–70, 91; steals queen, 92, 94; appears as black bull, 273–76; as evil being, 276; ridden by *garabonciás*, 279–80; relation to *garabonciás*, 347; mentioned, 76, 77

Dream: supernatural feats during, 206

Drinking: taught by devil, 180–81

Duna River. *See* Danube

Durkheim, Emile (French sociologist), xii

Dwarf: fights hero, 8–14 *passim*; is tied in knots, 30

Eagle, 21

Egyházaskozár, 327, 349

Elixir of life. *See* Water of life

Endings, etiological: origin of ants as transformed dwarfs, 15; origin of light, 27; lions' short hair due to snake's strike, 122; grouchy women created from dog's tail, 175; slovenly women formerly pigs, 176; good wives true descendants of Eve, 177; why sheep docile at midday, 182; why gadflies bother cows, 182; why horse always grazes, 183; why donkey seldom eats, endures cold, 183; knots in lumber as carpenter's punishment, 185; name of lake from hero, 215; as invention of narrator, 306

stylized: invoking God's blessing, 45; narrator's presence at feast, 45, 77, 99; hero still alive if not dead, 45, 77, 109, 126

Eördögh, Ferenc (narrator), 319, 350

Erdélyi János (Hungarian author), vi, vii, xxvi

Erdész, Sándor (collector), xviii

Estonian tradition, 319

Etiological: *See* Endings

Etes, 287

European tradition, 320

Eve: as mother of good daughter, 177

Evans-Pritchard (English anthropologist), xii

Exorcizing: devil exorcized by carter, 252; witch exorcized by throwing knife, 256

Extraordinary. *See* Supernatural

Fairies: freed by hero, 74; inhabit lake, 213; fearful of witches, 213–14

Falcon, 98

Farkas, Sándor (narrator), 306

Faustian scholar: legends of, 344

Fedics, Mihály (narrator), xxix, 309

Fejes, József (narrator), 312

Felsö-Zsolca, 332

Ferencz, András (narrator), 327

Ferenczi, Imre (collector), 330

Fiath, Pompejus: killed at Pest, 223

Fillies. *See* Horses

Finnish method. *See* Historical-geographical method

Finno-Ugrian relationships, xli

Fish: supposedly in bush, 148

Folklore: social function of, xix; as entertainment, xxi; as integral part of culture, xxix; research methods of, xxix; social basis of, xxix; as living art, xxviii

Folksong, xix

Folktales: indexes of, xvii; history of, xxiv; told as payment for food and lodging, xxiv; great length of, xxx, xxxiii; structure of, xxxi; as reflection of social context, xxxii; as entertainment, xxxiii

Folktales. *See also* Storytelling; Tales

Formulas: use of, in narration, xxxii

Fortuneteller: advice of, 289

Fostermother: cow as, 14

Foxes: as hero's helper, 102; ask for food, 102; destroy vineyards, 191; incur peasant's wrath, 191; afraid of cat, 192; afraid of half-flayed goat, 198; as game, 265

Frobenius, Leo (German ethnologist), xii

Frogs: eating of, brings magic powers, 257–58, 271, 345; fear of, 296; supernatural beings appear as, 296–97; midwife attends, 298

Funeral customs: for victims of
bewitching, 50, 51, 56; removing
corpse through hole in wall, 51,
56

Fülöp, Mrs. Károly (narrator), 340,
347

Füred, 249

Gaal, György (Hungarian folklorist), xxvi

Gajcsána, 285

Gál, Mrs. István (narrator), 327

Gallows: coachman's respect for,
141

Garaboncids: born with teeth, 272,
283, 306; appears as bull, 274;
destroys evil beings, 275–76;
drinks only milk, 275, 277, 283;
foresees future, 278–79; rides
snakes as horses, 281; legends of,
345, 347; etymology of, 346;
relation to dragon, 347

Garbolc, 306

Gégény, 244

Gerényes, 326

Gergely, Sándor (narrator), 332

Gesztén, Jóska: as outlaw, 226;
steals from rich, gives to poor,
227; escapes by deception, 228;
as folk hero, 333

Ghost: of surveyor, returns to redo
work, 290; of squire, returns to
hidden money, 295

Ghoul: devil as, 49

Giant: as gateman, 102; killed by
hero, 114

Goat: frightens wolf, 196; deceives
farmer, 197; eaten by fox and
wolf, 199

God: of the earth, 16; as provider,
33, 46; appealed to for help, 59,
60, 298; faith in is rewarded, 76,
101; invoked in christening, 111;
as creator, 175; as giver of difficult tasks, 186; sheeps' protec-

tion trusted to, 194; guides
mother to son, 217; man asked
to renounce, 255; help of, refused, 298

Godfather: Jesus as, 99–101; moon
as, 111

Goose leg: of supernatural lover,
287

Gratitude: shown by revenging
wrongs, 14; of children to parents, 15, 28, 109, 130; hero
sacrifices son to reward helpers,
125. See also Rewards

Greek tradition, 305

Grimm, Jakob and Wilhelm (German folklorists), v, xxvi, xxxi

Grozescu, I. (Rumanian scholar),
vii

Gyivák: help of, requested, 298

Györtelek, 345

Gypsies: as folktale hero, 15; as
musician, 123, 267, 344; as ped-
dler, 227; picture transformed to
orchestra of, 267, 344; as narrator, 306–7; as preservers of
folklore, 307

Hajdu County, 329

Halász, János (narrator), 331

Halmi, 265

Hangman: hangs innocent men,
141

Hapsburg Monarchy, viii

Hare: supposedly in tree, 148. See
also Rabbit

Hatvani, Professor: legends of,
344–45

Heaven: as place of bliss, 178;
reached by climbing tree, 203

Hedgehog: frightens goat, 198–99

Hell: as princess's prison, 118;
torments of, 178; wedding in,
301

Heller, Barnát (Hungarian folklorist), 323

Helpful animals. *See* specific animal

Herdboy: as lowly occupation, 27

Herdsman: offends Jesus, 181; as folklore bearers, 335; position in society, 335. *See also* Cowherd; Horseherd; Shepherd

Historical events: in legend and literature, 331

Historical fact; in legends, 330

Historical-geographical method, ix, x, xiii, xix

Hidden treasure: revealed by ghost of squire, 295

Hens: hatch out lizards, 277

Henszlmann, Imre (Hungarian folklorist), xxvi

Heroic epics: tales similar to, 311

Hetesi, Imre (narrator), 331

Honko, Lauri (Finnish folklorist), v

Honti, János (Hungarian folklorist), ix, xiii, xvii

Hovéds: fight Serbs, 223

Horger, Antal (Hungarian folklorist), xxvii

Horseherd: loses horses, 234

Horses: defecate ceaselessly, 36; decrepit nag chosen, 59, 83–84; kiss as humans, 72; reveals abduction, 92–96 *passim*; squire kills, 142; of hussar, stolen, 149; recovered by hussar, 153; refuses Jesus a ride, 183; killed to feed cat, 192; go astray, 234; lazy, 240; obey only coachman, 246; possesses magic power, 253; becomes weak at carter's demand, 253; received from devil, 253–56; of *garabonciás*, in lizard form, 277; man bewitched while pasturing, 289; as helper of hero, 313; history of, use of, reflected in tales, 313. *See also Táltos* horse

Horthy: fascist regime of, vii, xv

Hungarian folklore theory: role in building socialism, v; Soviet influence on, vi; Marxist-Leninist theory, vi; triumph of New School, xiii

Hungarian tales: number of, vi

Hungarian tradition: as intermediary between East and West, xli

Hunter: pursues bird seven years, 199

Hussars: as tale tellers, xxvi; as object of hero worship, 111, 316; given leave after twelve years, 149, 161; conceals self among swine, 150; hides under farmer's bed, 150; impersonates devil, 151; impersonates parson, 152; kills two men with one stroke, 157; forces disguised king to buy brandy, 162; hocks sword for brandy, 164; forces disguised king to steal, 164; abandon posts to assist *kuruc*, 222; sent from devil, 254; as cavalry, 313–14; portrayed as serving justice, 321; return to homeland, 331

Igaz, Mária (collector), 332

Illness: lovesickness, 42; cured by hero, 42; caused by eating bewitched food, 263; caused by encounter with ghost, 290

Illyés, István (narrator), 345

Immigrant folklore, xvii

Indian tradition, 320

Ingratitude: rescuer's death plotted, 27; rescued mother plots against son, 114–17

Inn (*csárda*): as locale for legends, 337

Innkeeper: stingy, 250; punished, 250

Ipolyi, Arnold (Hungarian folklorist), xxvi, 323

Iron shoes: travelling on until worn out, 54–55

Istvánovits, Márton (Hungarian folklorist), xvi

Jakó, Dénes (collector), 326

Jankó, József (narrator), 349

Janosík (Slovakian folk hero), 333

Japanese tradition, 319

Jealousy: older brothers, of younger, 58–60 passim; of rich man brings downfall, 170

Jesus: as godfather, 101; as old man in disguise, 101; advent of, mentioned, 178; wanders about the world, 181–83; grows tired of walking, 182–83; teaches Peter, 184; as legendary figure, 324

Jew: as innkeeper, 164

Jokes: increasing popularity of, xxiv

Kaiser: rewards officers, 219

Kakasd, xvi, 319

Kálmány, Lajos (Hungarian folklorist), xi, xv, xxvii, 323, 330

Kapos River: canal dug to, 221

Karancsság, 288

Karcag, 238–39

Karcsa, 234, 237, 269, 290, 328–29, 337, 339–40, 343, 345, 350

Karcsa, Lake, 213

Károlyi, Count, 228

Katona, Lajos (Hungarian folklorist), vi, viii, xvii, xxvii

Kecskeméty, Gábor (narrator), 341

Kecskés, Ferenc (narrator), 323

Kenézlö, 288

Kéthely, 323

Kindness: repairing wounds, 18; to dragon, 91; boy rescued from hanging, 130; king repays poor man's loss, 170; donkey shows, to Jesus, 183

Kisfaludy Society, vi

Kishartyan, 315, 328, 349

Kiskúnság, 324

Kiss, Gabriella (collector), 324, 327

Kisujszállás, 305, 320, 337

Kisvárda, 244, 321

Kodály, Zoltán (Hungarian music-folklorist), viii, xv

Korcz, József (narrator), 324, 327

Kórik, Gábor (narrator), 333

Korompay, Bertalan (Hungarian folklorist), xiii

Kossuth, Lajos: Hungarian patriot, viii, xxxvii; leader of kuruc, 223–24; punishes squire, 224–25; as former king, 225; in legend, 331; as symbol of freedom, 332–33

Kovács, Ágnes (Hungarian folklorist), vi, xiii, xvii, xxxvi, 305, 307

Kovács, Mrs. János (narrator), 340, 343

Kovács, László (collector), 306

Kökönyösd, 266

Kriza, János (Hungarian folklorist), vi, vii, xxvi

Krohn, Kaarle (Finnish folklorist), xii

Kuruc army: besieges Szatmár, 218; attacked by Austrians, 219; led by Rákóczi, 330; insurrection: as end to serfdom, 221; assisted by outside soldiers, 221–22; in legend, discussion of, 331

Labanc soldiers: fight Rákóczi, 219

Laughter: as indication of anger, 191

Laziness: hinders marriage, 142; as unbreakable habit, 144

Legends: popularity of, xxiv; as tradition, xxxv; assuming märchen form, xxxvi; historical, xxxvii, xxxviii; local, xxxix; explanatory, 324; derived from shamanism, 340; incorporation of numerous elements in, 342–43

Lénárt, László (narrator), 328–29, 337, 339, 345, 350

Lenkey, János, Captain: assists *kuruc* army, 222

Lenore tale, 309

Letters: from supernatural beings, 29, 32

Lidérc: as girl's lover, 286–87; as mythical figure, 349

Life token: dagger which rusts, 6, 14; mentioned, 306

Lion: as priest, 120

Lippai, Ferenc (narrator), 351

Lithuanian tradition, 309, 319

Lizards: as horses for *garabonciás*, 277

Lying, tales of: as comic interlude, xxxvii; popularity of, 327; told as bad dreams, 328. *See* Deception

Magic animals: food providing cow, 3; instantly appearing cow, 14; cow's tears produce flood, 14; golden pelican, 29, 32; ceaselessly defecating horses, 36; swans draw coach through air, 38, 30–41; skinny nag eats embers, 62; flying horse, 84; fox, 102; *táltos* bull, 102–9 *passim*, 273–74; instantly appearing wolf, bear, and lion, 115–16; lion carries hero to sun, 117; wolf, bear, and lion as bewitched prince, 124–25; cat as great eater, 192; cat predicts death, 193; horses, 245–47; dog, horse, bull sent from devil, 254–55; frogs request midwife's help, 297. *See also Táltos* horse

Magic helpers: as *deus ex machina*, xxxi

Magic knowledge. *See* Supernatural abilities

Magic objects: dagger as life token, 6; crackling forest, 17; rejuvenating lake, 31; revolving castle on cat's paw, 31, 34; glass mountain, 34, 70, 311; tall tree, 34, 78; fast growing beard, 35; nut containing armor, 37–40, 42, 43; flying coach, 34, 40, 41, 74, 86, 88; bean containing armor, 42; unpluckable flower, 51; diamond-studded horseshoes, 63, 70; belt of strength, 65–70 *passim*; water of life, 65–70 *passim*, 121, 124; healing grass, 65–70 *passim*, 121, 124; self-operating sword, 65–72 *passim*; devil producing loom, 73; meadow in which grass grows up overnight, 73; summoning ring, 75; tree branch wide as road, 78; sleeping potion, 81; rejuvenating apple, 99; diamond egg, 100; animal calling whistle, 115; flaming milk, 120–21; beautifying milk, 121; tree grows to heaven, 203; self-operating whip, 241; fatal horseshoe calk, 244; wheel rolls of itself, 250–51; blessed chalk as protection, 254; grass as protection, 254; coach from devil, 255; rejuvenating drugs, 272; rejuvenating jar, 272; book of charms, 276; salt as food, 281

Magic occurrences: food provided by cow's horn, 3–5; food from self-spread table, 23; protection by thinking of benefactor, 30; food from rose, 32; rose grows from grave, 51; girl (as rose) eats leftovers, 52; palace built overnight, 97; calf disappears, 102; hero controls bull by stroking horns, 103–4; pregnancy through stalk, 110; brush becomes forest, 119; handkerchief becomes sea, 119; pins become mountains, 119; blood of hero's son breaks spell, 125; lashing cape brings pain to thief, 232, 236; scratching ground brings blood on thief's back, 236; butterflies in cart tongue bestow power, 247; rag transforms horse, 253; knife taken by witch in whirlwind, 256; raising the dead, 258; striking with rag kills witch, 258–59; wedding party disappears, 265; gun fired backward hits target, 266; bull appears from cloud, 275; lizards hatched from hen eggs, 277; snakes care for man, 280–81; box burrows through earth, 284; sleeping man's shinbones removed, 289; mountain opens up, 297; man goes to devils' wedding, 301. See also Transformation

Magic powers. See Supernatural abilities

Magistrate: allegedly embezzles, 148

Magyar, István (narrator), 323

Magyarós Mountain, 297

Magyars: laugh when angry, 191

Makó, György (narrator), 326

Makra, Sándor (collector), 305, 320, 337

Malinowski, Bronislaw (Polish-English anthropologist), xii

Mancsalka, 255

Manikin: fights with hero, 8–14 passim; tied into knots, 24

Marót, Károly (Hungarian Homeric scholar), xi

Márton, László (narrator and collector), 322, 324

Marxist-Leninist theory, x

Mátyás, King: stories about, xxv, xxxvii, 161–68, 168–70, 171–72, 322–23, 333; as popular folk hero, 321

Merényi, László (Hungarian folklorist), xxvi

Mezőtur, 238

Midnight: as ghostly hour, 293

Midwife, mistreats frog, 296

Miller: climbs to heaven, 204; possesses magic knowledge, 269, 345

Minárcsik, József (narrator), 315, 328

Mogyorósi, István (narrator), 318

Moldavia, xvii

Moldavians, xl

Molnár, Ferenc (narrator), 324

Moral elements: characteristic of humorous tales, 319

Mutilation: supernatural beings remove man's shinbones, 289

Mythology: Hungarian, ix; collections of, 323

Myths: heroic, 306

Nagy, János (narrator), 310, 326, 339, 347, 350

Nagy, Sándor (narrator), 344

Nagyecsed, 330

Nagykároly, 228

Nagykúnság, 337

Nagyvázsony, 249

Narrators: cosmogonical concepts of, xviii; creative role of, studied, xix; recognition of, xviii, 311, 320; artistry of, xxx, xxxi, 312, 318; effect of environment upon, 307. See also Storytellers

Nationalism: as folklore heresy, vii

Necromancy: belief in, 309

Noah: mentioned, 44

Nógrád County, 315, 328, 333, 349

Nyögér, 324, 327

Oaths: taken on sword hilt, 17, 23

Obscene tales: collecting of, xxxvi

Obstacle flight, 119, 120

Ogres: hag with iron nose, 24, 25. *See also* Witches *and* Devils

Olaszi, 254

Ondrás: (Czech folk hero), 333

Origin: of sun and moon, 27

Ortutay, Gyula (Hungarian folklorist), vi, xxix; as collector, 309, 351

Ostriches: ridden by fairies, 74

Otherworld: Devil's Land, 71

Outlaws. *See Betyárs*

Oxen: killed by wolves, 138; killed to feed cat, 192; put in cart, 203; used to retrieve fairy bell, 214; eaten by wolves, 318

Pácin, 289

Palkó, Mrs. József (narrator), xvii, 319

Pandur, Péter (narrator), 316, 320

Papi, Lajos (narrator), 337

Parson: as poor man's employer, 136; fears wolves, 138; parsimonious, 139–40; punished for greed, 141; paramour of farmer's wife, 150–55; believes naked hussar is devil, 151; ridiculed in tales, 321; mentioned, 205. *See also* Priest

Páskuly, Mrs. László (narrator), 333

Passive bearers of tradition, xxxv

Peacocks: ridden by fairies, 74

Peasantry: idealized in folklore research, viii; as preservers of folklore, xxii, xxxviii; class divisions in, xxxviii

Personality study: as folklore technique, xi

Pest: besieged by Serbs, 223

Pest County, 316

Pig: man's love for, 3. *See also* Sow

Piper: deceived by witches, 287

Plowman: finds money, 147; gives king clever answers, 171

Poltergeist: dead squire returns as, 291

Pompejus. *See* Faith

Positivism, ix

Poverty: forces son to leave home, 28; caused by huge family, 99, 129

Prayers, recited before fight with dragon, 65–70 *passim*; not to be learned before christening, 111; learned from mother, 111; clothing as answer to, 111; feigned to disguise facts, 168; as form of entertainment, 179; offered for bewitched man, 255; said by *garabonciás*, 278–79; as means of protection, 297. *See also* Religious rites

Pregnancy: through stalk, 110

Priests: witness contract, 17; as performer of marriages, 45, 99, 144; lion as, 120; killed by horse, 135; allegedly makes unusual prophecy, 148; outlaws disguised as, 156; called to exorcize spirit, 135, 256; of devils, has cloven hooves, 301; mentioned, 39, 41, 86, 87, 89. *See also* Parson

Psychoanalysis, ix

Punishment, nature of: burying alive, 15; causing to burst, 22, 23; great thirst, 22, 23; insatiable hunger, 22, 23, 183; disowning, 27; beating, 35, 36, 225–26, 232, 251; relatives killed by devil, 49, 50, 56; mauling by animals, 90, 124, 141; casting adrift in barrel, 110; hanging, 129, 141, 248; bundling wife in straw, 146; scalding with hot mush, 154; beheading, 157, 167; mustache cut off, 165; loss of money, 170,

284; gadflies sent to herd, 181;
lumber contains knots, 185;
flaying, 198; needles stuck into
buttocks, 227; threat of permanent form as wolves, 233;
bloodying back, 236; bewitcher
blinded, 244; banishment, 262;
rats sent to infest house, 269;
tornado destroys house, 275; no
rest in grave, 290
Punishment, reason for: killing,
22, 124, 142, 157; unfaithfulness,
27; lying, 35, 49–56 passim, 124,
198; cheating, 129, 170, 251;
forgetfulness, 90; unwanted pregnancy, 110; greed, 141, 275;
laziness and stupidity, 146; dis-
obeying king, 167; rudeness,
181, 183, 227; beating St. Peter,
185; being paramour, 154;
cruelty, 224–26 passim; stealing,
157, 165, 233, 236–37, 269; bewitching, 232, 244, 248, 262;
making mistakes while living,
290

Quests: search for father's comrade, 59. See also Tasks

Rabbits: as game, 265
Rabies: false, easily cured, 239
Rákóczi, Prince: insurrection of,
xvii; as folklore hero, xxxvii;
leads kuruc army, 218; fights
Austrians, 219; as legendary
character, 330; belief in return
of, 333
Rats: follow miller's orders, 344
Rejuvenation: repeated, 308; tales
about, 313
Religious rites: christening by
Jesus, 101; christening by
mother, 111; christening as
prerequisite to learning to pray,
111; church service shammed,
120–21; baptism administered

by parents, 186; confession
required of bewitched man, 256.
See also Prayers
Religious symbols: sign of cross
removes curse, 23; sign of cross
causes transformation, 39, 41;
sign of cross as blessing, 101;
blessed chalk, 254; crucifix near
bewitching area, 254; rosary as
protection, 297; crucifix turns as
sign of Rákóczi's return, 330
Religious tales: related to anecdotes, xxxvii; satirical character
of, 323
Repetition: use of, in tales, xxxi
Resurrection: victims arise after
devil dies, 56. See also Unquiet
dead
Revenants: belief in, 309; abhor-
rence of, 317
Reward, nature of: half of kingdom and marriage to princess,
16, 27, 75–77, 106, 109; whatever desired by hero, 79, 80;
food, 101, 132, 155; helpful
animals released from bewitch-
ment, 125; gift of land, 136;
great riches, 101, 155, 161, 284–
85, 299, 302; sheep made docile,
182; great endurance given
donkey, admittance into heaven,
187; nobility conferred, 216;
brandy, 235; good wage and
pension, 246; marriage to squire's
daughter, 296; unspecified, 219
Reward, reason for: securing sun
and moon, 16, 27; freeing fairyland of devils, 75; having obtained unknown fruit, 77; faithful service, 79, 80, 246; kindness,
100–101, 182–83; plowing huge
field, 106; not having shamed
king, 109; having buried rich
man's mother, 132–34; silence
on cause of priest's death, 136;

ridding house of trouble, 155; saving king's life, 161; having made atonement, 187; killing Turks, 216; rescuing man, 219, 285; recovering goods, 235, 296; sharing food, 284; helping frog at childbirth, 299; being best man at devil's wedding, 302

Rich man: as negative hero, 318

Ricse: cattle market at, 236

Robbers: souls of, saved by child, 187. *See also Betyárs*

Róheim, Géza (Hungarian ethnologist), ix

Romanticism: as folklore heresy, vii, viii

Rooster: frightens fairies, 213

Rózsa, Sándor: outlaw leader, assists *kuruc*, 223–24; in legend, 332

Rozsály, 333, 344

Rumanian tradition, xl, 305–6, 319

Russian tradition, 319

St. Andrew: mentioned, 203

St. John: mentioned, 204

St. Nicholas: mentioned, 204

St. Peter: as Jesus' companion, 182–83, 325; beaten, is taught lesson, 184–85; as gatekeeper of heaven, 156, 186, 203; mentioned, 120

Sajtos, Imre (narrator), 329

Sára, 310, 312, 318, 326, 331, 339, 342, 347, 350

Sármellék, 336, 348

Sárospatak: college of, 240; castle of, 330

Satan: appears as teacher, 324. *See also* Devil

Satire: in folktales, xxxvi

Scholars: try to find answers, 171; are taught lesson, 172

Sebestyén, Gyula (Hungarian folklorist), xxvii

Serbs: attack Pest, 223; as invaders, 329

Serfdom: abolishment of, 331

Sharp, Cecil (English folksong collector), xix

Shams. *See* Deceptions

Shamanism: reflected in tales, 313, 314; as source of legends, 340, 345–47 *passim*; mentioned, xli, 306

Shepherd: gives Jesus water, 182; trusts sheep to God, 194; learns to feed dogs well, 196; gives advice on magic, 254

Siberian tradition, 311

Sisa, Pista: beaten by squire, 225; revenges self on squire, 226; takes from rich, gives to poor, 226

Slavic tradition, 305

Smoking: taught by devil, 178–79; as cause of quarrels, 181

Snake: as possessor of water of life, 121; denudes lion, 122; cares for man, 280–81

Social relations: reflected in tales, xxi, 317–19 *passim*

Soldiers: as disseminators of tales, 320

Solymossy, Sándor (Hungarian folklorist), viii, xxvii, 316

Somogy County, 323

Somogyi, Mrs. Sándor (narrator), 325

Soul: as owl, 44; departs through mouth, 44; resides in belly, 45; of girl in flower, 51

Soviet folklore theory, xi, xiii, xiv

Sow: contains magic box, 17

Spinning house: as courting place, 46–48, 142

Spying. *See* Deceptions

Squire: finds coachman is right, 142; mistreats serfs, 225; dies without a will, 291

Star: as supernatural lover, 286

Stealing. *See* Deceptions

Stinginess: of innkeeper punished, 250

Storytellers: correlation with audience, xxi; changing role of, xxiii; size of repertory of, xxxiv; rivalry of, 314; state recognition of, 320; as recorder of own tales, 322; style of, 324. *See also* Narrators

Storytelling: social context of, xxii; rivalry in, xxxiv; occasion of, xxxiii, xxxiv, 307, 312, 319–20, 322, 329; gradual disappearance of, 312; audience for, 316; in the military, 322

Strength token: chain mail shirt, 26; hero's first two fingers, 116

Stupidity: burning of washing clothes, 145; miller puts head on backward, 205; stupid servant, 207; man thinks grown boy is result of proposed intercourse, 208

Stylized endings. *See* Endings

Sümeg, 325

Supernatural abilities: obtained from devils, 254–56; of hero as characteristic feature of tales, 306
   great skill: tying dwarf in knots, 24; in climbing trees, 78; in caring for horses, 81; building palace overnight, 97; *táltos* bull freezes mud, 108; child catches sea fish by hand, 110; at stealing, 130; twelve killed in six strokes, 157
   great speed: horse flies as wind, 84; dragon overtakes fleeing hero, 93–95; horses overtake train, 245
   great strength: pulling up trees, 6; shoveling mountains, 7; kneading iron, 8; dwarf drags

tree stump, 12; fish as strong as men, 14; hurling mace great distance, 18, 20; wading through steel, 25; tying man in knots, 26; killing hundreds at one stroke, 73; hero controls *táltos* bull, 102–5; plowing huge field, 106; *táltos* bull blows sun backward, 107; *táltos* bull pulls huge cart, 108; prodigious swimmer, 111; cutting down tree with sword, 113; carrying huge tree on shoulder, 113; hero overcomes twelve giants, 114; killing giant with one blow, 116, 117; animals roll mountains over castle, 117; miller carries cord of wood, 206; horse carries huge load, 253
   magic powers: writing in gold with tip of finger, 17; sensitive smell, 20; nag eats embers, 62, 86–88, 95; living to great age, 83; cowherd bewitches cows, 231; devils exorcized, 231–32, 236; old man recalls horses by striking cape, 234–35; controlling animals from distance, 237–39 *passim*; uncanny knowledge, 238–39; coachman blinds bewitcher, 244; coachman alone controls horse, 245–46; turning men into horses, 247; drives cart with three wheels, 250; recalls cart wheel, 250–51; making horse strong or weak, 253; understanding animals' speech, 258; making doughnuts of dung, 259–62; blowing in gun barrel ruins aim, 265–66; recalling escaped game, 266; giving life to objects, 267; counting bees exactly, 268; detaining bees, 268; sending rats to infest thief's house, 269; instant knowledge of thievery, 269; driving out rats,

269; sending rats to gnaw pillows, 270; self-rejuvenation, 272; man flies after reading charms, 276; foreseeing future, 278–79; riding snakes as horses, 281–82; making thief stick to object, 344

Supernatural beings. *See* Devils; Dragons; Dwarfs; Ogres; *Táltos*; Witches; *also* Magic animals

Supernatural passage of time: three weeks as three days, 301

Surveyors: in legends, 350

Swans: draw glass coach, 38; ridden by fairies, 74

Swine: help conceal naked hussar, 150

Swineherd: undertakes king's difficult task, 78; unwittingly aids hussar, 150; angry at intruder, 208

Szabolcs, County, xxxix, 276, 309, 321, 326, 333, 351

Szatmár, County, xxxix, 228, 306, 330, 333, 344, 345

Szeged: chief justice of, visits outlaws, 224

Szeged University, xi

Székelys, xvi, xxxix, 319

Szenográdi, József (narrator), 333

Szentgál, 340

Szerdahely, 259

Szeregnyi, Péter (narrator), 321

Szolnok County, 305, 320

Szücs, Dániel (narrator), 330

Szucsáva River, 297

Taboo: against attending church, 54; not to speak, see, hear, 64–70 *passim*; broken by speaking, 65–70 *passim*; forbidden room, 91; broken, dragon is released, 91; not to step outside circle, 254; to give no greeting, 269; against speaking to creatures near midnight, 298

Tákos, Imre, Sr. (narrator), 305

Tales: spinning houses as sources of, 310; great length of 312, 313; as combination of numerous elements, 320, 325

Táltos: youngest son as, 17; writes with finger tip as gold pen, 17; needs no food, 23; needs no sleep, 26; needs no possessions, 27; cannot marry humans, 27; Rákóczi's daughter as, 219–20; born with teeth, 306; as shaman, 306–7; legends of, 345; impostor poses as, 348; strong belief in, 348

Táltos bulls: as prodigious breeder, 102, 104; as hero's helper, 102–9, 314

Táltos horses: ordered cleaned, 37; assists hero in task, 37; hides hero from princess, 38; flies through air, 38, 39, 41; becomes invisible, 39; dances to cure illness of princess, 42–44; nag changes into, 64, 84; pities hero, 309; discussion of, 311; represents hero's alter ego, 311; as cultural relic, in tales, 315; compared to coachman's horse, 338; mentioned, 253

Táltos legends: relation to coachman legends, 341

Táltos myth: as reflection of shamanism, 313

Tamás, Mrs. Gergely (narrator), 351

Tarcal: home of Lenkey, 222

Tartar invasions: in legends, 329

Tartars: brutality of, 215

Tasks: fix celestial bodies, 17; release imprisoned wasps, 17; currying horses, 36; cleaning Augean stable, 36, 37, 40, 42; finding father's magic articles, 63; to cut off helping horse's head, 65–70 *passim*; guarding meadow from devil's horses, 73; to find liberator of fairyland, 74; obtaining unknown fruit, 77; caring for horses, 79, 80, 85; to care for calf, 101; search for calf, 102; to plow a thousand acres in one day, 106; to empty castle in one day, 107; finding a bride, 117; bringing princess from Hell, 118; milking three golden mares, 120; hussar to behead prisoner, 167; to find meaning of clever answers, 171; to fill gourd with water not from sky or earth, 187; to sell whip, 242; to withstand frightening visitations, 254–55. See also Tests; Quests

Tatárfalu: Rákóczi hunts in woods of, 218

Tátos, Erzse, trial of as táltos, 347

Temesköz, 330

Tests: repeated in tales, xxxi; of strength, 6, 7; of faithfulness, 26, 27; bathing in poison milk, 120; of loyalty, 125; multiplication of, 309. See also Tasks

Thefts: of food from rich man, 131; great skill at, 131–34

Thompson, Stith (American folklorist), 305

Thread: used to track devil, 47, 48

Tisza, Lajos (Count), xii

Tisza River, xxxviii, 228

Tiszakarád, 235

Tiszalök, 333

Toad: eating of, brings magic powers, 271

Toldi, Miklós (Hungarian Hercules), tales of, xxv

Tolna County, xvi, 319, 331

Tornya, 330

Török, Mrs. József (narrator), 330

Totemism, xli

Tótvázsony, 250

Tradition: transmission of, xxii

Transformations: humans into animals: men into fish, 14; dwarfs (manikins) into ants, 15; robbers into wolves, 233–34; man into horse, 247; dead woman into horse, 258; boy into bull, 274

humans into objects: man into flame, 21; girl into flower, 52; girl into piece of wood, 265; musicians into picture, 267

animals into humans: fish into men, 14

animals into animals: nag into táltos horse, 64, 84; hen eggs into lizards, 277

animals into objects: dragon into flame, 21; horses into straw sacks, 247–48; rabbit into flame, 267

objects into humans: picture into musicians, 267

objects into animals: food into birds, 33; straw sacks into horses, 247–48; straw into rabbit, 266–67, 344

one object into another: shabby clothes into golden, 64; meadow into fairyland, 74; clothes and saddle into precious jewels, 86, 87, 89; cowdung into doughnuts, 259–62; doughnuts into horsedung, 265. See also Magic occurrences

Transylvania, xxxix, xl, 307, 326–27

Treachery: mother plots against son, 114–17; to discover strength token, 116; sleeping hero slain, 121; mother tries to kill son, 124; captain betrays leader, 220. See also Deceptions

Tree: in sky, as frame tale, 313

Trickery: spying with third eye, 5; dead woman made to appear as thief, 131–32. See also Deceptions

True stories: as new folklore genre, xxxvii
Turca, 268
Turkey: abducted child taken to, 217; death place of Rákóczi, 330
Turkish invaders: in legends, 329
Turkish occupation, 329
Turkish tradition, 320
Turks: as enemy, 215, 217; horse culture of, 316

Ukrainian tradition, xl
Unquiet dead: man thought to return from dead, 282; surveyor to redo work, 290; squire returns to reveal hidden treasure, 295
Unusual. *See* Supernatural; Magic
Ural-Altaic Turkish tradition, 306
Urfin, András (narrator), 332

Vajkai, Aurél (collector), 336, 340, 347
Vámos, Mária (collector), 349
Vampire: in Balkan tradition, 349
Var, János: brave fisherman, 215
Varga, Antal (collector), 329
Varjános, Lake: named for hero, 215, 329
Vas County, 324, 327
Vecsei, Ferenc (narrator), 336, 348
Veszprém, 249, 325, 336, 347–48
Vikár, Béla (Hungarian folklorist), xxvii
Virgin, blessed: man asked to renounce, 255

Wagers, 238
War of Independence, 225. *See also Kuruc* insurrection

Wasps: found inside sow, 17
Water of life, restores slain horse, 65–70; as element in tales, 311
Wedding party: magical, 264
Wild roses: Action of, vii
Wishes: foolish, 46; to obtain lover, 46, 55; last wish to blow magic whistles, 116
Witches: frightened by sound of bell, 213; inhabit lake, 213; pursue fairies, 213; destroy bell tower, 214; in whirlwind, 256; exorcized by throwing knife, 256; dead woman as, 258; make doughnuts of dung, 259–62; legends of, widespread, 341; characteristics of, 342; magic powers of, 343
Wolves: aid helpful hero, 115; kill parson's oxen, 138, 318; harnessed to load of wood, 138; afraid of cat, 192; steal sheep, 194; threaten to eat goats, 196; killed by dogs, 196; afraid of half-flayed goat, 198; carry off cows, 233; punished by cowherd, 233; as game, 265; transformation of, 336

Youngest as strongest, 17, 58, 60, 102
Yugoslavian tradition, 309, 319

Zemplén, County, xxxix, 310, 312, 318, 326, 328, 329, 331, 337, 339–43 *passim*, 345, 347, 350
Zsáró, 269